SOUTH BY SOUTHWEST

CAPITAL CITY MURDERS BOOKS 11-15

TROY LAMBERT

South by Southwest

Books 11-15 in the "Capital City Murders" series

Troy Lambert

Published by
CCMbooks
P.O. Box 45091
Boise, ID 83711 USA
www.capitalcitymurders.com

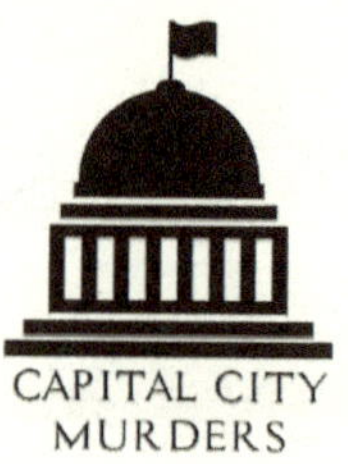

First Printing March 2020

CONTENTS

STUNG IN SANTA FE

AXED IN AUSTIN

CONTENTS

JOIN THE CAPITAL CITY CRIME SOLVERS, AND GET FREE PRIZES!

Nick is now on the assignment of his life.

Fast forward from *Fast Break*, and you'll find Nick O'Flannigan traveling the country from state capital to state capital, photographing capitol buildings and finding murder in each city.

> "At a time when we can't travel, Nick's story is a great escape."
> B. Worley, Amazon Reader

If you loved this book, I would love it if you would leave a review. It's one of the things we as authors love most.

If you want to keep up with Nick and his adventures, subscribe to our newsletter here. We'll only send you bargain books and let you know when new stories are coming. You'll never miss a release.

We also have audiobooks! Lots of them. Check those out here, and enjoy. Our narrator, Joseph Stevenson and the team at Larson Sound Studios do a great job on them.

If you want to join our exclusive review team, follow this link. (There is a test, but it's an easy one, I promise!)

In the meantime, be well. Nick and I will see you as we travel the country together!

SILENCED IN SALT LAKE CITY

BOOK #11

SILENCED IN SALT LAKE CITY

BOOK #11

PROLOGUE — SILENCED
WEDNESDAY

Kerry Lewis pulled his red 1965 Mustang through the garage door that opened as he turned into the driveway. His headlights illuminated an attractive woman in her early thirties guiding him in. She was not dressed in dental scrubs like when he saw her in a more professional capacity. Instead, she wore a red cocktail dress with a low v-cut neckline that showed off her cleavage and material that hugged her curves in a way he found very attractive.

This was the first time they'd met outside of the dental office where she normally worked even though they'd flirted several times during his visits there. He shut off the car and got out, absently grabbing the bottle of wine he'd brought with him.

"Hi," she said as she smiled at him.

"Hi," he responded. "Your dress matches my car."

"Two hot, fast machines," she said and propped her left hand on her hip.

"Vroom," Kerry replied, feeling silly as he did. "Thanks for the invite," he said as he moved closer to her. A hint of expensive perfume tickled his nose.

"My pleasure. Mm, a Pinot Noir." she said as she looked at the wine bottle he'd forgotten he had in his hand. "I love a good pinot," she said as she leaned forward and kissed him.

"I seem to remember you mentioning that once," he replied.

The woman turned around and went inside, holding the door open for him. Kerry absently removed his jacket and hung it on a hook next to the door and followed her inside.

He set the wine bottle on the kitchen counter. There were no signs that she'd been preparing dinner, his alleged reason for being here. "Was I supposed to get something on the way?"

"Oh, no," she replied. "We'll order delivery in a little while. It won't take long. They're usually a little slower on Wednesday evening. How about if we have some wine first?"

"Sure."

She opened a drawer and handed him a corkscrew. Two wine glasses sat ready on the counter.

"Thanks," he said as he sliced off the bottle's foil and popped the cork.

"I love that sound," she said.

"Me, too," he said as he poured the dark liquid into each glass, splashing a few drops onto the tile counter. "Sorry."

"Oh, that's okay," she said, handing him a sponge. Once he wiped up his spill, she lifted her glass. "Cheers."

"Ch-cheers," he stuttered as he picked up his and touched it to hers. His hands shook slightly. She was beautiful, and while he knew the reason she'd probably invited him, he wondered when and how things would happen.

"Come on," she said. "It's more comfortable in here." She held out her left hand for his wine glass and led him to the living room.

He handed it to her and sat down on the couch she indicated.

She took a slow sip of her wine. "Very good."

"I've had it before," Kerry said as he took more of a gulp than a sip from his own glass, nearly choking before he suppressed a small belch.

They made small talk as they drank. She asked about his Mustang and where he'd gotten it, and he asked about her desire to become a dentist and her current office.

Before he knew it, their glasses were empty. "I'll go get us a refill," she said. "You just stay here and make yourself comfortable."

He watched her hips sway as she walked into the kitchen.

"Okay." His palms were sweaty, and he felt his breath coming in shallow gasps. His heartbeat thudded in his ears. *Just breathe,* he told himself. *Everything will be fine.*

When she returned with the glasses, she set them down and moved to sit down next to him, but much closer than she had been before. She ran her fingers down his arm, and he felt the sharpness of her nails against his skin. "I've got an idea," she said. "It's still a little early for dinner."

"Oh?" he said, turning toward her.

"Yes," she said, slipping her arm around his neck. "I know something we can do to pass the time."

"Oh."

She moved closer to him, her lips nearly touching his. "Is that okay with you?"

"S-sure." Kerry stuttered again. He'd really expected to eat first, maybe even getting to know each other a little better.

"Come with me then," she said. She stood and held out her hand.

He took it, her skin soft in his, and she led him to a doorway that led down a flight of stairs. She turned on a light which revealed a dental chair, this one was outfitted with straps on the arms and footrests.

Various instruments sat nearby on one of those mobile stainless-steel tables he'd seen in her office and at other clinics as well.

"Is this your home office?" he asked.

She turned to him and smiled. "Of sorts. Do you like to play games?"

"Uh, kinda."

"Then get undressed and have a seat. I'll be with you shortly."

Kerry looked around nervously, seeing an area curtained off to the side, a cabinet filled with supplies, some of which looked like drugs, and a shelf attached to the wall next to it. A few clear jars sat on it, next to a few standard dental items, mostly molds of teeth he'd seen used to explain procedures to patients and a few vintage instruments.

"What are those?" he asked.

"Souvenirs," she said. "From some of the things we had to do in dental school."

"Oh," he said.

"Now, get undressed please," she said.

Kinky, he thought. *But maybe fun.*

He watched as she went through the curtain, pulling the red dress over her head as she went. She wasn't wearing anything under it at all.

My lucky night, he thought. He quickly undressed, and as he took his phone out of his pocket, he snapped a picture with the camera.

"The guys are not going to believe this," he said aloud.

"What was that?" she said from behind the curtain.

"Nothing," he said. "What—?"

"Call me Doctor," she reappeared, now dressed in pure white scrubs, but more the costume type than professional ones, the top tight and open in a large "V", the bottoms tight shorts as opposed to baggy pants. A stethoscope hung around her neck.

"Sit," she commanded.

He obeyed.

She strapped first one arm and then the other to the chair, and then she knelt, giving him a generous view of her chest, and strapped his feet in place.

Kerry felt incredibly vulnerable, naked, and trapped.

He was turned on and frightened at the same time. His heart raced, and he stared up at her.

"Do I scare you?" she asked.

"Y-yes," he stammered.

"Yes, what?"

"Yes, doctor," he said, catching on to the game, his gaze following her as she moved around him. Then he felt her hands on his head, and then felt a leather strap go around his neck, one with a plastic chin cup on it. She tightened and secured it, and he couldn't move his neck to the right or to the left.

"What are you doing?" he asked.

"Shh," she said, kissing him. She ran her tongue across his teeth, and he tried to stretch up into the kiss, but the strap held him in place.

A moment later, another strap followed, this one across his forehead. Now he couldn't move his head up or down. She disappeared from his vision, and he felt something tighten around his upper arm.

"What's that?" he asked. She reappeared, syringe in hand, and tapped the needle as she pressed the plunger.

"A shot to help you with this evening's performance," she said.

"You mean?"

"You'll last longer, trust me."

A moment later, he felt the needle enter his arm. Almost immediately, he felt aroused.

That must be an amazing drug she gave me, he thought.

But then she was gone, no longer over him. He could no longer see her but heard metal clanking against metal and he smelled some kind of chemical.

"Whash thath?" his words slurred, like she'd numbed his mouth, but she hadn't. Had she?

"Shh," she said. "Silence is golden."

"Sileth?"

"Yes, silence. Now, open wide."

Kerry felt metal in his mouth, an instrument pushing his jaw open. He heard it click, and his mouth was locked in place.

He tried to talk, but all that came out was a grunt.

"You see? Quiet is good."

He felt a pinch, like she actually had given him a shot in the mouth, but he couldn't feel or tell where.

"Hold still," she said, as if he had a choice. Her face appeared in his vision again, but now she was wearing a mask and some kind of protective surgical gown over her shoulders and chest. Safety glasses, the kind with the LED lights on either side, covered her eyes and when she turned right and left the brightness temporarily blinded him.

I've never heard of this intense of a game, he thought.

Then she disappeared, and he felt some kind of pressure on his tongue. He heard a click and it felt different than before, looser in his mouth. He pressed it forward, feeling like it might fall back in his throat and choke him.

"This part will be over in a second," she said.

He felt pressure in his mouth, and then saw a spurt of blood hit her just below her chin.

"Ooh!" she said, but he could see by the visible corners of her eyes under the glasses that she was smiling. "One more second."

Something felt really odd in his mouth. It felt—empty. *Was that my blood?*

The odd taste of iron and copper made him think it must have been. He swallowed without thinking.

He didn't feel any pain, but he felt like something was being pulled through the skin of his mouth over and over.

Stitches, he thought. He remembered when he'd been a kid and broken a glass in the sink while doing the dishes. His mom took him to the hospital for stitches. The feeling of having the gash sewn up in his hand had been identical.

"We can't have you bleeding out now, can we?" she said. "No way. I'd hate to kill you."

He heard her laugh. *Bleed out? Kill me?*

He nearly gagged as more liquid filled his mouth, but then the jaw vice, for he had no idea what else to call it, loosened.

His mouth sagged, but he found he couldn't control it or close it. He tried to explore things with his tongue, but it didn't seem to be working. As he tried to move it around though, he did feel liquid fleeing down his chin. She sat him up and he saw her using forceps to lift something and place it in a jar filled with some kind of liquid.

A tongue, he thought. *My tongue?* He tried to speak, but nothing happened. His eyes darted back and forth, and she stopped, staring at him.

"Yes, that was your tongue," she said. "Like the others, you've been silenced."

The others?

He felt weak and confused.

"It won't be long now," she said, approaching with another syringe. "Rest now."

She injected him in the shoulder and peaceful darkness took over.

AIRPORT RUN AND THEN THE HIGHWAY

Nick left the Denver Airport along Peña Boulevard, connected to E-470 North and continued on the nearly empty highway until it connected with I-25 North. There wasn't much traffic on the freeway for a Saturday morning, so he set the cruise control and leaned back in the seat.

He popped in a CD, hoping the music would help pass the time on his drive to Rock Springs, Wyoming. As the music began, he thought his journey, coming close to the end of the third month of his year-long assignment to visit each state's capital city. He was enjoying taking photographs of each capitol building and the surrounding areas for *Travel USA* magazine, but there was a certain loneliness to traveling by himself.

He thought of Sandra, the woman he'd met a couple months ago in Salem, Oregon, and who had just spent a week with him in Denver. Their time together in the Mile-High City was magical, filled with lots of holding hands, hugging, kissing, and conversation. They'd said, "I love you," as she entered the airport, and although it felt strange, it also felt comfortable. Nick hadn't been in a serious relationship with anyone since his divorce several years ago.

"It feels good having someone," Nick said out loud to himself. "I hope our next time together in a month is just as magical as this past week was," he thought as he hummed along with the music.

As much as he missed her, his friend Gerry, and her girlfriend who had visited with her, he was glad to leave the drama of Denver behind. A mistake on his part when selling his photos of the horrible events he'd witnessed there to what he thought had been local media turned sour. The website turned out to be a fake news site, and the oversight had nearly cost him his assignment.

Sandra and his friends had both witnessed the stress this caused and warned him off becoming involved in any other mysteries, something that seemed easier said than done on this trip. He hoped Salt Lake would be a much mellower city, as things appeared to be much more laid back there.

"Turn right on U.S. Highway Thirty-four," his navigation app said.

He'd actually put in directions to The Colorado Model Railroad museum in Greeley, a place he'd forgotten about. He turned down the music, exited the freeway and drove east until his app told him to go north on U.S. 85 for another two miles.

"How did we ever get around without Google maps and smartphones?" he wondered out loud as he pulled into the parking lot. "I should be able to get some great photos here for social media and my website." He parked the car, pulled his camera out of the bag, and went inside.

"Wow," Nick exclaimed as he took in the expanse of the exhibits.

"That's what we usually hear from the kids, not from adults," a museum volunteer said as she approached. "First time here?"

"Yes. I'm on my way to Salt Lake City, and wanted something exciting to break up the drive," he responded.

Her eyebrows lifted as she looked up and continued. "You're going to Salt Lake tonight?"

"Oh, no," Nick chuckled. "Just to Rock Springs, and then on to Salt Lake City tomorrow."

"Oh, that's good. Otherwise you'd have a long drive still ahead of you." The volunteer smiled as she looked at Nick's camera. "Photographer?"

"Yes. I'm on a one-year assignment to visit each state capital and take photographs for a major magazine."

"Sounds exciting," she replied. "Are you planning to take photos in here?"

"I'd like to, but not for the magazine, just my own site. Is that okay?"

"Of course, any publicity helps. Just be mindful of your flash. We get about twenty thousand visitors a year, but we could certainly accommodate more. Part of it is that we're not open seven days a week, and only three days a week during the winter."

"Let me take a brochure, and I'll put together a really nice post on my blog and social media with some of the photos and get you a little more exposure."

"Thank you very much, sir," she said as she extended her right hand.

"Nick," he responded and shook her hand. "Here's my card."

He wandered around for two hours, looking at the miniature exhibits, the hundreds of scaled locomotives, and even the dispatcher helping everything run smoothly. "Thanks a lot," he said to the same volunteer as he headed toward the exit. I'll have something up in a couple days."

"We'll look for it. We appreciate it," she said as she smiled and waved.

"Bye," Nick said, and he left the building and got in his car. He looked at his digital map, which showed him a faster route north to Cheyenne instead of going back to the Interstate. He got back to U.S. 85 and drove north.

"Kind of strange to be backtracking through Cheyenne after just being here a little over a week ago," Nick said as drove out of town.

It was just a few minutes over an hour's time when he crossed into Wyoming and pulled off the highway in Cheyenne. *Déjà vu,* he thought as he saw some of the places he'd been to recently. He'd helped the local authorities with a cold case, nothing compared to what he'd experienced firsthand in Denver.

His phone beeped as he pulled into a service station, glanced at the screen and saw a text from his friend Gerry, who'd landed him this assignment in the first place.

"Landed in Seattle. Drive safely." Ah, Seattle. His home. As great as this trip had been, there had been some down sides, and he missed home.

"Back in Cheyenne," he replied.

"Cheyenne? You've already been there."

"A roundabout way to Salt Lake City," he replied.

"Oh, okay. Hear from Sandra?"

"Not yet."

"Okay, drive safely."

"Always," he replied as he finished the text with a smiley face.

Four hours and one rest stop later, Nick arrived in Rock Springs, spotted a vacancy sign, and pulled into the parking lot of what appeared to be a fairly decent hotel.

His phone chimed again, revealing a text from Sandra: "Flights delayed. Home now. Love you. XOXOXO"

"Love you, too," he replied including a couple of heart emojis, and went into the office to register for a room for the night.

2

———————

FILLING TIME

I t was only about a three-hour drive along the interstate highway from Rock Springs to Salt Lake City, so Nick didn't worry about starting out too early.

"No real rush, but I should be able to check in early," he said as he loaded his bags into his car the next morning. "There should be a few places to pull off and capture some scenic photographs. I can always use more of those in my portfolio," he added.

Nick stopped several times along the drive into Utah. *This state is even more picturesque than I thought it would be,* he thought as he pulled off the freeway at Kimball Junction. He put the telephoto lens on his camera and took several photos facing south toward Olympic Park and the Park City and Deer Valley Resorts. "Must be gorgeous in the winter," he said to himself as he got back in the car. He opened the Marriot Bonvoy app on his phone and checked in, adding a note that he would be arriving early.

He then settled in the driver's seat for the final leg through the mountains and down into Salt Lake City. He opened the bag of black licorice he'd bought at the gas station and put one of the pieces into his mouth. He started chewing it, and then he stopped as his eyes opened wide.

He felt around inside his mouth with his tongue, and he felt an empty spot, where he was sure there used to be a filling.

"Crap," he muttered as he took the licorice out of his mouth. He kept his eyes on the winding road, but he rolled the gooey candy around in the fingers of his right hand.

A moment later he found the hard object in the candy, grabbed a tissue, put the filling in it, and used a napkin to try to remove the stickiness from his hand. He didn't think any dentist would be able to reuse it, but he wanted to have it with him just in case.

His app took him off the interstate to South State Street where he headed north to his hotel, the twelve-story Salt Lake City Marriott. He opened the hotel app, saw his room was ready and went directly to it. The door had been fitted with the newer smart locks with a proximity security feature, and he opened the door using his phone.

Technology, he thought, running his tongue along the inside of his teeth. A dull ache in his jaw told him he needed to get the tooth fixed soon. He didn't want a simple procedure to turn into a root canal.

Nick went back down to the lobby and approached the reception desk. "Checking in, sir?" the young clerk asked as she craned her head back to look up at Nick, something he'd gotten quite used to.

"No, I did that on the app. I need a dentist. I lost a filling on my drive in today."

"Hmmm," she mumbled. "I don't know of any open on Sunday, but I think we have a number for a dental hotline. Let me look," she said, typing on her computer keyboard.

"Hmm," she said. "There isn't one, but here are a few numbers for some dentists that list emergency hours."

She clicked her mouse. "I'll be back in a moment."

A moment later she returned with a printout. "I took a screen shot of the page, but you can see what I searched for, so you can probably find these on your phone."

"Thanks a lot," Nick said as he picked up the paper and went back to his room. He took out his phone and dialed the first number.

"Downtown Dental Group," a female voice answered.

"Hi, I arrived in town today and I had a filling fall out. Are there any dentists on call with your group that take emergency cases?"

"One moment, please," she replied and dreaded hold music started after a slight click.

"Oh," Nick groaned. He really hoped she could help him.

She came back on the line once Journey had been able to complete the first couple verses of "Don't Stop Believing."

"Sorry to keep you waiting, sir. "I have the number of a dentist who is not a part of our group, but she does take emergency cases, and she says she's available if you want to give her a call."

"Yes, please," he said, breathing a sigh of relief.

"Her name is Dr. Gordon. Here's her number."

"Thank you very much."

"You're welcome, sir. have a nice day."

"You, too. thanks," Nick said as he ended his call with her, and then dialed the dentist's number.

"Dr. Gordon," a woman answered.

"Hi," Nick said. "I got your name from the Downtown Dental Group. I just got into town today, lost a filling on the trip in, and I was wondering if I could come in and have it fixed."

"How soon?"

Nick looked at his watch. "I can leave right away. I'm at the downtown Salt Lake City Marriott. How far away are you?"

"I'm about ten to fifteen minutes away."

"Sure," Nick said eagerly. "What's your address?" He grabbed a piece of paper and scribbled it down as she spoke, reading it back to her to make sure it was right.

"It's my home office, but it sounds minor, and I should have everything I need to fix that filling for you."

"Oh, okay," Nick said a bit reluctantly. "I'll be there soon."

"Great, what's your name?"

"Nick. Nick O'Flannigan."

"Thanks, Nick. I'll be ready."

Nick ended the call and put the address into his driving app.

A little over fifteen minutes later, Nick found himself in front of an ordinary suburban house. As he pulled into the driveway, the garage door on the left opened, and a woman motioned him in. Tall, with dark hair, she wore a set of blue scrubs. A stethoscope hung around her neck, although he doubted she's need that.

Odd, Nick thought. *But I could see the benefit of being able to do dental work in your home if you are an emergency dentist. I wonder what the rules are when it comes to that.*

At this point, it didn't matter. He had an assignment this week, his tooth hurt, and he needed it fixed sooner rather than later.

"The office is right this way," she said. "My assistant should be with us shortly, although I doubt I'll need her help."

"Okay," Nick said, hung his light jacket on a hook just outside the door and followed her inside. She led him down a flight of stairs and into the basement.

In the center of the room was a normal looking dental chair. One of those portable stainless-steel tables sat beside it, a syringe ready. Behind the chair was a cabinet, filled with what looked like medication and some tools.

On a shelf underneath, he saw some odd attachments, what looked like leather straps of some sort.

"Have a seat," she said. As he did, she adjusted the headrest to its maximum extension. "You're almost too tall for this chair."

"It's a frequent complaint I get from dentists and doctors."

"Who's complaining?" she said with a wink.

Is she flirting with me? Nick wondered. Out loud, he just chuckled.

"So how did you lose the filling?"

"Chewing on some black licorice," he said with a wry smile.

"That stuff can be as hard on teeth as a frozen Snicker's bar. Let's have a look."

She laid him back, and he opened wide. She used a mirror to push his cheek to the side, and then put on a pair of safety glasses with an LED light on each side of the frame.

"Hmm," she said. "Middle molar left side. How long ago did you have this filling done?"

"It has to be at least five or six years, I would guess."

"Ah. Well, it was done pretty well. The hole still isn't too big. You floss?"

He tried to answer, but her mirror and a little hook were back in his mouth, and all he could manage was, "Hrrummpf."

"Good," she said, as if he'd said yes. "Many people don't. They lie to me about it, but I can tell."

He tried to nod, and then she was out of his mouth and sat him up again.

"Where are you from, Nick?"

"Seattle."

"Seattle? What brings you to Salt Lake?"

"Business. I'm on assignment with a national magazine."

She stepped back and looked at him. "Denver."

"What?"

"You were in Denver last week, right? I think I saw something about a photographer on the news, a tall red head. Are you that guy?"

Nick sighed. "Yeah, that's me."

"Oh, you're famous." She sounded a little disappointed.

"I wouldn't say so," he answered. "But lately I kind of feel like I am."

"Ah," she said. "Let me check on my assistant, and as soon as she arrives, we'll get you fixed up. Hang tight. You need some water or anything?"

"Sure."

She brought him a plastic bottle, and then picked up her phone, apparently sending a text message.

When she was done, he asked her, "So do many dentists have offices at home?"

"Not many," she said. "It's expensive, and you have to have your building inspected and get an occupancy license. Many HOAs don't allow home businesses, but many will waive that for doctors and dentists."

"I suspect you make a good neighbor, especially if someone loses a filling."

"I certainly hope so."

"Hello?" he heard a female voice say from above.

"Gloria, we're down here," Dr. Gordon said.

A blond haired, blue eyed woman appeared a moment later. She was curvy and tall, well-muscled and wore jeans and a t-shirt. She stepped behind the curtained area and emerged with a smock over her regular clothes.

"Okay, lay back and I'll give you a little shot," the dentist said. She titled the chair back, and then a big light swung over his head, lighting things up for her.

The rest of the procedure went much as it would have in any other dentist office. The dentist smoothed the area with a drill, installed a new filling, which took only minutes once he was numb, and then sealed it.

Gloria followed the dentist's instructions like, "Suction."

A couple times she told Nick to close his mouth around the sucking hose to remove the extra water from his mouth, and he did.

The pair worked together efficiently, and almost as soon as he sat up when they were done he felt better.

"You'll be numb a few more hours," she said. "Drinking water or eating might be an issue. Wait until you can feel again, so you don't bite your tongue or cheek without knowing it."

"Sure," Nick slurred a little bit. "Thanth a lot."

"Anytime," she said. "Do you have insurance to bill?"

"I'll just use my HSA card to pay today," he said. "Print out a bill, and I'll submith it lather."

The last part came out more slurred, and he felt like he was drooling.

"Sure," she said. She hit a couple of buttons on her phone, and asked Gloria to fetch the printout from upstairs.

On a shelf beside the cabinet, Nick saw four jars with strange objects floating in them.

"What are those?" he asked.

"Souvenirs, from dental school," she said. "All dentists seem to have them, and there's a story behind each."

"Ah," he said. Gloria came back with the printout, and he handed his card to the dentist. She ran it using an attachment on her phone.

"All set," she said. "Thanks for your business."

"Sure," he said. They all three walked upstairs. He walked out the door and grabbed his jacket off the hook outside the door. As he did, he knocked one off that had been already hanging there.

He picked it up and hung it back on the hook.

"Sorry about that." he said. "Hey, I have a pretty big social media following. You did such a good job I'd like to share that. Can we get an emergency dentist selfie?"

Dr. Gordon laughed. "Sure, why not?"

She opened the door to the garage to let in more light. He held his phone out at arm's length and the two women took places on each side of him. Nick bent his knees so he didn't tower over them quite as much, and then clicked a couple of photos.

"Thanks again," he said. "I'll share this far and wide."

"Thank you," she said. The two women waved as he got back into his car and drove back to the hotel.

So much for a eating a big dinner tonight, he thought. But at least I can concentrate on my assignment the rest of the week and not be in pain.

He smiled as he pulled back into the hotel parking lot. He'd have to see if he could get some soup somewhere. His stomach growled, and he hoped he'd be able to eat normally by breakfast time.

He grabbed a bottled soda from the machine in the lobby, and bummed a straw from the dining area, then headed upstairs. He saw a new text from Sandra.

"There yet?"

"Just getting back," he told her. "Had to run to an emergency dentist. I lost a filling."

His phone rang a second later, and he answered, retelling the story of the licorice, the filling, and his dental appointment in a basement.

By the time the call ended he was exhausted, but it was much too late in the day for a nap. He headed out to find something to eat. He walked around the corner to a place called Eva's, right next door to a Ramen Bar. He went inside, and since it was Sunday evening was seated right away, even without a reservation.

He ordered the shrimp and grits, something fairly soft, and found it delicious.

Trees outside the restaurant obscured the sky as he left, heading back to his hotel.

Two days of travel and a dental procedure had him quite tired. Once he got to the room, he flopped into the bed, finding the memory foam mattress quite comfortable, and turned on the television.

He logged into his Netflix account, reminding himself to log out of the SmartTV before he left on Friday, and put on a series he'd been watching. Two episodes in, he fell asleep.

3

CAPITOL TOURS

Nick ate breakfast in the hotel Monday morning more out of convenience that for any other reason, got his camera bag, and used the Uber app to set up a ride. Although his tooth was feeling better, his bad leg was still sore from all the walking he did in Denver. A shiny black car pulled up in front of the hotel two minutes later. "Nick?" the driver asked after he lowered the car's window.

"Yes. Hi. That was fast. As close as you can get to the East Entrance to the capitol building where the tours begin if you can."

"Piece of cake. Since you're taking pictures," the driver said, indicating his camera bag, "check out the two lion statues you'll pass as you head inside."

"Thanks," Nick said.

The driver made a left turn off East Capitol Boulevard five minutes later, pulled up past the buses and stopped next to one of the lion statues. "This is Integrity and the lion just past it is Fortitude. The tours inside run every hour and they start behind that door."

"Awesome. Thanks," Nick said, tipping the driver using the app, and grabbed his camera bag.

"Have a great day," the driver said.

Nick watched him drive away, and snapped some photos of the lions, including some up close of things like the paws and their facial expressions. The sign "Tours Begin Here" made it obvious where to start. He looked at his watch: 9:55.

The young female guide in her blue blazer smiled and nodded as Nick approached. "Here for the tour?" she asked.

"Yes, I am, "he replied. "Are there a lot of stairs?"

"Yes," she answered. "And we visit all four floors, but there is a central elevator you can use if you need it."

"I might because of my bad knee," he said, indicating his right leg.

"You won't be the only one," she said.

Nick nodded and moved to lean against the wall.

A couple minutes later, the guide looked at her watch and surveyed the group that had gathered. "Good morning, everyone," she said, projecting her voice. "Welcome to the Utah State Capitol Building. My name is Phoebe, and I'll be conducting your tour this morning. It will last just about an hour, we'll cover all four floors, and there are restrooms and elevators on each. We'll start by going to the central area over there that's called the Hall of Governors," Phoebe said as she pointed to her right and led the group to the middle part of the first floor directly under the dome.

Nick stayed near the back of the group and took photos as Phoebe talked about the history of the state and of the capitol buildings Utah had through its history. Four floors in one hour didn't leave much time to spend on each, so Nick stayed on the fourth floor when she announced the tour was ending. He took photos of the House and Senate Galleries, and then a few of the scenery visible through the windows.

He took the elevator back down to the first floor, went outside and took more photographs. The sun was mostly overhead now allowing him to get shots without long shadows. "Amazing symmetry," Nick said as he walked on the Philo T. Farnsworth Promenade, the oval pathway around the building.

He marveled at all the trees, shrubs, plaques, and monuments on the Capitol Grounds. He realized that he was limping, so he sat down on a bench and looked at his watch. "Didn't think it was this late," he said when he saw that he'd been outside for an hour and a half. His stomach growled, and so he decided to see where he could grab some lunch nearby.

He pulled out his phone and searched for nearby pubs. He was in the mood for something simple after his recent dental issue, and a cold beer would be really good with lunch. He selected Patrick's Pub, but saw it was a mile and a half away, a little longer distance that he wanted to walk. There were Green Bikes parked at a kiosk nearby, but he hadn't checked out how they worked yet. So he arranged for another Uber.

This may get a bit expensive, he thought to himself. *I'm going to have to either bring my own car or figure out the bikes soon.*

"You'll like Patrick's Pub," the driver told him after Nick shared his destination. "They don't have food, but you can go to J. Wong's across the hallway and get your food there. They'll even bring your order to the pub for you. They're always swamped during the lunch hour, but they are pretty fast."

"Thanks," Nick said as he closed his eyes and let the cool air conditioning flow over his face.

The short ride passed in relative silence, and the driver's music was soothing.

"Here we are," the driver said.

"Thanks," Nick said, grabbed his camera bag, and got out of the car.

The driver waved and drove away.

Nick walked through the doorway of the two connected businesses, a pub and a restaurant. He heard the noise of a crowd coming from the door to the pub on the left but followed his nose and turned right into the restaurant, J Wong's Thai and Chinese Bistro.

"Hello," the hostess greeted him.

"Hi," Nick replied as he looked up and scanned the lunch menu. "I'll be eating in the pub, if that's okay."

"Yes," was the short answer.

"Okay, let me have the Kung Pao Chicken with brown rice."

"Small, medium, or large portion?"

"Large, please."

"What soup?"

Nick hesitated. "Hot and Sour, please."

"Your name?"

"Nick," he replied as he paid. When the transaction was done, he headed over to the pub.

"Welcome to Patrick's," the bartender said loudly. He smiled and looked around. There was, indeed, a respectable crowd for lunch, but the pub wasn't too full. He found a seat at the bar, facing the television.

He hung his camera bag on the hook between his knees. The noon news was on.

"The investigation into the so-called Salt Lake Silencer continues," a reporter standing in a park said. Behind her, yellow crime scene tape fluttered in a breeze that also teased her hair. "The latest victim, found early last Thursday morning, died shortly after arriving at a Salt Lake area hospital. The victims have all been found at parks in relatively safe neighborhoods. All of them have been found naked, and with their tongues removed."

The picture changed to the reporter in the studio. "These are rather gruesome crimes. What are police saying about them?"

"Well, they have no suspects at the moment, although they say they are actively pursuing leads. They're also asking for the public's help. If you have any information please call the confidential tip line shown on your screen." A series of numbers displayed there.

"Thanks," the reporter in the studio said. "This is a developing story, and we will keep you posted."

"It's a crazy world," the bartender said. "The things people do to each other, am I right?"

"Believe me," Nick replied. "I've unfortunately seen worse, but you're right. Um, you have a porter on tap?"

"Sure thing," the bartender said, giving him a puzzled look. A moment later he returned with Nick's beer. "Did you order some food from next door?"

"I did. How is it?"

"Really good, although some of their hot dishes can be pretty spicy."

"That's okay with me," Nick said. The bartender left and Nick sighed. He took a long, slow draw on the beer as he enjoyed the taste of the frosty liquid.

A few minutes passed as Nick watched the rest of the news, including the weather.

"Order for Nick," he heard someone say, and turned around a waved.

"Over here," he said.

The young man brought the tray of soup and the chicken plate to the bar and set it next to Nick, who pulled a couple dollars from his shirt pocket and handed it over.

That's about all my cash, he thought. *I'll have to get some more.*

"Thank you, sir," the young man said and left.

"Another porter?" the bartender asked.

"Sure," Nick said. "Probably a water, too." He could smell the heat of the peppers, and he scanned the tray wondering where to start. He dug in.

"Those killings, they are odd for Salt Lake, right?" he asked.

"What?" the bartender replied.

"The guy whose tongue was cut out. The news said he was the fourth victim. Sounds like some kind of mob hit or something."

"The mob? Here?"

Nick shrugged.

"You're not from around here, are you?"

"Nope, Seattle."

"Well, we don't have a lot of mob crime here, especially on the East Side where those bodies were found. We have some drug cartels, but the cops keep them pretty much in check, and they operate more in the west valley."

"Interesting. I wonder what it is."

"My brother-in-law is a cop," the bartender said. "He says they think it is a serial thing, and they hate the 'Salt Lake Silencer' name the media has given the killer. Probably giving him just the attention he wants."

"Ah," Nick shuddered.

"How long are you here for?"

"A week," Nick said. "Photography assignment."

"Well, so far all the victims are from here," the bartender said. "But they've been happening once a week for the last month. So watch yourself." He winked.

I deserve that, Nick thought. *I probably freaked him out a bit, asking about that stuff.*

Nick forked the last few bites into his mouth. He saved his last sip of beer until he had eaten everything on his plate. Just as he swallowed, his phone dinged with a text from Sandra.

"Busy Monday?" it said.

Another reason to ignore the news and stop asking about that stuff. After Denver, she'd asked him not to get involved in any more mysteries.

"A bit," he said. "I'll text when I get back to the hotel. I got some great photos this morning."

He added a camera emoji. Sandra liked emojis, and he hadn't paid much attention to them until she came along, but he had to admit some of them were pretty fun.

She sent him back a thumbs up.

"Another?" the bartender asked, removing Nick's plate and placing it in a bin on the end of the bar, apparently for that purpose.

"Oh, no, thanks. It was great," he said, putting his phone away.

"You look like you've been traveling a while."

"How can you tell?"

"I have a knack for this stuff," the bartender said. "How long have you been away from home?"

"This is my eleventh week. I move to a different city every week."

"Wow, get boring?"

Nick chuckled. "I wish. A little crazy at times, but never boring."

"Sounds like a good gig."

"Definitely is," Nick replied.

The bartender set his check on the bar. "Whenever you're ready. Hope to see you back in here again."

Nick paid, then took an Uber back to the hotel, and sat at the desk in his room and opened his laptop. He pulled out his phone and sent a text to Sandra: "How's your day?"

"Good. I'll call when I get out of work."

"Perfect," he texted back. After hesitating for a moment, he added: "I love you."

He was more comfortable with those words every time he used them.

Sandra replied with a simple heart emoji.

He put the phone on the charger, closed the blinds and lay on the bed.

Just a quick pwer nap, and I'll upload pictures, he thought. He was asleep in a matter of minutes.

4

HERE'S YOUR SIGN

Nick woke after a quick twenty-minute snooze. He used the restroom, opened his laptop, and picked up his phone. A message from Sandra waited. "Is now a good time?"

"Sure." He typed back. "Two minutes."

It was only 3:30. He could talk to Sandra for a bit while uploading photos, and then find someplace for dinner. The show on the screen was some kind of court drama, and he ignored it.

He dialed her number, putting her on speaker to leave both of his hands free for the keyboard. *Multi-tasking at its finest,* he thought.

"Hey there," he said as she answered. "It's a bit early there. You're off work already?"

"I went in at four," she said. "Remember, my shifts rotate."

He'd actually forgotten. For a moment, he'd forgotten that she worked as a dispatcher for various service companies, rotated shifts often, and worked three twelve hour shifts one week, and four the next.

All she had to do was work seven days in a row, and then she could easily take a week off.

That's how Denver had worked out so well, along with the fact that she had a lot of paid time off accrued.

"I do remember now," he said. "I'd forgotten what week it was for you."

"Yep. They may be changing our schedules soon, which would be good for me. Less rotations, and more consistency."

"That would be good." Nick had been working as a freelancer so long, he often forgot about how other people's schedules worked.

"What are you up to?" she asked.

"Well, I went on a capitol building tour this morning, and I took a bunch of photos. I took a bunch more on the drive down, and I'm finally getting around to uploading all of them."

"Oh, good. Sounds like you're busy with your actual assignment. No weird stuff."

"No weird stuff," he said, looking at the photos he'd taken on the drive, and moving them all to his personal folder. A few were pretty good, and he figured he'd edit them and add them to his website later.

That was one good thing about this trip. Sales were up of prints and even digital downloads of his photos. He was getting exposure places he'd never been before. No pun intended.

He then got to the capitol photos, starting with the pictures of the lions. They were pretty solid too, something Emily would definitely like.

He and Sandra continued to chat. He told her about the filling incident, which reminded him that he needed to post his selfie to social media as he'd promised. There were also the photos from the museum in Greeley he hadn't loaded yet. His emergency dental visit really threw him off his game, and he needed to get organized again.

He also told her about his leg being sore, and his decision to take Ubers to the capitol building.

"Sounds expensive," she said.

"It's not too far, but I'm thinking about using the Green Bikes they have here. I would love to bike and still get some exercise without straining my knee."

"That's a good idea," she said. "I hear Salt Lake has a good bike program, and some good bike lanes."

"They do," he said. "I think it is similar to the program I saw in Boise, but I never used that one. I just have to figure it out."

"Other cities probably have it, too. But grab a helmet if you're going to ride around in the city," she said.

"You're right," he said. "I'll pick one up. Renting one in Helena was no big deal. But who knows how many people wear them here."

She laughed.

"I got some good shots today. I'll send them to you, and see what you think," he told her.

"I'll look for them. It is great talking to you, Nick."

"You too. I wish you could be here."

"Me, too," she said. "I'd be sure to keep you out of trouble."

Nick laughed. "I bet you would."

"I love you Nick. Talk to you tomorrow?"

"For sure," he said. "Once I get some photos, I'll head for dinner."

He ended the call, selected a couple photos, and emailed them to her as promised.

He then opened his social media app on his phone and added his selfie to his feed. "Filling fixed after hours, thanks to Dr. Gordon." When he typed the "@" symbol followed by the dentist's name, she came up right away.

He hit post, did the same thing on Instagram. then closed both applications, switching to his laptop. He quickly edited some of the railroad museum photos, and opened a word document to write a blog post.

He did a pretty respectable job on a blog post, ran it through a grammar checker. He then posted to his website, made a few more corrections with the proofreading tool there, and optimized it for SEO.

He scheduled that post to go live the next morning, when it would get more exposure, and set it up on his social media automation program with the right hashtags and tagging the museum itself.

"That should help them, I hope," he said to himself, glancing up from the little screen to the television, which had switched to the news.

He opened the maps on his phone to search for dinner as he watched.

Spitz showed up just around the corner, had great reviews, and was open until 10. He picked up the remote, and then paused. Instead of turning the television off, he turned it up.

"—developments in the Salt Lake Silencer case," the reporter said. "The police have a new lead. A video has surfaced of the victim being wheeled into the hospital the night he arrived, posted on social media by an anonymous account."

The video started, and Nick watched closely. A body was on a gurney, covered by a sheet except for the victim's face, hidden by an oxygen mask.

"What is that?" he thought, but he couldn't pause the video and study it. It was live.

The man passed into the hospital. "Police are looking for the person who posted the video. Again, if you have any information, please call the Utah State Police hotline."

Nick wanted to see the report again, but the newscaster had moved on.

They'll probably show it again later tonight or post in on their social media, he thought.

Sandra's words came back to him.

"I'd keep you out of trouble."

"Stay out of trouble yourself, Nick," he said. "Don't get involved."

Dinner turned out to be both great and affordable. One porter was all he allowed himself, thinking he would do some work this evening and not wanting to feel either full or sleepy.

He opened his laptop, doing some research on the area and even looking up restaurants and other things to do.

He watched the news again when it came on. He figured they would put the video online later, where he could look at it again.

They showed the same view of the victim, reaching up trying to get the attention of the first responders wheeling him inside.

"That looks like sign language," he said aloud. "The police will know that, though. Surely someone else will see this and know that same thing."

Still, he didn't want to take the chance. He opened his phone and called the tip line displayed at the bottom of the screen.

"I have a tip about the Salt Lake Silencer," he said. "But it may not be much."

"Anything helps," the person on the other end said. He could hear others talking in the background of her conversation, and he felt a little foolish, but he was already on the line.

"The video of the victim being wheeled into the hospital shows the man's hand dangling from the stretcher. It looked like it was just flailing at first, but I think he is using sign language to try to communicate to the paramedics."

"Interesting thought. Any idea what it might mean?"

"Not really. I had a deaf cousin growing up, and so I think that is what I see, but I never learned well enough to know what everything means."

"Well, thanks for the information. I'll pass it along."

The call ended before Nick could say anything more.

Just as well, he thought. At least I did my duty and called.

He shut off the television. It had been a long day, and he fell right to sleep.

5

JARRING REVELATION

Nick was getting dressed the next morning when his cell phone rang. It was Emily, his editor at *Travel USA* magazine. He cleared his throat and answered his phone. "Good morning, Emily," he said in an upbeat voice.

"Hello, Nick," Emily said in a monotone. "I had a nice chat with Gerry yesterday and she said you guys had a good couple of days once the press debacle got cleared up. How's it going in Salt Lake City? No more press or mysteries, I hope?"

"Yeah, we did have a good time. And don't worry, nothing's going on here aside from taking some great photos. I took a bunch yesterday both inside and outside. The capitol complex here is really nice, filled with statues and flowers and a nice oval walkway surrounding the capitol and other main buildings.'

"Sounds nice, have you uploaded them yet?"

"I'll get them up there today before noon. I'm going to get some more shots this morning."

"I'll check them out this afternoon. You're not taking any newsworthy ones this time are you?"

"Uh, no," Nick said. Technically, it was the truth. A video of the local newscast and an anonymous call didn't count. "I'm deleting duplicates and only sending you the best of what I have taken. All the personal ones I have so far will be on my social media and website today."

"Oh, okay," Emily said haltingly.

"One hundred percent transparency," he said and looked at his watch.

"Sounds good," Emily replied. The enthusiasm in her voice returned as she continued. "Gerry said that the three gals all hit it off great. What'd you think?"

"It was as if they'd been friends for years."

"That's good. Gerry also said she got a good idea for a feature story, but she wouldn't tell me what it was. She said she'd let me know when she was ready to submit it."

"Hmmm," Nick said. "It'll be news to me, too."

"She didn't tell you?"

"No, not even a hint that she was working on one or had one in mind."

"Everything she's done so far has been super, including recommending you, so I'm sure it will be good."

"Thanks."

"Well, I just wanted to check in with you to make sure everything was okay as you close in on three months on the road. Does it seem that long?"

"Not really."

"That's good," the editor replied. "Keep up the good work and let me know if you run into any problems."

"I will, Emily. Thanks."

"You're welcome. Talk to you later, Nick."

"Bye," he said and ended the call.

Nick grabbed his camera bag and opened the door to the hallway. He put the 'Do Not Disturb' sign on the door and headed out for breakfast at Elevations, a local favorite for breakfast near Temple Square.

It was only half a mile, and he noticed a Green Bike station next to the bus station outside his hotel.

He inserted his credit card, grabbed a bike, and took off, following his phone directions and arriving at another kiosk near the restaurant less than ten minutes later.

That was easy, he thought, noting the website for daily, weekly, and even longer rentals. *I'll check that out later. Well, that, and getting a helmet.*

After eating at Elevations, a nearby breakfast spot with great food, he headed for Temple Square. After taking photos of the Square and the surrounding areas for nearly two hours, Nick went back to the hotel where he uploaded his first batch of photos to the magazine's cloud folder. He looked at his watch. *Thanks to the hour time difference, Emily's got her photos before noon.* Nick smiled to himself.

He downloaded his newest photos to his laptop. "I can sort them later," he said as he grabbed his notebook and headed back out. He decided to go to J Wong's and Patrick's one more time before trying a new lunch spot tomorrow.

Hope the same guy's there, he thought as he walked the three blocks west. He turned into the vestibule and inhaled deeply. The aromas from J Wong's steered him right into the bistro. He scanned the menu and stepped to order. The woman there looked up, and then up some more. She peered over the top of her glasses at six-foot-six Nick.

"You're tall," she said matter-of-factly.

"Yes, ma'am," Nick replied as he bent his neck to look her in the eyes. "I'd like the Sweet and Sour chicken with white rice and the Egg Drop Soup, please. The name is Nick, and I'll be across the hall in the pub."

He pulled out his wallet and handed her his debit card. He'd forgotten to stop for more cash.

She swiped his card and handed him a receipt to sign. He wrote in a generous tip and handed it back to her.

"Welcome to Patrick's," came the familiar greeting after he made his way across the hall. He looked toward the bar and saw the same bartender he's seen the day before.

That's good, he thought as he weaved his way through the tables toward the bar.

"Welcome back," the bartender said as Nick sat on the bar stool. "Same porter?"

"Just an iced tea for now," Nick said as he looked around the bar area. He laid his debit card on the counter, so the bartender could start a tab.

The noise level increased as a group of construction workers entered. "Welcome to Patrick's," a server hollered. The group made their way to a couple corner tables and the waitress headed their way.

"More tea?" the bartender asked as he stopped in front of Nick.

"Yes," Nick said.

The bartender reached under the counter for a pitcher and re-filled Nick's glass.

Thanks," Nick said as he quickly scanned the bar again. "Yesterday we chatted a little about that guy whose tongue was cut out."

"Yea," the bartender replied. "Still, that's pretty damn creepy. Why are you so interested?"

"Just curious," Nick said. "You know anything about the other victims?"

The bartender looked around and then leaned forward toward Nick. "Haven't heard much except they were all found in the Sugar House area."

"Huh."

"Today's paper had a pretty good summary," the bartender said, handing it to him. "Try not to get your lunch on it."

"Thanks," Nick said. A moment later his food arrived, and he slid the paper aside while he ate. Then he picked it up to read the article.

It turned out the men had not been killed where they were found, each in their own car, in one of the parks in the Sugar House area. There were no fingerprints at the scene, but there wasn't enough blood for them to have died on the spot.

And none of them had actually died from blood loss. Everyone had died from an overdose of opioids.

Weird, he thought.

"You get the information you were looking for?" the bartender asked.

"Yeah," Nick said.

"What's your fascination anyway?"

"In almost every city I've been to on this trip, I've been involved in some kind of mystery, and while I keep hoping not too, things keep happening around me. So I've developed what some of my friends would call an unhealthy curiosity."

"Sounds right," the bartender said.

Nick left. He would definitely try elsewhere for lunch, not that this place wasn't cool, but the bartender seemed a little creeped out by him. And Nick didn't blame him.

Leave it alone, he told himself, resolving to do just that.

The afternoon sun felt warm as he walked back toward the hotel. *Tonight might be a good time to get some evening photos of the capitol and the surrounding park.*

When he was almost back, his mom called.

"Hello," he heard when he answered.

"Hi, Mom. How are you and dad doing?"

"Nick wants to know how we are!" she yelled to his nearly deaf father.

Nick quickly pulled the phone away from his ear.

"Tell him we're fine," Nick heard his father's familiar yell.

"He says we're fine," his Mom relayed.

"That's good to hear, Mom. It sounds like Dad's doing a lot better since his heart attack."

"He is. That has its good and bad points."

"That's great mom. I'm in Salt Lake now."

"How did you time in Denver go?"

"Great. Sandra said she really liked talking with you."

"She seems like a sweet girl."

"Yes, she is. Hopefully we'll be able to get together again in a month or so."

"That's nice. What does she do?"

Nick paused. "She's some kind of dispatcher. It seems like more than that though. She seems pretty well off."

"Whatever it is, she must be pretty lucky to be able to take so much time off to spend with you."

"Yeah, she can rearrange her schedule pretty easily." Nick's eyes closed as he pondered that thought. *And I'm pretty lucky that she wants to spend that much time with me.*

"How long have you been gone from Seattle?"

"This is week eleven, Mom. I head down to Arizona after this week, then to New Mexico, Texas, and Oklahoma."

"How's the car?"

"Everything's fine, Mom."

"That's good, Nick. Just stay safe out there."

"Always, Mom." He paused slightly before continuing. "Well, good talking with you. I love you, and tell Dad I love him, too. I'll call next week."

"Love you, too, son. Bye."

"Bye, Mom," Nick replied and ended the call.

He'd already scouted out a new dinner place, one within easy walking distance called From Scratch, a great looking place with burgers and pizza. He might grab a bike tomorrow, but for tonight he would walk there, and then head to the capitol building for some evening photos.

He got there and found a seat, one where he could see the television. He was anxious to see the news.

Just out of curiosity.

The burger was huge, but Nick's characteristic huge appetite allowed him to devour it as he watched.

The news started with a headline and a spinning, "Breaking News."

"Authorities have what they consider to be the first break in the Salt Lake Silencer case," the newscaster said. "We'll go out to Beverly, live at the police department after a late afternoon briefing."

"Thanks," Beverly said. A banner under her image also said "Breaking News" followed by a caption declaring new developments.

"An anonymous tip led police to be able to open the most recent victim's cell phone. It seemed he was using American Sign Language to communicate the code to open it, but everyone had missed it until the police got a tip sometime yesterday."

I did make a difference, Nick thought. That's something.

"They hadn't been able to open it to this point. Inside they found this photo, taken the evening before he was found. They don't know that the photo is linked to his murder, but it does seem odd. Before we show the photo, we do want to warn that it may be disturbing to some viewers."

Nick leaned forward, stopped, and put the French fry down he'd been about to put in his mouth. Then the image came up on the screen.

It showed a dental chair, but one with some odd strap attachments. Next to it was a silver table holding various dental instruments.

Once again, Nick kicked himself for being out, away from his computer when he saw this report.

Because he thought he'd been in that room just a few days before.

For an unusual dentist appointment in the basement of a suburban home.

Could he be sure it was the same one? The chair looked almost the same, and Dr. Gordon had said other dentists sometimes had offices at home. *Was that true?*

Suddenly Nick felt sick. Sick enough to lose his appetite.

Dr. Gordon had an assistant. They both seemed very nice. *Would they be capable of—this?*

Nick felt like he had to get back to his hotel room and look at this photo. Surely they would post it online, right?

"What else did police find?" the anchor in the studio asked.

"They did corroborate some text and phone numbers they'd gotten from the victim's cell phone provider, but they haven't told us what else that might mean."

"Thanks Beverly. As always, keep us posted."

"Will do."

The newscast moved on.

Nick raised his hand. "Check, please."

The waitress came over. "Was something wrong with the fries?" she asked.

"Nope," he said. "Just have to go."

He paid the bill, and then headed back to the hotel. He'd have to get night photos another evening.

As he entered the lobby, his phone rang. It was Sandra.

"Hey," he said."

"Hey," she said. "You okay?"

"Just headed back to my room to grab some things," he said. He felt bad about not telling her what was going on, but maybe it wasn't the same place after all.

Maybe Dr. Gordon had nothing to do with any of this, and he didn't want to look like an idiot, or like he was getting involved with something he shouldn't.

"Oh," she said. "You want to call me later?"

"Sure," he said. "I may duck out to take some sunset and night photos." Not a lie, he actually had planned to do that.

"Okay. Whenever you have a chance is fine."

Nick ended the call and headed for his room. He actually did hope this was nothing, and that he could just head out and take photos as planned.

When he got to his room he opened his laptop. One browser tab was on his social media page, and he saw Dr. Gordon had responded to his post. "Thanks for sharing."

It couldn't be her.

But he opened a new tab to the news channel's page. There, on the top of the feed in a pinned post was the photo. Nick clicked on it, and then right clicked and downloaded it to his computer. He opened it in his photo editing program, and zoomed in, looking around.

There. On the shelves behind the chair were a few jars. Three, to be exact.

All with dental school souvenirs.

Nick remembered the chair he'd been in didn't have straps, but had there been something, something on the bottom shelf of a cabinet.

Maybe.

He'd been in pain, desperate for help, and he'd had pain killers during the procedure. How could he trust his memory?

Still, he at least had to call again.

Give them a tip.

So he dialed the hotline again.

"I think I've been to the room you showed on the news," he blurted out as soon as anyone answered. "I had an emergency filling at a dentist on Sunday. That looks just like her home office."

"Slow down, sir. Can I have your name?"

"Can I remain anonymous?"

"Certainly, but—"

"I'd like to do that, then. Her name is Dr. Gordon."

Nick hung up the phone right away. His heart was racing. There was no way he could just go take some photos now and act normal. He decided to go to the gym, work off some energy. Maybe then he could sleep.

He changed and headed for the hotel gym. He then worked out as hard as he could, finishing with a quick few minutes on the elliptical.

His muscles were good and sore, and once he got back to the room, he took a quick shower.

Tomorrow would be another day. He set an early alarm to get some sunrise photos and went to bed without turning on the television again.

6

INVOLVEMENT

Nick awoke early the next morning when the sound of the alarm jarred him out of his restless and dream-filled sleep. He'd dreamed of dentists, dancing severed tongues, and being strapped to a chair. He was grateful to be awake.

He opened the drapes. The lights from the nearby buildings glowed and was absorbed into the pitch-black sky. He dressed warmly, grabbed his camera bag, phone, and car keys, and headed down for his car. There should be better parking this early, before the meters started to charge him, and he'd be back for breakfast before things got really busy.

There were very few cars on the roads, and he had his choice of any one of dozens of parking spots near the capitol building. Faint sunlight peeked over the Wasatch Mountains as he neared the south-western side of the capitol building. His photos of the mountain tops were followed by photos of the sun glancing off the capitol dome. As the sun got even higher in the sky, Nick captured photos of the elongated shadows cast by the various statues in the park surrounding the building.

Nick turned away from one photo and was almost struck by a jogger.

"Watch out!" he said, and memories of having his camera stolen in Salem rushed through his head. The jogger kept going, headphones firmly in place.

"Wow," he muttered.

He headed back to his car and the hotel.

He left the camera and his jacket in the room and went down for breakfast. He was enjoying the hot coffee, when he pulled out his phone and sent a text to Sandra: "Sorry about last night. Late one, and I fell asleep." The statement was not entirely untrue. But he felt bad. He should be simply telling her the truth, but he didn't want to upset her.

The national news droned on the television in the breakfast area, and he still felt faintly guilty.

Her reply was quick: "No worries. I had to get up early anyway."

"Talk this afternoon?" he said.

"Sure!" she replied, a heart emoji on the end.

"Miss you," he replied.

And he did miss her. *I'll tell her what's going on this afternoon,* he told himself.

He looked at his plate of food plus a yogurt and a banana and devoured them all. He got one more cup of coffee, put a lid on it, and took it to his room. After downloading this morning's photos to his laptop, he went through and started to edit them.

When most of them were done, he switched to his browser, and typed in "The Salt Lake Silencer."

Hundreds of hits appeared immediately. Several national media outlets had picked up on the story and were running it in the secondary headlines. He read several of the articles, but there was nothing really new from the night before.

Maybe it really wasn't her.

Then his phone rang, an unfamiliar Utah number.

"This is Nick," he answered.

"Nick O'Flannigan?" the gruff male voice asked.

"Yes?"

"This is Detective Worthen, Utah State Police. Do you have a moment?"

Crap.

"Sure, how can I help you?" he asked, trying to keep innocence in his voice.

"We got an anonymous tip yesterday about a dentist, and we got your name from her patient records."

"Dr. Gordon?"

"Yes. Did you recently have a procedure done by her?"

"I did. I lost a filling on the way into town and needed an emergency dentist. She was recommended to me."

"Did you go into her office?"

"I met her at her home. She has an office there."

"She does?" the detective said.

"Yes, in her basement. That's where the room on the news—" Nick just realized what he had done.

"So you called in the tip?"

"I—Yes. I thought I recognized the room when I saw it on the news."

"And you are from out of town."

"Seattle. I'm here on a photography assignment." *The less information I share, the better,* he thought.

"Where are you staying?"

"The Marriott downtown."

"Can you meet me out front in say, fifteen minutes?"

"Sure," Nick said.

The call ended and he sighed. This was the time, before things went any further.

He texted Sandra. "Can I call?"

"Can it wait until after I'm off work?" she answered.

Nick signed. Technically, yes it could. He hoped.

"Sure," he said.

He went into the bathroom, splashed water on his face, and headed downstairs.

An unmarked Dodge Charger waited at the curb. The passenger window rolled down.

"Nick?" a man called.

"Detective Worthen?" he answered, bending down to look in the car.

"You're as tall as you seem on social media," the man said. "To your credit, you do look just like your photos. Some people are a little more obtuse."

"You checked me out?" Nick said.

The detective shut off his car, got out and stood.

"You want to get a coffee?" he said. "We could use your help, and I'm just waiting on something."

"Sure," Nick said.

"Have you tried Beans and Brews yet?" he asked. "Right around the corner."

"I'll give it a shot."

"Funny guy," the detective said with a chuckle. He reached in his car, put a tag on the rear-view mirror, and left his car parked where it was.

Nick laughed at his unintended joke. They walked the short distance to the coffee shop.

They ordered, and then he turned to the detective. "I'm a little nervous here. How can I help you?"

"Well, I'm waiting on a search warrant, but it seems you were one of the last ones in Dr. Gordon's home office, which is a slight bit illegal by the way."

"She said something about HOAs not liking it."

"Well, it wouldn't be illegal really except for the drugs. Inadvisable maybe, but not against the law. But she isn't allowed to have controlled substances, at least not in the quantities she seems to have on the shelves, in her home."

"Ah."

"Didn't you think it was odd for her to have a basement office in her home?"

"I did, but she actually told me other dentists do it too."

"Hmm. Not that I know of, but maybe they are all doing it these days," the detective said with a smile. "When did you say you got into town?"

"Sunday."

"The same day as your appointment."

"Yeah. I lost a filling on the drive from Denver. Black licorice."

"Disgusting habit," Worthen said.

"I'm beginning to think so," Nick said.

"Tell me what happened."

"With the filling?"

"The dentist, Mr. O'Flannigan." The detective, jovial at first, seemed to be losing his patience and his sense of humor.

"Ah. I arrived, she opened the garage for me, I went in. She took a look, asked some questions, and then sat me in the chair. Her assistant arrived a little while later—"

"Her assistant?"

Nick just nodded and kept going. "She just gave me the usual shot in the gums, drill and fill, pretty quick actually. Then I left."

"What did you talk about before her assistant arrived?"

"My reason for being in Salt Lake City. Where I was from. Stuff like that."

"Huh."

The detective typed some things into his phone, and then looked up.

"We've got the warrant. I've got to go. Once we've been inside, I may call you again to look at some photos. Would that be okay?"

"Sure, whatever you need."

"You don't seem to be too shaken, Mr. O'Flannigan."

"Oh, I'm used to dealing with the police, and the media," he said.

"You'll have to tell me about that sometime."

"It will have to be later in the day, and with something stronger than coffee," Nick told him.

"I may take you up on that. In the meantime, have a good day Mr. O'Flannigan. I'll be in touch."

The detective stood and left. Nick made his way back to the hotel, suddenly tired.

But he had work to do, and that work would definitely keep his mind off of this, and how he was going to explain it to Sandra and Emily if he turned up on the news again.

7

COMING CLEAN

Nick started by uploading the personal photographs he'd taken so far to his website MacroPhotography4U.com and scheduling some on his social media. His phone began vibrating on the hotel room desk, and he hoped it was Sandra, but it was Gerry.

"What's up?" he answered.

"Not much, Nick. I heard you had a good call with Emily."

"Well, it could have been better. She seemed a bit concerned about my getting involved with cases and being in the media. I assured her I wasn't and that her photographs were my top priority. I've already sent some great photos to the cloud, plus I got some stunning photos at sunrise this morning. She's going to love this city."

"That's good. How's it going there? Heard from Sandra?"

"Yes. We've been in touch, if you must know."

"That's cool. Anything new?"

"Between us? No, just seeing where things go after the week in Denver," he replied.

"What about in Salt Lake, anything going on there?"

"Well, it is a really great place. I rode a bike once, and plan to use the ones they have here again. I just need to get a helmet, or Sandra—"

"Come on, Nick," Gerry replied. "You know what I mean."

Nick exhaled deeply and looked around the room. "Well," he began after a lengthy pause, "there was this fellow whose tongue had been cut out, and it turns out that he's the fourth in four weeks."

"I heard about those on the news. That is kind of why I asked."

"I actually did call in a tip, because I saw something in a video the police released to the public."

"How did that go?"

"Fine, but—"

"But what?"

"It seems to be turning into something more. I saw something, and I tried to stay out of it, and stay anonymous, but a local detective tracked me down."

"Nick!"

"It's a long story. So I have to tell Sandra this afternoon, just in case I can't stay in the background."

"Okay. Don't let this get in the way of your main job there, and don't let anything get in between you and Sandra."

"I won't. I'm trying to stay as far out of it as I can," he said.

"Good. She's a great gal, Nick."

"You like her, don't you?"

"Of course I do. She's awesome, and I think you two would be great together long-term."

"Hmmm," Nick murmured. "I've been thinking that, too. I'm hoping we can get together again in a few weeks."

"Super," exclaimed Gerry. "Let me know when and where, I just might send flowers with your name on them."

"I'm not sure I need your help, Gerry," Nick said.

"Trust me, Nick. Girls love flowers."

"I don't doubt you, but I can do this on my own."

"Well, you have a good afternoon, and call me if you need my help with anything."

"Sure will, my friend. Thanks for everything. I can't wait to get back to Seattle and spend some quality time with you guys."

"Let's talk again soon."

"Sounds good. Bye for now."

"Bye, Nick," she said as the call ended.

Nick got up, went into the bathroom, and while in there, he heard his phone beep.

It was Sandra. "Talk now?"

He took a deep breath and called her.

"What's up, Nick?" she asked. "What was so urgent earlier?"

"I've become involved in something," he said.

"Oh, Nick."

"I didn't mean to, honestly. Remember I told you about my filling?"

"Yes."

"And have you heard about the Salt Lake Silencer?"

"Who hasn't? Some serial or spree killer, national news. Nick, don't tell me you are involved in that?"

"They think it was a dentist."

"The dentist you saw?"

"A photo was on a victim's phone. It showed her home office. The same one I went to."

"Nick! So were you in danger?"

"I don't think so. She had an assistant come help her. I'm not sure she even did it, but a detective tracked me down. I left an anonymous tip, but—"

"You what? Nick, you promised you wouldn't get involved."

"That's why I tried to stay anonymous. But I was listed as one of her patients, and he figured it out."

"So it's not your fault, I suppose?"

"Well, it's not really."

"C'mon Nick."

"I'm sorry."

"Yeah, okay. Listen, it was a long day. I gotta go."

"Okay. Talk later?"

"Sure," she said. She hung up before Nick could say more.

"Love you," he said to the blank screen. "What have I done?"

Just then his phone dinged again.

It was a text from an unknown Utah number. "Call me."

Nick checked and found it was the same number from earlier. Detective Worthen.

Reluctantly, he dialed.

"Hi, Mr. O'Flannigan."

"Can you call me Nick?"

"I'm sorry?"

"Can you call me Nick? Mr. O'Flannigan sounds like my dad. Tell me you have good news."

"I wish," Detective Worthen said. "We served the search warrant. The chair was normal, like you said it was. There was no evidence of straps, and there were no odd jars on the shelves like in the victim's photo."

"There were some jars when I was there," Nick said. "I'm almost positive."

"Almost?"

"I was in pain. She did give me drugs, but nothing too bad. I just don't want to say for sure."

A long sigh followed. "Okay. Maybe it wasn't even her after all. Maybe other dentists or some other wacko does have a similar basement office."

"Sorry it didn't pan out," Nick said.

He was generally speaking sorry. He didn't want her to be the killer in a variety of ways, and for a number of reasons that all meant he wasn't involved after all.

Now he just had to convince Sandra and Gerry of that, and hope Emily didn't hear about it.

He decided tonight would be a good night to take some sunset photos. He'd been up early, but one long day sure wouldn't hurt.

He packed up his camera and headed out, but not before he searched for "bike shops near me."

He needed to pick up a helmet before he took one of the city bikes again.

There was at least one way he could set Sandra's mind at ease. Before he left the hotel room, he bought a four-day pass, which gave him a code for unlimited thirty-minute rides until he left.

He headed for the Trek bike shop he found, checking out a bike for the short ride, knowing it would be his last one free of head protection.

While he was there, he bought some gloves, padded bike shorts, and a riding shirt too. He didn't need all those here, but the gloves would come in handy, and the rest he could use along the way.

He strapped the helmet on his head and headed for the capitol building.

The streets were crowded. There were other cyclists too, but even as he rode along with them, he felt lonelier than he had in a long time.

The sunset shots of the capitol building and the park were incredible, and he got lost in the job for a few hours. He then headed for Temple Square, where he took some more great shots.

Emily would love this city and these photos, but he was falling in love with it himself despite his unwilling involvement with law enforcement.

Oh well. It seemed like that was over, and maybe the rest of the week would be uneventful. He could live with that.

He climbed on a green bike, put on his new helmet, and took a quick selfie with the temple framed well in the background. He edited it quickly on his phone and then sent it to Sandra.

"Behaving myself. Wishing you were here."

The message showed sent and received.

But she didn't answer.

8

———————

DISTRACTION

With nothing on his schedule for Thursday morning, Nick didn't set his alarm. He rarely slept in, so it was a rare treat when he was able to let himself do so. He slept longer than he thought he would.

What woke him up was his stomach making "Feed me" noises that he couldn't ignore. He rolled to his side and looked at the nightstand clock. 9:14. "Wow," he exclaimed. "That felt good."

Nick got out of bed, opened the drapes, turned on his phone, and got dressed. He hurried downstairs for the complimentary breakfast, not remembering if it closed at 9:30 or 10:00. He was relieved when he saw the sign "Breakfast Served 6:00 - 10:00." He fed his hungry stomach and used the dark roast coffee to kick his brain into gear. He cleared his items away and went to the front desk.

"Good morning, sir. How may I help you?" the cheerful clerk asked.

"Hey there," he said. "I'm only here for a few days longer, and I want to see something other than just the Temple Square and the capitol building. Do you have a little map or something?"

"I can make some suggestions."

"Shoot."

"Liberty Park isn't far, and it's pretty cool. So is the Gigal Sculpture Garden, and Pioneer Park too."

"Those sound cool."

"They are in opposite directions."

"That's okay, I got hooked up with the Green Bike program."

"Oh good. It's a great deal."

Nick went upstairs, changed into appropriate clothing and headed back to the lobby on the main floor. As he walked out of the hotel to the station he sent a text to Sandra: "Biking this morning and visiting some parks. All quiet."

There was no response.

Nick adjusted the seat and handlebars, no small feat even though he'd selected a large bike and used the map to lead him east and south to Liberty Park. He returned the bike at the station near the northwest corner of the park, and then walked south to 1300 South and then east one block to The Park Café. It hadn't been long since he'd eaten breakfast, but the hunger pangs returned with the biking.

After a quasi-healthy snack that included a juice and a bowl of fresh fruit, he thought about riding down to the Sugar House area where the four victims had been found.

Then he remembered what he had told Sandra. "Stay out of it," he mumbled. He walked around for a little bit, and then decided to go visit the sculpture park, and then try to get some more interior photos of the capitol building.

He followed the directions on his phone, and made his way to the sculpture garden, where he took even more photos. The garden was small, but there was an amazing sculpture of a sphinx with the head of Joseph Smith.

He then headed for the capitol building after a quick rest and stop for an iced coffee on the way. He also grabbed a water bottle, remembering to stay hydrated.

He went inside, and took the elevator to the top floor, working his way down as he took photos along the way. The light was different than the first time he'd been here, softer, and he took his time, resting his sore legs along the way.

But they felt better after a few even brief bike rides, and he resolved to do more biking whenever he could. All the walking in Denver had been rough, this was much better. And the stronger his leg felt, the more likely he would be able to walk more too.

He reached the bottom floor and the Hall of Governors. He spotted his guide from earlier in the week and waved. She waved back with a smile before returning to her tour, this one filled with several seniors who were taking the elevator, the same thing Nick had done his first day here.

The air outside was just warm enough for comfort, but not too hot. The ride back to the hotel was quick and pleasant, and he felt good as he docked the bike and headed inside.

He saw the same young clerk at the front desk who'd been there this morning.

"Hey, there," he said slightly out of breath.

"Go biking?" she asked.

"Yeah, it was good. I might do more tomorrow if I have time. Thanks for the recommendations."

Nick headed back upstairs, and thought about taking a shower, but he wanted to check his email quickly first. There were several new ones, but none from the police, and still nothing from Sandra.

He texted her again, but simply said, "Let me know when you're ready to talk."

Normally eager for the news, Nick was hesitant to turn it on. He wanted to know the Silencer had been caught, and that he wasn't in the news, but at the same time he was afraid to look.

He hadn't seen any reporters or talked to any. Check one for good. But technically he was a witness. He could be named.

He'd hardly looked at social media all day. Several of his photos from the day before were getting likes and traction. But there was an odd note about halfway down his notifications. Dr. Gordon had removed the tag on his photo, and her comment had been deleted.

He scrolled a little further and saw a video come up from the Salt Lake News channel. "Breaking News on the Salt Lake Silencer."

Reluctantly, he clicked.

"Police served a warrant on this home in East Salt Lake today. We've since learned it belongs to a local dentist. The detective in charge, Detective Worthen, offered no comment other than that they found no evidence in the search to connect the dentist to the case."

"We had a tip," Detective Worthen said on the screen with the words "Recorded Earlier" under his photo. "But we didn't find any evidence related to the crime at this location. We ask that the public not be discouraged. If you have any tips, please call."

"The homeowner asked that we leave her name out of the broadcast and would not offer us any comment."

"It sounds like police are back where they started, Beverly," the anchor said.

"It appears so," she answered. "Although at least they have eliminated one suspect at this time."

"Thanks, Beverly. We'll keep you posted on this developing story."

Nick's shoulders sagged. In a way, he was glad the dentist was not involved, and he was no longer a part of the investigation. Secretly, he had been hoping the killer would be caught and he could stay out of the news at the same time.

He decided to change and go for a walk. He checked his phone. Still no word from Sandra. He was starting to get worried.

9

———

MOTIVE?

N ick showered and went out for a walk. He chuckled when he saw the neon sign up ahead for, "Beer Bar" right next to "Bar X."

"Well, that's pretty descriptive," he said as he stopped and went inside Beer Bar. It was crowded, and it was early Thursday evening. His height gave him a literal advantage over the others in the crowded room. He saw an open spot at the bar and made his way to it. "What's it like on a busy day?" he hollered to the bartender as he sat on the stool.

"Doesn't matter what day of the week, it's this way every afternoon. What can I getcha?" the bartender said loudly over the crowd noise.

"A porter?"

"Sure thing."

Nick turned his head and looked around the bar. The crowd was pretty mixed. There were the professionals in dress shirts and loosened ties, some twenty-somethings who looked like college students, and one large table filled with a group who appeared to be construction workers. "You get all kinds in here," Nick said as the bartender his beer in front of him.

"Yeah, typical crowd. Start you a tab or close it?" he said, as Nick handed over his debit card.

"Leave it open."

"Sure. Enjoy," the bartender said.

Nick said as he picked up the glass and enjoyed the first sip. He felt the vibration first, and then he heard the ping. Nick pulled the phone out of his pocket and looked at the display, hoping it was Sandra. Instead, it was an email from a list he subscribed to. The headline read "Opioid Statistics."

Nick looked at his phone. "I'll read it later," he said to himself. He looked at his glass of beer. His mind went back to fraternity days, and nights, at Boston College. *An overdose of opioids, the reporter had written. Odd, considering the method of murder.*

He'd known kids addicted in college. A few in the fraternities had even died when partying with them. At least they kept their tongues. "Shit!" he exclaimed. This case was seriously getting to him, but his hands were tied, and he couldn't do a thing about it.

"Is everything okay?" the bartender asked.

"Sorry, just thinking about some old friends," Nick replied as he picked up his glass and finished the beer.

"Another?" the bartender asked.

"Sure," Nick said.

He sat and thought for a few minutes. "Why would someone cut someone else's tongue out?" he mumbled.

"Because they talk too much," a woman, who had come up to the bar to get a drink, answered his quiet question to himself, grabbed her drink, and left.

Nick hadn't thought about it up until that moment, but he reviewed in his head what he knew from reading detective novels, watching television, and what he'd learned on this trip. His dad loved Columbo, and he'd been subjected to the series more than once growing up.

He often said something that here made a lot of sense. "A killer needs three things. Means, motive, and opportunity."

To the police this might be obvious. To Nick, he needed to think about things for a moment to really get it.

Means. Simple, whoever this was cut the victim's tongues out. He obviously gave them drugs as well, but why? For the pain?

So they won't move, he thought. Cutting out a tongue can't be easy. And it would be near impossible if the person was still alive and moving around. Nick had a hard enough time sitting still for his six month cleaning, let alone long enough to have his tongue removed.

And that would hurt way more.

Thus the reason for the drugs. And the straps on the chair.

The straps on the chair. Nick opened the photo the last victim had taken with his phone, and enlarged it, looking closer at the chair.

There were straps for the arms and legs, and on the headrest too.

Interesting, but not proof of anything. Why had the victim taken this photo anyway?

He looked even closer at the cabinet. In the glass on one of the doors, he could see an image, a faint reflection.

He zoomed in. The quality wasn't the best, but it was good enough that he could see what looked like a naked man holding the phone. The victim. Had he been naked already when he took this photo? He couldn't see exactly, but he thought maybe so.

That meant he didn't think he was getting a dental cleaning. Had the victim's clothes been found?

To answer that, he looked online. There was a photo of the victim from the day of his murder, a selfie from his phone, it looked like. He wore a grey jacket and a light blue polo.

Maybe he should call the tip line. Maybe he should call Detective Worthen. Maybe he should just stay out of it.

Then he remembered the jacket he'd knocked off the hook in the garage. What color had it been? He'd been slightly drugged, and the memory was faint.

But he had a picture.

He swiped to his own social media page and pulled up the emergency dentist selfie.

He zoomed in on the hook behind them. There it was. A gray jacket.

He opened his phone and called Detective Worthen. Nick felt a sudden urgency. There had been a killing every single week for the last four weeks. And the killer was one day overdue.

10

———————

OPPORTUNITY

"What do you want, Mr. O'Flannigan?"

"I have another clue for your case."

"Really? Is it as good as the last one?" A little bit of sarcasm and stress showed in the detective's voice.

Nick put his finger in his ear so he could hear better. The bar had suddenly gotten louder if that was even possible.

"Look, I know, okay. Sorry you didn't find what you were looking for. But you don't even have to meet me to see this one. You have the last picture of the victim from the day of the murder?"

"Yes."

"Go to my social media profile and look just a few photos down for the emergency dentist selfie."

"Give me a minute."

Nick waited.

"Got it," he heard a minute later.

"Zoom in on the coat hook by the garage door. Behind us in the photo. Doesn't that look like the victim's jacket."

"It does. But there could be a thousand—"

"Isn't it worth another look?"

"O'Flannigan, I don't have a search warrant to go back there again. There's no way I can get inside again."

"I can."

"What?"

"I'll call her. Tell her my filling is loose again or something. I can get in, and then if something is in plain sight or something happens, you can come get me."

"I can't let you do that."

"Why not?"

"I can't involve a civilian in an investigation and then follow you inside without a reason. Any evidence we find would be inadmissible."

"What are we supposed to do then?" Nick asked. "The killer is one day overdue if they are going to stick with killing one person a week."

"Actually more than that. We found the other victims on Thursday morning. We assume the assault that resulted in their deaths happened the night before. I'm painfully aware, Mr. O'Flannigan, and I appreciate your enthusiasm, but there's nothing more you can do."

The call ended. Nick sat, and considered his options, if he had any.

He looked at his phone again. Nothing from Sandra.

He had a few more photos to get the following morning.

He should just head back to the hotel and get some rest. The police were on it, and he'd been told his place in the investigation: none.

He paid his tab and left the bar and started walking. His limp was back. He'd have to take a bike in the morning.

That would be just fine with him. He smelled the clean air, looked around at the well-lit city, and made his way back to his room.

He took a quick shower and called Sandra.

"This is Sandra," the recording said. "Leave a message, and I'll get back to you."

"Please call me," he said. "I'm sorry, and I love you."

He ended the call and looked at the time. She'd already be sleeping if she had an early start tomorrow.

He headed to bed himself, and as he drifted off to sleep, he thought he heard sirens go by outside his window.

11

MEANS AND MEANING

F riday morning began early with Nick's phone ringing, waking him. He rolled over and looked at it. It was 5:00 a.m., and it was Sandra.

"Hi," he said, as enthusiastically as he could.

"Hi, Nick. I'm sorry I haven't responded sooner."

"It's okay, I was a jerk. You were right—"

"It's not that," she said. "My brother is in the hospital in Connecticut."

"Connecticut?"

"Long story. So I am here, too. I flew over the other night."

"Ah. So sorry. I thought you were mad at me."

"Oh, I was. But not mad enough to shut you out for two days."

"Oh."

"I'll never be that mad, Nick. It's unfair. Our relationship is not leverage I'll hold over your head. Are you okay?"

"Yeah. It's five a.m. here, but I went to bed fairly early last night."

"How are things there? Did you disentangle yourself from that case?"

"You could say that. Or I was disentangled."

"That's good, right?"

"Yes, it is actually. I feel much better this morning. It was tough not hearing from you. What's going on with your brother?"

"He was in an accident. He scared us all, but he will be fine. I'll be flying back to Salem Monday or Tuesday. My sister-in-law seems to be handling it well, and he should be able to go home today."

"What was he doing?"

"He works for my dad's company. He was driving a company truck across town and got hit head on. He has a broken leg, some broken ribs, but overall he is pretty lucky."

"Your family lives in Connecticut?"

"Yes."

"Ever think about moving back there?" Nick couldn't believe they had never talked about this before.

"We're not close," she said simply. "So, no."

"Okay," he said.

"Listen, I have to go, Nick. Things are a little crazy. But I do love you, and I promise I will call again when I can."

"Love you, too," he said simply. He hung up and stared at the dark screen. He learned more about her all the time, and he reminded himself not to be so self-focused.

He was awake anyway and decided to take a quick shower.

He got out and turned on the television as he dried himself. He had time this morning. He could treat himself to another good breakfast once he uploaded photos from yesterday. He could then get a few more photos at the capitol, anything he might have missed, and maybe go to Pioneer Park at some point.

The news opened with Breaking News about the Salt Lake Silencer, and he stopped, nearly dropping his towel.

"Late last night, another victim was found, naked and deceased in their vehicle, this time parked on a side street near downtown. Police refuse to comment at this time until they have more information. In the meantime, Salt Lake residents, particularly single males, are encouraged to be vigilant and report anything unusual to the police."

"I tried that," Nick said out loud.

He dressed quickly, noting that he needed to do some laundry either here or his first day in Phoenix. Since it would take him two days to get there, he was inclined to do it here, or have it done for him.

He looked up laundry services really quickly and made a call to one not far from his hotel. They offered pick up services as well and could have his items done by this afternoon. He gathered everything into a laundry bag and got it ready to take downstairs.

His phone rang, and he answered it without looking.

"This is Nick."

"Mr. O'Flannigan, Detective Worthen."

"Good morning. What can I do for you?"

"Can I buy you breakfast?"

"I suppose so."

"I do have ulterior motives."

"Yes?"

"I want to see your take on the photos you described to me yesterday."

"Sure. I'm dropping some laundry at the front desk, and I have some work to do today, but I'll meet you."

"See you downstairs in twenty minutes?"

"Sure."

Nick didn't rush, but he thought very carefully about what he would share with the detective.

He'd show him what he thought was the naked reflection for sure. And the coat. Those made sense.

Then he would roll with what the authorities needed but ask them to leave his name out of it. He'd told Sandra he'd been disentangled, but he made a resolution to himself.

If he was involved in anything, he had to be honest with her above all. She had to accept him for who he was, morbid mystery curiosity and all.

They couldn't start a relationship built on lies.

He grabbed both his laptop and camera bags, knowing he would bring the computer back to the hotel before he went out.

He arrived outside the hotel lobby just as the detective pulled up. The passenger window slid down, and Nick was invited into the car. He slid inside, impressed by the computer gear and the gadgets inside.

"Good morning," the detective said.

"Good morning. Where are we headed?"

"Have you been to Elevations?"

"I have. But I will go again."

"Okay."

It was only a few blocks, and the detective grabbed a parking spot easily. They went inside.

Once they ordered and sat down, the detective looked at him, staring.

"So, O'Flannigan, can you show me what you were talking about last night?"

"Sure," Nick said, pulling out his laptop. He opened it, and opened the photo he had downloaded, the one the now previous victim had taken.

He proceeded to show the detective the reflection he'd seen. When asked to email it, Nick did so. He then switched photos and showed him the jacket.

"That's interesting," the detective said. "And this other woman is the assistant?"

"Yes."

"Okay, good."

"What's going on Detective? Can you tell me?"

"Well, we had the dentist under surveillance. Just on the off chance she led us somewhere. But she didn't."

"What?"

"Last night, Dr. Gordon was at a friend's house in Latah. All night."

"So—"

"She didn't do it. She was also out of town last Wednesday too. She has an alibi."

"Rock solid?"

"Yep."

"Then who did this?"

"Someone else has access to her home office. Her assistant."

"Does she have an alibi?"

"We don't know. We can't find her, but we're looking."

"Thanks for letting me know."

"One word of this, O'Flannigan, one photo in the media, and I will ruin you."

"What?"

"I know about Denver and what happened there. This conversation is a courtesy, call it a thanks for what you've shared with us."

"Understood. I—"

"That's enough. Can you make your way back to the hotel, or do I need to give you a ride?"

"It isn't far," Nick said. "I'll walk."

But he didn't.

After the detective left, he took a Green Bike back, slinging both his bags over his shoulder, sans helmet, but he thought he could be forgiven this time. As he got to the hotel, he lost his balance when approaching the bike station. He tried to catch himself, but he fell, and hit his head lightly on the side of another bike. He stood, made sure his camera and computer hadn't taken too much of a hit. He shook his head, and touched the side, wincing. A small knot had formed at the site of the impact.

That hurt. Another argument for a helmet for sure, to protect even from a minor fall.

Nick deposited his computer at the hotel, grabbed his helmet, and spent the rest of the day taking more photographs around the capitol building and then made his way to Pioneer Park using his Green Bike pass. He decided to try somewhere new and headed to the Copper Onion. On the way, he stopped and grabbed a small bottle of ibuprofen. His head still hurt a little.

The food was good, and there was no news visible anywhere. Nick had hope, but he kept it to himself.

His phone buzzed, and he saw a text from Detective Worthen. "Found the assistant. She confessed. Thanks again."

Nick headed back to his hotel and sat at the desk.

He uploaded the best of the shots to the magazine's cloud folder and then texted Sandra.

"Can we talk?" he asked.

"Sure."

He called her. "What's happening?"

"Listen, Sandra, I don't want to lie to you, ever."

"Okay. That's an odd way to start a conversation."

"The thing is, I like mysteries. I really did try to stay out of this one, but it seems like they follow me everywhere."

"I know that Nick," she said softly.

"I want to promise you I won't get involved in things as I travel around, but I don't want to make promises I can't keep. If I get accidentally involved or sucked in somehow, I promise to tell you."

"I appreciate that, Nick. But—"

"Let me finish. I like you. I love you, and I hope we have a future together. I need to start by being honest."

"Nick!"

"What?"

"I love you. Just the way you are. I love your curious spirit. I just want you to avoid stuff like Denver. Be smart. Be safe. You can even call me if you have doubts about what to do next."

"I can?"

"Nick. I don't want you to get involved in things, and I don't want you to jeopardize your career or assignment. But I do want to support you. We're a team, right?"

"Yes."

"Okay. Enough said. I love you."

"I love you, too."

"Are you headed for Phoenix tomorrow?"

"Early tomorrow morning."

"Okay, get some rest. We can talk when you are on the way."

"I will. I'm headed for dinner, and then I'll probably hit the sack early."

As he was about to leave, Nick heard a noise in the hallway, and opened the door. His laundry had been delivered. He brought the bag inside and decided he would pack it in his suitcase in the morning.

Nick took two more pain relievers and headed out for one last dinner in Salt Lake. He decided to treat himself and headed for Takashi, a Japanese restaurant with great reviews. He was in the mood for sushi and maybe some lamb, and this place offered both.

The lamb was tender, the sushi fresh and well made. Nick drank a lot of water, and his head hurt a little bit if he moved it too fast, but other than that, he enjoyed the dinner and even a small glass of Saki.

When he got back to the room, he headed straight for bed, turning the television on as background noise. He had a long couple of days of driving ahead.

He heard the laugh track of a sitcom faintly in the background as he closed his eyes. He fell asleep as soon as his head hit the pillow.

12

ON THE ROAD AGAIN

Saturday Nick woke to light coming through the window between the drapes he'd forgotten to close the night before. His head still hurt a little, but it was better than it had been the day before.

He turned on the news as he packed, and he turned up the volume. The headline showed breaking news and said underneath: "Salt Lake Silencer Caught."

"Beverly, finally there is some good news in this case," the anchor said.

The now familiar Beverly stood near the dentist's home. Nick recognized it easily, but the driveway and front door were both blocked by yellow crime scene tape.

"There is," she said. "Police have a suspect in custody. They have what they are calling significant evidence that this is indeed the killer."

"Have they identified her yet?"

"They have not, but the police promise a press conference later this morning, where they will release more details."

Good, Nick thought.

He showered and dressed, grabbed his phone and went out for breakfast. He walked a few blocks west to Mollie and Ollie. He ordered their Best-of-the-Southwest Scramble along with a Fresh Fruit Bowl and a cup of coffee.

The drive to Phoenix would be a long one, another two-day trip. But there were things to break it up, and he thought he would probably enjoy it. Phoenix would be another great place to enjoy some biking as well.

His food came, and he took his time eating. He finished, paid the bill, and walked back to the hotel. He packed his bag, his camera, and his computer. Then he took a couple of Tylenol for the trip and headed out the door, stopping at the front desk to check out.

He was sorry to leave Salt Lake City, but looked forward to his next adventure, a quieter week in Phoenix.

THE END

FACTS ABOUT SALT LAKE CITY
AND UTAH

Utah --

I'm glad to be here where the mountains rise
Dazzling white 'neath the clear blue skys [sic.]
From crimson dawn 'til the dear day dies
Way out west in Utah.
Where the mountain air is pure and sweet,
Where fresh, cool water flows down the street
And the climate! Friend, it can't be beat;
Delightful, magnificent Utah.
God made Utah and He made it grand,
The beauty spot of His glorious land,
Where plenty supplies with a generous hand
All of our needs and wants in Utah.
Mighty mountains, sylvian [sic.] vales,
Picturesque canyons and rugged trails,
Joy's your companion, health never fails,
Happiness dwells in Utah.

-- Minnie J. Hardy

- The capital of Utah, Salt Lake City is sometimes referred to as SLC or just Salt Lake, misleading some people to confuse it with the Great Salt Lake. The southern tip of the lake itself is about twenty miles from the city.
- The authors extend our thanks to Kerry from Heber City, Utah, who volunteered his name for use in this book. We hope that "his role" in the book doesn't silence him. Keep on writing, Kerry!
- Salt Lake City is known by many as the "home" of The Church of Jesus Christ of Latter-day Saints, and was founded in 1847 by followers of the church and led by Brigham Young. Tourist and other information about Salt Lake City is available at https://www.visitsaltlake.com/
- Sitting at the foot of the Wasatch Mountains, the residents of, and visitors, to SLC enjoy many outdoor activities. Hiking, biking, rafting, skiing and other winter sports are very common and contribute to the bustling economy.
- Although Utah didn't gain official statehood until 1896, the U.S. Congress established the Utah Territory in 1850. The territory's capital city then was Fillmore in the county of Millard—both of then named after U.S. President Millard Fillmore. Salt Lake City became the capital city of the territory in 1856. and then continued on after Utah's 1896 statehood.
- Street addresses in SLC are based on a North-South and West-East grid system whose beginning point is at the southeast corner of Temple Square in the downtown area.
- The Green Bike program mentioned in the story is a vital part of the city's effort to reduce traffic emissions and encourage a healthy lifestyle. In addition to the marked bike lanes, there are over twenty-five miles of paved multi-use bike trails in the city.
- The oval path circumnavigating the 100-acre Liberty Park is popular for both bicyclists and walkers. The park contains the Tracy Aviary, two lakes, and is a popular spot for outdoor gatherings, festivals, and picnics.

POISONED IN PHOENIX

BOOK #12

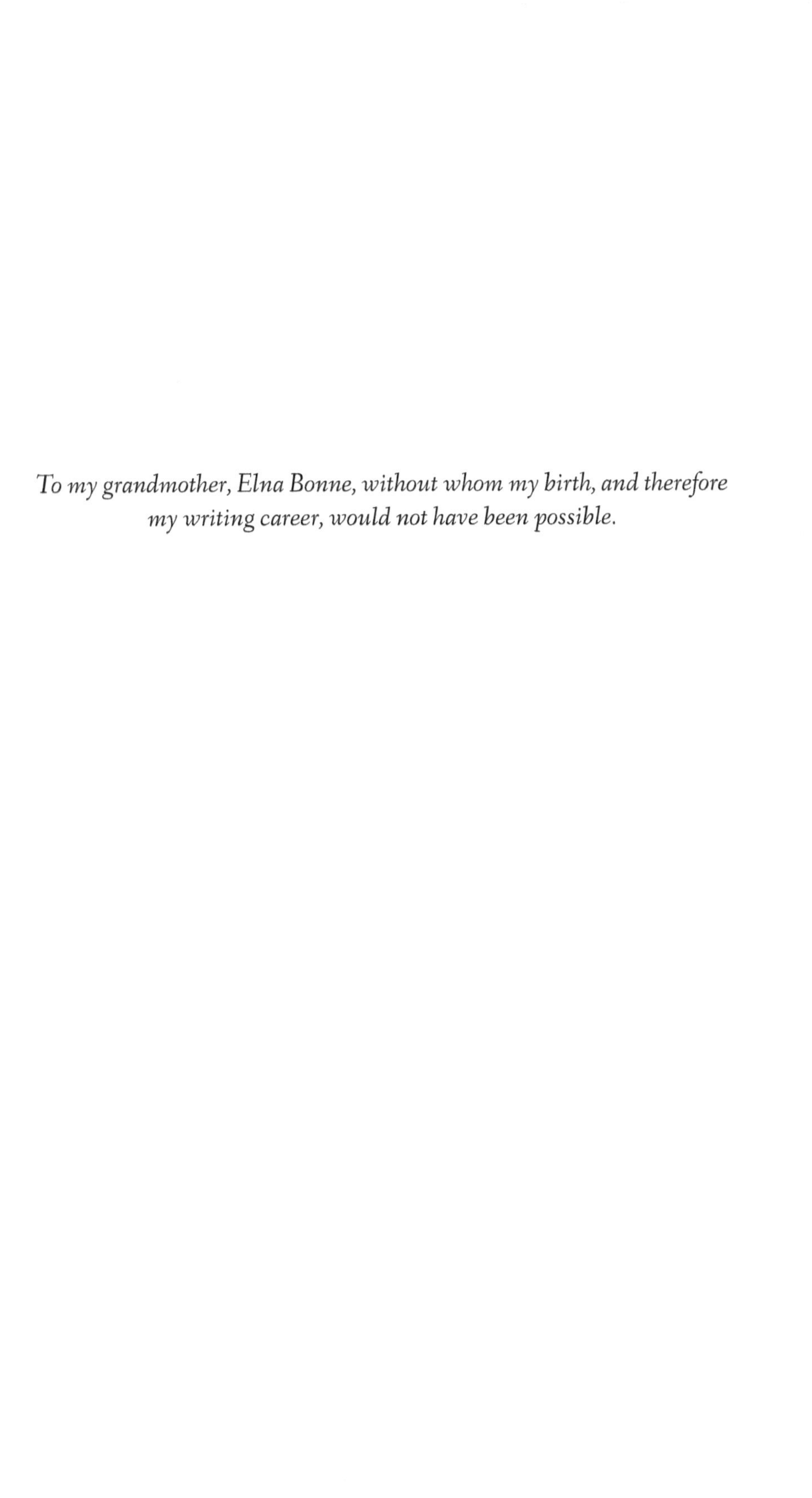

To my grandmother, Elna Bonne, without whom my birth, and therefore my writing career, would not have been possible.

PROLOGUE: THE DEVIL'S TRUMPET

His phone beeped and Jeff glanced at it.

"Party tonight?" the text message read. It was from Crazy Rhonda, his recent ex-girlfriend.

Jeff knew all about the hot/crazy scale. Originally made popular by a comedian as a joke, it became a law many men lived by.

Boiled down to the essentials it meant, simply, that if a girl was hot enough, you could ignore a certain level of crazy. The two things, on an X/Y scale could help you determine how dateable a woman was. For sure, it told you a lot about long-term relationship potential.

A senior at Arizona State University in Tempe, a suburb of Phoenix, Jeff thought about the long-term often.

Thus, the motive for dumping Rhonda. Her crazy was tolerable at first, because she was hot - at least to him, even though his taste in women was often contested by his friends. As their relationship progressed though, the crazy became more pronounced, especially when it came to jealousy. When Jeff told her it was over, she'd flipped out. In fact, this was his first text from her since the breakup, and the moment he'd changed her designation in his phone from "Crazy Hot Rhonda" to simply "Crazy Rhonda."

So, he weighed his options. He could answer, and even say yes to the party. He knew one of Rhonda's friends, Becky, was equally hot, and not nearly as crazy, as far as he knew.

For a shot at dating her, the party might be worth going to.

"Where and when?" he texted back.

"My parents' place. They're out of town." The text was followed by a winking emoji.

Uh oh. Trouble.

Still, her parents had a huge house, a pool, and her dad was notorious for having a well-stocked bar.

Time to take a risk.

"Will Becky be there?"

There was a pause, but three dots showed she was typing a reply.

"Of course. And a bunch of other girls, too. You on the prowl, Lone Wolf?"

Relief. Lone Wolf had been a pet name, but she seemed okay with him looking around. Still, he sensed a mine field here. If he stepped wrong, he'd likely be half the man he had been.

"Not particularly. But as you know, I like to look."

The message that followed was simply an emoji sticking its tongue out. Another message followed.

"Starts at 7. Come over whenever you want."

Jeff smiled, shouldered his backpack, and headed for his next class.

Maybe this breakup wouldn't be so bad after all.

Music thumped from the speakers around the pool. Jeff remembered at least eight from his previous trips here. The "yard" was made up of gravel, cactus, and other desert flowers, and crisscrossed by paths made of stone pavers. A few stubborn weeds made their way up through the small rocks, including one bright yellow dandelion.

Rhonda's dad was big on parties, mostly adult parties, but as an art dealer and the owner of his own gallery, he had plenty of reasons to entertain. Jeff had attended a few as the dutiful boyfriend and had even met some cool artists and photographers.

Even though his major was engineering, he loved art, and carried a minor in art history. He hoped to use his "day job" designing software as a springboard for traveling to the world's museums and seeing master-pieces in person.

Even though he'd come in through the back gate, he used the excuse of needing to change into swimwear, a valid one, and a need to use the bathroom to walk through the den and one of the hallways in the massive house. He marveled at the originals and prints Rhonda's dad had hanging there.

In that way alone, it was too bad they hadn't worked out as a couple. Jeff would miss him, if not his daughter.

Once he changed, Jeff stuffed his day clothes in a backpack, and walked out back in swim trunks, flip flops, and a towel. There were hooks on the patio, and he hung his bag on one of them.

He turned to head for the pool. Rhonda was there, but busy on the other side, talking to a well-tanned and muscled guy Jeff had never seen before.

Becky was there too, and she walked out of the water wearing only a turquoise bikini.

"Hi, Jeff," she said.

"Hi," he said. "I was hoping to see you here."

"Rhonda told me. Do you have a drink yet?" she grabbed a towel and started drying her hair.

"Not yet," he said.

He followed Becky to an area where there were coolers set up, some with beer, others with wine coolers and even alcohol infused seltzer water, which he found to be disgusting.

Behind the coolers was a section of flowers, more like a bush really, in the middle of the otherwise desert landscape. It was about two feet tall, and the various branches looked more like vines than anything. The flowers themselves were white and purple and had broad leaves with several points on each.

Pretty, he thought. *Rhonda's mom must have some influence here.*

He grabbed a beer, not his favorite, but probably the best of the selection, and turned to Becky.

"So, you come here often?" he joked.

"Only when invited," she said. "Nice place, huh?"

"It is."

"Why'd you break up with her?"

He shrugged. "Things didn't work out, I guess."

"You think things would work out with me?"

Jeff took a swig of his beer while he considered his answer. Her line of questioning was not exactly what he'd expected.

What did you expect? he asked himself. *That she didn't talk to Rhonda at all, and you'd both ignore the facts plainly present at this party?*

Fair enough.

"I can't say, Becky. I don't know you well enough yet, but I'd like the chance to get to know you. I'm graduating soon, looking to the future. I just couldn't see Rhonda and I working out long term."

"I see," she said, suddenly cold. "I'll see you around."

"Great," Jeff said, drained his beer and grabbed another one.

"Hi, Jeff," Rhonda stood behind him. She was wearing a red bikini in the same style as Becky's, and it clicked that they must have gone shopping together, or at least coordinated outfits.

Crash and burn.

"How's Becky?"

"She's fine," he answered. "Where's your new friend?"

"Over there," she said, tilting her head over her shoulder. The newcomer was talking to another one of the girls at the party, and as he watched, both started laughing.

Exactly what I should be doing, Jeff thought.

"Can we talk for a second?"

"Why not?" he said. He had a feeling it was either talk and settle things with her, or he'd never have a ghost of a chance with any one in her circle of friends.

"Come with me."

She led him toward a wooden gazebo, one just a little way from the pool, where no one seemed to be hanging out at the moment.

She sat down and gestured to a spot on the bench.

Jeff sat beside her, and she smiled at him. He smiled back. "So," he said. "What's up?"

"I'm glad you broke up with me, Jeff."

"You are?"

"Yes. It gave me some perspective." She reached inside a small box on the bench and pulled out two joints. "Smoke?"

Jeff wasn't a big fan of pot, but it did almost nothing for him, so he also rarely refused.

"Sure."

She handed him one and clicked a lighter. As the smell wafted across to the pool, several other people came to join them. Soon, there was a fog around them.

"You wanted to say something to me?" he asked her when some of the crowd drifted away.

"I did. Jeff, I know you like Becky. But she's a lot like me. A little high on the crazy side of the hot/crazy scale, am I right?"

"Who—?" he groaned.

"Did you think guys were the only ones who know about that stupid scale? Do you think we really care what you think?"

"N-n-no." he stammered.

"You leave her, and my other friends alone. I'm sure you can find someone here I don't know, someone fits your 'standards'," she said, complete with air quotes. "But when it comes to anyone close to me, anyone in my friend circle, you're black balled."

"Why did you invite me here?"

"That, right there," she said, indicating his face with a sweep of her hand. "The look on your face. I wanted to see it."

"Damn," Jeff stood. But not before she did, and he watched her disappear into the crowd.

He sat back down and finished smoking the joint as the sun dropped behind the horizon, and the lights around the pool came on automatically.

He felt a little funny and hungry, so he deposited the tiny butt in the can set by the gazebo for the purpose and headed for the food table.

Might as well eat, he thought. He filled a plate with chips, baked beans, and two hot dogs, sans buns.

The world wiggled a little bit, and he felt woozy. He stumbled toward a chair on the patio and sat down.

Thinking back, he realized he hadn't eaten since lunch. Maybe he just had low blood sugar or something.

As he stuffed the food in his mouth it didn't seem to help. In fact, the light headedness seemed to get worse. The last bite of beans seemed to balance on a tiny little airplane headed for his mouth. It was purple, and a little trail of smoke followed it.

He laughed, and a few people turned to stare. Even to himself, the laugh sounded like a cackle.

What's wrong with me?

The poles around the pools seemed to be bending and dancing in an invisible wind he could not feel at all. The music sounded muffled in his ears.

The air around him felt cooler than it had when he sat down, but still he felt hot from the inside, almost feverish. Sweat beaded on his forehead.

Shit.

He stood. "I need water!"

His voice thundered in his ears, but no one turned to look at him at all.

"Water!" he said again and tried to walk toward the coolers.

The pool decking under his feet kept bending and flexing, and it reminded him of those videos you would see of bridges dancing in earthquakes.

Was that what this was? An earthquake?

But he didn't feel anything. He looked at those around him. No one else seemed to notice the shifting ground at all.

Some even pointed at him and laughed.

Was it the weed? Weed hadn't ever had that kind of effect on him before.

Water. I need water.

He stumbled to the cooler and managed to get it open and pull a plastic bottle from it. The top seemed to be stuck, and he twisted as hard as he could.

The bottle itself seemed to warp and twist. His hands felt so hot. As he held it, the water in the bottle appeared boil and then turn purple.

"What the hell?"

He struggled, turning the cap the other way, and finally managed to get it off the writhing bottle. Ignoring its appearance, he put the bottle to his lips and drank the purple, boiling liquid. It went down cool and refreshing and seemed to help for a moment.

Maybe I should have another one of those, he thought.

When he opened the cooler this time though, he saw it was full of snakes. Writhing, gray snakes, their backs decorated with black diamonds.

He heard the rattles, and looked around, but everyone else seemed entirely calm.

"Snakes!' he shouted. Everyone looked at him, and he pointed at the cooler. "Snakes!"

"You're crazy," the tanned man said, and reached for the cooler. One of the snakes coiled, preparing to bite him.

"No!" Jeff said, and lunged forward, tackling him. They rolled onto the gravel, and Jeff felt it bite into his skin.

"Get off me!" the other guy said and rolled to his feet.

Rhonda appeared in his vision. "Jeff, maybe you should just go."

"I'm so hot," he said. He was burning up, like an oven had turned on inside him. "So hot."

"Calm down, okay?" she said.

But Jeff saw the answer. The pool. That would cool him off.

He stood and staggered to the side. A figure tried to stop him, and he shoved it aside.

The water swirled in some kind of whirlpool like something from a movie, something you would see in the middle of an ocean, not a back-yard pool.

But the only thing that mattered was the water would be cool. It would put out the fire inside him. Jeff jumped.

The water surrounded him and steamed away from his overheated body. It felt so good on the outside. But that's not where the fire was.

The fire was inside him. Inside.

Jeff ducked beneath the waves, mouth open, taking in as much of the cooling water as he could. He tasted chlorine, but it didn't matter.

It was working. The more water he breathed in, the cooler he got.

He felt himself struggling. Looked up to see lights, shadows moving frantically.

He fought them. He wanted to stay here in the cold, refreshing water.

Then he started to shiver underwater. Something he didn't think was possible. His vision narrowed, first to a tunnel with a large light but one that got smaller and smaller.

Jeff felt hands grabbing him, under his arms, around him.

Then he felt nothing at all.

1

____

THE HEAT IS ON

From the time Nick O'Flannigan entered Arizona on his drive down from Salt Lake City to Phoenix, he could only think of two words to describe the state: beautiful, and hot, and not necessarily in that order. The drive would take a total of ten hours, so he planned to stop somewhere along the way. His first stop involved a small detour where he chose to take 89A south out of Kaibab to Jacob's Lake, where he turned south on Highway 67 toward the North Rim of the Grand Canyon, which he found to be gorgeous and much less crowded than he imagined.

"Why aren't there more people here?" he asked one park ranger.

"Well," she said. "Most people come in the morning or the evening, when it is a little cooler outside. Second, most people visit the South Rim, closer to Flagstaff and Phoenix. This site is a little more out of the way."

"Makes sense. If I'm headed to Phoenix from here, where should I stop along the way?" He'd already been on the road for six and a half hours, and the windy roads were wearing him out.

"Well, you know you have to backtrack a bit to Jacob Lake, and there isn't much there in the way of lodging. Are you camping or staying in motels?"

"Motels," he said, regretting his lack of camping gear for the first time on his trip.

"Oh bummer. Really, the next place to stay is in Marble Canyon. There is a lodge there with a pretty good restaurant, and that's only a couple of hours away. Unless you want to stay in a cabin, that is, but it might be a bit uncomfortable without any gear."

She gestured towards a low row of log buildings and Nick smiled. "Ah, no thanks," he said. "I think I'll just grab some photos and move on."

"Okay," she said. "Nice camera, by the way."

He thanked her, then headed down the trail toward the overlook, limping only slightly from his old basketball injury. His week in Denver, a part of his year-long assignment to photograph every state capitol building for *Travel USA* magazine, had been rough since both his girl-friend, something that still sounded strange to him in his own thoughts, and his contact and friend from the magazine who'd actually gotten him the gig had visited him there at the same time.

That trip had involved a lot of walking and drama. Salt Lake had offered a little respite, and he'd forced himself to take more Uber rides and even use the elevators in the capitol to make his way around.

It seemed that no matter how he tried to avoid mysteries and crime, they seemed to follow him in every city, something he secretly liked a little bit. But this time, he hoped Phoenix would be better. He'd hoped to get lost from the limelight in Denver, and that hadn't happened. Now in the third big city in a row, he wanted to ambitiously avoid mysteries, the cops, and the press. A few days of taking photos and a few days by the pool were just what he needed.

Provided he wore plenty of strong sunscreen to protect his pale skin, something that came with his bushy red hair and his Irish last name.

At the overlook, he found the canyon to be breathtaking. It was one thing to be told about a mile deep and mile wide trench in the earth, but to see it with his own eyes was something else. There were telescopes at the overlook and he used them to look around.

Nick pulled the zoom lens from his bag, and while he was usually into more macro photography, this seemed to be the right place to use a long lens first and then switch to a wide-angle lens for some panoramic shots.

At sites like this, it was hard to get shots someone hadn't already taken. Nick resolved to try his best.

As he turned to the side, he saw several other tourists with high end cameras as well. He paused.

Maybe macro photography was the answer. Everyone was focused on what was over the edge rather than on the edge of the canyon, yet there were some gorgeous wildflowers there.

So he ventured off the platform and hiked down the trail a little way. He sat down where he had a good view of the flowers, and took several shots of them up close, the background of the canyon blurred, but still present.

He moved further down the trail and did the same thing with several different plants and flowers of varying colors, including reds, purples, yellows, and more.

He spent more time taking photos than he anticipated, and so rushed back to his car. Realizing how tired he was, he took one last look at the cabins.

"Not a chance," he told himself.

He decided to call ahead to reserve a room in Marble Canyon. But he had no service.

"I'll just have to wait," he said aloud. "I hope they aren't sold out."

An hour later, he got service and reserved a room a mere twenty minutes before he arrived.

The low adobe building was quaint, and by the time he pulled into the parking lot, the sun was setting, and the temperature had dropped significantly. Orange decorated the horizon, but from the east, he could see dark clouds moving in. The building was flanked by a long, low stone bluff, one that would be amazing to climb if he had the time and his leg wasn't so sore.

Several motorcycles, most Harley Davidson models, were parked outside. He could only imagine the winding roads he'd just traversed from the back of one of those. If this hadn't been such a long assignment spanning all four seasons and so many areas of the country, a bike might not have been a bad idea.

He stepped out of his car, stretched for the sky, and bent to touch his toes.

"Ain't you a tall one?" a man asked. His salt and pepper beard reached his large chest, ending just above his ample, and likely beer-built belly. He wore a black shirt with the lower half of an eagle visible under his beard, holding a ribbon bearing the words, "Live free or die" winding through it.

Below that were faded jeans and hard leather boots clearly in need of a polish.

"I suppose I am," Nick said. "I'm Nick."

"Dale," the man said, holding out his hand to shake. "Long drive?"

"From Salt Lake, and including a stop at the North Rim, it did make for a long day," Nick said. "It's my first time ever in Arizona."

"It's a pretty cool state. You got a room?"

"I reserved it about half an hour ago," Nick said.

"Must have been right before we rolled in. They're near full up now. You headed for Phoenix?"

"Yep."

"Us too. I don't suppose you're headed to the bike rally?" the man asked, pointing to Nick's car.

"Nope. I'm on assignment traveling to every state capital to photograph them for *Travel USA* magazine."

"Nice. We'll be at the capitol building this coming Friday for a rally. You should get some photos of that."

"I'll keep my eye out," Nick said.

"You probably haven't been over the Navajo Bridge yet, since you came from the canyon?"

"Not yet."

"It's a site. If you're leaving early tomorrow, plan some time to stop, take pictures, and look around. It's pretty amazing, and the Colorado River is gorgeous at sunrise."

"I'll do that for sure."

"Maybe we'll see you around Phoenix?"

"I hope so. Nice to meet you."

"You, too."

He went inside, grateful to have escaped the inevitable question, "Did you ever think about playing ball?"

With the inevitable response to follow: "Yep. I played in college until I hurt my leg." He'd point, they'd notice the limp, and then it would end. When people were around him for long enough, they gave it a rest, but the one thing that held true on this trip was that the same conversation repeated itself in every single city, sometimes more than once.

He needed to have a business card made, one he could just hand over that told them the story. Then at least he would have an answer ready for them.

At the front desk, he asked for his room key. He'd been hoping for a pool, spa, or even a gym where he could get in a quick workout, but the offerings here were definitely basic accommodations.

The bed was newer, the linen older, and the decor more than a little retro. Still, he was comfortable, and he sat down on the bed, kicked off his shoes, and laid back.

He flipped on the television to the local news, took out his phone, and texted Sandra, a gal he'd started talking to in Salem, who helped him for a week in Sacramento, and who'd visited him in Denver and solidified her position in his life as his girlfriend.

"What's up?" he typed. "In Marble Canyon, Arizona. Long day."

"Did you see the Grand Canyon yet?" the reply came back right away.

"The North Side. I guess most people go to the South Rim, but not sure if I will have time for that," he texted back.

"You should make time," she said. "I wish I was there."

"I wish you were, too," he texted back.

This trip would be so much easier with a companion, but that would be a tough way to start a relationship. They wouldn't only be living together but living together on the road.

Besides, she had her job and apartment. He wasn't even sure what their future would look like beyond this trip, but he had planted some seeds for her to think about in their last several conversations.

"How's the hotel?" she asked.

He sent her a photo he took of his feet stretched out on the bed, the television on. He noticed the channel was a Phoenix based news station. A headline under a photo of an ambulance and fire truck outside a home with a rock yard said, 'Strange Teen Drowning Investigated." He turned up the sound only to hear the last of the report.

"—police say that several witnesses mentioned there were drugs at the party, but it's unknown if they were involved at this time."

The report moved on to the weather, which simply showed a giant sun in the frame for each day, each with triple digit temps underneath.

He snapped a photo of the screen with his phone and sent it to Sandra.

"Ew, hot," came her response.

"Just a little," he said.

"Can I call you?" she asked.

"Sure," he said, and muted the television right before the phone rang.

They talked for an hour or so before Nick let her go so he could go find some supper and get some sleep.

As he sat alone in the restaurant, he realized how great it would be to have her traveling with him. Maybe she could take another week off soon.

That night, Nick dreamt of driving with Sandra by his side, followed by a separate dream of strange drownings and partying teens.

He woke at 5:30 before his alarm went off, rested and ready for the final part of the drive. He thought he might stop at the Grand Canyon after all and mapped the route on his phone to see how much time that would add to his travel.

Turned out it would only stretch his trip to just under six hours, and that should give him a good couple of hour stop at the canyon for some photos.

2

SUNRISE TO SUNSET

The Navajo Bridge, a short way out of town, was more majestic than Nick expected, and he spent a good thirty minutes taking photos there as the sun rose. He got some great wide-angle shots and followed a small trail to get a few looking under the bridge as well. The span over the Colorado River was amazing, and a sign reminded him why he'd had to drive so far around to get into Arizona. This was one of the few bridges for several miles.

Following the maps on his phone, he turned and headed for the south rim area of the Grand Canyon, finding himself stuck behind several recreational vehicles and campers headed the same direction.

"This is going to take longer than I thought," he mumbled to himself, but it seemed silly to be this close to the world-famous attraction and not stop.

So he kept following the others, until he finally arrived at the parking lot in the main tourist area. The place was packed, so he parked in the back of the lot at the first spot he found, grabbed his camera gear, and headed for the restroom. His stop would have to be quicker than he wanted, but he needed to push on to Phoenix tonight for his reservation at the downtown Marriott.

However, he did some math in his head after looking at his watch. While he had no real experience with Phoenix traffic, he'd read about it. It was about 10:30 now. It would take him a little over three and half hours to be in Phoenix if he just took I-17, or an hour longer if he took the more scenic route along state Highway 89 though Prescott or 89A through Payson.

In theory, he would be going against the flow of traffic, which would primarily be headed out to the suburbs, but a strained infrastructure meant the actual rush hour started closer to 3:30 than 5.

It also lasted a bit longer, more into the 6 o'clock hour. If he spent two hours here, he would still make it to his hotel in plenty of time to grab a late dinner. Then he remembered it was Sunday, and normal traffic might not be much of an issue after all.

He took a couple of ibuprofens from a bottle in his pocket, dry swallowed them and walked over to the visitor center. His bad leg, the result of a basketball injury that had ended his NBA hopes, felt pretty good, but his head still hurt from a minor fall he'd suffered on a bike a couple of days before in Salt Lake. He purchased a big bottle of water and walked toward the rim itself.

The temperature already had to be near 100 degrees, and for a Seattle city guy, it was a little overwhelming. He felt himself sweating from places he didn't even know he had.

Tourists roamed everywhere, but his height gave him the advantage of seeing his way through them to the first lookout area. It also allowed him to take photos without having to jostle his way to the front of crowds, although he got better photos when he was able to.

Most people seemed to be staying at the top of the canyon, but there were trails that descended into it. One was called Bright Angel, and Nick started down it. It immediately got pretty steep, and he stopped at a water station not far down. It was there he saw a map detailing the length of the trail, and that advised carrying a couple of gallons of water per person.

A string of donkeys went by as he sat there, that or burros. He wasn't sure what they called them here, but that would be the way to travel down this trail and, of course, back up.

There was a little platform not far from the water area, and he hiked to it, taking a few panoramic shots, and then he focused on his macro-photography. A small yellow flower grew from between two rocks, and next to it was a purple and white flower, one that was long and protruded from a small bush-like plant. He got close ups of both but included the majesty of the canyon behind them.

The small juxtaposed against the large made him smile.

These were the moments he loved.

Then he started back up the trail. His leg already ached, and the steepness of the trail quickly got to him.

It must be a higher elevation here, he thought to himself. *The air seems thinner.*

About halfway to his destination, his water ran out. He shook the bottle, but there was no more left. He could see the rim of the canyon and the spot where the trail peaked, and he put his head down and kept going. When he got to the top, he staggered as he reached the level ground. He made a beeline for the shade and went in to purchase another bottle of water.

"Are you okay?" the clerk asked.

"I'll live," he said, only slightly uncertain.

"Well, there is a restroom over there and some benches you can sit on. They have ice cream next door."

Nick grabbed a hat and t-shirt combo from the shelf next to the checkout counter. "I'll take these, too."

"Good idea. You probably should have had a hat for your hike."

He completed his purchase and headed for the restroom. He looked in the mirror, and saw his face was red, much redder than could be attributed to the heat. Sunburn.

"Shit," he said.

He pulled off his sweaty shirt and used a few paper towels to wash and dry his armpits, and pulled the new shirt on over his head. He put the hat on, wincing a little as he did so. There was still a tiny knot from his little mishap with the bike.

After leaving the restroom, he checked the time. 2:00. That hike had taken more time and energy than he thought.

He grabbed some ice cream and another water from the shop the clerk had indicated, and headed for his car.

The air conditioner felt good. Before he took off, he took another two ibuprofens, and got on the road, deciding the straight route would be the simplest.

A quick fuel stop in Flagstaff gave him a quick break, and he couldn't help but notice the altitude drop as he went along the winding highway. As he drove, his headache subsided some.

By the time he got to Glendale, just outside Phoenix, traffic was pretty light, and he arrived at his hotel a little before seven.

The Marriott Complex on Madison and Central was domineering and impressive. He found the parking garage, gathered his bags, and walked inside.

There were several check in stations, but only one was occupied.

The woman there was either exceptionally tall or wearing heels. She wore the typical Marriott uniform, but as she looked up at him, he could see she was trying to control herself. She'd been crying.

"Hi," Nick said. "Are you okay?"

"Yes," she said, struggling. "How can I help you?"

"I have a reservation for Nick O'Flannigan."

"Okay, Mr. O'Flannigan," she said.

"Call me Nick," he said.

"Sure," she said, typing his name into the computer and pausing to wipe her eyes. "Sorry."

"It's okay—Sharon," he said, checking her name tag. "Are you really okay?"

"It's just tragic," she said. "My nephew passed away the other night. A drowning. He was staying with friends, since both his parents are out of the country. I can't even reach them."

"A drowning? You mean the one that was on the news?"

"You heard about it?"

"I was in Marble Canyon last night."

"Oh. Yes, that is the one. He was so young. The same age as my son."

"That is tragic," Nick said.

"I hope they catch whoever did it," she said.

"Did what?" he asked.

"He was killed. It wasn't just a drowning; it was a murder. Someone drugged him."

A part of Nick wanted to ask why, what happened, and so many other questions. The last he'd heard on the news it had been a simple drowning, although—hadn't they said there were drugs at the party?

He wanted to ask how she knew the boy hadn't taken the drugs himself. But he wanted to stay out of it.

Phoenix was a big town. Nobody knew that he, Nick O'Flannigan was anything more than a freelance photographer here on a national assignment. Mainly because that's exactly what he was, nothing more.

No one knew of his interest in sleuthing, and after all the events that happened in Denver, he wanted to keep it that way. In Salt Lake he'd been an unwitting witness in a case. Here, he intended to have the most normal week of his trip so far.

"That is awful," he said out loud. "I hope they catch whoever did it."

He picked up his bag and headed for the elevator. As he did, his phone rang.

"Hi, Mom," he answered. "How are you? How's Dad?"

3

FALLING DOWN

Nick woke to a pleasantly cool room and opened the shades to let in the sun. The room, at least that half of it, got almost immediately warmer.

"Wow," he said to himself. "This is going to be a sweaty week."

He turned on the local news and saw from a graphic in the corner of the screen that it was already 89 degrees. No wonder everyone had a pool around here.

He decided to try a close breakfast spot and found the closest was a quirky spot called the Breakfast Club. He took his camera bag with him and walked. Even the short distance had him overheated. He wasn't used to this kind of heat at all, and even the heat coming off the sidewalk was almost too much to handle.

He glanced at his watch. It was only 9 a.m. He couldn't imagine yet what things would feel like in the heat of the day.

Nick found the A/C in the restaurant welcoming and cool, but not as cool as he liked. They probably kept it set a little higher than he'd prefer, but natives seemed pretty used to the temperature. He opted for an iced coffee and an egg sandwich on a bagel and found both to be satisfying. His head still hurt a little, and he swallowed two Tylenol before heading out toward the capitol.

He saw on his phone it was about a five-minute drive, but he could see from how busy things were that parking could be an issue. So, he decided to take an Uber.

He opened the app and summoned a car, waiting in the shade he could find. When the car pulled up, he dropped inside.

"Hot one today, isn't it?"

"Is it?" the driver said. "Well, not yet, but it will be. Supposed to be pretty brutal later in the week."

"Great," Nick said.

"Not used to it, huh?"

"Not at all."

"Where are you from?"

"Boston originally. Seattle now."

"Ah. You're used to liquid sunshine, then?" the driver laughed at his own joke, and Nick laughed with him. That was one way to look at things.

"What are you doing in Phoenix?"

"I'm on a yearlong assignment," Nick replied. "I'm photographing every state capitol building for a book being put together by *Travel USA* magazine."

The driver whistled. "Sweet gig. Are you driving or flying?"

"Driving. I have it all mapped out."

"Sounds like a long trek. How far are you in, four or five?"

"This is number twelve."

"Wow. Impressive. Got a card or something? I'd like to see that book when it comes out."

"Sure," Nick said as they arrived on the curb. "Here you go."

"Thanks, Mr. O'Flannigan."

"You're welcome," Nick said. As he got out, it felt like a hand filled with heat pushed on his chest.

The driver sped away, and Nick looked at the capitol. Two sidewalks led to it from where he stood on 17th street. On either side were palm trees, and in the center section was a grassy strip interrupted occasionally by a saguaro cactus. A few had yellow flowers blooming on top of them.

A family stood to one side, and an older lady in a pantsuit was backing up to try to get them all in the frame. She was bent forward a little bit, and crossed from the sidewalk to the grass, and took another step back, nearly hitting the cactus right behind her.

"Watch out!" Nick said. The woman straightened and stumbled, nearly falling, and just as suddenly she shot forward.

From where he stood, Nick could see a cactus needle protruding from her thigh.

"Oh, no," he said, shaking his head and walking forward.

She turned to look at him and kept looking up. She wasn't short, but not overly tall, and as red as his hair was, hers was white. She looked at him through thick bifocals.

"Thanks, that could have been much worse," she said, looking at the cactus. A woman who looked enough like her to clearly be her daughter stepped up behind her.

"Mom, what were you thinking?"

"I have no idea," the woman said. "I suppose I wasn't watching."

"Well, you have a—"

The older woman looked down. "Well, so I do. I thought that hurt a little bit." She pulled the needle free and tossed it on the ground.

Nick winced just watching it happen. For a moment, the encounter took his mind off of how hot it was. He wiped his brow.

"Is it a little hot for you?" the woman asked.

"Yes," Nick said. "But I'll manage. I'll be in the Southwest for a few weeks."

"Oh," she said, glancing at his camera. "Could you do us a favor?"

"Sure."

"Could you take a picture of us all together?" she handed him a small mirrorless DSLR, a nice consumer level camera.

"Okay," he said. "Everyone gather up."

He saw why she had been struggling and had the large family back up a little and get closer together. He took a series of shots, hoping at least one would be a good one for them.

He handed the camera back to her.

"Are you headed inside?" she asked.

"Yes. I'll have to get some photos outside later, but for now, I think I need some air conditioning."

"Don't we all? Join us. We are going on a tour."

"Sure," he said. "I'm Nick."

"I'm Janice," she said. "Nice to meet you."

"You, too."

The rest of the family introduced themselves, and Nick followed them inside. The capitol was breathtaking, and Nick was amazed to learn right away that while most state capitol buildings were working capitols, the Arizona capitol building was actually a museum. The government offices were in other surrounding buildings in the area known as the Government Mall.

The initial tour was an hour long, and afterward Nick hung around for a while longer, taking photos nearly everywhere. The floors were all open in the center, providing a view upward to the dome and downward to the state seal in the center of the capitol floor, and he took several photos of that from various angles.

In the once operational areas, furniture and other artifacts combined with interpretive language told him a lot about how things used to work. He pretty thoroughly photographed the top floor and the one below it, and decided he would come back for more pictures later.

For the moment, his mouth felt really dry and he was pretty hungry. He headed downstairs. On his way, he saw a security office.

He went inside.

"Hi there," the lady behind the counter said. "Can I help you?"

"I hope so," he said. "I'm a photographer from Seattle. I'm traveling around the country—"

"Oh my God," she said. "You're that guy."

"Um, maybe?" Nick answered.

"The one who has been traveling all over. You got in some trouble in Denver, didn't you?"

"Well," Nick started. "I'm hoping to have left that all behind me."

"I hope so, too. It seemed like you were just trying to do the right thing."

"Well, that doesn't always work out. I was wondering—"

"If you can get a media parking pass," she finished for him. "Sure. How long are you here for?"

"A week," he said. "This place is really neat."

"But hot, yeah? For someone like you, from where? The Northwest somewhere?"

"Well, I live—"

"I hear that. It is sweltering, but you get used to it after a while."

Nick was frustrated that she would not let him finish a sentence. But he filled out the form she handed him and traded small talk until she handed him a pass for his window with a number on it.

"Here you go. Did you park today?"

"No," he said. "I took an Uber."

"Well, good to meet you," she said. "You stay out of trouble in Phoenix, okay?"

"I'll certainly try," he said, and walked outside.

He decided to try La Canasta Capitola, a nearby Mexican place that would not only be close but offered reportedly great food. As with many other places he'd been, he wanted to see for himself.

By the time he arrived, he needed water, and went through four glasses and two baskets of complimentary chips and salsa before his food arrived, a giant enchilada.

Nick polished it off, left a tip, and ordered an Uber. He waited inside until the app showed the driver "arriving" and went outside.

He slid into the air-conditioned car with a sigh.

"The Marriott, huh?" the driver said.

"Yep," Nick answered.

"They have a great pool."

"I'll have to check it out," Nick said, resting his eyes. His head hurt again.

When they arrived, he tipped the driver, and then headed inside. His eyes felt really dry, and he felt himself almost panting.

He entered the hotel lobby and looked around. There was the same clerk at the desk, and he vaguely saw a family gathered by the elevators, talking excitedly.

He felt himself sway a little bit, his vision blurring.

What's happening? he thought.

He fell toward the floor, and everything went dark.

4

A HELPING HAND

Nick woke to a view of the ceiling interrupted by Sharon, the desk clerk, the woman who had been at the hotel when he arrived.

"Are you okay?" she asked.

"Sure, sure," he said, trying to sit up. "I think I'm just dehydrated."

"Okay, well, we have someone on the way to check you out."

He laid back and closed his eyes. He didn't feel any horrible pain anywhere, but his head did hurt a little.

Could I have a concussion? he thought to himself. He thought back to Salt Lake City and returning the Green Bike outside of his hotel. He'd taken a little spill, and he hadn't been wearing his helmet, thinking it would be a quick trip and it wouldn't matter.

He wouldn't make that mistake again, that was for sure.

Nick opened his eyes, and another female face entered his vision. It was round, surrounded by long black hair, and it topped what appeared to be medical scrubs and a white jacket.

"Hi, Mr. O'Flannigan. I'm Kelly, and I'm a nurse. How are you feeling?"

"My head hurts a little and I feel a little weak."

"Understandable. Seems like you passed out. How much water have you had today?"

"Not enough, apparently," he said. But he really did try to think back and realized he probably had neglected getting enough water. Not smart in this hot of an environment.

"Okay, we're going to sit you up."

"Okay," he said, and pushed himself up to his elbows and then to a sitting position.

"How does that feel?" she asked.

"Better," he said.

She handed him a bottle of water, and Nick promptly drained it.

"I'm going to help you to your room," she said. "I recommend you stay there for a while, rest up, and drink lots of fluids before you go out again."

"Deal," he said. He felt a little nauseous. "Can I ask you something?"

"Sure," the nurse said with a smile.

"I bumped my head last week, a small bike accident. Do you think that could be contributing to this?"

The nurse immediately looked concerned. She took out a light and shined it first in one eye, and then the other.

"Where did you hit your head?"

He pointed to the spot. "Right here. I wasn't wearing my helmet at the time."

"Does it still hurt?"

"Not really. I've just had headaches off and on."

"Okay. I revise my previous advice. I'm going to recommend you go to a hospital and have that checked out just to make sure. Sometimes concussion symptoms take a long time to show up, and they can be made worse by dehydration."

"Okay. I will do that."

"I'll take you if you want. I'm certainly not going to let you drive."

Nick thought about that for a moment, too. He'd driven from Salt Lake, possibly with a concussion, with a stop at the Grand Canyon, where he'd probably been dehydrated too.

"That would be better than an ambulance ride, I suppose," he told her.

The nurse and Sharon helped him into her car after she pulled it around, and she took him to the nearest facility, Phoenix Memorial Center. She got him to the front desk, where they checked him in, and got him back to a room quickly, as it appeared to be pretty slow. The nurse left but gave him her card.

"Kelly Luna," the name said.

"Once they spring you, give me a call if you need a ride. I just finished my shift, and I'm off tomorrow, too."

"Thanks," Nick said.

The next few hours were a blur. They hooked him up to an IV to hydrate him, and told him they would be running a series of tests. First there were x-rays followed by a CT scan. At the end of it all, a doctor appeared beside him.

"Good news, Mr. O'Flannigan," he said. "You have a mild concussion, but nothing serious."

"That's good."

"What are your plans for the next few days? I see you are from Seattle."

"Yes," Nick told him. "I'm on a photography assignment."

"How extensive is that? What do you need to do?"

"Take photos of the capitol building and surrounding areas downtown. I don't have to do much else."

"Okay. I'm going to advise you to take it easy for the next few days. Rest when you need too, but above all drink lots of water. Gatorade or other stuff with electrolytes. If you don't like those, take salt tablets. This heat is probably a bit much for you, and if you don't acclimate, at least a little, you'll find yourself on the floor again. This time, you might hit your head again, and you don't want a second concussion anytime soon."

"Agreed," Nick said. "I'll do my best."

"Good," the doctor said. "I hope I don't see you again while you're here, unless it is somewhere you are buying me a drink. Deal?"

"Absolutely."

"Okay. A nurse will be by with your final paperwork."

"Okay," he said.

The nurse appeared a few moments later, had him sign papers and get dressed. She reminded him to stop by the front desk and talk to them about billing.

"Hey there," the receptionist said, looking up at him. "You're a tall one. Ball player?"

"Nope. College injury ended that dream for me," he said.

"Well, the tallest guy I ever met was Joe Kline, when he was with the Suns," she said. "You're not quite as tall as him, but close."

"Yep. I think he is about six inches taller than I am, if I remember correctly."

"Probably. Where do you want me to send the bill, and do you have insurance I can charge?"

Nick did, but it was a freelancers' policy with a high deductible. This visit might help him meet it. But where did he want the bill sent?

He thought of his parents, but didn't want them to worry, or to pay it for him, even though he knew they probably would.

Sandra. That was who he could trust with this.

He called her.

"Hi, Nick," she said. "How are you?"

"Well, I just got out of the hospital ER," he said.

"What?"

"Don't worry. I was a little dehydrated, and they were worried about the fact that I might have a concussion from my spill last week."

"Are you alright?"

"Yes, and I can explain more later. For the moment, I need a place to send the medical bill, whatever my insurance doesn't cover, and I wondered if I could have them send it to your address?"

"Sure," she said. "I didn't think about you getting mail while you were on the road."

"Most stuff is online anyway, but this is unusual," he said. "Shoot me your address, and when you get the bill from Phoenix Memorial, send it my way."

"Sounds good," she said. "I'll text it to you."

"Okay, call you soon. Love you."

"Love you, too, Nick. Talk soon."

He hung up, got the address, and gave it to the woman at the desk.

"Thanks," she said. "Take care."

Nick looked at the nurse's card but decided to opt for an Uber instead. He used the app to summon one, and less than fifteen minutes later, he was back at the hotel.

Sharon was still at the desk. She must be on a long shift. He approached her.

"Hey, thanks for earlier," he said. "You've been here a long time."

"Someone called off," she said. "I'm working a double."

"That's too bad," Nick said.

"My son is here," she said. "The one who was at the party with my nephew." She called the boy over, who was sitting with another young man, probably college age, watching the television in the lobby.

"Hi," Nick said. "Nice to meet you. Sorry about your cousin."

"Yeah," he said. "It is a real bummer."

"It is. He was your age?"

"Yes. And I hope they catch whoever did it. His ex-girlfriend and her new boyfriend were at the party, too."

"You don't think they would have killed him?"

"Maybe not on purpose," he said. "But there's a rivalry there for sure."

"Well, you should share that information with the police."

"I did," the boy said. "But I don't know if they are doing anything with it. My mom hired a private investigator. We still can't reach my aunt and uncle."

"Really?" Nick said. "Where are they?"

"In Africa. Some kind of missions work or something with their church."

He shook his head. "Well, I'm glad your mom is handling it."

"Yeah."

"Well, good luck. And I'm sorry." Nick felt pretty tired. He turned to Sharon. "Thanks again for your help," he told her. "Let me know if I can help you in any way."

"I will," she said. "You can count on it."

Nick headed up to his room, drank a full bottle of water, and chased it with a second. He laid down, turned on the television, and ordered pizza. The restaurant offered bottled water and other drinks, and he ordered two giant water bottles and two bottles of Gatorade so he wouldn't have to go out again.

He called Sandra and filled her in on the day's events. He would need to give Emily, his editor, a 'heads up', too. This was going to be a tough week, as far as his assignment was concerned. He emailed her after his conversation with Sandra. Then he set an alarm for early in the morning. He had a feeling that either early or late was going to be the best bet for him.

He rolled over and was asleep in minutes. After all the water, he woke up at least twice in the night to pee.

When his alarm went off, he headed for the shower. He wanted to get all the photos outside that he could this morning before temps reached triple digits again, which they were forecast to do.

5

GETTING BURNED

Nick headed out to the capitol building and the complex around it early. He was relieved to see that Sharon was not at the front desk after her long shift the day before. He took an Uber again, because parking seemed to be at a premium, and because he wanted to be able to jump right into a cool car for the ride back to the hotel.

He also took a huge water bottle and drank from it often. He didn't want to pass out again, and he also wanted to feel better and have more energy this afternoon. He figured two things: hydration, good food, and rest were all key to that.

He worked his way around the outside of the Arizona State Capitol Museum first, getting shots of each side in the morning light. Since the government in Arizona was set up so differently, he also took photos of all of the other buildings in Government Square, working his way around those as well. The sun rose quickly, and places that had been in long shadows emerged into great light for photography.

The temperature rose with the sun, and he quickly found his water bottle empty. *That's good,* he thought. *It means I am drinking water and staying hydrated.*

As soon as the building opened, Nick headed into the gift shop, where he bought a large Hydro flask emblazoned with the word 'Arizona' printed over a large cactus. He filled it at a water bottle station near the restrooms, one that had a digital counter showing the number of water bottles those using the station had saved.

The water was cool and clean, and he took a large drink, then filled it up again. He found he needed to use the restroom and figured that was also a good sign.

When he was done, he headed back into the gift shop. "Hey there," he said.

"Hey there," the clerk said, looking up. "Something wrong with the water bottle?"

"Nope, it's great," Nick said. "I was wondering if you have a good recommendation for breakfast."

"If you're looking for something a little different, try the International House of Food. They have Asian, Mexican, and pretty standard breakfast food. The owners are amazing people."

"Sounds like just what the doctor ordered," Nick said. Then he mumbled to himself, "No pun intended."

It was a short walk, but by the time he arrived, Nick was already sweating.

The food was as advertised, and after wolfing down a breakfast burrito chased by some great sourdough toast, he was pretty full. As he set his card down to pay the check, he ordered an Uber, and by the time his transaction was complete, he only had to wait for a minute or two for the car to arrive.

In a matter of minutes he was back at his hotel, walking into the air-conditioned lobby.

He waved to the desk clerk and headed upstairs.

On the way, his phone rang. "Hey, Emily," he said, after seeing it was his editor at *Travel USA* magazine calling.

"Hey Nick. How are things going?"

"Well, good, but interesting," he said as he got into the elevator.

"What kind of interesting?" she asked.

"Oh, not that kind. I overheated yesterday and ended up in the hospital."

"In the hospital? Nick!"

"I'm fine. I should have been drinking more water. They also checked me for a concussion after my little bike accident in Salt Lake."

"You need to be careful."

"I am. Trust me. I have a big water bottle, and I can't stop using the bathroom."

"Well, it is hot there."

"It is. And I'm not used to it. I'm trying to get good shots as early as possible, and as late in the evening as I can. In fact, that's where I just got back from. I'll have some photos uploaded for you early this afternoon."

"Sounds good. Be careful, Nick."

"Will do," he said. As he hung up, he reached the door to his room, and used his phone to unlock it. Proximity technology. You had to love it.

He let himself in, thinking he might take a shower before working on photos.

Before he could head to the bathroom, the hotel room phone rang. That was unusual. It was rare when anyone called those anymore.

"This is Nick," he answered.

"Nick, this is Sharon, from the front desk."

"Sharon?" he said. "How are you?" Nick swore she had not been at the front desk when he just went by.

"I'm okay. How are you feeling today?"

"Good. Better. Thanks for checking in."

"You're welcome. So actually, I'm not working today. But I have a question for you."

"Sure," Nick said, but feeling a little guarded.

"Did you mean what you said yesterday?"

"About?"

"If I needed help, just to ask?"

"Yes, I did. What can I do for you? Do you need some photos taken or something?"

"No. I need you to look at some."

"Look at some?"

"I've read up on you, Nick. I know you have helped the police with cases as you have travelled across the country. I saw the article about you in Denver. You're on the front page of Google for that one."

"Great," Nick said. "What does that have to do with...?" then he remembered. Her nephew, the party, and his unusual death. What was it her son had said - something about a private detective? "Is this about the murder of your nephew?"

"Yes," she answered. "I wondered if you would be willing to help the private investigator by looking over photos of the crime scene. There are a ton of them he has gathered from social media and other places, but he could use your eye for detail."

Nick sighed. The last thing he wanted to be involved with this week was a murder investigation. But he wouldn't truly be involved. Just looking at some photos, right? She had really helped him out. What would be the harm?

"Okay," he said. "But only looking at photos. I've been involved in way too many mysteries on this trip, and I've promised both my editor and my girlfriend that I will stay out of things."

"I understand," Sharon answered.

"I appreciate your help, and I do want to help you, too. So I'll make an exception."

"Thanks," she said. "How about we buy you dinner tonight?"

"Sure," he said. "I have to get some capitol photos this evening, so a late one?"

"Okay," she said. "Eight o'clock. Do you like sushi?"

"Love it."

"Okay. Meet us at Harami over on Adams. It isn't far, and their food is awesome."

"Okay," Nick said. He ended the call and headed for the shower.

A few moments later, he felt much cleaner and cooler, and sat down to upload photos. He sorted the ones he had taken over the last couple of days, edited them, and removed duplicates. He uploaded the best of them to the cloud file he shared with the magazine.

He closed his laptop and noted that, despite his large breakfast, he was hungry for lunch. He didn't want to have sushi, since he would be having that tonight, but sandwiches sounded good. He looked up a few local sub shops and found one who would deliver.

As he placed his order on their app, he looked out the window, and saw people relaxing by the pool. The blue water looked refreshing, and there seemed to be plenty of shade.

Maybe a couple hours of relaxation and reading by the pool were just what he needed.

As long as I stay hydrated, he thought to himself.

He gathered his water bottle, a towel, and dressed in his swim trunks. He applied generous amounts of sunscreen, and headed downstairs.

As he got to the pool, his phone rang again. It was Gerry, his friend from Seattle and the connection who had gotten him this gig in the first place.

"Hey there," he said.

"Nick! I heard you made a trip to the hospital?"

"Who told you? Emily or Sandra?" Nick asked.

"Emily. Are you okay?"

"Just dehydrated. No big deal," he said. "I'm fine now. Actually, I'm trying to rest a bit on this trip. I'm headed for the pool."

"Is that a good idea for someone who's dehydrated?" she asked.

"Well, I'm recovered, and they have misters and plenty of shade. I'm just going to read, drink water, and stay out of the sun."

"Okay. Be careful. Everything else going well?"

"Absolutely."

"Okay. I'll let you go, but if you end up in the hospital again, and don't call me, I may never speak to you again."

"I promise," he said.

"Have a good afternoon, Nick."

He hung up and headed outside. The heat hit him right away, but there were tables and chairs under misters, so he headed to one of those, and dropped his book, phone, and towel there. Then he dove into the pool and did a couple of quick laps. The water was cool and felt great, and he walked to the chair he had chosen, dripping all the way. He looked back to see that the footprints he left behind disappeared almost right away, the water evaporating in nearly an instant.

But the shade did feel good. It felt at least fifteen degrees cooler under the umbrella, and he settled in to read after drying his hands.

Soon, his eyes felt a little heavy. He stood and went for another quick dip in the pool, thinking that would wake him up a bit, and drained most of his water in a long drink.

I'll read a few more pages, he thought. *Then I'll go back inside.*

A few moments later, his eyes closed, and he fell asleep. He woke to a tapping on his shoulder.

A woman stood next to him, looking concerned. She held a Danielle Steel novel against her chest and wore a wide-brimmed straw hat and a flowered one-piece swimsuit.

"I didn't want to bother you," she said. "But the sun has moved a little, and it looks like you are getting a little burned. You may want to move if you are going to stay outside."

Nick looked down. Most of his body was still in the shade, and was fine, but his lower legs were in the sun, which had hit them at an angle. The tops of his feet, and his shins, bisected by a 45-degree shadow, looked a little pink.

"Um, thanks," he said.

The woman laughed. "I hope it isn't too bad," she said. But her eyes showed concern.

His legs were warm. And they did sting a little. It was past time to go inside.

Nick stood, and that was when the pain and tightness of his skin hit him. It hurt to walk.

Sheepishly, he gathered his things, and tried to leave the pool area as normally as possible. The surface around the pool was hot, and nearly burned the bottoms of his feet.

Once inside, he looked down again. His lower legs looked ridiculous.

And they hurt. He thought quickly about what he had in his suitcase. He would be in the Southwest for a few weeks, so he should probably buy a couple of pairs of shorts. From the look of things, he might need some sandals, too.

Putting regular shoes and socks over what looked like a doozy of a sunburn would be nearly impossible.

He shook his head and headed upstairs. From the corner of his eye, he saw the hotel clerk at the front desk look at him and shake her head. She covered her mouth, but he could see the smile in her eyes.

As if being a six-foot six redhead wasn't enough, he told himself. *Now I have a crazy sunburn to draw attention. So much for keeping a low profile.*

He waved and headed gingerly for the elevator. Time to go shopping.

6

ALOE THERE

The store was crowded for a Tuesday afternoon. He'd looked for and found a big and tall store on Camelback Avenue, a twelve-minute drive from his hotel, so he put on the only shorts he had, a pair designed for working out, painfully pulled on socks, and tied his shoes as loose as he could. Fortunately, they were having a sale, and Nick used his credit card to pay for three pair of khaki shorts and picked up a couple of light polo shirts at the same time, those made of a breathable fabric.

They didn't have any sandals, and so he went down the shopping center to a shoe store, where he found a couple of nice pair that seemed to fit him well. Once he got to his car, he ditched his running shoes and socks, and put the sandals on right away.

The straps still bit into the sunburn in places, but they were much better than his athletic socks and running shoes.

He walked back into the hotel, and saw a girl sitting in the lobby. She first looked up at him and then down at his legs. When she saw the sunburn lines there, she snickered.

"Oh, my," she said. "I am sorry, but that is funny."

Nick looked down, aggravated at first, and then saw what she must see. He laughed, too. "It is isn't it?"

"You fell asleep, didn't you?"

"I did," he said. "And it is pretty painful, as funny as it looks."

"I'm Cindy," she said. "My mom works here."

"I'm Nick," he said, shaking her outstretched hand. He would guess her at nineteen, maybe a little older, but the older he got, the harder it was to guess a girl's age. She had dark hair, dark eyes, and was well-tanned. She was dressed what he was calling 'Arizona style', in shorts sandals similar to the ones he'd just purchased, only pink, and a sleeveless white cotton top.

"Sharon wouldn't be your mom, would she?"

"No, although she and my mom are friends. My mom works in house-keeping. She has some herbal stuff that works well on sunburns."

"No worries. I'll get something."

"Ah, it's no trouble," the girl said, texting on her phone.

Nick waited patiently. His feet hurt, even in the sandals, and he wanted to put them up sans shoes for a little while before he went to dinner.

A short but rotund woman came out of the hallway a few moments later. She had a small bottle in her hand.

"Hi there," she said in broken English. Her daughter was the mirror of her features, although the young girl was much slimmer. "My daughter says you have—," she stopped, and chuckled after she looked down. "Oh. I see."

"Yes," Nick said. "It is pretty bad."

"This will help," she said, and held up the bottle in her hand. "It is aloe and some other herbs. It will help with the pain, and it should heal faster."

"Thanks," Nick said. The substance he could see was green and thick, but he figured it was worth a try. "I appreciate this. I'll give it a shot."

"No problem," she said, glanced at her daughter, winked and walked away.

"Thanks to you, too," Nick said to the young girl.

"Let me know how it works," she said.

"Will do. See you around."

Nick headed upstairs, wincing as he walked. It was going to be a rough week, but he figured he would survive.

When he got upstairs, he set the small bottle in the bathroom, kicked off his sandals gingerly, checked his email, and turned on the television. He had a little time before dinner, and he wanted to put his feet up, which was tricky it turned out. The best way was to lay flat, his feet on a pillow at the foot of the bed. He didn't want to turn them side to side, and there was a distinct line between the pink front of his legs and his still-white calves.

He looked at the diagonal line across his shins and smiled. How silly could he be? He snapped a photo with his cell phone and texted it to Sandra.

Three laughing emojis came back, the kind with the tears coming off their faces.

"Does it hurt?" the message followed.

"A little," he said. "Going to dinner shortly. I bought some shorts and sandals to ease the pain. Good news is, I'll fit in with the local fashion."

"But your legs are so white," came back.

"I'll stay away from poolside. And they won't take long to adapt and tan up."

"I'm sure," she texted back. "Be careful of getting too much sun on that burn."

"Will do," he texted back.

As he finished typing his phone rang. "Hi, Mom," he said when he saw who was calling.

"Hi there, Nick," she said. "How are you?"

"Okay. I'm in Phoenix."

"Is it hot?" he heard his father yell from the background.

"He asks if it is hot," his mom repeated.

"Yes, it is. Very. I nearly passed out the other day." He figured he would not worry her by telling her he actually did pass out. "And I have a sunburn."

"Oh, Nick, do be careful."

"I will, Mom."

"How are things otherwise? How is that girl, Sandra? Are you still talking?"

"Of course we are, Mom."

"Just checking. I want you to be happy. Is it hard to be apart from her?"

"It is. But we are making it work so far."

"That's good to hear."

"How's Dad?" Nick's father had recently had a small heart attack. He was home, but Nick worried not only about him, but the toll it took on his mom.

"He's getting stronger, Nick. Don't worry about us."

"Yeah, don't worry about me," his dad yelled from the background.

Nick smiled. He did seem to be doing better, but clearly his heart attack had not helped his hearing at all. "I love you guys," he said.

"We love you, too, Nick. Be safe, okay?"

"I will," he said, and ended the call.

He looked at his feet and took a quick sniff of himself. He needed to shower, but he couldn't imagine the pain of the water on his sunburn.

He sighed. He'd have to do it anyway.

As he stood to go brave the process, he spotted the early evening news. He turned it up.

"New developments in the drowning death that happened over the weekend. The police have ruled this was not an accident, and they say they now have new video evidence from witnesses. We can only show you a fraction of that footage here, but we will be posting it on our website and social media. Police are asking anyone who has tips to call them in."

Nick looked at his watch. He'd have to look at that later, after dinner, but he figured it might be a part of the topic of conversation.

He had to admit as reluctant as he was to get involved, he was looking forward to seeing what the private investigator had found.

He took a quick shower and dressed in his new clothing to prepare for dinner. As he headed out the door, he remembered the lotion he'd been given. Maybe he would use that after dinner, too.

After all, his skin felt even tighter and stung more the longer the day went on. He only hoped dinner wouldn't take too long.

He'd look at a few photos. Point out what he saw and move on.

He needed to tell Sandra what he was up to afterwards, too. No more hiding anything from her, he'd determined. That was a promise he intended to keep.

7

―――――

DINNER TIME

He arrived at Harami on time, wearing khaki shorts and his new sandals, and a nice, light polo. The temperature had dropped, but not to what Nick would consider to be normal or comfortable for him. After this, he would be headed to Santa Fe and Austin, so as closely as he could tell, he was in for some more heat over the next few weeks.

The restaurant felt cool though, and he looked forward to eating something cool rather than a hot meal.

Sharon sat in a corner with a man he did not recognize but assumed to be the private detective. The man had dark hair, large hands, and Nick bet he would be tall when he stood, but not nearly Nick's height.

He put a smile on his face as he approached, even though he saw Sharon put her hand over her mouth and giggle a bit as he approached.

"Hi there," the detective said, rising and confirming Nick's suspicions about his height. "I'm Casey. Nice to meet you."

"Nick," he said, and shook the man's outstretched hand, seeing it was almost as large as his own.

"It's nice to meet you. Sharon says you are from Seattle, on a trip around the country, and you're something of an amateur sleuth?"

"Not intentionally," Nick said. "At least the sleuth part. I've promised to stay out of mysteries."

"After Denver, I don't blame you," Casey said. The look on his face was cold and hard. "Don't worry about it. We all make mistakes. But I do want to get one thing out of the way."

"What's that?"

"These photos are between you, me, and Sharon here. They go anywhere else, we're going to have some issues. If we find something, I'll share it with the cops. One slip to the media, and this could turn into a disaster. We have a clever killer here, more than likely, who is trying to pin the murder on someone else, and if we let them get away—"

His voice trailed off, but the threat was clear.

"Understood," Nick said. "Trust me, I don't want to be in the paper here for a number of reasons. I will tell you that I do love the thrill of 'solving' a crime, or at least helping. But in this case, the credit is all yours."

"Good," Casey's shoulders relaxed. "It's not that I am a credit hog, but I have seen what the media does. No offense to freelancers like yourself. They're looking for news and sensationalism. I'm looking for answers."

"I'm okay with that." Both men sat.

"Let's order," Sharon said. "Then we'll see if you can help us."

They did, Nick ordering a Fire Roll, and something called a Dragon Roll that looked incredible and promised to be spicy.

"So, that's quite the sunburn you have there," she said to Nick after their food was on the way. "Fall asleep?"

"Yes, I did," he said. "Thus the new clothes. I guess I will fit in anyway, and the next few cities on my trip promise to also be hot."

"You'll adapt and then, with your schedule, next thing you know you will be back in cooler territory."

"Until I hit this area. I didn't think much about the climate changes I would experience when setting up this route."

"You'll be surprised how fast the time passes."

"I'm sure. Your friend at the hotel, the one in housekeeping, gave me some lotion to put on it, some herbal stuff."

"Oh, that is nice. Her daughter was also friends with my nephew."

"Really? She is the one that suggested her mom's cream. She was in the hotel lobby."

"She does that often, waiting for her mom. Have you tried the stuff she gave you yet?"

"No. I was going to, but headed here first."

"Be careful with it. Some of her stuff is pretty powerful."

"Hmm. Okay."

Casey interrupted. "While your sunburn is fascinating, you want to take a look at some pictures?"

"Absolutely," Nick said.

Their food arrived, but Casey brought out a tablet, and it was big enough that Nick could still look at photos while shoveling sushi in his mouth. He found himself to be hungrier than he thought and ordered a third roll as he looked through the various pictures.

Some were good, taken with either advanced cell phone cameras or other digital devices. Most came from social media. There was even a short drone video over the party, showing an overhead view of the back yard, the kidney-shaped pool, and the various tiki torches burning around it.

He saw several kids sitting in or near a wooden gazebo smoking what he assumed was marijuana. The posts had captions and hashtags like #partytime and #goodtimes. One even said, "High as air, and I just don't care." It was a sentiment Nick found humorous despite the inaccuracy.

Everything looked normal, pretty much, until he saw a video of a young man dancing oddly, and a group staring at him.

"That's the victim," Casey said, popping another piece of sushi in his mouth. He was also clearly enjoying the food.

"My nephew," Sharon corrected.

Nick nodded. He could see the benefit of the detective being objective, but this was a person who had been killed, not just a "victim."

The next few photos showed more of him dancing, followed by another video. The detective had put these things in order intentionally to show Nick the progression of events. He saw now there were time stamps next to several of them.

The video showed the victim drinking a bottle of water and then staring into a cooler. There was no sound, or it was turned off in consideration for those around them, something Nick thought rather wise from the look of things.

The boy shouted and ran, shoving a couple of people, and stumbling as he went. He wiped his forehead several times with his arm and spun in circles a few times.

Casey's finger tapped the screen to stop the video. "If you zoom in here, you can see by this point he was sweating, we assume from whatever drug is in his system. He seems to be either really drunk, really high, or both. He was probably hallucinating at this point."

"What makes you say that?" Nick asked. He glanced over and saw that Sharon wasn't looking at the video. There were tears in her eyes.

"Just the way he was acting. In the next video, he jumps in the pool. Several people try to save him, and I will let you watch those for yourself in a bit."

"You want me to take them with me?"

"I think it would be better," he said. Casey also looked over at Sharon.

"I think I will go now," she said. "You two let me know what you find later, okay?"

She signaled the waiter, paid her check, and left.

Nick looked at Casey, and the private detective studied him. They remained silent for a moment.

"I appreciate your help, Nick," he said. "I know you want to stay out of this kind of thing, and I get it. But that woman and her sister need guys like you and me."

"You and me?" Nick said.

"I see the way you look at those photos. You can avoid the limelight all you want, but you like this stuff. I can tell."

"I'm beginning to wonder," Nick said. "Looking at things like this is tough."

"You're getting used to it, though. Aren't you?"

Nick thought about it for a moment. "I hope I never get too used to it."

"We all do," Casey said. "I'm trusting you. Here is a thumb drive. You can listen to the video with sound, look through all the photos. If you find anything, let me know. If you don't or don't even want to look, that is fine, too."

"I'll look," Nick said. "I'll help if I can."

"Thanks, man. And hey, whatever you do, if you can avoid it, stay out of the P.I. game."

"Why do you say that?"

"It's the toughest job you will ever do. And it makes you hard. Too hard sometimes."

"I'll take your word for it," Nick said.

"I hope you never find out differently for yourself."

Nick took the thumb drive and Casey's card with his phone number and email address. Casey closed the tablet, they paid their bill, and left, Nick grabbing an Uber back to his hotel.

The whole way back, he couldn't get Casey's words out of his head. "This job makes you hard." He'd also said, "I hope you never find out for yourself."

Nick put the thumb drive next to his laptop on the desk in his hotel room, and called Sandra's number.

"Hey there!" she said.

"Hey there," he said back. "I just got back from dinner, and I need to fill you in on something."

"Okay," she said.

Nick filled her in on what he was doing and why. He left out Casey's final warnings.

"I admire you, Nick. Be careful, alright?"

He agreed. Then he went to the bathroom, took a quick rinse in the shower, and put the lotion the housekeeper and her daughter had given him on his shins, slathering the sunburn thoroughly, putting on a thick layer. The gel-like substance cooled the burn almost instantly. He rubbed the excess on his face and neck, and his skin felt moist and smooth as soon as it touched his skin. He smiled, because he hadn't realized how dry his skin had been until that moment.

He dressed in shorts and nothing else and laid down to go to sleep.

He woke up abruptly some time later. The room was tilting at an odd angle, and he felt like he was going to roll out of the bed and land on the floor. He gripped the covers and tried to steady himself as the room righted itself, and then tilted the other direction.

Something was seriously wrong.

8

TRIP WITHIN A TRIP

The room tilted again, and the colors of the walls swam in front of his eyes. He was nauseous and needed to get to the bathroom or thought he did.

He struggled to a half sitting position and looked at the floor. It had turned from a regular carpet to a pulsing, purple ooze. It would be impossible to walk on, but he had to.

Had to.

The temperature had risen what felt like twenty degrees since he laid down. He was shirtless, sleeping in only shorts, but it felt like a jungle in here.

As soon as he thought the word "jungle" a giant tiger appeared, guarding the bathroom door. Even if he could get across the floor, which had now transformed to a grass-green color that tilted at crazy angles as he looked at it, he would be eaten alive.

But he was going to be sick. And it was so hot. He would have to risk it.

How did it get so warm?

He was sweating but managed to get his feet on the floor. It certainly felt more solid than it looked.

He got to his feet. He found that if he closed his eyes, or kept them closed to tiny slits, the room looked more normal.

He made his way slowly to the bathroom, stopping from time to time to let the room settle into something steady. He stood in the doorway, where the tiger had been but now had disappeared somehow, and stared into the bathroom, totally white and overly bright. It tilted and swirled, and it looked like snow was falling inside.

Nick knew something was wrong. Had it been the sushi? Impossible. He hadn't eaten anything unusual, at least not for him. He wondered how Sharon was doing, or the detective.

Were they sick, too?

The bathroom seemed even hotter than the hotel room. He turned on the fan and then the shower on to full cold. Standing left him dizzy, so he pulled off his shorts and sat in the small tub.

As the water washed over him, he started to feel better. He sat in the tub for what felt like forever, until the cold water started to actually feel cold. He shut it off and stood.

He felt a little better. The room was stable now, and the temperature felt a little more normal. In the mirror, he could see that his eyes looked odd, almost dilated, and that explained why the light felt so bright.

What in the world?

He looked around the bathroom and thought, *What had he done that was out of the ordinary?*

He drank plenty of water. The sushi he ate was normal, no funny smells or taste that he had noticed. Then he saw the bottle of lotion on the counter.

"Be careful," Sharon had said. "Some of her stuff is pretty powerful."

Why would she say that?

He looked at the bottle again. There was a tiny label, and it had a small list of ingredients. The first one was aloe, and that one he knew. The second was datura.

Datura? What was that?

He made his way unsteadily out to the desk and looked at the clock on the end table.

Three-thirty.

It didn't feel like he'd been either asleep or awake for that long. Nick opened his laptop. The screen seemed way too bright and he turned down the brightness. He typed "datura" into the search bar.

A whole series of articles came up, and Nick first read two of them and then looked at the photos.

He looked up "datura absorbed topically." In small amounts, it appeared to be very useful. But in large amounts, the natural substance was a hallucinogen. "Trips" could last for hours. In some states, it was considered a controlled substance.

No wonder Sharon said some of her stuff was powerful, but Nick wondered if she'd known about this at all.

He looked at the label again. There were recommendations, and one said that a thin layer was plenty. A small warning said, "Do not over-apply."

Nick smiled at his own foolishness. Reading directions had never been his strong suit.

He felt cooler now, and tired. He looked at the bed. He'd have to try to get some sleep, and tomorrow he'd have housekeeping change the sheets.

He'd have to share his experience with the housekeeper and Sharon in the morning.

Nick laid down. At first, he had vivid dreams about odd monsters. But he fell quickly into a deep sleep.

When he woke in the morning, he sat up to bright light. He looked at the bedside clock again.

8:30.

He would have to get out and take some photos before it got too hot. He grabbed the water bottle by his bedside and drained it. He headed for the bathroom and a normal shower, he hoped.

He felt almost hung over, not something he felt often, but other than that, he felt normal.

Once he got some capital photos, he would come back and look at the video for the private eye. But on the way, he planned to get some normal lotion.

He hoped Sharon was working today, and that he could talk to the housekeeper at some point. He wanted to know more about her formula and the side effects.

He wondered if what he'd experienced was normal. Because it didn't feel like it.

By the time he got out of the shower, Nick found that he was pretty hungry. It was 9 a.m. and his phone told him it was already ninety-two degrees. At least it hadn't hit triple digits yet.

He grabbed his camera, his water bottle, and rushed out the door.

9

POOLING RESOURCES

The sun seemed especially bright even for Phoenix, and Nick winced even behind his sunglasses. The outside temperature seemed to be rising by the minute.

He drove to the capitol area, hoping beyond hope that there would be parking. As luck would have it, he found a space about a block away, although the meter told him he had a two-hour limit.

That was fine. Nick figured by then he would be a puddle of goo on the sidewalk. He stuck to the shaded areas where he could, stepping out to get photos with the right light. Thankfully, even being an hour or so later than the last time he visited the complex gave him some new light and yielded some photos he was truly happy with.

That was great, because he wanted to finish up any outdoor photos as quickly as possible. He found the heat, though supposedly a dry one, to be hard on his body, but particularly the sunburned areas of his legs.

Walking down one of the streets next to the Government Mall, he spotted a vendor selling some cooling neck wraps and bottled water.

He shook his own bottle, finding it nearly empty. He might as well refill, and look into almost anything that would cool him down.

The vendor smiled as he approached. "Hey there," he said, first looking up and then down at Nick's sunburned legs. He suppressed a laugh.

"It's okay," Nick said. "It is kind of funny now."

"Probably stings like crazy," the man said.

"Yeah, a bit," Nick said.

"Well, you need some sunscreen and some lotion," the vendor said. "And to protect your neck and keep it cool, you might want one of these."

The man pointed to a bandana he wore around his own neck, but one that seemed thick and almost cylindrical. Nick saw a large pitcher that said, "SAMPLE" in big letters. In it was another one of the devices floating in ice water.

Nick had seen them before, but never in person. He never needed one in either Boston or Seattle, nor anywhere else he had traveled. Even though Sacramento had been hot, it had not been this kind of hot.

"How does that work?" he asked.

"It is filled with these gel-type beads," the man said. "It retains water for a long time and stays cool. If you use it around your neck or on your head, it will help with the heat for hours." He handed Nick the one from the pitcher. It felt cool in Nick's hands.

"You can even freeze them overnight," the man said. "They will last even longer that way."

"This is really cool," Nick said.

"Here, check this out," the vendor said. He handed Nick a bottle.

Nick turned it over, looking carefully at the ingredients. The three primary active ones listed were zinc oxide, aloe, and hydrocortisone. He simply nodded to himself.

"It's totally safe," the man said, apparently reading Nick's expression.

"I get that," Nick said. "Just checking. I had an odd reaction to some a housekeeper at my hotel gave me. Some natural stuff that I think I might be allergic to or something."

"What would that be?" the vendor asked as Nick handed him his card to pay for his purchases.

"Datura, I think?"

The man laughed as he pulled a new bandana from a cooler, where it had been sitting in ice water and handed it to Nick along with the bottle. Nick stayed in the shade of his enclosure and put his leg up to apply the lotion.

"Datura can be a hallucinogen," the man said. "If you take high enough doses. You say it was in some kind of lotion?"

"Yes."

"And you only put it on your legs?" the man seemed puzzled.

"Yes, but—" Nick stopped. He remembered putting the sunscreen on his face and neck, and it feeling good.

"Did you wash your hands when you were done?"

But Nick already knew the answer, sort of. He still didn't know what datura did exactly, but the word hallucinogen was familiar enough for him to understand that he'd been drugged, or accidentally drugged himself.

He laughed, a little at first, and then harder. It was funny now.

"Did I say something funny?"

"I just realized what happened," Nick said. "I've got to get moving. But thanks. You've helped more than you know."

The vendor handed his card back, smiled, and waved.

Nick walked away, shaking his head. He had to admit the new sunscreen and the neck wrap did help, and he was able to take photos for quite a while longer than he thought.

He was rounding the last corner of the capitol and realized he never had stopped for breakfast. He was starving and needed something to fill the hole in his stomach.

A burger sounded excellent.

He glanced at his watch. He had only ten minutes to get back to his car or risk a parking ticket.

He decided to get there first and then find a place to eat.

As he approached his car, he could see an official looking parking attendant about five cars away, writing a ticket for someone else.

Nick waved as he got to his car, seeing there were three minutes to spare on the meter. He got in and started it up, putting the air conditioner on full-blast, glad he'd had that repaired in Boise, seven weeks behind him and several degrees cooler.

As he pulled out, his phone rang and he answered it without thinking, using the hands-free feature in his car.

"This is Nick."

"Nick, this is Casey. You have time for lunch?"

"Yep. I was just headed to get something to eat. I haven't had a chance to look at the photos you gave me yesterday."

"I have something new, and a question for you. Let me buy you a burger and a beer."

"I'm game," Nick said. "I'm in my car down by the capitol now. Where should I meet you?"

"I'll text you an address. It's about a fifteen-minute drive, but I promise you it is worth it."

"Deal," Nick said, hoping wherever it was had some big plates. He was starving.

The name came up simply as Cold Beer and Cheeseburgers on North 7th Street.

He headed that way, encountering almost no traffic until he got close, and pulled into their parking lot. It was a quick dash to the door, and inside it was cool and dark. He removed his sunglasses and marveled at all the taps and the screens behind them. The place was amazing.

Casey was already there and waved him over to a booth.

"Hey," Nick said. "Thanks for the invite."

He ordered a porter, which arrived in a frosty mug, a large burger and a mountain of fries. Casey ordered something similar.

Once they had their food, Nick said, "So, I feel bad because I haven't had a chance to look at your photos or videos. I accidentally slept in a little and I planned to go over them this afternoon."

"No worries," he said. "I've got another video for you, but this one is a little different and more sensitive."

"More sensitive?" Nick asked, taking a large bite of his burger.

"Yeah. I got this one through a connection at the police department, and I'm definitely not supposed to have it. I especially should not show it to you, but I need your help. I didn't see anything, but my gut tells me the clues I need are in it."

"Why do you say that?" Nick said, swallowing and taking a huge drink of the cold beer.

"Because it's from the victim's cell phone."

Nick nearly spit out his beer and choked as he swallowed. "What?"

"Yeah. And he wasn't the one taking the video. Someone else was."

"Who do you think that was?"

"I'm not sure yet. But I suspect whoever was holding that phone was also the killer. Will you take a look as soon as you get back to your hotel?"

"Absolutely," Nick said, agreeing before he even thought it through.

Casey set a thumb drive on the table, and Nick wiped his hands with a napkin, picked it up, and slipped it in his pocket.

It seemed to weigh a lot, and Nick couldn't get his mind off of it as he finished his burger and beer.

As he did, Casey's phone rang. "Call me if you see anything," he told Nick, and excused himself with the check.

Nick swallowed his beer in one giant swallow and headed back to the hotel. He couldn't wait to get there and look at this new evidence.

As he walked into the lobby, he saw Sharon and the housekeeper huddled in conversation.

They looked up as he approached.

"Nick, have you made any progress with the photos?" Sharon asked.

"No, but I—" Nick said, turning toward the housekeeper.

Sharon gripped his arm like a vice. "You have to hurry if you can."

Nick stared at her and saw she'd been crying. The housekeeper had a look of shock on her face, and Nick could see she'd been crying, too. "What's wrong?"

"It's Cindy," the housekeeper said breathlessly. "She's been arrested."

10

THE DEVIL'S TRUMPET

Two things happened simultaneously. Nick's phone rang, and he saw that Sandra was calling. The housekeeper looked behind him, her hand shot to her mouth, and she fainted. Sharon caught her on the way to the floor.

Nick turned to see two police officers coming through the hotel lobby. Both looked very confused, and while one looked up at him, the other rushed over to the housekeeper.

"Stay right there!" the first officer said to him.

"But I—"

Then he heard a small voice from his phone. "Hello? Nick, what is going on?"

He stood, unsure what to do. So he froze. He could still hear Sandra, asking what was happening through the phone, but everything else seemed to move in slow motion.

Officer #2 knelt by the fallen housekeeper.

Sharon stood and made a motion to the police officer, waving her hands at him and pointing at Nick.

Nick felt the weight of the thumb drive in his pocket, the one he should not have. He wondered why the police were here at all if Cindy had already been arrested.

It took a moment, but Sharon's quick explanation about Nick being a guest seemed to calm the officer down. The housekeeper sat up against the wall, recovering.

The second officer explained they were just here to ask her some follow up questions about her daughter, nothing more.

They let Nick go. His phone rang again as he headed for the elevators and he answered it.

"My God, Nick, what is happening?"

"Just a misunderstanding," he told Sandra. "The police are here, and they were confused by what they saw."

"The police? Nick?"

"Can I call you back in five minutes?" he asked. "I'm about to get on the elevator. I'll fill you in when I get to my room."

"Okay."

Nick used the ride up and a quick visit to the restroom to compose himself. He took the thumb drive out of his pocket and set it next to the other one and his computer on the desk. He also sat his camera next to both.

Then he took a deep breath and picked up his phone.

He told Sandra the whole story, from the private eye to his strange experience the night before with the housekeeper's ointment, the new evidence he'd been given to look at, and the fact that the housekeeper's daughter had been arrested.

"I'm sorry," he told her. "I was doing a favor for the desk clerk who helped me when I was dehydrated, and I thought I would not be involved in anything, but suddenly I am. I don't like it any more than you do, but now I feel like I have to finish things."

"Do you think the daughter had anything to do with this?"

Nick thought for a moment. "Honestly, I have no idea. I haven't really looked at any of the evidence. She seemed nice enough, but murderers aren't always what they seem, or so I have learned. The police must have some reason to suspect her."

"What if the victim was having the same type of experience you did? You said you were overheated and hallucinating, right?"

"True. So that might be the case. I'll have to look at photos to find out, and maybe the private eye or the police have a tox screen by now."

"Possibly. Nick, how do you feel about working with this P.I. instead of the police, even just looking at photos? I mean, you said the latest stuff he gave you is something you're not supposed to have."

"I've been thinking of that. I'm not sure what the right thing to do is. He seems genuinely interested in getting to the bottom of things."

"As long as you trust him. But be careful, Nick. Just look at photos, nothing more."

"That's the plan," he told her, and ended the call.

Nick opened his computer, inserted the first thumb drive, and opened the folder on it labelled social media.

There were over one-hundred photos and seven videos. The files had been named by time order, so he followed through with them starting at the beginning.

The first few were wide shots of the party and the scene. It was still light outside in them, although the light was fading. There were several tiki torches lit around a pool area. Several long tables occupied the gravel area around the pool, but there was some grass as well, unusual for the typical lawn-free Arizona home.

On one was a punch bowl and several types of drinks. Many of those who'd arrived early at the party were either vaping or smoking. Nick didn't understand the appeal of either, not that he had ever tried them.

As an athlete, keeping his lungs in shape had always been high priority for him.

He zoomed in on each of the photos, looking at various things, but didn't see anything he would consider a clue.

He refilled his water bottle from the sink in his room, determining the water must be filtered, because it tasted pretty good. He craved a diet soda or something but figured he could get one from the machine shortly.

The first twenty photos or so didn't really show him anything. The last couple showed Jeff, the victim, apparently arriving but at that time everything looked pretty normal. He grabbed a drink and walked around.

In the background of one shot, Nick could see him talking to another young man. He was large and muscled compared to Jeff. The large individual stood next to a young woman who looked uncomfortable.

Nick panned around each new photo. He was looking for details, but details of what? He had no idea.

He spotted Cindy, the girl who had given him the sunburn lotion in one of the next photos. She was standing behind Jeff, apparently watching him as he talked to another girl.

"She wasn't the ex-girlfriend, was she?" Nick asked himself.

He checked his notes from the private eye and found the name he was looking for: Rhonda. He wasn't sure which one she was, but he didn't see Jeff interacting with one girl more than any of the others.

A few photos later, he saw Jeff talking to the girl who had been with the large man in one of the first photos. They were sitting in the wooden gazebo. She smiled and handed him something.

In the next photo, he was smoking something, what looked like a joint when Nick zoomed in. He wondered if marijuana was legal in Arizona. He hadn't really checked.

He opened a browser on his laptop and learned that it was, but only medicinally not recreationally. Interesting. Then he remembered his intention to look some other things up, so in a new tab searched "datura."

He stopped as soon as the first photo came up, his water bottle halfway to his lips. It was a close up of a plant that had purplish-white flowers and thorny looking leaves. The initial information said it was a bush-like plant and was a foul-smelling and invasive weed in some areas. It was called by several names, the most common of which was jimson weed, a name that came from a poisoning that happened in Jamestown during the early colonization of North America.

He clicked on the article and read further, seeing that it was used in medicine but also as a hallucinogen.

The list of symptoms fit almost perfectly with what he had experienced himself the other night after applying the sunscreen lotion. It probably would not have affected him so strongly from just a topical application, but he'd put it on his face, and gone to sleep. On his face, next to his mouth, eyes, nose, and he hadn't washed his hands after using it either.

It could be that he was very sensitive to it as well, and Nick suspected he might be. But that's not what caught his attention the most.

He saved the image from the article to his computer, and opened it, zooming in. He moved it to one side of his screen and studied it for a moment. It looked familiar. He opened the file of photos he'd taken at the Grand Canyon.

There it was, front and center, the background of the canyon blurred behind it. A datura plant, the now distinctive white flowers he'd taken only days before.

He moved that one to the side as well, and opened the photos from the party, scrolling until he found what he noticed.

There it was. In the background, behind the table, a large plant in the middle of the gravel.

It had purple-white flowers. Thorny leaves. Datura.

Nick clicked off the photo in the article and read further.

It listed another common name of the plant: the devil's trumpet. He clicked back to the photos from the party, and cropped the photo of the plant, isolating it.

Then he clicked back to the other party photos. The plant was there, and likely the victim had been poisoned with datura. It made sense. He watched the video, the clip of Jeff falling into the pool. Something looked off about that, but he couldn't see what it was from this angle. He shut it off as several people rushed to try to pull him to safety while whoever had been holding this phone looked on.

Nick scrolled backwards through the photos and concentrated on the one of the girl handing Jeff something. A joint which he then smoked. Could the datura have been in that?

Nick considered it. That girl might be the killer. But she might not. Before he jumped to any conclusions, he wanted to look at the other video. He ejected the thumb drive and inserted the second one.

He wanted to see who had control of the victim's phone, and who shot that video.

As he opened the file and it appeared on his screen, his phone rang with a 602 number, the Arizona area code.

"This is Nick," he answered.

"Hi, Nick. This is detective Olson, Phoenix P.D. Do you have a few moments to chat?"

"Sure," Nick said, pausing the video before it could play. There, on the screen, he saw Cindy walking through the shot toward the pool.

He closed the lid of his computer quickly as if the cop might be able to see through his phone.

"How can I help you?" he asked.

11

SEEING THINGS

This was exactly what Nick had been trying to avoid. He didn't need another interaction with the police, the media, or anyone else in authority. What he needed was a quiet week with normal things like a sunburn and passing out from dehydration.

But no matter how hard he tried to avoid it, he ended up in the middle of some kind of crime. He'd wanted to look at the photos and help Sharon out, but how could all these people in Phoenix be connected? He knew the girl who'd been arrested, had received what might be considered a controlled substance from her mother, and had in his possession a video from a P.I. that he wasn't supposed to have.

And now the police were on the phone. They'd called his cell phone. They knew who he was.

So much for keeping promises and staying out of things.

"How can I help you?" he'd replied to the call.

"We understand you've had contact with one Cindy Cruz?" the voice of authority said.

"I didn't know that was her last name, but I have had contact with a girl named Cindy at the hotel where I am staying. How did you get my number?"

"We're just reaching out to anyone who might have had contact with her in the past few days."

"What is this regarding?" Nick decided to play innocent. Maybe they didn't know that he already knew about her arrest, the murder that looked like an accident at first, and the fact that she had been at the party.

"C'mon, Mr. O'Flannigan. We know you've had contact with a private investigator working on behalf of the victim's family."

"How do you know that?"

"Has he shared anything with you that we should know about?"

"As far as I know, he's shared everything he has with the police. Listen, I'm just a photographer on assignment."

"I know who you are. You may be just a photographer as you say, but you have been involved in mysteries on your trips, and despite your misadventures, you have helped police from time to time."

"I have. But in this case—"

"Let me guess. He just asked you to look at some photos, right?"

"Yes."

"Is he paying you to do that?"

"No. I just said I wanted to help."

"Casey is great at getting other people to do his work for free. You know what he is charging that family?"

"Hey," Nick said. "This sounds like an issue between you and Casey. I don't know what this has to do with me, why you've contacted me about it, and what you expect me to do for you."

"I just wanted to let you know who you are working with or rather, working for."

"I'm not working for anyone," Nick said.

"If he was paying you, you would be operating as a private investigator without a license."

"Wait a minute," Nick said. "Is this some kind of threat? As I said at the start, how can I help you? I'm not doing this for money and certainly not to get noticed at all."

"Right. Like your little adventure in Denver?"

"This conversation is over," Nick said, and ended the call.

He stared at his phone and at the paused picture from the video that was still on his screen. It was Cindy, the girl he'd met at the hotel. There she was, at the party, walking toward the pool, and holding a joint in her hand.

It looked similar to the one the victim had been smoking.

In the background he could see the Datura plant, but when he hit play, the video swung away from that and to Jeff, the victim. His eyes were red, and he was dancing in circles as whoever held the phone laughed loudly.

That laugh belonged to a male, Nick knew that much. He paused the video and zoomed in on Jeff's face. He was sweating profusely.

Nick's phone rang again, a Phoenix number a couple of digits off the one that had called a few minutes ago. He ignored it. Until he had something figured out here, he wasn't going to deal with the police or anyone else for that matter.

Okay. So, a few things he knew or thought he knew. So far, he'd just heard the boy had been drugged, but now he guessed from his experience and from the photos he'd seen the drug was datura, the substance in the sunscreen that sent him on a trip of his own.

But that raised some serious questions. There was a "devil's trumpet" jimsonweed plant in the yard where the party happened.

But how had that gotten in Jeff's system?

There were a couple of options. The joint could have been laced. According to the information Nick had found on the web, smoking was one way the drug was ingested. Besides topical applications, it was also often brewed into a tea.

Nick doubted the boy could have consumed the tea without knowing it. He would have smelled or tasted something off, right?

The detective thought whoever had shot the video with his phone was likely the killer, but Nick had his doubts.

I mean, it was probably whoever gave him the joint or whoever made it, or rather rolled it, he thought to himself.

Then he stopped, hand hovering over the mouse, realizing what he was doing. He really was only supposed to look at the videos and photos and see if he could spot details others might have missed. Like the plant, the sweating boy, the people in the background.

It wasn't his job to connect the dots. The private eye was getting paid to do that.

Getting paid. Nick sat back in the hotel desk chair and closed his eyes. He wasn't getting paid, the investigator was, or the cops were, or whoever. He was being used, just like the one cop had said.

His job wasn't even to look things over, although he did owe Sharon that favor. But his real job was to take capitol photos and photos of the surrounding area. Upload them. Find facts and interesting things about the city he was in. And move on to the next. And so on.

He sat forward and hit play on the video. One last look, and a report of what he saw, and he would be done with this. He'd call the police back, share with them what he shared with the private investigator, and that would be that.

The video jiggled as whoever held the phone moved around. Nick watched in horror as Jeff roamed toward the cooler, grabbed a bottle of water and chugged it.

Then he stood up, and yelled, "Snakes!"

Jeff ran toward the screen, shouting "Snakes!" again and tackled the person shooting the video.

For a moment, the viewpoint swept up to the sky.

"Get off me!" he heard the person holding the phone say. "Dude! Dude! Come here!"

But Jeff turned and looked directly into the phone. "You stole her! Keep away from me!"

The first girl, the one he'd been smoking a joint with, appeared. The camera was pointed straight up at her. "Jeff, maybe you should just go," she said.

"I'm so hot," Jeff said. "So hot."

Nick could relate.

"Calm down, okay?" the girl said.

But Jeff walked toward the pool. A few others tried to stop him. Nick stopped the video on a still shot of Cindy trying to grab his arm. He took a quick screen shot, and hit play again.

Jeff turned again. "Why is it so hot?" he asked those around him. "It is supposed to be cooling down."

The camera angle was still low, as if the person shooting it was either still laying there, or they had propped up the phone and left it.

Then Nick saw the large man the girl had been talking to. He reached for Jeff after Cindy did, but also wasn't able to stop him.

Then Nick saw something, the flash of tanned skin, a turquoise bikini, and a small hand. He couldn't see the owner of that hand in the shot, but he did see it shove Jeff into the pool, and he thought he saw that person, at least from the waist down, jump into the pool after him.

Shoved him into the pool.

Nick saved the video to his computer and ejected the thumb drive.

He inserted the first one and scrolled through the photos. Then he spotted the girl in the turquoise bikini in one of the early shots before Jeff had arrived.

She was handing the girl Jeff had been smoking with two rolled joints. In the photo, she pointed specifically at one of them.

In the next photo, the two girls stood side by side, laughing.

Nick zoomed in on the girl in the bikini.

He was pretty sure he'd found the killer, and it wasn't Cindy. Nor was it the first girl, or the person holding the camera.

But he had no idea who she actually was. But he knew who would.

He picked up the phone, and dialed Casey's number.

"Nick, tell me good things," Casey said.

"I think we need to meet," Nick said. "I found something."

"Good," Casey said. "How about breakfast in the morning?"

"Sounds fine," Nick said. He felt things were more urgent than that, but he agreed, and looked at the time on his computer. It was already 7:30, he was hungry for dinner, and he hadn't uploaded a single photo that was part of his real job yet.

He ended the call with Casey, agreeing to meet at a place called Matt's Big Breakfast, then ejected the disk and connected his camera to his computer after using a delivery app to order dinner.

He called Sandra as he sorted and edited photos for upload to the magazine.

"Can I run something by you?" he asked her.

"Anytime, Nick," she said. "What's on your mind?"

He outlined his idea, and shared his thoughts about the private eye, the police, and the investigation while he ate.

"Those are good thoughts, Nick," she said. "I say go for it. Just be careful."

"I will," he said. By the time they hung up, the photos were nearly uploaded, and Nick was exhausted.

He left his computer open and went straight to bed.

He woke the next morning to his alarm going off. It was Thursday and time for him to put this odd case behind him.

He opened the curtains, and when he saw the sun rising, painting the clouds orange, he stepped out onto his balcony with his camera, and captured some spectacular shots of the city skyline.

Today was going to be a good day.

PAYING IT FORWARD

Matt's Big Breakfast offered just what the name promised: a big breakfast. So he ordered a plate of waffles with eggs and bacon, coffee, and waited.

Casey walked in a few minutes later, waved, and came over. Nick had selected a larger table, and already had his laptop open.

Casey sat down, signaled for coffee, and looked over the menu, placing his order before he turned to Nick.

"So what do you have for me?" the detective asked.

"First things first," Nick said. "I have a serious question for you, and I want an answer before we go any further."

"Okay."

"How much are you getting paid?"

"What?"

"How much are you getting paid for this case?"

"I don't see that's any of your business," Casey said, putting his coffee mug down and folding his arms. "What's this about, O'Flannigan? You looking for a payday? Something like your deal in Denver, huh?"

"No. I just want to know."

"I don't see—"

Nick shut his laptop. "I'll just take this to the cops myself, then." His food had arrived, so he dug in.

Casey stared at him for a minute without saying a word. "What makes you think they'll listen to you?"

"Well, an officer called me yesterday afternoon. They don't seem too fond of you."

"They don't like it when a P.I. solves their case instead of them, that's all. It makes them look and feel incompetent, which they often are."

"You don't think they might be a little overloaded from time to time? What you do could be helpful, but it seems to me like you don't have much respect for the police force."

"Wait, Nick. Wait. That's not it at all. I may be a little cynical, yeah. That's because I come in with a fresh look at the evidence and fill in blanks the cops can't or won't. I know they're often overloaded, and I can help them close cases they might not otherwise."

"But you make a lot of money off what you do, right?"

"Sometimes."

"And then you call me in to help you, as a consultant, right?"

"If someone like you or with skills I don't have is around."

"So what does a consultant like me usually make?" Nick asked.

"Oh, there it is. You want money? Okay, name your price."

"I don't want money for me. Let me lay it out for you. I've found something on this video, probably who the killer is, even though I don't know who she is—but I am sure you or the police can put a name to her face."

"That's good, I suppose."

"I can show it to you, or to the police. I assume if they solve the crime first, you probably don't get paid as much."

"True. Although I don't— "

Nick held up his hand. "I don't care how you structure your fees right now. All I want to know is what you would pay a consultant like me. Because if I give these photos to you, I want you to donate that amount of money."

"To a charity, in your name, right?"

"No. I want you to leave my name out of it. Not a word about who I am, or that I had anything to do with any of this."

"You want to remain anonymous, and you want me to donate the money I would have paid you?"

"Those are my terms."

"You're an odd one, O'Flannigan."

"I don't mind that. Do we have a deal?"

"Yes."

"I'm counting on your honesty. I want you to give my fee to Sharon's family, her sister, the kid's parents."

"Okay. Deal."

Nick opened his laptop again, wiping his hands with a napkin first. The food was delicious.

As he ate with one hand, Nick explained his theory between bites, and showed Casey the videos and the shots where he'd zoomed in and cropped.

"That's good work, O'Flannigan," Casey said. "You sure you're in the right line of work?"

Nick popped the last strip of bacon into his mouth. "Positive. I have a great eye for detail, and I'm happy to use it. But everything else to do with solving mysteries has been nothing but a pain and hinderance to me. Just once, I'd like to have a normal week just doing my job."

"Good luck with that, man. Seems like mystery follows you everywhere."

Nick saved his cropped versions of the photos to the thumb drive. "The cops can call me if they have any questions, but they shouldn't. Good luck, Casey."

The investigator stood and grabbed the check. Nick stood too. "Thanks for all your help. I'll let you know how it turns out."

They shook hands, Nick packed away his laptop and left. It was already warm outside, but he was at the point where he expected it and almost welcomed the warm, fresh air after the canned air conditioning everywhere.

He headed back to the hotel and picked up his camera. He wanted more indoor photos of the other buildings in the government mall, just for reference, and figured he would get some sunset shots that evening. As he walked between buildings in the complex, he picked out various spots where he'd be able to have a clear shot to the west and see the sunset behind the capital. A few stray clouds dotted the sky, and he hoped they would stick around for his final shots.

As he stepped inside the Arizona State Capitol Museum, his phone rang. It was Sandra.

"How did it go?" she asked.

"It went perfectly," he said. "I just have to trust that Casey will do what he said he would."

"That's all you can do," Sandra said. "I'm proud of you, Nick."

"Thanks. I appreciate that. I love you."

"I love you, too," she said. "I have to get back to work, but we can talk tonight, right?"

"Yep. I plan to get some sunset shots tonight, and some final sunrise shots of the capitol building tomorrow morning. Then I should have this about wrapped up."

"Great job, Nick. How are you feeling?"

"Good. No headache, the sunburn is—" he looked down at his legs. "Fortunately or unfortunately, it's fading into a tan."

Sandra giggled. "Send me a picture of that."

He smiled. "I will."

They ended the call, and he snapped a photo of his now peeling and oddly tanned legs and sent it to her.

He took a few more photos inside, mostly close up macros he'd spotted but hadn't actually taken yet. The light was perfect, and he was in and out in very little time.

As he walked out he saw a big group of motorcycles on the street out front. It was the group he'd run into in Marble Canyon.

Someone shouted his name, and he turned.

"Dale?" he said. The large biker he'd met outside the hotel stretched out his hand. Nick shook it.

"You did come to take photos of the rally," the big man said.

"Not exactly," Nick said. "But I'm here, so I can."

"How did your week go?" the biker asked as they walked toward the group. "Aside from your unfortunate sunburn."

Nick laughed. "A little more eventful than I would have liked it to be," he said. "But it's almost over now."

He followed the man to the rally, where he was introduced to several new bikers. He took a bunch of photos and got an email address where he could send them to the organizers.

"Thanks a bunch, Nick," Dale said as Nick prepared to leave. "Maybe we'll see you around."

"Maybe," Nick said.

He headed for a late lunch. This afternoon, maybe he could relax for a bit once he uploaded photos. Just not by the pool.

He'd been burned more than enough times already on this trip.

13

____

BURNED AGAIN

Lunch was good, but it was hot, so Nick headed back to the air-conditioned hotel where he could upload photos and relax before going to take the final sunset photos he would need. Maybe his Friday would be pretty open for photos for his social media and website stuff, and he could catch up a little bit on that.

As he entered the hotel, he saw Sharon and waved. She was with another guest but motioned him over. He waited patiently, feeling pretty relaxed about the rest of his day.

The guest left, and he stepped forward.

"You met with Casey this morning?" she asked. "How did it go?"

"Well, I had a few things to share with him. He should be giving them to the police and hopefully helping them wrap this up."

"Oh, good," she said. "I knew you could help."

"How is Cindy's mother holding up?"

"Pretty well, all things considered. Hopefully, Cindy will be released later today once Casey shares your information."

"I hope so," Nick said, wondering how Sharon knew so certainly that his information didn't point to Cindy.

She just believes strongly in her innocence, Nick thought. Out loud, he said, "Have a good afternoon. I'll check in later to see how things are going. How late do you work?"

"Seven," she said.

"Good," Nick said. "I'll be headed out before that to get dinner and to set up for some sunset shots at the capitol."

"Okay, talk to you later," she said.

Nick walked toward the elevators and stopped. Standing by them was Janice, the woman he'd met by the capitol building, the one who'd run into the cactus taking her family's photo. He smiled at her.

"I had no idea you were staying here," he said.

"Well, my daughter and her family are. I actually live out in Mesa, about 45 minutes away. But I have a small house and the kids like to stay where there is a pool."

"That's great," he said. "It's good that you get to spend time with them like this. My parents are in Boston. It will be a few months still before I will be on the East Coast and can see them."

"Yeah, it seems like they don't come often enough. The photos you took of us turned out awesome. Do you want to see our favorite?"

"Of course," Nick said.

The older woman took out her phone and opened her photos, holding it up so he could see. He looked closely and saw someone in the background he hadn't noticed at the time.

"That is great," he said out loud. "Can you send that to me?"

"Absolutely," she said, and asked him his number. Nick gave it to her, and a moment later the photo was in his text messages.

"I might just add that to my portfolio," Nick told her with a smile. Inside, he had an odd feeling. He could just see someone in the background of the picture, and he wanted to see who it was. The shape, the way the person was standing looked oddly familiar, but he didn't want to seem strange, so decided to study it later.

She laughed. "If only you had a more photogenic family for that shot."

"You guys are great," Nick said. "Thanks for this."

"No, thank you. The kids will be leaving today and having photos of us all together means a lot. Good luck on your trip."

"I may need it," Nick said. Janice gave him a quick hug that surprised him. "You're a good guy, I can tell," she said.

As they finished talking, the elevator dinged and her kids and grandkids poured out of the doors, the haggard looking father pulling a luggage cart along.

Nick smiled, waved, and got on the elevator.

As soon as the doors closed, he sagged back against the wall, and counted the seconds until he got in his room.

He looked at his phone right away, saving the photo and zooming in on it. There, behind the family, was a man watching them. Nick could see, despite the large sunglasses, that it had been Casey. Why had he been watching him then? It made no sense. But there he was.

He decided he needed to do some detective work on his own, stuff he was good at. He went back to the photos of the party, leaving his camera and the photos he needed to upload on the desk for now. He set an alarm though, one for 5:30. He wanted to have time for supper and to get his sunset photos in, and he knew he could lose track of time doing stuff like this.

But something felt off about this morning, about Cindy, how Sharon just knew she was not guilty, and Casey.

Something felt off about the whole thing, like he had been targeted, chosen somehow. But why?

There were bags on hooks by the edge of the pool, and he zoomed in, seeing a couple of them had logos, some kind of mascot.

He looked up local schools on Google and found that at least a few of the bags were from a private school in Peoria, a suburb not far from where the party had happened.

He looked online but found that you needed a login from the school to view past yearbooks, so instead Nick turned to social media, where he found a student page. There was a list of several members of the group, and he put that page on one side of the screen and the photos from the party on the others.

He started to write down names as he zoomed in on faces. The big guy was named Thad. There was Jeff, the victim. Cindy. Rhonda, the joint girl. Becky, turquoise bikini.

Rhonda Guthrie. That name sounded familiar.

He scrambled, looking for Casey's card. "Casey Guthrie," it read.

"What in the world?" he said out loud. "If they are related, why would he not say something? Why would he show me the video and photos?"

Then it clicked. The connection, everything. He looked at the clock. It was only four. Sharon should still be at the desk.

Nick rushed to the elevator and down to the lobby. He almost ran to the desk, and Sharon came out from a back-office area.

"Are you okay?" she asked, looking up at him.

"Yes, I just need to know. How are you so positive Cindy isn't guilty?"

"Casey told me you figured out it was someone else using the video he gave you."

"When did he tell you that?"

"Yesterday."

"Thanks," Nick said, and turned to go.

The whole thing made so little sense, but then maybe it did. The video did prove that Cindy wasn't guilty. But did it really prove anything about Becky?

"What's wrong?" Sharon asked.

"Not a thing," Nick said. "Just overthinking something."

"Okay," she said.

Nick went back to the room and watched the video again. He zoomed in. Becky, the girl wearing the turquoise bikini. He saw the tiny hand, and a shove into the pool.

The same person who'd given the joints to who he knew now was Rhonda Guthrie, the ones that had been shared with Jeff.

Guilty.

There was something else though. Something didn't add up.

He looked again. The devil's trumpet plant seemed whole. Every angle he looked at it, there were no obvious leaves or flowers missing. He zoomed in, looked every way he could, but unless they had been taken from an area he could not see, which he had to admit was possible, the datura didn't come from there. And the joints Becky had handed to Rhonda were already rolled. So maybe the poison wasn't in them.

Then where? And where did it come from?

Frustrated, Nick went back to the beginning of the photos, of the various people arriving at the party. Then he saw it in the background.

Rhonda and a man, near the house. The man was handing her something. He zoomed in. It was Casey.

Obviously the house wasn't his, so Nick needed more information.

So he looked up Rhonda's social media profile. It was pretty secure, but some things were public, including relatives. It listed her father, Jerome, an art dealer. Nick clicked on his profile, because it seemed fairly public, the way many of those of public figures were. On his page, Nick saw a photo of Jerome with his arm around another man, Casey. The hashtag was #siblingday. His brother.

Rhonda's uncle. Who had been there just before the party and handed her something. Drugs?

There were way too many angles of this thing for Nick to figure out on his own, but he had to share what he'd found with the police.

Becky might have pushed Jeff into the pool. But the drugs may have come from elsewhere.

They may have come from Casey himself.

He looked at recent calls on his phone, and called the most recent 602 number, the one from the police department.

"Phoenix P.D., homicide," the person answered. "How can I direct your call?"

"I'd like to talk to whoever is in charge of the recent drowning case," he said.

"And your name?" the voice asked.

So much for being anonymous, Nick thought to himself. "Nick," he said. "Nick O'Flannigan."

"Homicide," a voice answered after a brief hold.

"I have some information to share about your case," Nick said. "It involves Casey Guthrie."

He explained what he had learned and set a time to meet the detective and hand him the files he had. Nick took the photos and videos he had cropped and edited, and dropped them on a new thumb drive, a cheap one he figured he would just give the police. If he was lucky, that would be the end of his involvement.

His alarm went off. It was time to get moving. He'd meet the detective, grab dinner, get his photos, and be on his way.

Nick grabbed his camera bag, the new thumb drive, and just for good measure the other two thumb drives Casey had given him too and headed out the door.

14

CAPTURED

Nick handed off the photos and the thumb drives with no issue. The detective thanked him, and Nick moved on with his evening. He grabbed a burger and headed to the capitol building to the spots he'd already selected to get his shots. There were just enough clouds for him to get a sky painted pink and orange behind the dome, and he knew these would be a hit with Emily, his editor.

He took some macro shots too, and snagged a quick sunset shot with his phone.

When he felt he'd gotten all he could, he sent a quick text to Sandra with the sunset photo attached. "Thinking of you."

His earlier encounter with Janice and her family made him miss his parents and want to call them, but it was too late. That would have to wait until morning.

He headed back to the hotel, deciding to edit and upload files in the morning.

He dropped into bed, flipped on the television for background noise, and set a timer for it to shut off after an hour. He lowered his head to the pillow and went to sleep.

When he woke, it was still dark, but someone was knocking on the door of his hotel room.

Confused, Nick pulled on a t-shirt and went to open it. On the way, he glanced at his phone on the desk, and without really thinking about why he did it, opened the voice memo feature and hit record.

"Good morning, Nick." Casey stood there, face angry and arms folded. "Mind if I come in?"

Nick tried to shut the door, but the detective was much quicker, and blocked it with his foot, stepping inside anyway.

"What are you doing here?"

"You find anything interesting last night looking at pictures and video?" the investigator asked.

"I did," Nick said, seeing no point in lying.

"Anything you want to share with me, per our agreement?"

"I figured it might be a conflict of interest for you, so I shared it with the police," Nick said. He backed slowly to the desk, leaning one hand on it, careful not to touch his phone or reveal what was happening on the screen. The detective looked—threatening—and Nick wasn't sure what he would do if the detective took any kind of action.

He evaluated his chances. Nick wasn't much of a fighter, never had been, and especially not after the injury that had ended his professional basketball chances. He was taller than his potential opponent, but probably could not outrun him no matter what. He could only hope the recorder was actually on and getting all of this.

"I know you did," the detective said. "They called and want to talk to me. But I figured I would stop by here first and find out what I might be up against."

"I saw you in a photo, at the party where the victim died."

"So? It's my brother's place. I stopped by to see my niece."

"Okay. If that's all you have nothing to worry about."

"I didn't have anything to do with any of it, O'Flannigan."

"If you're innocent, just explain to the police."

"That kid, Sharon's nephew? He was a punk. My niece deserves way better."

"I didn't know him."

"I know. I can't figure you out. You're just a photographer. You get involved in these cases, but you couldn't just do what you were told in this case."

"I think this is way more complicated than it looks," Nick said. "I wanted to be sure the police had all of the information they needed. Why did you involve me anyway?"

"It was bound to come out that I was Rhonda's uncle, and that I was at the party. I wanted any evidence to come from a source that wasn't me. You just happened to be in town."

"And an easy target, since I just took what you gave me at face value at first."

"Yes. Sharon told me you were an amateur but had a good eye. She was right, but you're more than that."

"Thanks, I think."

"I like you, Nick. What do you think happened here?"

"I think you gave your niece some drugs, even if they were just to party with. I think she gave them to Jeff, maybe intending to hurt him, maybe just thinking it would be funny to see how he reacted. Then I think someone else saw an opportunity and pushed him in the pool, and he drowned."

"So it's a big accident?"

"Or a few people wanted him dead, or to hurt him, but things didn't go exactly as anyone expected."

"Interesting theory. You sure you aren't a real P.I.?"

"No. I just don't like seeing people like you use other people. You already knew some of what happened when you took the case."

"Maybe."

Then it dawned on Nick. The real motive for the investigator enlisting him. "You wanted me to point the finger somewhere else. Because you didn't know what happened, but you did know your niece drugged that kid."

The P.I. shrugged.

"Even if his death was an accident after that, she'd still be guilty of manslaughter, or something. Maybe—"

"Negligent homicide," the detective answered. "Or a similar charge. Either way, it's not worth her ruining her life over someone like him. Not someone as young as her."

"With what I gave the police, I did just that."

The detective smiled. "I'm not going to confirm or deny anything you just said. I'm going to leave it to the police to sort it out. Based on your 'evidence' I know what's likely to happen."

"I guess it's in their hands now," Nick said.

"I hope they get it right, O'Flannigan."

"Me, too," Nick said.

The detective turned to go. "I hope we don't see each other again."

"I'm leaving tomorrow, so I doubt it."

"And our little deal and your way of paying it forward? That's off."

The door closed behind Casey, and Nick rushed to the desk, tapping the screen of his phone. The counter sat at 00:00. It hadn't recorded a thing.

He sat on the corner of the hotel bed and lowered his head into his hands. "What have I done?" he said out loud.

Not knowing what to do, he called Sandra's number. It went to voice mail. It was 8:30. He thought about his options. He had none. He'd given the police everything he had, and either they pieced it together or they didn't.

Any more involvement on his part would only mess things up further and would risk his own reputation.

The phone read 8:30. Plenty of time to go snap some outdoor photos before it got too hot. He might as well use his last day in Phoenix to do his real job.

He headed out with his camera bag, careful to make sure the hotel room locked behind him.

The morning passed quickly. Photos, breakfast, and a brief walk around Government Square. He heard police sirens go by, and wondered how the case was coming, and what the police thought was happening.

He'd been avoiding the news, but when he sat down to a late lunch around one o'clock he brought up the local Phoenix paper on his phone. There was nothing about the drowning, nothing about any arrests.

He went back to his hotel, broke out his laptop, and sorted, edited, and uploaded the last of the magazine photos. He uploaded others to his own website, and scheduled some posts on social media, including a series of photos that included some local hashtags. He was surprised to see that his followers had increased significantly in the last couple of weeks.

By the time he was done with all of those things, he looked to see that is was 4:30. He tallied and sent his expense report for the week and turned on the early news.

"Local police have announced a break in the drowning case we have been following this week. An anonymous tip combined with some photos and videos gathered from social media have led police to make an arrest. A young woman is suspected of drugging the victim with a laced marijuana cigarette, then supposedly pushed the victim into the pool.

"Police have not revealed the motive, but say they are seeking another person of interest, and that more details will be revealed once the investigation progresses further."

The unidentified person was probably Becky, Nick assumed. *Casey and his niece were probably involved and would also probably get away with it.*

He hadn't really worked up much of an appetite, and reached for his phone, thinking he would call his parents, when his phone rang.

It was a 602 number.

"This is Nick," he answered.

"Mr. O'Flannigan, this is Sergeant Olsen of the Phoenix police department. How are you this evening? I just wanted to thank you for your help on this case."

"Thanks," Nick said.

"I can't share details with you," the officer said. "But this is a complicated case. There will be more charges brought than those that have been announced so far."

"More charges?"

"I can't tell you more, but I know you leave the area this weekend, right?"

"I do."

"You did the right thing. Have a good trip."

The call ended. Nick called his parents first, talked for a bit, and told them how much he loved them.

Then he called Sandra. They talked for a while too, and Nick told her about the conclusion of the case, and his last bit of involvement.

"You going to leave tomorrow?" she asked him.

"No," he said. "I'll stay around and rest for a day," he said. "It's only a seven-hour drive. I'll leave Sunday morning."

"Sounds good," she said.

"I'm finally hungry," he said. "I think I'll grab a late dinner."

"Okay. You did the right thing, Nick. Good job."

"Thanks," he said.

Nick ended the call, ordered Chinese food on a delivery app, and ate in his room.

He went to bed shortly after that, exhausted.

15

MOVING ON

The next morning, Nick headed downstairs after sleeping in. He wanted to just take a breather day. No computer, no photos, no pressure. He figured he might catch a movie, something like that. It felt like forever since he'd just taken a day off to do nothing.

When he reached the lobby, Sharon was there. She smiled and waved, and he approached the front desk cautiously.

"Thank you, Nick, for helping," she said.

"Anytime," he said. "I just hope the police got it right."

"Well, Cindy is free, and it seems like they have my nephew's killer in custody. I'm so glad you were able to work with Casey to resolve this."

At the mention of the detective's name, Nick shuddered even though the lobby was quite warm.

"What's wrong?" she asked.

"Oh, nothing," he said. "Goose walked over my grave or something."

She laughed. "Haven't heard that one in a while."

Nick just smiled. "Well, I am glad things worked out, and I am sorry about your nephew."

"Me, too," she said.

Nick waved and left quickly. He found a brunch spot and used his phone to buy a ticket to a matinee movie. At least the theater would be cool.

The movie was good, if a little long, and as he left, he noticed there was a message from his friend Gerry.

"Hey, Nick!" she answered when he called her back. "How was your week?"

"A little too wild for my taste," he told her. "I got dehydrated, visited the local hospital for a minute, had an odd drug experience from a natural sunscreen, and helped solve a murder, sort of."

"I thought you were going to stay away from that kind of thing," she said.

"Me, too. Luckily, I didn't get too involved."

"You sound tired, Nick."

"I am. I just got out of a movie. I decided to take the day off, and just relax."

"Good for you. You deserve it. You headed to Santa Fe in the morning?"

"Yep. I'm going to take my time. It's only a seven-hour drive."

"Well, take care. Call me when you get there. I miss you."

"I miss you, too," Nick said.

He ended the call. Nick looked around the half-empty parking lot. He missed home, and the cool, damp air of Seattle. All the green. He missed his friends, his new girlfriend, and his parents. At that moment, he felt lonely and all alone.

He headed to dinner by himself but took the time to send a photo of his food to Sandra and post it to Instagram.

Nick walked back to the hotel, and turned on the television, selecting another movie to watch. He really just wanted to hear another voice in the room.

Before too long, he fell asleep. When he woke the next morning, he packed his lone bag after a shower, and checked out of the hotel. As he got in his car, he called Sandra.

"Hey there," she said. "What's up?"

"Not a thing," he said. "Just driving, and I would love to just have someone to talk to."

"You miss me, huh?"

"I do," he said. "What's up with you?"

They talked as he drove, and her voice filled some of the void Nick felt inside himself. At least for a while.

THE END

FACTS ABOUT PHOENIX AND THE ARIZONA STATE CAPITOL MUSEUM

Facts About Phoenix and the Arizona State Capitol Museum

Unlike many other state capitol buildings, the Arizona State Capital was the last home of the territorial government until Arizona became a state in 1912. The original idea behind the capitol building was to prove that the young territory was ready for statehood, and a design competition was won by James Riley Gordon.

However, due to budget constraints, the capital plan was reduced, and the planned dome was replaced by a lead/alloy top. The legislative wings were discarded, and the building is much smaller than other state capitol buildings.

Construction started in 1898 and the building opened a mere three years later in 1901. Additions were made as the state grew, one in 1918 and another in 1938. Initially, all of the branches of government occupied the building, but it quickly became too crowded. So in 1960, the legislature relocated to the two new buildings constructed on site, known as the Government Mall. The governor moved his office to the newly constructed executive tower in 1974.

At that time, the state had the idea of turning the old capitol building into a museum dedicated to Arizona history, and Governor Bruce Babbitt announced the opening at his inauguration in 1978. Work began on the museum, and it reopened again in 1981. In the 1990s, many rooms in the capitol were renovated to match their original design. However, due to budget concerns, a few rooms on the third floor still remain unfinished.

The building is on the National Register of Historic Places, and tens of thousands of visitors see it every year, along with many school children on field trips.

There are extensive plans in the works to remodel the entire Government Mall, but to leave the capitol intact and preserved.

Oh yeah. The older woman with the white hair, in the beginning of the book? The one that runs into a cactus and gets a thorn in her thigh? That was my grandmother, and this is only partially a fabricated story. This story is dedicated to her memory, as one of my fondest and most humorous experiences with her involved a trip to the state capitol museum.

You should visit too, if you get the chance.

STUNG IN SANTA FE

BOOK #13

PROLOGUE: STUNG

Miguel Alvarez smelled perfume and then looked up. Alicia Hernandez, a co-worker he'd recently started dating, walked by, closer to his desk than she needed to, turned her head, and smiled.

Employee dating was not forbidden by Apis Vaccination Labs, but they'd decided to keep their relationship on the down low for now. For one thing, they had just started dating, and had no idea where things would go. For the other, a co-worker had kind of a crush on Alicia, and they didn't want him to get jealous.

But it was hard not to react to her at work. Miguel was, for lack of a better word, smitten.

A recent graduate with his Master's in Entomology with an emphasis in immunology, he was a doctoral candidate. Alicia had a bachelors and was still exploring her master's degree. They'd both been hired right away by the startup, AVL for short, who was working on developing advanced vaccines for the astonishing number of people allergic to bee and wasp stings.

The job meant that you were almost certain to get stung. While most of the employees were not themselves allergic, they knew multiple stings could cause a similar reaction, and so everyone carried EpiPens, both at work and when on their personal time.

It was close to quitting time, so he gathered his things, noticing that Ronald, another researcher, seemed to be staring his direction. Miguel looked behind him to see if there was someone there, and when he turned back around Ronald was gone.

At 7,200 feet, Santa Fe felt hot. It cooled down in the evenings, but the eighty-five degree temps felt much hotter in the thinner air. Miguel had moved here from Phoenix, so after some adjustment, the temperatures were actually pretty refreshing. Triple digits were nearly unheard of here.

He saw Alicia across the parking lot at her car, talking on her phone. They had a date later tonight, so he merely waved from a distance, and headed for his own vehicle. A sunshade depicting a tropical beach filled his windshield.

Miguel had a routine, developed while living in the more intense Phoenix heat. He unlocked his car, hit the remote start, which turned on the air conditioning, too.

He opened the door, reached in and grabbed the sunshade, folding it up and tossing in into the back seat on the passenger side before he slid into the driver's seat.

As he did, he felt a slight sting in his right thigh. He looked down and saw a wasp.

"Shit, little guy! Why didn't you just fly out of the way?"

He flipped the wasp away, but instead of taking off, it fell onto the floor on the passenger side of the car.

Poor bugger must have been dying already, he thought. *Usually the lone ones don't sting.*

He moved to stand but suddenly found it hard to breathe. His face felt stiff and frozen in place. He coughed but couldn't clear his throat. In fact, it seemed to be swelling shut.

Allergic reaction, he thought right away, and popped open the glovebox where he knew he had an EpiPen. He grabbed it and looked at it before stabbing himself.

It was empty. The cartridge normally there was gone.

He didn't think he'd used it, but he must have at some point.

Have to get to the front door, he thought. His vision narrowed and black spots danced before his eyes.

Using the open door and the edge of the windshield, he pulled himself upright. His thigh hurt more than it should. He staggered, struggling to keep his balance.

Carefully, he moved around the door, supporting himself on the hood of the car with his right hand. He stumbled, and looked up, seeing a car coming toward him in the parking lot. He couldn't be sure, but it looked like Alicia's aging Toyota. He raised his hand to wave and that was enough to send him tottering off balance.

With a jerk, he fell forward. Squealing tires followed.

"Oh my God, Miguel! What happened?" Alicia's face swam into his vision and wobbled there, blurry.

"Stung," he wheezed.

"Did you use your EpiPen?"

He tried to answer but descended into a coughing fit and could only shake his head.

"Okay, hang on," she said. She disappeared and he heard her car door opening.

"I've got you covered," she said. He felt a sting in his thigh.

His breathing didn't get any easier and he felt himself slipping away.

Don't pass out. Don't pass out, he told himself.

But darkness raced toward him, and he found himself falling into it. Through the thick blackness he heard Alicia talking.

"Yes. A wasp sting, possible multiples at Apis Labs. Male, mid to late twenties, no response to EpiPen application. Yes, I'll stay on the line. Starting CPR now."

No longer able to see and feeling like he was breathing through a tiny straw, Miguel felt hands roll him on to his back. He heard other voices, ones he did not recognize, and felt strong pressure on his chest. He tried to respond, to draw breath, but the straw was closing rapidly.

He heard sirens, distant and for some reason growing fainter rather than louder.

The darkness took him, and he saw nothing, felt nothing, heard nothing, smelled nothing. Then nothing became everything.

1

PHOENIX TO SANTA FE

It was only an eight-hour drive to Santa Fe from Phoenix, but Nick intentionally planned his trip through Payson, Holbrook, before eventually joining I-40. An overnight in Holbrook would let him take in some of the sights along the way.

The drive went smoothly. The desert gave way to forests, which were gorgeous, but there were patches where they'd been recently scorched by forest fires.

"Global warming," he said aloud as he reached Payson and stopped at a grocery store. He didn't need fuel yet, but a bathroom stop and a snack wouldn't hurt.

"Driving through?" the cashier said, looking up at him.

"How'd you guess?"

"You asked for the bathroom first, grabbed some snacks, and you're playing with your keys. Also, that strange sunburn on your leg tells me you're not a Phoenix native up for some weekend recreation."

Nick laughed. "Very observant. The sunburn was courtesy of falling asleep by a pool, and I am, indeed passing through."

"Where you headed?"

"Holbrook tonight, on to Santa Fe tomorrow."

"You still have some climbing to do. Are you headed there for business or pleasure?" she asked as she scanned his can of potato chips, his soda, and a small pack of chocolate chip cookies that proclaimed they were "baked in store" on a little red sticker.

"Business, mostly," Nick told her. "I'm on a photography assignment."

"Oh, well, then you have to stop on the Mogollon Rim."

"The what?"

"Just east of town. You'll know when you get to the top of the hill, there will be a sign for Woods Canyon Lake. Follow it and you'll find several pullouts and paved trails you can use to check out the views from the rim."

"Hey, thanks."

"It may be a bit crowded. It's Saturday, and all the tourists are up from Phoenix."

"The highway did seem busy on the way up."

"That's pretty normal. Hey, have a nice trip and get some good pictures."

"I will," Nick said, digging in his pocket for a card. He handed it to her. "You might see some of them on my website or social media if I get some good shots."

"Thanks," she said, taking the card. She waved as he left the store.

Good, small town hospitality. He loved it.

Nick knew exactly what she was talking about as he left a small town called Star Valley and started to climb. Near the top of a particularly large hill, he saw the sign she mentioned, and took a left.

At the first pullout, he stopped and checked out the sign: the Mogollon Rim. Pronounced mugghee-on, the rim extended for over 200 miles diagonally to where it ended near Flagstaff and featured several lakes along the way. The elevation here was just over seven thousand feet, but the rim crested eight thousand in places according to the map on the sign.

Nick could see the road he'd driven up on as a tiny ribbon far below. It was much cooler here. Arizona had a lot more to offer than he thought. He made a mental note to come back and visit someday.

He took several photos, some landscapes off the road, but several macro shots of flowers growing from the rocks, dead trees clinging to the side of cliffs, and more. He moved his car several times to different pull outs, each providing him with a different view.

I best get back on the road, he thought to himself. As he got in his car, his phone rang. It was Sandra, his girlfriend. He'd met her in Salem, she'd helped him when his camera was stolen in Sacramento, and they'd developed a friendship that had turned into more two weeks ago when she visited him in Denver. He'd witnessed a horrible crime there, but despite the stress of the week, their relationship had only gotten stronger.

"Hi, gorgeous," he said.

"Hey," she answered. "How's the sunburn and your head?"

He'd suffered a mild concussion just over a week ago in Salt Lake, and an incident of dehydration in Phoenix resulted in some concern, but he was improving.

"I'm better," he said. "Taking my time getting to Santa Fe. I'm going to stop in Holbrook tonight."

"Where are you now?"

"A place called the Mogollon Rim in Arizona, just northeast of Payson. I think the only reason I have any cell coverage at all is I'm up pretty high."

"Nice. You'll have to send photos. How are you feeling about the case in Phoenix?"

Nick paused. A private investigator, a drowning, and an uncertain outcome left him feeling less that satisfied about his visit, even though he'd gotten some great photos. He'd managed to stay on task with his freelance assignment, taking photos of every state capital in just a year's time. He only had a week in each location, which seemed like plenty at first. But in every city, a mystery of some sort had nearly derailed him, and one nearly landed him in trouble with the police. Phoenix had been fairly trying, and just thinking about it made him tired.

"I'm okay," he said. "I just hope Santa Fe doesn't have anything like that in store for me."

"Me, too. I love you, Nick. How are your parents?"

The conversation descended into one about his mom and dad, their health, and what she'd been up to. Nick didn't want to move from the spot, sure he'd lose cell service any distance from his vantage point.

"I'll let you go," she finally said. "Text me when you get to Holbrook."

Nick got back on the road, and a few hours later entered the small town of Holbrook. He checked into his hotel, got some supper, and took a late walk.

He turned on the television to ESPN and watched whatever was on, falling asleep while listening to the sports announcers. He forgot all about texting Sandra.

Early the next morning he woke, dressed, and made his way down to the lobby. The clerk directed him to Joe and Aggie's Cafe, where he found a solid breakfast to fuel his morning, and strong coffee to keep him awake.

As he walked out of the restaurant, he looked at his car. There was something odd on the windshield. He looked closer. A wasp?

At first, he thought it was dead, but when he looked closer he saw that it was still moving. As it fluttered his wings, he jumped back.

Behind him, he heard a laugh. An older gentleman wearing coveralls and a hat decorated with the sun rays of the Arizona state flag stepped up beside him. With gentleness seemingly opposite his large fingers, he plucked the wasp gently from the wiper, and tossed it away. Nick heard a buzz as it flew off.

"Wow," he said.

"Ah, hell, son. They won't usually attack people. Unless you stare at them too close and irritate 'em."

Nick smiled. "Like I was."

"Yep. We have a lot of them around here. High elevation, warm enough most of the year in the high desert for them, and lots of stuff for them to feed on. We have a pretty good population of bees, too."

"I see."

"On vacation?" the man said, pointing to his Washington plates.

"Business trip," Nick said. "Thanks for the information."

"Which way you headed?"

"Santa Fe."

"You'll like it. Cool little town. Safe trip, ya' hear?"

"Thanks," Nick said. He got in the car and drove off.

It was only a little over four hours to Santa Fe, and he drove pretty much straight through, stopping for some quick photos in the Petrified Forest National Park.

He stopped once after that at a large truck stop for gas and a corn dog. Tempted by some fresh cinnamon rolls, he bought a pack of them, promising himself he'd hit the gym tonight at the hotel.

As he drove, clouds gathered overhead, and as he reached Albuquerque for his final gas stop, rain pelted the windshield with large drops. Nick thought about how he'd love to come back to take the *Breaking Bad* tour. The show, though disturbing, had turned him into an Aaron Paul fan.

No time. He checked it off as another place he'd like to come back and visit after his trip was over. He got back on the road to Santa Fe.

Just before town, orange cones indicated construction, and the traffic squeezed down to a single lane. The speed limit said thirty, but most of the traffic was moving about forty-five. A second later he heard a thump and then a crack.

A small rock struck his windshield leaving a small chip.

Dammit, he thought. Then considered how far he'd come. It was a wonder he hadn't had any car trouble since his air conditioning issue in Boise, and he hadn't taken a single rock to the windshield this whole way.

Still, he'd have to have that taken care of as soon as possible.

A short drive and a few turns later, Nick ended up at his hotel, a Residence Inn. He darted through the rain into the office.

The clerk looked up and then looked up some more. At six and a half feet tall, Nick was used to it. This trip had made him even more conscious of his height.

"Hi," he said. "I've got a room for the week."

"Nick O'Flannigan?"

"Yes, that's me."

"You're the photographer taking the capitol pictures."

"How did you guess?" Nick smiled, but inwardly sighed.

"Well, you're famous. Sort of. Our modern photography professor has been following your trip. He showed us some of your photos and told us about you being in the news."

Nick groaned. Not another one. Out loud he said, "That's quite a compliment."

The clerk gestured for him to lean closer. "You're not chasing any bad guys in Santa Fe, are you?"

Nick chuckled. "It doesn't quite work that way. I'm really hoping for no trouble at all while I'm here."

"Oh." The clerk looked almost disappointed. "Well, we've upgraded you to a suite for the week."

"Sure," Nick said, taking the keycard he was offered.

A few moments later he found himself in a two room suite with almost a full office at his disposal. A separate seating area, two televisions, and a large bed made him smile. It was almost like a small apartment.

He headed back to the lobby. "Hey, thanks for the upgrade," he said. "Can I trouble you for a supper recommendation?"

"Sure. The tapas bar is closed on Sundays, so I would try the Coyote Cafe. Normally, I'd recommend seating on the rooftop outside, but the rain may stick around until around midnight."

"I'll give it a shot. Do you have those guys around here who fix windshield chips, too?"

"We do. There are some on street corners, but there are several mobile ones, too. I'll have a short list waiting for you when you get back from dinner. Sound good?"

"Deal," Nick said. "Thanks for being so helpful."

"Anytime. One thing though?"

"What's that?" Nick said.

"Mind if I get a selfie with you for my Instagram?"

"Sure," Nick said.

He smiled for the shot and headed for dinner. The food and the atmosphere were as promised, and by the time he got back to the hotel the downpour had tapered to a mere drizzle.

He thanked the clerk, took the offered list of mobile chip repair businesses, and headed up for bed.

It had been a long two days of travel. Tomorrow would be another day.

2

MORNING FLOWERS

Nick had set the coffee maker to brew automatically before he went to bed, and although the coffee wasn't the greatest, it was a great smell to wake up to. Besides, it would get him through his morning routine, which, he reminded himself, needed to include a trip to the hotel gym.

He downed a cup of coffee, a large bottle of water, and after brushing his teeth headed downstairs for a quick workout. He had a pair of Bluetooth headphones and paired them with the television on the stationary bike while he rode.

He'd found in Helena that riding a bike was much easier on the leg he'd injured in college, the reason he was a photographer and not a candidate for the NBA, and despite his small accident in Salt Lake, he found he loved to ride.

He rented bikes when he could, but it just wasn't always feasible everywhere, and buying one and bringing it along would just complicate his trip.

He found himself a bit winded, *probably due to the elevation*, he told himself. He'd experienced the same thing in Denver and figured by the time he really acclimated to altitude, he'd be heading downhill into middle America and the flyover states, many of which he'd never visited.

Ah well, he thought. *Such is the life of a freelance photographer. This is about the sweetest gig you could hope for.*

He headed back up to his room when he was done, took a shower, and gathered his camera to head out for the day. A different clerk directed him to the Old House Restaurant of Santa Fe, and recommended he try the blue corn pancakes.

They were much better than he expected. *Who knew there was even such a thing?*

He then headed to the capitol building. After facing difficulty parking in various cities, he'd scoped out the parking garage, and found they had plenty of spots. Thankfully, the information he found on the web was doubly true on a Monday morning, and he had no trouble at all. He walked the short distance to the capitol, taking photos along the way.

While many capitol buildings looked similar, he often found unique things about each. Where Arizona's capitol building was actually a museum, and not the functional seat of government, Santa Fe had a round building.

Without the typical dome on top, it looked truly different from the rest. Nick wished, not for the first time, that he had a drone to get some aerial shots. Not that he was known for that. His macro photography and eye for detail were the things that won him this assignment, not the gimmick drones often seemed to be.

"They hired a photographer for the job, not a drone pilot," he told himself. But he still thought one might prove useful from time to time.

To start with, Nick decided to walk around the outside of the capitol building, one he learned was called "The Roundhouse" locally.

He knew Santa Fe had a rich and robust art community, but he was in no way prepared for the amazing sculptures surrounding the building.

He snapped several close ups of a bronze statue of five children playing, three girls and two boys, who appeared to be pulling each other back and forth.

He'd seen some shots of this online but tried to get some unique angles and some close ups. There were several other sculptures, so he consulted the brochure, found them, and took photos of each.

The rain the night before had clearly benefited the flowers, and they were blooming in the gardens surrounding the building.

He leaned in close to study one flower, a bloom a couple inches across. The center looked like a sunflower, except the petals were orange toward the middle, and faded to yellow at the tips.

"That's called Indian Blanket," a voice said beside him. Nick turned to see a man in a tan uniform. A name tag over his right breast pocket revealed his name: Luis. Over the left an embroidered section declared him to be New Mexico Capitol Staff.

"It's beautiful," Nick said.

"It's rare for this altitude, but for some reason these grow well here."

"I'm glad I got to see them in bloom," Nick said.

"Well, thank the rain. There should be a lot of flowers flourishing over the next few days. We do our best to keep things watered, but honestly there's no substitute for Mother Nature."

"True," Nick said. He turned back to look at the flower again, and raised his camera to capture another close up, this one from a lower angle.

As he did, he felt a pinch, then pain.

"Ow, what—" he said, standing. He slapped at his neck and caught something there. A fly?

He pulled it away and looked at it. A wasp. Damn.

The gardener grinned at him. "You were in his territory, I guess."

Nick smiled back or tried to. He tossed the insect to the ground and grabbed at the place he'd been stung. It really hurt, and he felt the skin swell under his fingers.

He tried to take a step, and then staggered. Suddenly, it was hard to breathe. The sting really hurt, but his vision swam. That wasn't normal.

"Are you okay, sir?" Luis asked.

"I—" Nick couldn't get any air. He wanted to sit down, so he did, right there in the middle of the pavement. He grabbed at his camera, but it fell to the sidewalk with a thump.

Then Luis was beside him. The man's face came into his vision.

"Are you allergic to bee stings?"

Nick shook his head. He didn't think he was.

"I think you might be," Luis said. Nick saw the man reach into his cargo pocket, and a second later he felt a new sting, this one in his thigh.

Only a second later, he was able to breathe a little better. He could hear the air squeaking in and out of his throat.

His vision cleared a little, but his eyelids sagged.

"Hey, hey." Luis slapped the side of his face gently. "You with me?"

Nick tried to sit up, not remembering when he'd laid down.

Maybe Luis laid him back.

He saw several faces behind Luis's, all of them looking down at him wearing various degrees of shocked expressions.

Inside, he laughed, even though it felt like he hurt all over. He could imagine what they'd seen. A giant red head with a camera around his neck, staggering, sitting on the sidewalk with no apparent reason.

Then the laughter stopped. Everything hurt. Exhaustion washed over him. He laid his head back. A pollen-rich smell filled his nostrils.

"I'm gonna get you some help," Luis said. Nick heard him talking, into a phone or radio he wasn't sure which. His ears felt like they were stuffed with cotton, and everything sounded far away.

Then Luis turned his attention to Nick again. He did feel better, but he really wanted to close his eyes. The groundskeeper wouldn't let him.

"Stay with me partner. What's your name?"

"Nick." The single syllable took a lot of effort.

"Is there anyone I can call for you?"

"I'm traveling—on my—own."

"Anyone back home you want me to contact?"

"S-s-sandra," he managed. "Phone, pocket."

"Okay. Hang in there."

He heard voices. "Yes, ma'am. He's okay. We're sending him to the hospital to have him checked out."

"No, ma'am. I will have him call you as soon as possible, and I'll have the EMTs let the hospital know they can talk to you about his condition."

"Sure. I'm sure he would be fine if you let his friends know what is going on. Do you know if he is allergic to bees or other stings?"

"No? Okay. Thanks."

"Hey, Nick," Luis said. "I see your mom is a contact in your phone. Can I call her and ask her about allergies?"

Nick sighed. He didn't want them to call her, didn't want to worry his parents more than they already were about him on this trip. They were in Boston, retired, so they were likely to be home. She would have answers for sure.

"Go ahead," he said.

As Luis connected the call, Nick heard sirens.

He saw Luis smile and nod but couldn't hear his end of the conversation.

A few moments later he found himself on a stretcher and headed to the hospital. His phone was back in his pocket, and his camera bag sat on his chest.

"My car," he said to the EMT.

"We'll make sure you get back to it," she said. "Just relax. We got you."

He heard her talking to someone, apparently at the hospital, a moment later. "Yes. Vitals are stable. The Epi seems to have helped, thanks to a quick-thinking bystander.

Yes. We'll be there in less than five."

The sirens were no longer on. Clearly, he was in no danger, but they transported him just to be sure.

They wheeled him into a room. "You look exhausted," a male nurse told him. "Let me give you something to help you rest, and then we're going to take a little blood and run some tests, okay?"

Nick nodded, and a few moments later he was asleep.

3

LAYING LOW

Nick woke to a beautiful face staring back at him. The woman had deep brown eyes, dark black hair, and a deeply tanned complexion.

"Hi there," she said. "I'm Alicia."

"Hi, Alicia," he said.

"I hear you had a little scare at the capitol."

"I did."

"Well, I'm an Apis allergy specialist, or rather, a venom specialist. I am working at a local lab, and I volunteer here at the hospital from time to time. They almost always call me when they have sting cases."

"Nice to meet you," Nick said, attempting to sit up.

"Let me get that for you," she said. He heard a whir and the head of the bed pushed him to a sitting position.

"You are probably fine to head back to your hotel, but I'm going to recommend you carry an EpiPen with you from now on. We'll have your blood results back relatively quickly. I rushed them to our vaccine lab. But you likely had an anaphylactic reaction, which is a severe allergy."

"Okay."

"We basically measure the Immunoglobulin E in your blood or IgE. It's an immune response to things like a bee or wasp sting or even something as simple as peanuts."

"So, I'm allergic to bee stings?"

"To their venom, yes. Although probably you were stung by a wasp, not a bee."

"I see."

"There isn't much difference, as far as you are concerned. But I work for a company here in town that is developing a vaccine."

"A vaccine?"

"Yes. Stings, like other allergic reactions, can be fatal."

"Fatal?"

"Yeah." Her eyes fell. "Unfortunately, one of my colleagues at the lab passed away this past weekend from one."

"Really?"

"Most of us carry EpiPens. We aren't allergic—if you are you can't work in the lab, but we do get stung often, and enough stings can actually make someone who isn't allergic develop a similar reaction. The EpiPen he had with him was empty. I didn't get to him in time with another one."

"I'm so sorry."

"It's okay. It's a risk. It's just—" Alicia stopped, and wiped her eyes. "We were close. He was a nice guy."

"Again, I'm sorry," Nick said. "That must be tough, I mean to go back to work there."

"There are things about it I don't like," she said. "But overall, it's worth it to get to work in this field."

"Doing something you're passionate about is great. I get to work in my passion, too."

"What do you do?"

"I'm a freelance photographer. With all the phone advances, it's hard to make a living at it these days, but I have a great assignment."

"What's that?" she asked.

"I'm traveling to every single state capital over a year, spending one week in each location, taking photos for *Travel USA* magazine. They're going to compile them into a coffee table book."

"Sounds amazing."

"It is. Did—is my camera bag handy?"

"I'll ask for you."

"Also my phone?"

"I'm sure they're nearby. I'll get the nurse and find out."

"Thanks."

"Are you at the beginning of your week in Santa Fe?"

"Just arrived yesterday."

"Here's my card. Come check out the lab where I work while you're in town. You'll find it fascinating."

"I might just do that," Nick said.

"Please do," Alicia told him. "No stings, I promise."

She left. The male nurse came back in a few moments later.

"Well, I have good and bad news for you, Mr. O'Flannigan," he said.

"Call me Nick, please," Nick smiled at him.

"The good news is, you're cleared by the docs to leave. You just need to rest for the next twenty-four hours or so."

Nick groaned. One week with a concussion, the next with a bee sting. Travel was taking its toll. He patted his belly.

It was taking its toll in weight gain, too.

"And the bad news?"

"Well, I have your camera bag. But it looks like one of your lenses was damaged in the fall."

"Oh man!" Nick said. He sat up further on his own, and his head didn't spin.

More good news to offset the bad.

The nurse handed him the bag apologetically. "Your phone is in the side pocket. We shut it off so you could get some rest. I'll get your discharge papers while you look that over."

Nick nodded and pulled out his camera first. He'd been shooting with his macro lens, and he looked at it closely. The glass appeared to be cracked, and there was a dent in the front of the lens. It probably could not be repaired.

Damn.

He'd need to get a new one. One chipped windshield and a broken camera lens.

Welcome to Monday in Santa Fe.

Speaking of which, he needed to get his car.

The nurse came back a moment later holding an iPad and a couple sheets of paper.

"So, here are your instructions,' the nurse said. "Rest for twenty-four hours, hydrate, eat normally, and avoid bees. There's a prescription for an EpiPen, but I've got one here you can take with you in case you need it before you can get to a pharmacy."

"Thanks," Nick said. "Appreciate it. I do have an odd question, though."

"Yeah?"

"My car is in the parking garage at the capitol. My hotel is downtown, the Residence Inn. Is there a simple way for me to get a ride to one place or the other?"

"Sure," the nurse said. "I'll see if I can line up our shuttle driver. He usually goes to nursing homes and other places, but he can probably give you a lift."

"Thanks."

"All of your insurance information up to date on those forms?"

Nick nodded. Two weeks of hospital visits should get him close to his deductible, at least.

Nick signed the offered iPad. He then sat up, and grabbed his phone, turning it on.

He had several messages. Emily, his editor, Gerry, his friend and the social media manager for *Travel USA* magazine, Sandra, and two voice-mails from his parents.

He wondered if he could put off answering that one, and attribute it to avoiding stress. But the longer he waited, the worse that return phone call would get.

He sighed and decided to answer them once he got back to his hotel.

The nurse ducked back in a few moments later and let him know the shuttle was ready.

The nurse wheeled him out in a wheelchair, even though Nick didn't really need one. He climbed into the shuttle with the driver, told him where his hotel was, and closed his eyes.

He could take an Uber to get his car later. Driving right now was prob-ably a bad idea.

A few moments later, they arrived, and Nick gathered his belongings, made his way to his room, and laid down on the bed.

He was restless. The forced nap in the hospital had satisfied his need for sleep. He answered the first couple of text messages, Gerry first and then Sandra, who must have called Gerry, who then let Emily know what was going on.

That one would require a phone call, but first he dialed his parents.

"Hi, Mom," he said. "How are you and dad doing?"

"Nick! How are you doing?"

"I'm fine."

"He says he's fine!" she shouted to his father, who was already almost deaf. He'd had a stroke recently, which had complicated the problem, but he'd been steadily improving.

Nick held the phone out from his ear. When he put it back, his mom continued.

"Nick, people who are fine don't go to the hospital. What happened?"

Nick recounted his encounter with the wasp, what Alicia had told him, and his instructions from the doctor.

"Well, we knew you might be allergic. That's what I told that nice man who called."

"What, Mom?"

"That one time at Hampton Beach? Remember, you got stung, and your father had to take you to the doctor. It wasn't that bad, but you did have quite the lump on your arm the rest of the trip."

Nick thought about it, and he did vaguely recall the incident, but he'd probably been five years old.

"They say allergies can change with age," he said. "The one gal is working for a company working on a vaccine."

"Your dad was almost in a study for those once."

"What?"

"Yeah, your father and grandfather are both highly allergic to bee stings."

"Really?"

"Yes," she said. "They both carried EpiPens all the time. Your father almost used his on you that time at the beach. But you were little. He didn't know what the dose would do, and you were still breathing fine."

Nick heard his father say something in the background.

"What did he say?" he asked his mom.

"He said he could tell you were breathing fine because of all the screaming."

"Oh, great," Nick said, laughing. "I've got to go get my car, but I plan to lay low today, and get it tomorrow."

"Sounds good."

"Is Dad really okay, Mom?"

His mom hesitated, and Nick noticed, but let it pass. "He's fine," his mom said. "He gets tired faster than he used to, but he'll be okay."

"Okay, thanks, Mom. I'll call again soon."

"Avoid those bees," she said. "We love you."

"I love you, too." He hung up, wishing not for the first time that he was closer, or could take a weekend to go see them. But he was already over a quarter of the way done with this assignment. The rest of the year would pass quickly.

Speaking of his assignment, he needed to call Emily, his editor. He dialed her next.

"Hi, Emily," he said when she answered.

"Nick, how are you? First, I have to tell you to stay out of mysteries on this trip, and now I have to tell you to stay out of the hospital." She laughed, and Nick joined her.

"Yeah, I guess I am allergic to bee stings. Who knew?"

"How are things otherwise? Is your hotel good?"

"It's great. I got upgraded to a suite. The perks of membership rewards and living in hotels for the last few months. The Santa Fe capitol building is unusual. I like it, and there is a lot of art inside. I can't wait to get in and take photos of what I can. It's restricted for some of the artwork, but there is a lot of it, and I might be able to get some special permissions."

"That would be awesome."

"I got some shots of some sculptures and the outside already. I'm supposed to lay low this afternoon, but I will get them uploaded as soon as I can."

"No worries. Take care of yourself. Seriously, try to stay out of the hospital."

"Will do," Nick said.

He ended the call, and then dialed Sandra's number.

She answered on the first ring, and he filled her in on everything that had happened since their last conversation.

By the time he ended the call, Nick was exhausted. Maybe there was something to laying low after all. He could call for takeout, stick to his room, and get his car in the morning. The doctor had said 24 hours, but overnight should be plenty.

An Uber wouldn't be that expensive, and he could get the windshield fixed at the same time.

In the meantime, he went to the Olympus website and looked for a local dealer. His zoom lens might not have been as big of a deal, but his macro lens was his bread and butter.

He opened his laptop, an decided to upload a few photos to his website, macrophotography4u, and his social media while he was at it.

As he did, he opened a browser tab for the local newspaper. He wanted to check the weather for the rest of the week, and make sure he wouldn't be hampered by the type of rain he'd seen Sunday night.

Right on the front page, he saw the story that piqued his interest.

"Officials Advise Watching for Wasps After Mysterious Death"

Nick read the story. It detailed the death of Miguel Alvarez, his empty EpiPen, and the story Alicia had told.

"'It has been an extremely active wasp season,' Ronald Giles, of Apis Vaccination Labs told us," the paper said. "'If you are allergic, carry an EpiPen, check it often. Even if you are not allergic, watch for symptoms if anyone around you is stung, and call 9-1-1 right away if they have shortness of breath, faintness, blurred vision, or if they pass out. Mr. Alvarez is an unfortunate lesson we can all learn from.'"

Nick immediately set a reminder on his phone to pick up his EpiPens first thing on his way to get his car in the morning.

He didn't want to be the next news story.

He ordered food next and then laid down to watch some television. The anti-histamine they'd given him was supposed to make him sleepy, but it still took him three episodes of the latest Netflix documentary on the psychology of murderers to put him to sleep.

He dreamed of giant wasps chasing him around "The Roundhouse", finding the doors locked, and being unable to get inside.

4

STINGS AND VACCINES

Nick woke with a start to a bright room, the television still on, but displaying a message with a question.

"Still watching?"

"Shut up, Netflix," he said aloud. His head ached a little, and his sinuses felt a little swollen. Other than that, he felt fine.

He felt even better after a shower. First order of business, get his car. EpiPens after that. Then a new camera lens, if possible.

Then to the job: capitol photos. He would call Alicia sometime today. He really did want to tour the lab and learn more about his recently discovered allergy, but more importantly about the vaccines that were being developed.

It would be better for him if he didn't have to rely on EpiPens just in case, especially traveling around the country.

He wondered how quickly he could get one at the pharmacy, and if he could maybe be a test subject at Apis Labs.

It was worth checking into.

What he hoped would be a normal week was turning pretty busy, and it was only Tuesday.

Nick took an Uber to his car and looked at the windshield. Discouraging.

He decided to head for some breakfast and then to get EpiPens. He probably wouldn't get stung eating a plate of pancakes, or better, a local Mexican omelet. That was one thing about the southwest, so far he'd found some great Mexican food.

A place not far away called The Burrito Company had great ratings, and so Nick headed that way. He arrived to find some cute red umbrellas for outdoor seating, a friendly staff, and a variety of offerings.

Instead of an omelet, he ended up with a monstrous burrito. He was able to finish it, washing it down with coffee and water, but he was stuffed when he was done.

He called a local pharmacy, who told him they would have his prescription ready shortly, and he gulped when he heard the price, even with his insurance.

As he pulled into the parking lot, he saw a stand in the corner of the lot.

"Free Chip Repair," the sign said. He pulled over that way, and a young woman walked out from under an awning.

"How can I help you?" she asked.

"How does this work?" Nick said, skeptical. "You repair these rock chips for free?"

"Yes. We bill your insurance, if you have full coverage."

"I do."

"I'll just need your insurance card then, and to make a quick phone call."

Nick waited, and within minutes, the gal was at work on his windshield with some kind of suction device and a form of epoxy.

The process looked fascinating, but he had things to do.

"Hey, I'm going to run inside and grab a prescription. Is that okay?"

"Sure," she said.

Nick entered the air conditioned store, finding it almost too cold for his taste, walked back to the pharmacy counter and grabbed his prescription. As he went to pay, the cashier looked at him.

"You have a high deductible plan, even for prescriptions."

"It's the price of being a freelancer."

"Let me see what I can do about that," the man said. He moved back to another computer and pulled up a coupon. "Here, I'll enter this for you. Should save you quite a bit."

The man typed some numbers into his computer. "There. That brings it down to eighteen dollars."

"Thanks," Nick said.

"Hey, it's a service we offer."

"Do you know of a good camera shop around here?"

"I do," he said, taking Nick's card. "What do you shoot with?"

"Olympus."

"Well, there is a shop that carries used lenses. There isn't an official Olympus dealer in Santa Fe, but one of the chain stores might have one. Which lens?"

"My macro. That's what I shoot with a lot of the time."

"What happened?"

"I got stung by a wasp, apparently. I found out I was allergic when I fell over."

"Man, that's bad news. Did you hear about the guy from Apis Labs?"

"I did. Odd that his EpiPen was empty."

"It is. We sell them their supply, in bulk of course. We double check to make sure they're good before they leave here. I don't know why anyone in that industry would ever have an empty one with them. They have plenty and can just trade used one out if they need to."

"A tragedy."

"Yep. Keep one of yours close at all times, and if you run out, get refills."

"Will do. Thanks for the camera advice."

"Sure thing."

Nick smiled as he walked out. He'd been able to get away without answering a whole bunch of questions about his assignment, and he had a shop recommendation and a backup idea if not.

The young lady waved him over, and the spot on his window was barely visible any more.

"There you go, sir," she said.

Nick thanked her. "This is great. I'm glad I could get this fixed this fast."

"You're welcome."

Nick waved to her and backed out, stopping only to look at his phone and type the name of the nearest camera shop into his phone.

It was only a few moments away, and when he got there he found they were closed.

"Back tomorrow," the sign said, with no other explanation.

Nick saw no choice, so headed for one of the big box electronics retailers. He walked straight to the camera aisle. Luckily, they had Olympus, so he wouldn't need any adapters.

He picked the lens he wanted and took a little card on the shelf to the cashier, as instructed. A few moments later, another associate brought him the lens, and he gulped as he paid for it. It made quite a dent in his travel budget.

Once the transaction was complete, he headed to the capitol. It was lunchtime, but the burrito he'd had for breakfast kept him full, so he decided to take a bunch of photos first.

He took the new lens out of the box and went to put it on the camera. It didn't fit. It wasn't even the right brand, even though the box said Olympus.

Damn. He'd just have to take some inside photos and go back to replace the lens later.

He made a call to the store, received an apology for the lenses being switched, grabbed his camera, and headed inside.

As he reached the doors, his phone rang, a New Mexico number he didn't recognize.

"This is Nick," he said.

"This is Alicia Hernandez, from the hospital. How are you doing?

"Good," Nick said.

"Do you think you'd have a chance to come by the lab this afternoon?" she asked. "I have something I'd like to show you. You're taking it easy today anyway, aren't you?"

"Sure," he said, only lying a little bit. "I'm just taking a few photos at the capitol and then I can head your way." He checked the time on his phone. "Three-thirty be okay?"

"Sure," she said. "See you then."

Nick hung up, grabbed the door handle, and headed inside "The Roundhouse" hoping to get some photos quickly. He could always come back, but he wanted to get a good idea of the layout and what he needed to get later.

As he ducked inside, he looked back and saw the same staff member, Luis, who'd helped him when he was stung. He raised his hand in a wave and reminded himself to thank the man next time he saw him.

5

———————

THE LENS

The inside of the New Mexico state capitol building felt like a museum. There were literally dozens of pieces of art. He grabbed a second brochure and decided to start on the fourth floor and work his way down. Before venturing upstairs, though, he took the nearly obligatory shot of the rotunda from below. This rotunda was unique, and he liked the look right away.

Again he wished for a drone, so he could take photos of the building from above. The ones on the brochure looked incredible and it told him the building was designed to look like the Zia Sun symbol when viewed that way.

The fourth floor held mostly offices, those of the governor, lieutenant governor, and legislative counsel. The hallway around was lined with art, and the flags of all thirty-three New Mexico counties were displayed there as well.

The third floor held more offices and even more art. Nick took photo after photo, often wishing for his macro lens. As time passed, he started to get hungry.

He would have to come back later for the rest and was looking forward to getting some views from the legislative galleries on the second floor. This place was impressive in a number of ways.

He read about renovations, updates, and all of the local art pieces available for viewing.

There was a lot. To really cover this place thoroughly would take at least one more visit inside, a checklist, and at least two more outside shoots, plus morning and evening photos.

All the work would keep him busy and away from any trouble.

He headed down and out the front door, glancing at his phone again. Already 1:30. He better hurry if he was going to get the lens exchanged, grab some lunch, and get to the lab in time for his appointment with Alicia.

As he walked by an area filled with flowers, he saw Luis wearing a mesh mask and gloves. He had some kind of box, and he was putting what looked like a hive into it.

It wasn't the typical gray, paper wasp hive, but had a different look.

Bees or maybe wasps buzzed all around him.

"Huh," Nick said, and kept walking, even speeding up a little. He didn't want to try out his new EpiPen. Not just yet.

After grabbing some fast food, something he hated to do, and that made his stomach roll a little, Nick headed back to the store to exchange his lens. As he headed to the returns counter, the clerk recognized him right away.

"We're sorry, Mr. O'Flannigan, but this one was apparently returned by a customer, and no one noticed it was the wrong brand in the box."

"I understand," he said, handing it back to him. "Do you have another one?"

The young man blushed and stammered. "No, we don't. And currently the lens is on back order. The manufacturer told us they can rush one and have it here in five days."

"I'll be gone in five days. I need this for my work. Is there anywhere else?"

"There's a local camera shop. They have some used lenses, some vintage ones mostly, but they might be able to help you."

"They were closed today."

"Oh, that's odd. I'm sorry. You could try ordering one online."

"Okay, thanks," Nick said. "I'll figure something out."

Inside, he seethed. One of the local stores had other brands of cameras, but he didn't want to buy a new one, at least not yet. Or did he?

He remembered mixing up photos, uploading personal and crime scene ones to the cloud, and how upset Emily had been.

He'd thought at that point about buying a second camera but hadn't done it. He hadn't felt like he had enough money to make that work at the time.

Now, maybe. He'd have to check. As he sat in the parking lot, he pulled out his phone.

With a quick search, he discovered there were no authorized Olympus dealers in New Mexico. He looked at his camera and bag, on the seat next to him, and took a minute to really think things through. He entered a new inquiry.

There were Olympus dealers in Austin, Texas. His next destination. He just had to make it through this week.

He opened his bag and looked at the lens again. Maybe it could be repaired, or the local shop would have a used one, even with an adapter from another manufacturer. Either that, or he'd have to take all his shots without that lens this week.

Only time would tell, but even though it was only Tuesday, he felt pressure creeping up on him.

He put his car in gear and punched in the address of the lab. He didn't want to be late, and he really was curious about what they did and what is was Alicia wanted to show him.

6

———————

AND THE LAB

Less than fifteen minutes later, he pulled up to the security gate at Apis Labs. He had to show his ID, and the guard made a call, but once he was in the gated parking lot, things got easier.

There were several cars parked around the lot, but one car, close to the door, had two empty spots on either side of it.

Nick pulled into one of those, grabbed his camera, and headed inside. The receptionist looked up and smiled at him.

"You must be the photographer, here to see Alicia."

"I am. Nick O'Flannigan. But please, just call me Nick."

"Hi, Nick. I just need you to sign these forms here. They're standard procedure. You can take your camera with you, but as you tour you can only take photos authorized by the staff, so please ask first. Will you be doing a story on the lab?"

Nick hadn't thought that through yet, but he'd made a little extra money already on this trip selling photos on the side, even though that had gone wrong in Denver, and partnering with his old college buddy in Salem.

As long as the story wasn't crime related, he didn't see why he shouldn't write something up, maybe sell it to the local paper or something.

"I may," he answered.

"Just be sure to run it by someone before you print anything, okay? The company is very touchy about that."

The form in his hand was a standard non-disclosure agreement. He looked it through briefly, signed, and handed it back.

Just then Alicia walked out from the back area of the lab.

"Hey, Nick," she said. "Welcome to Apis Vaccination Labs. How are you feeling?"

"Good," he said. "Better. I slept well with the antihistamines, and I now have EpiPens."

"Good," she said. "You won't need them here. I see you have your camera. Did you get your lens fixed?"

"Not yet." Nick briefly told her the story as they headed through a metal door.

They entered an open room where several people were working. Some were huddled over microscopes; others were using centrifuges and other equipment he did not recognize.

"This is Ronald," she said, turning to a man near the front of the room. He was staring at a computer screen and looked up at Nick.

"Hey there," he said, standing. "I'm Ronald Giles, head of research."

"Nick O'Flannigan," he said. "But call me Nick."

"Welcome Nick. Alicia will show you around. Just don't take any photos without permission."

"I won't," Nick said. "Thanks for letting me see what goes on here. I'm fascinated."

"Alicia says you got stung the other day?"

"Yes, at the capitol."

"They have some bees on the grounds there. All the flowers, you know. One of the staff is a beekeeper, but they have a wasp problem this year, too. We're hoping to help."

"So, the difference?" Nick asked. "I know wasps can sting more than once, and I also know bees are endangered in some places, but do they do different things?"

"Well," Ronald said, glancing at Alicia and smiling. "Bees often help pollinate plants, something like 80% of crops and flowers. Of course, that's an estimate, but that is why many farmers and gardeners are also beekeepers. As you said, they can only sting once, and usually do so in self-defense.

"A wasp on the other hand is a predator. They keep insect populations in check, so they can be a good thing, but around people's homes they can be pests, and even fatal ones. We lost one of our employees to a sting just last week."

"Alicia told me. I guess I got lucky."

"Things could have been worse for sure. The irony is that here we are working on a vaccine, one designed for people like you with severe allergies. If you got stung, it would still hurt, but it wouldn't kill you."

"That's good news."

"It is. We want to prevent things like what happened to Miguel from happening to anyone else."

"Thanks for the information," Nick said. "I appreciate it."

"Sure," Ronald said. "I'll see you when you're done with the tour, Alicia?"

"Sure," she said, clearly uncomfortable.

"What's that all about?" Nick asked once they had moved to the next room, what looked like a small storage area. There were boxes of test tubes, beakers, and syringes arranged on shelves, along with gloves and other protective equipment.

"He asked me out once, and I said no. Miguel and I tried to keep the fact that we started dating quiet, but this is a small place, and word gets around."

"Oh, I'm sorry. I'd forgotten the two of you went out."

"It was new, but still. Ronald didn't like Miguel much anyway. They didn't get along well for whatever reason. But Miguel was really good, so Ronald couldn't afford to not have him on the team."

"I see," Nick said. A thought tickled the back of his head.

Leave it alone, he thought. *This wasn't a murder. It was an accident. How would you make a wasp sting someone?*

"How do you make a vaccine for stings? I know with disease, you take a little of the disease itself, and create some kind of formula? It makes your body build up anti-bodies, right?"

Alicia laughed, and Nick was glad to move on from the topic of her deceased friend. "That's a very simple way to put things, but yes. One of the reasons we set up here in Santa Fe is that we can study wasp and bee populations year round, but we can also harvest them and harvest venom for when we are ready to go into production, if that happens soon."

"Harvest them?"

"Essentially, we take a wasp colony and do what is called 'smoking' them. We wait until they are less active, usually at night, fill the colony with a smoke compound that essentially puts them to sleep, and then we freeze them."

"Like, freeze the bodies?"

"Yes. Let me show you."

They moved from the storage area into another room, one full of glass fronted industrial freezers.

Alicia stepped up to one, opened it, and showed him what was essentially a tray of frozen wasps.

Nick shuddered involuntarily.

"I know it looks a bit creepy the first time, but they won't come back to life and come after you, I promise."

Nick laughed nervously at himself, but also felt his body relax when she slid the tray back into the freezer and closed the door.

"That is amazing. All of these freezers are filled with—wasps?"

"Yep. We use a lot of them in testing, trying to get the vaccine just right, and also work with what to combine the venom with that won't harm the venom, but also won't be harmful to the person we inject with it."

"Sounds complex."

"It is. Much more so than people think. We have some great minds working on it here."

"Including yours?" Nick smiled.

Alicia blushed. "I do okay," she said.

"How do you get the venom out of—well, this?" Nick asked.

"It's easier to show you that, too," she said. "If you're comfortable."

"Lead the way," Nick said.

They headed back to the lab, and to a table where a woman in a lab coat was working with what Nick would best describe as a pile of wasps.

She had a small needle and a microscope. As he watched, she took a wasp from the pile, put it under her scope, carefully put the needle in its abdomen, and pressed a button. A tiny bit of liquid, really just a few drops, appeared in the syringe.

The woman pushed the plunger as he watched, putting the extracted venom through a sealed lid into a small test tube that was only about a quarter of the way full.

"How long does it take to fill one of those?" he asked.

"Quite a while," Alicia told him. "This is one of the dullest parts of the job."

As Nick watched, the woman took the "used wasp" and set it aside. Nick noted that the abdomen of that wasp looked thinner than the ones on the pile. There were several next to it that looked just as thin.

"We actually pass along some of the bodies to other places doing research, entomologists and even some schools that do dissection in classes. Nothing goes to waste."

"That's amazing," Nick said. "This has been very—well, enlightening. Was this what you wanted to show me?"

She smiled. "You'll see."

They moved on to other stations, Alicia explaining what each worker did as she went along.

Nick only took a few photos, but he did take some notes in his phone. He took photos of the freezer tray, the wasp pile, and a few other things, but Alicia asked that he not take photos of any of the proprietary equipment, or any papers.

"Before you use photos for anything, please run them by us," she said.

"I will," Nick told her.

"There is one last thing," she said. "But no photos."

She used her badge to open a door, and inside Nick saw a series of shelves. On them were trays that held little test tubes. One on each tray was filled with an amber looking liquid. The rest of the tray had several syringes filled with clear liquid.

"What's this?" Nick asked.

"Our first batch of vaccine for human testing."

"What's the amber liquid?"

"That's pure wasp venom, the basis for the vaccine. The clear tubes are the vaccine itself."

"Can I join that study?"

"Ha. You'd have to live in Santa Fe. We'd have to monitor you, as we think this will be a several step process."

"Oh, bummer," Nick said. "I would love to be part of something like this."

They stayed in the room only a moment longer, and Nick wished he could take photos. But they left and headed for the front of the lab.

They stopped, and Nick thanked Ronald, shook his hand, and then Alicia showed him out.

"Thanks again," he said. "I'll contact the local paper and see if I can collaborate with one of their writers on an article."

"That would be great," Alicia said. "Call me if you need anything while you are in town."

"Will do," Nick said.

He walked out the front door. When he got to his car, he looked at the car parked by itself. The windows were rolled all the way down.

That might be a good idea in this heat, and in a secure parking lot that might not be bad, but he looked at the rest of the cars in the lot.

They were all locked up tight, at least they appeared to be. Many had those sunshade things in the windshield.

Nick looked inside and saw one of the windshield things in this car too, but it was tossed in the back seat. He ducked down to get a better look.

On the passenger side of the car, he saw a wasp on the floor. He raised his camera and took a picture, then zoomed in all he could with his short lens and watched it for a moment. It didn't move, but still, he thought maybe he should warn whoever's car this was that there might be a wasp inside.

He looked around. He was the only one in the parking lot. A short distance away, he could see the security guard in his little kiosk by the gate.

Nick got in his car and headed that way. As he came up to the gate, the guard just waved, but Nick stopped and rolled his window down.

"Can I help you?" the guard asked.

"Yeah, maybe," Nick said. "You see that car over there? The one with the windows down?"

"Yes?"

"I saw a wasp inside. It looks dead, but you might want to warn whoever it belongs too—"

The guard held up his hand. "That's Miguel Alvarez's car, the employee who died last week from a sting."

"I heard about that."

"No one has picked it up yet. You probably saw the wasp that stung him. I'll let someone know. They might want to clean it up a little before his family shows up."

"Alicia—I mean, Miss Hernandez might be a good one to let know. She seemed to know him the best."

"Good idea," he said. "Thanks for the heads up."

"No problem."

Nick drove away, looking at the clock in his car. Damn.

It was already time to find some supper to replace the horrible lunch he'd grabbed on the run. And some evening photos of the capitol. Maybe he could get lucky and get ahead on other photos until he found a lens solution.

He waited until he was downtown, close to the capitol, and searched "restaurants near me."

As he did, his stomach growled.

7

SMOKE AND MIRRORS

The restaurant, called Radish and Rye, featured great food and a wide bourbon selection. Since he was walking and would be around the capitol for a while, Nick ordered an Old Fashioned, made with the bartender's recommendation for bourbon.

It was a bit pricey, but Nick figured he'd earned a good night out. He looked at all the couples around the room though and missed Sandra. It would be great if she could just travel with him all the time.

But it might not be so great. Their relationship was new, and although this was a great gig, there were stresses. Nick thought they would be fine, but it was really hard to tell since they'd only really spent two weeks together, one in Sacramento and one in Denver.

He took photo of his food and sent it to her.

"Talk to you soon," he added. He did want to fill her in on his day.

He finished his meal and his drink, resolving to come back later, maybe even take a taxi, so he could sample more from their bourbon selection.

Then he walked the short distance to the capitol. He decided to shoot with his standard lens, since most of these would be simple outdoor shots, more landscapes, but he did have his zoom if he needed it. He wanted to focus on some of the flowers and some other macro shots, but they would just have to wait.

That's probably why his eye seemed to catch opportunity after opportunity.

"Tomorrow is another day," he told himself. As he walked along, he saw a van parked along the curb, and a man with some kind of wand with smoke coming out of it near a group of trees.

Nick took photos from a distance. The smoke provided an eerie look to the trees, and while he was unsure if he would use those for the magazine, he just found the pictures to be cool looking.

When the smoke dissipated, the man got a bag of sorts from the van and walked toward the trees. Nick watched as he used a long device, something like a tree pruner, to pick up the gray colored wasp nest from one of the branches and drop it in the bag.

Once he closed it, Nick approached.

"Hey there," he said. "I see you are 'smoking' these wasps. Do you work for Apis Labs?"

"No," the man told him. As he turned, Nick saw it was Luis. "Oh, I didn't know it was you. I'm a bee keeper her on the grounds, but I also handle the wasps

"What do you do with them?"

"I sell the ones I can capture to the lab. They pay me for them."

"That's cool. I was just there today."

Luis tilted his head and looked at Nick. "How are you feeling after your sting the other day?"

"Better. Really, thanks for your help."

"You're part of the reason I'm here tonight. Another tourist was stung, too. So we had to move this nest. There are a few others I'll have to come back and deal with later, but this was the biggest."

"That must make some long days for you. Someone said this was a bad wasp year."

"Yep. More stings than last year for sure. Then there was that guy from the lab who died, and you, a pretty close call, both in the last week. The governor wants us to keep this under control."

"The governor?"

"He even made me move some of the bees that pollinate the flowers."

"You can do that?"

"Yeah. My dad is a beekeeper too. We actually took one hive away and brought in a smaller one. The honey bees hardly bother anyone, and I actually collect the honey from them on site."

"That's actually pretty neat."

Nick noticed a wasp, clearly dead, laying on the sidewalk.

"This is going to sound weird," he said. "But can I have this?"

"Have what? The wasp?"

"Yes."

"Um, sure. You want something to put it in?"

"Do you have something?"

Luis took out a small, plastic vial, almost like a pill bottle. "This is what we use if we collect individual ones, especially if they are an unusual species. Then we can get them identified. Apis is really helpful with that."

"Sounds like a good company."

"They are."

"You ever accidentally kill bees with that smoke?" Nick asked.

"Rarely. I try to be really careful. But the smoke can't tell if something in its path is a bee or wasp. It just goes where it goes."

"Huh," Nick said. "Interesting. Thanks for the information. And the wasp."

"Anytime." As Nick walked away, he saw Luis shaking his head.

"I suppose I do seem oddly curious," Nick said, mumbling to himself. The little something tickled at the back of his head again, though. Something about Miguel's death didn't feel right to him.

Leave it alone, Nick, he thought. But he thought of the wasp in his pocket, in the plastic container. In his mind's eye, he saw the pile of wasps by the microscope.

But then he looked up. The light was just right around the capitol building itself, and he started to take photo after photo.

As he moved around the building, he was soon lost in his work.

The moon had risen by the time he made a full circuit, and so he went around again.

By the time he headed back to the hotel, he was pretty tired. But he had a lot of material to work with.

He decided he would sleep in a bit the next day, then get some sunrise shots on Thursday. Hopefully, tomorrow would provide him with a lens solution.

He emptied his pockets onto the desk in his hotel room, including the vial with the wasp. He went to lay down and turned on the television for background noise as he texted Sandra.

He sent her a few messages, but his eyes kept going back to the desk, and that vial.

He knew the wasp was dead. The vial was sealed. He'd carried it here in his pocket.

But it didn't matter. He got up, went to the bathroom, emptied a Ziplock that usually held his toiletries, and put the vial inside. He sealed the bag, then covered it up with his laptop bag.

He went back to the bed, sent Sandra a good night text, and then set a timer on the television.

He was asleep in moments and dreamed of trays of frozen wasps coming to life and chasing him.

He woke to sunlight and a buzzing sound, but discovered it was only the hotel clock on the nightstand. Someone had set the alarm for eight in the morning.

For Nick, that was sleeping in, and he got up ready to start his day.

Unfortunately, before he could get to looking through the capitol photos, he had to sort out his personal ones.

That meant looking at all the shots he had of wasps, which were now the subject of his nightmares.

8

IMMUNITY

Nick sorted through the photos, even though it did give him the creeps a little bit.

When he had those sorted, he turned to the photos he'd taken at the capitol. It turned out he had quite a few good ones. He needed second floor and first floor photos if he could get them, but he was really hoping to have a macro lens before going back inside. He uploaded what he had to the Cloud folder the magazine had set up for him.

Then he looked through his own photos, the ones of the wasps on a tray, in a pile, and more.

He looked at the photo he'd taken of the wasp in the victim's car, the man who'd died. Something about it looked different, yet familiar. It was just—off. Just like he thought the rapid conclusion of the authorities that this was an accidental death also seemed off. He couldn't say why, it just felt wrong.

Nick told himself again that he was just being paranoid. *It's not your business. If the police didn't find it odd, why should you?*

He tried not to think about it as he uploaded the files to his personal Cloud folder, taking care not to mix them up with the magazine photos.

After the process was complete, he jumped in the shower and took extra time to massage his bad leg. It didn't bother him as much since he'd been working out and riding a bike when he could, but the injury that had sidelined his NBA hopes still ached from time to time.

It reminded him of how he'd gotten here, to his job as a freelance photographer. His choices had been basketball first, accounting second, and photography had just been his hobby.

But his unique eye and his ability to run his own business made him well suited for the entrepreneur and freelance life. He'd jumped in with both feet, first building small clientele in Boston, but then deciding to move to Seattle, nearly as far from home as he could get, to start over.

It was one of the best decisions he'd ever made. Yes, at some point he'd have to go back and care for his parents, probably. He hoped that day wouldn't come for a long time.

He didn't miss Boston at all.

Just as he finished getting dressed, realizing he really needed breakfast, his phone rang.

"Hey there," he answered. "How are you, Mom?"

"We're good. I just wanted to check on you. Are you okay now?"

"Yes, and I have the EpiPens just in case."

"Did you ask them about a vaccine study?"

"I toured a lab. They told me about one, but I would have to live here to participate in theirs."

"Bee venom can be good for you, you know."

"I got stung by a wasp, Mom."

"I know. But they use bee venom for all kinds of things. My friend, Dorothy, is into all that herbal stuff. She uses it for her arthritis."

"Really?"

"Yeah. I told her about you getting stung, and she told me all about it."

"You're kidding?"

"You should try some for your leg."

"I'm not sure how that would work for someone who is allergic," he told her.

"Oh, well. Yes. I suppose you should check."

"I will, Mom, I promise."

"Well, I just wanted to check in. I'm taking your father to that fishing store he likes today. Even though he doesn't fish much anymore."

"That's good, Mom. I love you."

"Love you, Nick."

He ended the call. *Bee venom. For arthritis.*

He sat down at his laptop for a second, and did a search. Sure enough, people used bee venom to help a variety of ailments. There was a caution on most websites for people who were allergic, but he thought he should check into it anyway.

The breakfast burrito had been so good the day before, Nick considered going back to that place. The food had definitely hit the spot and held him through the day.

But he wanted to try something different, so again he turned to the search engine on his phone.

Tia Sophia's looked good and wasn't far, so he headed there, stomach growling on the way. As he ate, he watched the local news, something that had become a habit.

The local station had a segment on Apis Vaccination Labs, the death of the employee, and the emphasis that put on the development of a vaccine. He listened with interest and noted with a smile that the announcer mentioned the use of bee venom for various medicinal purposes.

Once he finished the hearty breakfast, good coffee, and had treated himself to a glass of fresh orange juice, he was ready to go.

He patted his belly, reminding himself that he hadn't been to the gym since the sting. That wasn't good.

He promised himself he would go this afternoon. It was only Wednesday after all, and the events of the week had thrown off his rhythm. He'd be fine.

The first thing he wanted to do was look for a lens at the local shop, provided they were open today.

He headed that way and found an open sign on the door. He stepped inside to find a minor heaven: there was a rack of straps, a case with used vintage gear including many film cameras. On the wall behind the counter were several types of film for sale.

A menu in the middle even offered film development options.

As much as Nick liked being in the digital era of photography, he often thought he would have enjoyed the hands-on tactile experience of developing film, and waiting to see what photos came out well, and what others would need to be reshot. Such an endeavor would have made this trip a much longer one.

What he was doing now would not even have been possible a couple of decades ago.

He stepped over to another counter, one with a glass top which revealed lenses inside. He spotted an Olympus one right away, not the newest one, but one that would be compatible.

A man stepped out of the back. "Hi, can I help you?"

"Yes. I would love to look at that lens."

"That's a nice one."

"My other macro got broken the other day."

"It's not fixable?"

Nick pulled it from his camera bag and handed it over. "I don't think so."

The man, bearing a name tag that read, "Mike" looked the lens over carefully.

"Nope, you're right. That dent is pretty deep. What happened?"

"I got stung by a wasp. Found out I was allergic when I fell over."

"Oh man. They are bad this year."

"So everyone keeps telling me. How much for the lens?"

"You a pro?"

Nick nodded. "Freelance. I'm on a year long assignment from *Travel USA* magazine."

"Hmm. Okay. This one goes for around $500 new, but I'll sell it to you for $375. A customer used it, but only a few times before they sold it back to me."

"Deal," Nick said. It was substantially less than he paid at the huge box store.

He used his card to pay for the lens, and looked at some other items in the shop, but didn't see anything he needed. He did see a brochure for the newest Olympus model.

Maybe soon, in the next few weeks. He'd have to weigh the pros and cons. He thanked Mike, took the brochure, and headed out.

Nick headed to the capitol with the new-to-him lens and new focus. He wanted to get some more outside shots. This evening would be good time for some sunset and night shots, and this afternoon or tomorrow he could focus on the last two floors inside.

The one thing he didn't envy was the person who'd be selecting what photos went in the books. There were so many to choose from here, so many great pieces of art, he felt like "The Roundhouse" could have a book all its own.

One of the greatest things was the landscaping. Sacramento had a park next to the capitol, and many cities did similar things, but this one was immaculate.

He put his macro lens on the camera and shot a few close ups with it. He checked them out on the small screen, and they looked amazing. He couldn't wait to look at them on his computer later. The lens wasn't the newest macro, but it worked exceptionally well.

It felt good to have his full lens compliment back.

He took some close up photos of flowers, and even one with a bee on it, although that made him back away slightly. That photo was good, but he was too nervous to get a better one.

He rounded a corner, and as he raised his camera for another floral closeup, he heard a buzzing sound. He blinked and looked closer.

There, close to the trunk of the tree right in front of him was a gray, wasp paper nest. He backed rapidly away, and as he did saw a group of the stinging beasts fly out and around the tree.

He quickly switched lenses to his zoom and took some photos of the buzzing beasts from a distance. He looked at a few in his screen, and again thought of the man who'd died from a sting at Apis.

It just didn't make any sense.

Something, something—the wasps here looked different than the one he'd seen in the car.

Different species? He didn't think so. Different body shape? No, that wasn't it.

In his hotel room, he still had the wasp he'd picked up. He could look at photos later and figure out what was tickling at his brain.

For now, he wanted to find the groundskeeper, Luis, and let him know about the wasps' nest.

As he walked toward the door, Luis came around the corner.

"Hey there," he said. "I was just looking for you."

"Oh yeah?"

"Yeah. There is another wasp nest over by that tree," Nick pointed.

"You didn't get stung again, did you?"

"No, thank goodness. But I thought you'd want to know."

"Thanks," Luis said. "Damn things keep coming back."

"I get that," Nick said. "I guess Apis can take them off your hands."

"They can," Luis said, almost brightening.

"The other night, you mentioned local honey."

"I'll grab a jar at home and give it to you next time I see you. It's really great stuff."

"I'd be happy to pay you for it."

"It will be your consolation prize for getting stung."

"Deal," Nick said.

He went inside, hoping to get some pics from at least one more floor today.

Again, he was astounded by the art, and the way the capitol was laid out. The art collection was well curated and presented exceptionally well.

He was about to leave when he was struck by an idea. He went up to the fourth floor and headed for the legislative counsel's office.

He knocked, and a well-dressed woman invited him in. "What can I do for you?"

"I'm Nick O'Flannigan, a freelance photographer."

"The one who got stung outside the other day?"

"That's me."

"How are you feeling?"

"Good. Much better now, thanks."

The room wasn't large, but was well appointed with an oak desk, a leather executive chair behind it, and a smaller pair in front of it, facing the wall. The wall itself was covered with a bookcase filled with serious looking volumes.

"How can I help you, Mr. O'Flannigan?"

"I was wondering if I could get into the legislative floor downstairs. I know it's not usually open to the public, but I'm on assignment from *Travel USA* magazine, and I'm sure they would love to share some exclusive photos with our readers."

"Sure. I'll have to have someone go with you. Do you want to set up an appointment?"

"Sure," he said. "Tomorrow morning?"

"I'll call security and set it up for you. Do you have a card?"

Nick handed one over.

"They'll call you with all the details. Enjoy the rest of your week, Mr. O'Flannigan."

"Thanks," he said. "Appreciate it."

His stomach told him it was time for a break, and his watch said that it was two in the afternoon, and the large breakfast was wearing off.

Gym, tonight, he promised himself.

He left, in search of some lunch. He saw Luis on the way out, and waved to him, but the groundskeeper either didn't see him or ignored him, because he didn't wave back.

9

―――――――

WASP MAN

Nick headed for a place called The Burger Stand. On the way, he thought again about the wasps. What was it he had heard, or read? "Solitary wasps seldom sting," he said aloud as he walked.

When he'd been stung, he'd heard buzzing from a group in a nest. Today, another nest, and a group or "swarm" of wasps.

In Miguel's car there had been only one.

No one had said anything about there being a swarm or a nearby nest.

And what else had he been told? The higher the IgE level in your blood, the more allergic you were, or the more stings you had received. In his case, one sting had been enough to send him to the hospital.

Miguel had not been allergic. "People get stung all the time," Alicia had said. Multiple stings could lead to an "induced" allergic reaction.

How many times had Miguel been stung? Why am I even asking these questions?

Because something about the wasp in the car looked wrong. Something in the details, something small.

His phone rang just before he reached his destination. It was Sandra.

He sat at one of the outside tables under a green umbrella. He'd go in and order shortly, but Sandra might be the perfect first one to bounce his wasp thoughts off of.

The problem was that no one was calling this a crime. Not the lab, not Alicia, not the police as far as he knew, and not the press.

As far as he knew, he was the only one with suspicions.

That made this more of a challenge. Quite literally, this was none of his business. He wouldn't be assisting with a case, or asked to help with one, but instead would be starting an inquiry.

"Hello there," he said.

"Hi, Nick. How are you feeling? No more stings?"

"Nope. I managed to replace my damaged lens and got some great shots this morning."

"Why do I sense there is more there you want to say?"

Nick hesitated, and then dove right in.

"Look, I know I said I would try not to get involved in any mysteries, but—"

"Oh, no. Nick, what is going on?"

"Here's the thing," he said. "Before I got stung, a guy at a local lab died from a wasp sting."

"I think you told me."

"I went to the lab for a tour. It's a really cool place, and they're working on some great stuff, including vaccines."

"Oh, that would be amazing for so many people who are allergic."

"Exactly. The guy who died worked there, but there has been something off about the way he was stung, and I couldn't put my finger on it. Still can't."

"Aren't the police looking into it, if his death was suspicious?"

"That's the thing. No. Everyone is calling it an accident."

"And you don't think it was."

"No."

"You feel obligated to share your suspicions."

"I do, but I need more than just a hunch."

"Do you have anything besides that?"

"No, not yet, but I have some photos I'm going to look over again. Something feels wrong about the wasps in the photos."

She sighed. "Okay, Nick. I'm inclined to help you look at them at least. One way or the other, we can put this to bed."

"I appreciate that."

"If we find nothing to support your hunch, Nick, you have to make me a promise."

"What's that?"

"That you'll drop it. Move on. You have enough to do without getting wrapped in another mystery, especially something no one else is calling a crime."

"Deal," he said. "I'm eating lunch now, and then heading back to my room. I'll upload magazine photos first, and then work on looking these over. You aren't working today?"

"Sort of, but I have some freedom. I just have a couple things I need to finish this week, so my schedule is pretty flexible."

"Sounds good." He hung up, still not sure exactly what she did for a living. Something in a family business, he did know that.

He ate the large burger, every last one of his fries, and chased it all with a chocolate shake piled high with whipped cream.

The gym - somewhere between photo analysis and night photos - he'd go.

He walked back to his car. All of this walking was good for him, but his leg was a little sore. He needed to stretch as much as he needed a workout.

Only a few moments later, he was in the room, uploading magazine photos, which he did as carefully as always. He made sure his personal ones were not included but did include the one with the bee on the flower, because it had turned out so well. He didn't caption all of them but labeled that one "Stung in Santa Fe."

He then turned his attention to the wasp photos.

He pulled up the photos he'd taken today of the wasps buzzing around the nest he'd accidentally discovered.

He zoomed in on several and cropped them. They all looked pretty much the same. Then he pulled up the photos from the lab, including the tray of frozen wasps, and the photo of the pile of wasps near the microscope. They all looked pretty similar, too.

He got to the photo of the wasp on the floor of Miguel's car.

It looked—different. He couldn't figure out why.

He turned it back and forth, thinking maybe it was the angle.

Then he emailed a few of the photos, and the one of the wasp in the car, to Sandra.

She called a moment later.

"So, what are we looking at?" she said after the usual pleasantries.

"Something about the wasp in the car looks—different."

"It does, but it's really hard to tell what. It could be the angle. Are these the only shots you have of it?"

"Yes, the ones I took through the open window."

"Well, Nick, I don't see how, without more shots from other angles, you can say anything definitive about this one."

"You could be right. I just—"

"Look, if you're really concerned, call the police, offer them the photos and your idea. Let them take it from there. Or the woman from the lab, Alicia."

"Yeah, maybe even her boss. Ronald, I think his name was."

"Yes, sure. Whoever. Just let them check it out. You concentrate on your job. Are you going out again today?"

"I'm going to try to get some sunset and night shots."

"Sounds good. I hear wasps aren't as busy at night. It should be easier for you to concentrate."

"Thanks for keeping me headed the right direction. I love you."

"Love you, too, Nick."

He closed the laptop. And sighed. She was right, but he didn't want to take something this thin to the cops or anyone else.

He'd been made to feel like a fool often enough.

His late lunch meant a late dinner would be fine with him. He decided to hit the gym after all.

An hour and a half later, he returned to the room, showered, and grabbed his camera bag.

His evening was spent taking photos, which included a spectacular Santa Fe sunset with the capitol in the foreground.

Once darkness fell, he walked around the capitol one more time, taking some cool shots that included the light pouring from the windows creating odd shapes on the ground, shadows that walked with him, talked to him, and projected images of giant, stinging wasps into his mind.

As he came around the last corner before heading to his car, he saw Luis, smoking the wasps near the tree where he'd spotted them earlier today.

Nick watched for only a moment. The process was the same as it had been before. The smoke, and whatever it contained, made the sluggish wasps even more so. He could see the equipment nearby, the same items he'd used the last time to collect the nest once they were neutralized.

As he walked toward his car, he happened to look down. There on the sidewalk was a lone wasp, dead.

Lone wasps seldom sting, he thought. *Most often, others sting humans in self-defense. If you kill one near the nest, the others come after you, defending their home.*

The swarm, their fellow insects must give them confidence, strength in numbers.

Nick understood that. He still had his suspicions, but with no evidence, nothing to back them up, he felt like the solitary wasp himself. Alone, and powerless.

10

SOLITARY

Nick woke to his phone ringing, a common occurrence. It was his editor, Emily.

"Good morning," he said, the best he could do under the circumstances. It had been a late night at the capitol, and his dreams had been odd.

"How are things coming?" she asked. "I saw some great outdoor photos, and some great day shots and interior shots. But how are you doing on the sunset and sunrise sets, and the rest of the interior?"

She was okay to be concerned. It was Thursday, and he hadn't uploaded the other shots from the night before yet.

"Well, I have some night photos from last night I haven't uploaded yet. But I will this morning. I'm supposed to get a call so I can get some exclusive shots of the legislative floor, an area that's usually not open to the public. And I plan to get sunrise photos tomorrow."

I better, he thought. *That's my last good shot at it.* The week had flown by.

"Sounds great. How are you feeling?"

"Okay. No more stings, and I seem to have fully recovered."

"Good to hear. Keep up the great work, Nick."

She ended the call, and Nick stood, stretching. The gym had been good for him, but he was sore.

He'd hoped for some bike riding this week, but that hadn't worked out.

C'est la vie, he thought. He jumped in the shower as hot as he could stand it. He figured he'd stay in this morning, grab some hotel breakfast, and then, hopefully, he would hear from security so he could get into the lower level of the capitol.

It's a good thing that mystery did not pan out, he thought. There was no time for distractions this week.

He sent a quick text to Sandra and headed down to the lobby where he gathered a plate of eggs and bacon, two bagels complete with packets of cream cheese, some orange juice, and a cup of coffee.

He scarfed it down in the breakfast area, where he watched the local news and weather, and headed back to his room.

His laptop waited, and he slid his finger across the trackpad to open it, grabbed his camera bag, and turned around, sliding his laptop bag out of the way as he did.

The vial with the wasp, the one he'd taken from the exterminator, fell to the floor.

He'd forgotten all about it. He picked it up and then looked at his computer screen.

The photo of the wasp in Miguel's car filled the monitor. Nick glanced from the one in the vial to the one on the screen. Then he saw it.

The abdomen of the one in the car looked—thin.

The one in the vial looked—normal. Not fat, but...full.

It's just the angle, Nick.

Was it?

Thoughts of uploading photos fled his mind, and he took the vial with the wasp in it and held it up to the light.

He shook it.

"I know you're dead," he said to it. "But if I let you out, you can't sting me for revenge."

With a sigh, he popped the top and poured the wasp onto the desk. He looked it over carefully, then took his camera, and focused on it. He snapped a photo. Walked away to get a different angle and took some more.

Standing as tall as he could, he took few shots from above. Studying the photo from the car, he tried to imitate the angle, and clicked the shutter a few more times.

Then he plugged in the camera and transferred just the photos he'd just taken.

With the wasp from the car on one side of the screen, zoomed in as close as he could, he flipped through the photos of the wasp on the desk. No matter what the angle, no matter what it he did, the wasp on the left looked thinner, the one he'd gathered at the capitol looked—full was the only word he could still think of.

But he'd seen wasps like the thin one before the one in the car. Where? The lab was really the only place he'd seen other wasps in significant numbers.

Leaving the car photo up on the left, he pulled up the file with the lab photos on the right side of his screen and worked his way through them.

Frozen wasps equaled full. Pile by the microscope, waiting for the venom to be extracted, full too.

One of the wasps by the microscope after the venom was removed? Thin.

Drained.

Is that what a wasp would look like after it stung someone?

He turned to the search engine on his laptop. Nope. They could sting several times, as he had been told, and replenished venom quickly. The victim, as Nick now called him, had been stung once.

Once. By a solitary wasp. The type of wasp that seldom stung someone.

And that one sting had killed someone who wasn't allergic?

Nick didn't think so.

But what should he do with the information he had? The police? The news? Neither of those things had worked out perfectly for him in the past. Suddenly he was tired. Not sleepy tired. Mind-weary tired.

Why me? he thought.

Sandra was right. He could leave it alone and walk away, but he suspected someone had killed this man, and if he didn't say anything, it might happen again.

He couldn't do that.

As he reached for his phone, it rang showing a Santa Fe number.

"Nick O'Flannigan," he answered.

"Mr. O'Flannigan, this is Dennis, head of security at 'The Roundhouse.' How are you today?"

"Good."

"The Legislative Counsel contacted us and said you'd like to get some photos of the legislative rooms."

"That would be great. I am on assignment from *Travel USA* magazine, and they would be a great addition the book they are creating with my photos."

"Yes, she filled us in. Can you be here at 12:30? There is a brief session late this afternoon, so we need to be out of there by then."

"Sure," Nick said, checking the time on his computer. He would need to upload the photos for the magazine quickly and then head out. There was no time to mess with the wasp dilemma, at least, for now.

"Okay." Dennis gave him instructions about where to meet him and what he would be allowed to do, and how much time he would have.

"Thanks," Nick said. "I'll see you soon."

"Looking forward to it," Dennis said.

The call ended and Nick quickly switched gears. He plugged in his camera to transfer photos, put a couple of batteries into his quick charger, and got to work editing and deleting. When he had a pretty solid group of sunset and night photos, he hit upload and sat back to think while he waited.

As soon as the upload completed he would have to leave. The photos this afternoon and another quick shoot should have him done with the inside of the capitol building.

The sunrise shots tomorrow should offer him a chance afterward to finish the outside. Then he could really have the weekend off.

That meant he had this afternoon and this evening on his own.

He called Alicia, thinking she would likely be working and not answer.

"Alicia Hernandez. How can I help you?" she answered.

"Hi, Alicia. It's Nick O'Flannigan."

"Hi, Nick."

"What are you doing later this afternoon? I have something I would like to run by you."

This was the best course of action. His only course, if he wanted to stay out of any entanglements.

"Oh yeah? What would that be?"

"It's really something I have to show you."

"Sounds mysterious."

"It's wasp related, and it could be nothing. I just have some questions, that's all."

"I can probably answer them, or find the answers," she said. "Where do you want to meet?"

"Why don't we meet at the lab? I have a special photo shoot at the capitol, but I should be able to meet you around 3:30."

"Sounds good. I will let them know up front that you are coming."

"I'll need to bring in my laptop."

"No problem. We can meet in the conference room."

"Sounds good. I've got to go. I'll see you this afternoon."

Nick ended the call as the upload finished. He unplugged his camera, put in a fresh battery, threw a second one in his camera bag, and grabbed his laptop, too. He took a deep breath and scooped the wasp back into the vial. He wouldn't need it, but he didn't want to leave it laying in his room either.

He flipped the card on the door handle to let the staff know he could use maid service and left.

A short time later, he arrived at the capitol building. He met Dennis in the designated area. The man led him to a locked door and used a key from a large selection to let him into the legislative area.

Nick took his time, working counterclockwise, noting where he started. He took dozens of photos from every angle. He changed lenses frequently, catching macro shots of the seats, the table, the speaker's bench and more. These were photos that not just any tourist could take.

He checked them on the small screen as he made it around to his starting point, noting that they looked pretty good.

Hopefully, they would look even better on his laptop and please his editor too.

Especially in light of what he was about to do this afternoon.

Which never completely left his mind as he talked to Dennis.

"Thanks, man," he said. "I do appreciate this."

"I look forward to seeing these pictures in a book someday," he said. "Can you take a shot of me in here?"

Nick smiled. "Sure."

He knelt a little, and took several headshots of Dennis, ones he thought looked pretty decent, even though portraits were not his strong suit.

"Can you send them to my email?" Dennis asked, handing him a card.

"Of course," Nick said. "Thanks again."

Dennis let him out, and Nick exited the private entrance and entered a world of intense sunlight. On the horizon, he could see the kind of towering clouds that might turn to thunderheads later.

It would be awesome if he could catch a storm over the capitol grounds.

Luis worked away in a flowered area, and Nick approached him.

"Hey, how are things?" he asked.

"Good," Luis said. "Storm coming this afternoon, maybe."

"No more wasp issues today?"

"Not so far."

"Good," Nick said. "I'm glad."

"Hopefully it stays that way," Luis groused. "Sometimes I wonder if Apis harvesting them just makes more wasps come back, stronger."

"That would be odd, wouldn't it?"

"Well, who knows what they are really doing there?" Luis said. "I sure don't. And I don't like it at all."

"Well, I know very little about it," Nick said instead. "I'll be here a couple more days, so maybe I'll see you again."

"Sure," Luis said. "I didn't forget your honey. I'll have some with me tomorrow. Have a good afternoon."

Nick looked at the building clouds one more time and wondered if it meant anything beyond some spectacular pictures. For a moment, he reconsidered what he was doing next, but glanced at his phone. Two o'clock. He had an hour, maybe to grab a bite to eat, and finalize what he would tell Alicia.

It suddenly weighed heavier on him than he thought it would.

Maybe there was more than one storm brewing, and this wasn't so great of an idea after all.

11

DRAINED

Nick headed for Apis Labs after grabbing a burger nearby, passing on an afternoon beer. His stomach churned. This was new territory for him.

No one else had asked him to help out. No one was pressuring him, but instead he was bringing up something entirely on his own.

If word got out, if this spread somehow, how would he justify it to Emily? To Sandra? But it was important.

He parked in the same place he had before. Miguel's car was still parked in the same spot and appeared not to have moved. Nick wondered when the family or whoever wanted it would be picking it up. *Probably soon,* he thought.

He glanced in the window and saw the wasp was still there. As he entered the building, Ronald was leaving.

"Hey, there," Nick said.

"Hey. What are you doing here?" Ronald asked.

"I have a meeting with Alicia."

"You aren't seeing her are you?"

"Seeing her?"

"Dating or anything."

"No, of course not. First, I already have a girlfriend, and second, I'm on a long assignment. I'm not the kind of guy to have a girl in every port, so to speak."

"Good. I think she was seeing Miguel, and she seems pretty affected by his death. I would hate to see her get hurt again."

"I see," Nick said, looking down at the smaller man. "Well, I would never do that."

"Just looking out for a friend," Ronald mumbled. "Have a nice day, Mr. O'Flannigan."

Nick shook his head and went inside. People were certainly odd at times, and he was sure he'd never understand them. From what Alicia had told him, he was sure she wasn't interested in Ronald. In fact, quite the opposite.

But he seemed to be interested in her still. He shrugged and went inside.

The receptionist smiled at him. "Mr. O'Flannigan! Welcome back. I'll let Alicia know you're here."

"Thanks," he said.

The curse of being recognizable, pretty much anywhere. There were few communities filled with six and a half foot tall red heads. If they did exist, he hadn't found one yet, which meant there was no place he really blended in.

Which was also a blessing at times.

Alicia came out a second later and showed him to a conference room.

"So what's up?" she asked. "What questions do you have?"

"This is going to sound crazy," Nick said. "But stick with me. If I'm right, it could be big. If not, just tell me it means nothing, and I'll move on."

"Okay. Now you have me intrigued."

Nick opened his laptop and set up the photo of the wasp from the floor in Miguel's car on one side, and the photos of the other wasps on the other.

"You want to project that on the screen?" she asked, pointing to a large television on one wall.

"Sure," he said. "That will make this easier to see."

He plugged a cable into a port on his laptop while she powered the television, and there it was. His photos, bigger than life.

He took a deep breath.

"When I left the other day, I took a photo of the wasp on the floor of Miguel's car. I didn't know it was his at first, until a guard at the gate told me. It just seemed odd for the windows to be down, and a wasp to be there like that."

"Okay," she said.

"That's the wasp on the left side of the screen. I didn't think it looked quite right, but it took me a bit to see what was different."

"Your eye for detail. Macro photography."

"Exactly," he said, blushing. "Look at this."

He brought up the photo of the wasp on his desk, the one from the same angle as the wasp in the car.

"They are different," she said.

"The abdomen," he said. "The abdomen of the one in the car is thinner than the other one."

"So it is," she said, leaning forward.

"That's what bothered me, but then I realized I'd seen a wasp like that before. Here."

He flipped through to the frozen tray photo. "These all look like the one on my desk, before they have been drained of venom."

"Yes," she said.

"But this one looks like the one in the car."

As he flipped to the next photo, Alicia's eyes opened wide, and her mouth followed suit.

"It's been—"

"Drained," they said at the same time.

"Yes, drained," Nick said. "Could it look like this after stinging Miguel once?"

"No," she said.

"Then where did it come from?"

"I don't know. Someone here? Miguel's blood levels were off the charts. He was either highly allergic, so he must have become so, or he was stung several times close together."

"But there was only one sting wound, right?"

She nodded. "And he was not likely to be allergic even after working here as long as he did."

"What does that mean?"

"It means—can we go look at his car?"

"Sure," Nick said. He left his laptop set up on the table but put it to sleep so the photos wouldn't still be visible.

"I want to check something out," she said.

"You have gloves, right?" Nick asked.

"Yes, why?"

"We should wear them. From my involvement with the police lately, I've learned it's a good idea to protect a crime scene."

"A crime scene?"

He shrugged. "Maybe it is, maybe it isn't. Either way, we need to make sure we don't disturb anything the police might want to look at later."

"I'll grab a couple pair. Extra-large for you?" she said, staring at his hands.

"Please," Nick said.

They headed out the front doors and walked straight to Miguel's car.

Nick bent to look in the window. The wasp that had been on the passenger floor was gone.

He swore it had been there when he walked in earlier.

He looked again.

"The wasp is gone," he said.

He pulled open the driver's side door, using his gloved hand, and leaned over as far as he could to see if it had blown under the seat or something, but the wind was still gentle, even though clouds loomed on the horizon.

As he started to back out of the car, he felt his foot slide, and put his hand on the driver's seat near the center console to catch himself.

"Ouch!" he said, as something poked the palm of his hand. "That hurt. What was that?"

"What happened?" Alicia asked, opening the passenger door and looking inside.

Nick looked at his hand. It was bleeding inside the glove from something that had poked him.

He knelt level with the seat and looked closely. Barely visible, he could see a needle protruding from the cloth upholstery.

"What is the world is that?" he asked. "And where did it come from?"

"I don't know," she said.

"It seems to be sticking up through the seat," he said. "Do you have a Band-Aid and another glove?"

"I do."

The pair went inside to the front desk. Nick's heart pounded, but he didn't feel short of breath. It was probably excitement more than anything else.

Alicia looked over the needle stick, and saw there was no swelling, and no apparent reaction. After applying a simple bandage, Nick pulled on a new pair of gloves and went back outside. He opened the back door and looked under the seat.

An odd contraption sat there, one with a syringe in it. It looked like...

"Grab my camera, would you?" Nick popped the lock on his car, parked right next to Miguel's. He took his camera, set it to low light mode, and used it to snap photos of whatever was under the seat at angles he couldn't get his head down to.

He worked without brushing his red hair on the back seat, and possibly leaving false evidence in the car, or destroying any.

Once he'd snapped some photos, Nick pulled the camera close, shaded the small screen, and looked at them. Alicia came around to look with him.

The gadget appeared to be some kind of mechanism. It held a syringe, but the plunger was against a stopper at the very bottom of the device. If someone sat in the driver's seat, the needle would pierce their skin, assuming they were not wearing heavy jeans and the plunger would be pushed, injecting the liquid.

The syringe was half empty.

Miguel had been poisoned, but by what?

The only reason Nick hadn't been was because he hadn't sat on the seat, but had run his hand over it, only pricking himself with the needle without injecting himself.

He shuddered.

"What is that, Nick?' she asked.

"I was hoping you would know. It looks like some kind of injection mechanism."

"We don't have anything like that here."

"It means Miguel was probably poisoned. With what, I don't know. What poison imitates a wasp sting?"

"Wasp venom," she said. "Full strength, not diluted, wasp venom. He wasn't allergic. He didn't suffer several stings. He was injected with a large volume and high concentration of wasp venom."

"Wouldn't that have shown up in a blood test?"

"Just the amount of anti-bodies his body produced, not the reason for them being elevated."

"Are you sure?" Nick asked. It sounded far-fetched as she said it out loud, but her explanation also made the most sense.

"No. But I am sure that whatever happened to Miguel wasn't an accident."

"So our next call is the police," Nick stated.

"Yes," she said, her phone already out.

Nick looked at the passenger floor of the car. The wasp was gone. Someone had removed it, or maybe it had just blown away. That didn't seem possible, though.

If the killer had removed it, why hadn't they removed the syringe as well.

He had no idea, but he walked over to the guard shack as Alicia talked to the police on the phone.

Thunder rolled in the background. The police better hurry, either that or they needed to roll up the windows on Miguel's car. Otherwise, a very soggy crime scene might greet them.

Nick knocked on the window and the guard looked over at him and slid it open. He felt the air conditioning rush out of the tiny enclosure.

"Hey," Nick asked. "The police are on their way. We found what might be a clue in Miguel's car."

"A clue?"

"His death may not have been an accident after all. I wanted to give you a heads up."

"Thanks," the guard said. "I wondered what you guys were doing over there." He pointed to a tiny screen showing a scene from a camera.

"Are those recorded?" Nick asked.

"No. We inherited them with the facility and haven't updated them. They're view only, just for us to keep an eye on things."

"I see," Nick said. "While I have your attention, did anyone else go near that car today? Besides Alicia and I?"

"Ronald walked that way just before he left. I assumed he was just checking to make sure everything was still secure. The family is supposed to have the car towed tonight."

Nick looked at the sky. "I would hope they get here before the storm hits, but the police might change that timetable now."

"Well, thanks for the heads up. Let me know what they say. I don't want to let the wrong people tow his car or anything."

"You bet," Nick said.

As he turned to walk back toward Alicia and the car, an unmarked car pulled up to the gate.

Nick stepped up his pace, and a moment later, the cop pulled up next to him. Two men got out.

Nick and Alicia started by explaining what they'd found, and Nick showed them photos.

"I think I get how it works," Nick told them. "But I can't be sure."

"We'll get our own photo guy out here, but can you send me those?"

"Sure," Nick told the detective, taking his card. "I'll email them to you as soon as I get back to my hotel."

"Hotel?"

"I'm a freelancer, here on an assignment. But I leave Saturday morning."

"So, how did you—" the detective stopped. "I'm not sure I want to know, actually."

"Alicia helped me at the hospital when I got stung. Look, I have some more things to show you as well, the photos that led us to looking at the car at all."

"I'd love to hear the whole story," the detective said. 'But we need to work fast, close the windows on this car, and protect the crime scene first."

"Of course," Nick said.

"Do you have any idea who would have wanted to wish Miguel harm, miss?" the officer said, turning to Alicia.

"Only maybe. Ronald, one of the managers here, didn't like him much."

"Why was that?"

"Ronald asked me out. I turned him down. Miguel asked, I said yes. We tried to keep things, quiet, but you know how these things are."

The detective nodded. "I see. That's it?"

"That's all I know."

"The security guard did say Ronald was around this car as he left work today," Nick said. "I passed him on my way in. And when we came out to the car, the wasp was missing."

"The wasp?"

"Part of the rest of the story I have to tell you."

"Okay. You have the keys to this vehicle?"

"I can get them," Alicia said. She disappeared inside. The second detective opened the back door of the car and studied the device under the seat.

"This is an ingenious device," he said. "I can't wait to look closer at how it works."

"You'll have to forgive my partner," the first detective said. "He's a little on the nerdy side."

"I understand," Nick said. He'd been fascinated himself many times on this trip by the methods people used to kill each other.

Some of them were truly gross. He shuddered. He'd seen decapitations, tongues being removed, and even witnessed a man being pushed from a window.

Alicia came back, and the officer carefully put the keys in the ignition, rolled up the windows, closed the door, and locked it.

"Now," he said. "Before we all get soaked, let's go inside and talk this over."

"Absolutely," Nick said. "My laptop is already set up in the conference room."

The detectives exchanged a glance.

"It will all make more sense inside."

As they entered the building, thunder crashed, and the rain started to fall. Or rather, it came down in sheets.

Darkness had come early with the storm. Nick only hoped tomorrow would be a brighter day.

In so many ways.

12

———

THE BAIT

"**N**uts!" the detective exclaimed as he came back into the conference room and disconnected his phone call.

"What's wrong?" his partner asked.

"Neil's gone camping. All weekend."

"He'll be getting drowned like a rat."

"I hope so. Mr. O'Flannigan?"

"Yes?" Nick said.

"Would you be willing to help us out by taking some crime scene photos —probably tomorrow considering the weather? It seems our guy is currently unavailable."

"Sure," Nick said. "I have a few photos to get for my assignment tomorrow morning, early, but I should be available after that."

If the storm clears, he didn't add. *The disadvantage of putting off photos he really needed until the last minute.*

'Now, can you share with us the events leading up to your calling us? We understood this was an accident."

"I thought so, too," Nick said. "But let me explain."

He then told the officers how he'd been stung, met Alicia, and how things just didn't seem to add up.

"I knew something looked wrong about the wasp in his car."

"The one that is missing now?" The detective said.

"Yes, that one."

"You have a photo of it?"

Nick woke up his computer and walked them through the same comparisons he'd walked Alicia through.

"Great eye for detail," the second detective said. "Are you sure you didn't miss your calling?"

"Pretty sure," Nick said. "Any detective work I've done so far on this trip has only gotten me in trouble."

"Other detective work?" the cops glanced at each other again.

"Yeah, long story," Nick said. "I could write a book. A whole series of them, in fact."

The detective laughed. "Maybe a photo book?"

"Maybe," Nick said with a smile.

"Okay, how about the photos you just took? Can you put them up on the screen?"

Nick hooked up us camera to his laptop and projected them there.

"Stop. Stop. Back one," the detective said. "There."

Just visible in one of the shots was a single hair. "I hope that belongs to the killer, not Miguel," he said.

It was under the seat, next to the syringe. It had to be.

"Tell me more about Ronald," the cop asked Alicia. She went on to explain their relationship and what had happened.

"Well, he may have excuses for his behavior. Even a single hair might be circumstantial, unless he left prints on that syringe."

"Doubtful," the other detective said.

"What if he confessed?" Nick said quietly.

"Why would he do that?" the cop asked.

"He wouldn't, not to you. But he might, to her. Or he might give himself away."

Nick outlined a plan.

"And you could take photos of all this happening?"

"I could."

"Okay. Can we meet here tomorrow morning at ten?"

"Yes," Nick said. "Alicia?"

"Yes. And I'll hang the keys back up and make the call."

"Okay," the detective said. "We just have to hope he takes the bait."

Everyone left. The detectives stopped and collected the hair for evidence from under the seat, using an umbrella to shield themselves.

Nick drove away. He stopped at the guard shack and told him to let the family know not to pick up the victim's car until they heard from Alicia. On the way to dinner, his wipers worked overtime. There was no walking in this downpour. He hoped it would clear in the morning. He hoped Ronald would show up.

He hoped his plan worked, and the man would confess so they could all move on, especially Alicia.

After dinner, he headed to his hotel, sent the photos to the detective, and went to sleep early after sending a quick good night text to Sandra. He'd have to explain this to her later.

He set his alarm before six, and he went right to bed.

But it took him a while to fall asleep.

His alarm woke him from uncomfortable dreams. Up until this point in his life, he'd never dreamed so much, or at least, he hadn't remembered his dreams upon waking.

But as this trip went on, they got worse and worse. They started in Carson City with a headless body. Since then?

Burials, hangings, shootings, human brandings, all kinds of killing.

His little datura-induced trip in Phoenix had made things worse rather than better, at least, as well as he could tell. That was only last week.

Maybe he was just having a bad day. Maybe the sting had affected him in some way. He wondered what bee venom did when it interacted with other substances. If you were on certain medications, were you at higher risk for side effects?

What did it matter?

He wasn't on drugs. *Get a grip, Nick,* he told himself.

First things first. A quick shower. Sunrise photos. Complete the assignment.

Go help the police. Hope for no new gruesome sightings to add to his dreams of giant wasps, drowning, and others.

Keep it simple.

Then, he remembered the night before, and the rain. He opened his hotel curtain slightly.

Clouds, but no rain. Were they breaking up? He couldn't tell. But he had to try.

He dressed quickly after a shower, grabbed his camera bag, some cheap coffee from the carafe in the hotel lobby, and then drove to the capitol grounds.

As he did, the clouds parted further. He could see the remnants of a waning crescent moon peeking through the clouds.

He set up his tripod this time, in a place where he could face either slightly southeast or slightly southwest, and still have "The Round-house" in his viewfinder.

And he waited. From time to time he would "wake" the camera and look at the little screen.

The light was getting better. He took a couple of shots looking each direction.

Then it happened. The sun peeked over the horizon, pushing through some clouds, and turning the sky spectacular pink, orange, and red. Nick moved quickly, swiveling his camera back and forth, doing his best to capture the entire sky as it changed and evolved. Purples replaced some of the red, the pink got lighter, orange changed to yellow and back again.

These were the money shots. Then he had an idea.

What are you known for, Nick?

Macros.

His website even said it: Macrophotography4u.com.

He lowered the tripod, and moved to his right, so he would be facing southeast. He focused on the Indian Paintbrush, the flower he had been near when he got stung.

He lined up the shot perfectly. Flowers in the foreground, capitol in the middle, sunrise behind that.

Each click of the shutter captured perfection.

He turned to leave, and saw Luis, the groundskeeper. He waved.

"Hey, Nick," the man called him over.

"Yes?" Nick asked, walking toward him.

"Sorry if was grumpy with you a couple of times this week. It's been hot and rough for all of us, but I don't want to send you away from Santa Fe with anything but good vibes. I'm sorry for all your trouble, getting stung and all."

"No worries. Thank you."

"Anytime, really. Here's the local honey I promised you." Luis pushed a small bottle into his hand. "If you're ever back through, look me up."

"I will."

The two shook hands, and Nick walked away feeling lighter. He just had time to grab a light snack before he had to meet the police.

He could only hope Ronald fell for their ruse.

Nick stopped with one cup of coffee. He put a fresh battery in his camera, brought his laptop in case the police wanted anything he had on it, and headed for Apis Labs.

Alicia was inside already, according to plan. The two police detectives from the day before waited in their car under some trees. Nick parked next to them. He didn't know or remember their names and didn't care. He just wanted this to be over.

The faster the better. He'd love to just relax for his last afternoon in Santa Fe before moving on.

Nick put his long lens on his camera but had the bag over his shoulder just in case he needed to switch.

And they waited for the signal. Alicia came out the front doors and walked toward Miguel's car. She hit the unlock button, opened the driver's door, and waited a moment.

It was on. Nick tensed as she raised her cell phone to her ear.

From here, he couldn't hear her, but he knew what she was saying, at least, the gist of it.

The detectives had started to move already, staying low and behind the other parked cars. But there was a huge open space between them and Alicia if Ronald went nuts.

"Ronald, you have to come help me," she'd been coached to say.

He would be concerned.

"I went to Miguel's car to get something for his sister. I sat in the driver's seat, and I think I got stung."

We could only hope for the right response.

She dropped the phone to her side.

Ronald ran out the front door. Nick snapped photo after photo, catching every moment as Ronald sprinted to her. Asked her an inaudible question.

She said something. Pointed to her butt cheek.

Ronald moved her aside, and opened the back door, bent down, and looked under the driver's seat.

We had him.

Alicia ran for the front door of the building. Ronald stood and yelled.

Nick walked rapidly forward, adjusting his camera lens and still taking photos as he went.

Two officers appeared, rushed forward, told Ronald to hold still. One officer pulled his weapon.

Ronald looked at Alicia, and then right at Nick.

Then he screamed, not words, just a primal, angry scream. Nick stepped back, lowered his camera and stared.

One of the police officers grabbed at him, but Ronald twisted away, and ran towards Alicia.

Nick paused, and then ran to intercept him.

It didn't matter. Alicia met her potential assailant herself. She struck out with some kind of punch, Ronald spun and reached for her, and in some judo move Nick only glimpsed, she tossed him over her hip, and he landed on the pavement, hard.

He simply laid there.

A moment later, Nick joined the cops, who turned the fallen man over and cuffed him.

"Well, that was fun," Alicia said. "He's had that coming for a long time."

13

____

MOVING ON

"**I** was looking for the wasp that stung her," Ronald said.

"Under the seat?" the first detective, the larger of the two, asked.

"I thought maybe it fell back there, since I didn't see it right away on the driver's seat."

Everyone but the smaller detective sat in the conference room in Apis Labs. He was out, carefully removing the device from the car. Nick was listening as he transferred the photos he'd taken of the trap to a memory stick the police had provided. They said he might be called back to testify, but he hoped not.

Mysteries had interfered enough with his assignment already. He didn't want to have to explain that one to Emily.

"Well, that's a convenient excuse, but it sure looks like you knew something was under the seat."

Just then the smaller officer walked in carrying the device from under the seat in a bag.

"It's a clever device," he told his partner.

Nick studied it. The syringe in the center still had liquid in it. The detective had capped the needle so it wouldn't poke through the evidence bag.

"I wonder what's in that syringe?" the larger detective said.

"I can tell you really quickly," Alicia said. "If you'll let me test it for you."

The detectives looked at each other. "How much of it do you need?"

"Just a little bit," she said. "Less than half of what's left."

"Can you test it in front of us? We need to document the chain of evidence."

Ronald shifted uncomfortably. The cops had switched the cuffs so his hands were in front of him, but he looked like he had an itch he wanted to reach but couldn't scratch.

"Do you have something you want to say?" the smaller detective asked.

"I didn't mean to kill him," Ronald said. "I just meant to scare him. I figured if he got stung bad enough, he might quit. Or if the company thought he was allergic, they might let him go."

"What about his EpiPen?" Alicia asked. "It was empty."

"I swapped it out. I figured he would get inside in time, get another one."

"I'm not sure I believe you," the larger officer said.

Nick watched.

"It was an accident," Ronald said.

"That's the story you want to stick to?"

"Yes. And I think I want my lawyer now."

"You can call him when we get to the station."

By then, the photos were done transferring, and Nick handed them the memory stick, and a card with his information on it.

"Hopefully, we won't have to call on you," the officer said. "But if we do, we'll try to give you as much notice as possible."

They left, and Nick was alone with Alicia. He looked at her.

"I'm so sorry about your friend," he said. "And I'm sorry about Ronald, too."

"None of it is your fault, Nick. And he would have gotten away with it without your help. You noticed the wasps."

"I'm not sure how much of a good thing that was."

"Think about it, Nick. If Ronald would kill someone over someone he wouldn't ever have been with anyway, what would he do the next time he was jealous of someone?"

"True."

"Thanks, Nick. For everything. If you're ever in Santa Fe again—"

"I'll look you up," he finished. "And you're welcome."

Nick left and headed back to the hotel. Uploading the sunrise photos, as beautiful as they were, seemed almost anti-climactic, and he needed to talk to someone.

Sandra was the only person who came to mind.

He picked up his phone and called her.

"Hi, Nick," she said. "Are you pretty much done in Santa Fe?"

"Yes," he said. "But I need to tell you something. I just need to talk to someone."

For the next hour, he told her about his involvement in the solution to the mystery and the solution.

"You actually took your idea to the police?"

"Eventually, yeah."

"And they arrested this guy as a result?"

"Yeah." Nick felt bad. He'd told her he would stay out of it, and he'd tried. But he just couldn't leave well enough alone. Not once he knew what he thought to be the truth.

"That's great, Nick," she said quietly.

"Great?" he asked. "Did you say great?"

"I did. Look, I know you don't want to be involved in more mysteries, and I'm happy about that. After the last few places you have been, I totally get it. But this time you did some good. You didn't interfere. You didn't try to be a detective instead of a photographer.

"You didn't even have any help. You solved a crime, one that would have gone unpunished without your help. That's different, Nick. That's good."

He smiled. "Thanks. I needed to hear that."

"I know you did," she said. "I love you, Nick. Even when you do step outside the lines a little bit. I'm proud of what you did."

"I love you, too."

He ended the call, and his phone rang right away. It was Gerry.

"Hey there," he said, his voice cheery. He was feeling much better after talking to Sandra.

"Hey, Nick. Emily is ecstatic. The photos you got in Santa Fe are the best yet. She's very impressed."

"I'm glad. I worked hard at it."

"She says you deserve some kind of bonus."

"That would be nice," he said. "But not necessary. I really am loving what I'm doing."

"How did the rest of the week go for you?"

"Pretty good," he said. "Not a bad week at all."

"No mysteries to unravel, huh?"

Nick hesitated. He thought of Sandra. What she'd said about being proud of him.

"Nothing to speak of," he said.

"Good. Have a safe trip to Austin, Nick."

"It's a long drive," he said. "I'll leave early tomorrow."

"Okay, Nick. Talk to you later."

Nick ended the call and headed out to dinner. He'd turn in early, get a good night's sleep, and start his drive the next day. It wouldn't be the most scenic drive, but if he pushed himself he could make it in a single day.

He looked forward to a week in Austin. He'd heard the music scene there was to die for, and there were a few local bands he would love to see.

SOME FACTS ABOUT SANTA FE

Known as "the Land of Enchantment," the state of New Mexico has used this phrase since 1935 as part of its Tourist Board outreach. The phrase was first used in 1906 in a travel guide, but at that time it was referring to a collection of southwestern states, not just New Mexico.

At an elevation of 7,199 feet, Santa Fe is the highest capital city in the U.S. Next highest is Cheyenne, Wyoming, at 6,062 feet. Denver, Colorado's "Mile High City," comes in third at 5,280 feet.

The state of New Mexico has a population of 2.1 million, and the largest city in the state is Albuquerque with a population of 550,000. The city was made popular by the AMC series Breaking Bad, and there are "Breaking Bad tours" offered in various places throughout the city.

The population of Santa Fe is 85,000, making it the 4th largest city in the state. It covers an area of 37 square miles. The mean average elevation in New Mexico is 5,700 feet, and the lowest point is 2,842 feet above sea level, at the northern end of the Red Bluff Reservoir on the Pecos River.

Santa Fe, founded in 1610 as the capital of Nuevo México, is the oldest state capital in the U.S., even though New Mexico didn't gain statehood until 1912, approximately six weeks before Arizona became the 48th state. The name of the city of Santa Fe means "holy faith" in Spanish, and the city's full name as founded remains La Villa Real de la Santa Fe de San Francisco de Asís ("The Royal Town of the Holy Faith of Saint Francis of Assisi").

The capitol building in Santa Fe, locally known as "The Roundhouse," is the only round state capitol building in the U.S. It is home to multiple sculptures and paintings and showcases just a fraction of the great artwork to be found in Santa Fe.

In fact, there are several outstanding galleries and museums, including the world-famous Georgia O'Keefe Museum, in the city. If only Nick had time to visit them all.

As railroads were built across the nation, it was naturally assumed that the route would go through Santa Fe. When that didn't happen, the city fell into a general population and economic decline for several decades. Artists and tourists who liked the charm and the beauty of the surrounding area began to infiltrate the area, and the city's prominence, slowly, came back to life.

In 2008, New Mexico was the first U.S. state to officially adopt a Navajo textbook for use in public schools.

There are some great sights and activities in and around Santa Fe:

Tent Rocks National Monument (about 40 miles west): Unique formations with tent-like shapes were created from volcanic eruptions more than one million years ago.

Most people don't think of Santa Fe, or even New Mexico, as a grape-growing area. Join a wine-tasting tour of several local vineyards with New Mexico Wine Tours.

The World famous Rodeo de Santa Fe is an annual event drawing top professionals and audiences from around the world. If you're in the area in June, check it out; it's fun for the entire family!

La Cieneguilla Petroglyph Site (about 16 miles west): Pre-Columbian representations of birds, deer, hunters, and even some early Native flute players.

Check out more of what Santa Fe has to offer at its official travel site: https://santafe.org/ .

AUTHOR'S NOTE: WRITING TRAVEL FICTION DURING A PANDEMIC

As of this writing, the world of travel is locked down, and while it is slowly reopening around the world, travel in the United States is still extremely restricted. It's doubtful that a journey like Nick's could actually happen right now.

If you're reading this in some literature or United States history class years from when this actually happened, first I apologize. Try to pay attention. After graduation, when real life starts, you'll long with nostalgia for this time in your life. Or you won't. I have no idea about your situation, and perhaps you, like me, will actually start to thrive and live after graduation.

But I digress.

It is strange writing about travel right now. I'm creating stories as if restaurants are not closed or take-out only, a world where wearing masks in public is neither mandated nor recommended, and where people are going about their lives as if nothing is globally wrong, the economy isn't in a strange state of disaster and recovery simultaneously, and gas is still reasonably expensive because people are actually driving from place to place.

But I feel like I need to. Sure, I could modify the stories not yet written, insert a global pandemic and the obstacles that would present to our photo taking sleuth.

I don't think that's the best idea.

We write fiction and read fiction for a variety of reasons, but one of the chief ones is hope and escape. We step outside of our world, and into one where things are better or even sometimes worse.

But at the end, the bad guys lose, the good guys win, and the journey of life continues, just like Nick's trip around the country.

As we read, and as the story carries us to its inevitable ending, we leave it with hope.

Hope that the virus raging across the world will be contained. Hope for a vaccine. Hope for return to a new normal.

A normal where an ordinary guy, a photographer, travels from state capital to state capital, taking photos, taking in the sights, and solving murders along the way.

For as Nick often says, tomorrow is another day. And in the next city, things will be better.

He hopes. So should we.

AXED IN AUSTIN

BOOK #14

PROLOGUE: AXED

Jared needed a break, and ax throwing seemed like just the thing.

He'd come to Austin to pursue one dream: playing his bass on stage for hundreds of fans. Rock, country, jazz? He could play it all, but rock was his first love, and the music scene on sixth street and the opportunity for session gigs kept him going.

Jared's big advantage when it came to playing bass? His exceptionally large hands. He had reach other players simply didn't have, but fortunately for him, things hadn't started that way. He began playing stand-up bass at the age of seven, sitting with his father, who played guitar, trying to mimic his music and find the strength to push the thinner strings on the kid-sized instrument hard enough to create a note.

He excelled not only in the school band but beyond to community orchestras and a symphony gig by the time he turned twelve. But the hard-hitting, creative bass lines in rock sent him in another direction, and his talent earned him credit everywhere.

That's how he'd come to Austin. And after a long-term relationship with a band mate, and then a shorter one with another bass player, he'd met

Cathy. The Texas native, a full foot shorter than him, and likely half his weight, wore her black hair long, and her green eyes sparkled. A talented audio producer, she played a mean keyboard too.

A long day of work in the studio led them both to the need for a break. No stage, no audience, no performance, just a time of plain fun.

"Ask and you will receive," said the Austin vibe, and lucky for them, a new indoor ax throwing, paintball, and a small flag football field offered them something completely different.

"You have to throw axes," Cathy told him. "It's the best stress relief ever."

Jared held the door for her. "So you've done this before?"

"Of course. The last place was outdoors, up near Fort Hood, and it was hot as blazes, but a blast."

"Are you good?' he asked her.

She snorted. "You'll see."

The blast of the air conditioning hit them as soon as they walked inside, but the building was so vast, it couldn't compete with the Austin heat. In a couple of hours, maybe, it would be more bearable. Giant fans placed strategically throughout the room roared in the distance.

"How far do you think you can throw an ax?" he said to himself, noting that the lanes were around 20 feet long.

"What was that?" Cathy asked.

"It's smaller than I expected."

"It's also harder than it looks."

Jared let the obvious sexual jokes in those lines pass. Cathy was a friend, and although he thought there might be more, and that's really one of the reasons he'd come here with her for this break, he didn't want to be overly crude.

Only a couple of lanes were occupied in the throwing area, but a large man with a long, dark beard stood in one. Jared noted that he used several techniques for throwing. His first toss was one-handed, kind of an overhead thing, and the ax spun several times before hitting the target dead center.

The targets were neatly cut stumps, heavy and thick. And true to form, a red circle filled the center of a bullseye on each of them.

The man retrieved the ax, and his next throw was two-handed, this time starting in the center over his head. Again, the ax embedded in the wood dead center.

"Impressive," Jared said.

"That's the owner," Cathy told him. "We, um, dated for a bit back in high school."

"Oh, yeah?" Jared was only mildly jealous. He was at least as good-looking as this guy, and he kind of owned his own business with the music work he did. He and Cathy were not dating, not yet anyway.

But he'd be damned if the guy would show him up.

Both of them got their passes at the desk and made their way to the lanes. The owner, who introduced himself as Tony, took them through a quick safety briefing. No crossing the line at the front of the lane, no two people throwing at once, and several other small rules. He also demonstrated techniques, including one underhand method that looked interesting.

Jared studied each technique, mentally warming up. Tony assigned them a lane and they found two small throwing axes hanging on a pair of nails beside it.

Cathy started, and her first toss was a bullseye. Dead on.

Jared's first toss was a one-handed, overhand strike. Dead center in the red.

"You're a natural," she said.

He smiled at her. "I try."

Her next throw struck the bullseye. His shot landed barely outside the inner ring, not bad for a noob.

Another couple at the lane next to them was doing well, too. The girl, a shorter woman, used the underhand method with astonishing success. Nearly every shot was a bullseye.

"Nice," Jared told her.

"Thanks," she said.

Jared saw a shadow behind him. The owner had arrived between the two lanes.

"Mind if I join you guys?" he asked. "We could have a contest."

"Sure," the woman said, and Jared nodded. The younger man with her seemed unsure but agreed.

"That could be fun," Cathy said. "Tony, this is my friend, Jared."

Jared took his offered hand and shook.

"Okay. So winner gets a free round of paintball, on me," Tony said. "But if I win, y'all are buying me drinks after I get off work."

"I'll do you one better," Jared said. "You know the concert next Saturday?"

"Eight bands? All-day, with meet and greet times?" Tony asked.

"Yeah. I'll put up two tickets against your paintball experience."

Tony laughed. "You're on. I want to go, and someone else might as well pay." He winked at Cathy.

"Deal." The two men shook hands again. Tony explained the scoring, a method similar to darts.

The contest went back and forth. Tony rarely missed. The under-hand method started to falter for the woman next to them, and she quickly fell in the scoring ranks. Her partner dropped out too after a throw where he strained his shoulder. He glared at both Tony and Jared.

"Jerks," he said, and went to sit down.

Cathy fell behind, too. She seemed a little nervous, and Jared wasn't sure why other than that the competition between him and Tony got pretty heated.

It turned out he had a decent arm, and they stayed neck and neck, score for score. Tony would pull ahead, and then Jared would catch up. Soon a crowd had gathered and sweat poured over Jared's face. His arms shook with every single toss.

"Damn," he said to himself quietly. He wiped his face with his t-shirt.

"It's all tied up," Tony announced loudly. "Whoever scores next, wins. That, of course, means me."

Rather than facing the target, Tony faced Jared. "I don't even have to look," he said.

The ax left his hand and spun, but the handle, not the head, struck the wood. It fell to the floor.

Jared smirked, turned and faced the target, and threw a perfect bullseye. "I win."

Tony spun on his heel without responding. "Give him the tickets," he told the cashier and disappeared into the back.

"What's that all about?" Jared asked.

"He doesn't take losing well. It's one of the reasons we broke up."

"Oh," he said. "Maybe I'll offer him tickets anyway."

"You should. That would be very kind."

The two of them moved to the paintball area. There, they got another demonstration of the face masks, gear, and rules for playing the game, and were advised not to take point-blank shots. Through the entire demo, they didn't see Tony at all.

"It's all in fun," the instructor told them. "No one wants to get hurt out here tonight."

Once they put on goggles and masks, nearly everyone looked the same.

"Catch me if you can," Cathy said and ran into the darkness.

The area was lined with hay bales, wooden walls, and obstacles. The overhead lighting was much like that in a stadium, creating a lot of shadows and providing natural hiding spaces. Jared ran forward and then slowed, moving with caution from obstacle to obstacle. A would-be shooter popped out from behind a barrier, but Jared saw him, raised his rifle, and shot first. A blue dot appeared on the man's chest, he swore and ran away.

This was going to be fun.

The aisle widened as he went, narrowing at the back of the course. Another smaller figure, one he thought might be Cathy, fired at him and missed. He fired back and missed as well.

By the time he reached the third turn in what was apparently a maze, he'd shot and taken out three people, and been shot at four times by people who missed, one quite narrowly.

From behind, he heard someone clear their throat.

He turned. A paintball rifle was pointed at him from maybe ten yards away. The barrel lowered, and the person fired a paintball at his feet. It was dark, and he could only make out a vague shape. The shot just missed, clearly on purpose.

"What the hell?" he said and raised his own rifle to fire back.

The figure ran at him.

"Come get me, then," Jared said, turned, and fled.

He dodged a couple of shots, one at his feet again, but the person chasing him was likely missing for a reason. He could have been shot in the back any number of times. This was a different game.

He glimpsed other figures around him. Some watched him run by, apparently enjoying the show the chase produced. A few cheered.

"Get him!"

"Run! You got this!"

The conflicting cries sounded, but fairly quickly Jared couldn't hear them over his own breathing, air rasping in and out of his lungs. They burned, and his arms, already tired from ax throwing, ached from the simple act of carrying a paintball gun at a full sprint.

He wanted to turn, to give up, and just let the person shoot him. But something felt more sinister than a simple paintball game. It felt--wrong.

Jared lost track of where he was. Soon, the shouting of the other players seemed far away. This place looked huge on the outside, but now it felt even larger.

It was time to end this, one way or another.

Jared stopped abruptly and turned, standing right under one of the stadium-like lights. He raised his rifle. Shoot, or be shot, either way, he was done running.

He moved to pull the trigger, hesitated, and then looked, or rather studied the person following him. The shape looked vaguely familiar.

"Hey--"

An ax spun out of the darkness. Jared felt it strike his arm, and he tried to roar in pain. A scream escaped his lips instead. The ax stuck, embedded in his bone.

He reached for the handle, or tried to, and then heard the soft whistle of air passing over metal.

A second ax struck his other shoulder and lodged there. Warm liquid seeped under his paintball armor. His vision clouded, cleared, and clouded again. He fell and heard a thud as his head hit the ground.

His eyes closed. He was suddenly tired. More tired than he had ever been.

He couldn't hear anymore, but the light overhead seemed to get brighter and brighter. Jared floated toward it. The closer he got, the fainter the pain got. So he let himself go until he became a part of it.

And then there was nothing.

COMING IN HOT

The simplest word to describe Austin was the same one Nick had used to describe Phoenix. Hot. Lubbock had been warm, even early in the morning. The journey would normally have taken him six hours, but Nick had stopped a few times on the way to take various photos, and he regretted that decision now. The mid-afternoon temps were well into the triple digits.

He opened the door of his car, never more thankful for the fixes to his AC that had happened in Boise what seemed like an eternity ago, but in reality only a couple of short months before. So many things had happened since then: he'd traveled through eight different state capitals, taken some amazing photos, helped local officials solve murders, and even been a witness in two cases.

The word exhausted came to mind, but it was more than physical tiredness. His reaction to being stung by a bee in Santa Fe, New Mexico had certainly taken a physical toll, but that was not the only one. That sting had led him into yet another mystery, and he was emotionally exhausted too. It was one aspect of travel no one liked to talk about, but he was discovering first hand.

It would make an interesting post for his blog, a great story later on, and even perhaps his own series of books about his adventures to go with the giant coffee table book being created by *Travel USA* magazine. And in his travels to Austin, he intended to focus on just that.

His real assignment had nothing to do with murder or any crime-solving at all. His friend Gerri, the social media manager for the magazine, had recommended him for this assignment, one where he would travel to every single state capital in a single year. He was to capture the capitol building and surrounding areas in each, giving readers of the planned edition a glimpse into the heart of every city.

That did not include the police department, murder, crime, or the underbelly of the cities. Instead, it was to inspire people to travel to these fabulous capitals. It was something he thought he had been doing well, and Emily, the head editor on the project, seemed pleased overall, although unhappy about his extracurricular activities.

He pulled his six-foot-six frame from his car, stood, and stretched for the sky. His height and his bright red curly hair made it hard for him to remain anonymous, and news of his exploits and travels often preceded him. His route wasn't public anywhere, but it was pretty easy for anyone thinking clearly about what he was trying to accomplish to determine his next logical step.

And his timeline only gave him a week in each location, meaning he had to stay on track in order to accomplish his task. He'd almost missed dead-lines only a couple of times, but that was due to his work ethic, not the ease of the assignment.

He sighed, wiped the sweat from his face, and headed inside. Air conditioning hit him in the face, and he shivered with the change in tempera-ture. The woman behind the desk stood, and he found he was nearly eye to eye with her.

"Hi there," he said. "I-um-I'm Nick O'Flannigan, and I have a reservation."

"The Nick O'Flannigan," the woman said. Her brown eyes sparkled, and her milk-chocolate skin glowed. She extended a large hand, and he shook it.

"I've been looking forward to your visit. Boston College, right?"

Nick nodded, feeling the familiar ache in his right leg as he did so. He was most often recognized now as a photographer, not as the college star and NBA candidate he once was.

"Yes, ma'am," he said awkwardly.

"Injured against Georgia Tech. Shame. You would've made a great NBA player. You ever play now?"

"Uh, no. Not much. Now I stick to bike riding." Nick felt awkward saying that. He'd only recently rediscovered bicycling in Helena, Montana, but he was unsure what else to say.

"Running and jumping are hard?" she asked.

"Yep. Did you ever--?" Nick felt silly asking and didn't finish the question. So she was tall for a woman. That didn't make her a ballplayer.

"I did," she said with a smile. I was WNBA bound. I tore all the ligaments in my knee my junior year."

"Oh, man. I am sorry to hear that."

"It's okay. I had a backup plan. Hospitality and hotel management. It's paid off with a great career. I referee kids' games from time to time."

"Sounds fun," Nick said. He'd never thought of refereeing games before. "My backup plan was accounting, but I accidentally fell into this photography career, and it stuck."

"Macro stuff, mostly, right?"

"Pretty much. Although my current assignment is a little different than that."

"Loving it?"

"Most of the time," he told her. "There are challenges I didn't anticipate."

"That's usually the way it is. Let me get you checked in."

She tapped a few keys on a keyboard and smiled at him. "I'll also be happy to upgrade your room to a suite, with a kitchenette. Although I don't recommend you cook here unless maybe you want an early break-fast. There are two things you can't miss in Austin."

"What are those?"

"The food and the music."

"Ha!" he said. "I have been looking forward to exploring the music scene."

"There are some other cool things, too," she said. "Here's a brochure, and I would be happy to serve as your guide if need be."

"Sure," he said, glancing at her left hand. There was a ring on her finger, and he breathed a sigh of relief. His long-distance girlfriend, Sandra, who he'd met in Salem and kept in touch with, was a source of stability on this trip. She'd even come to see him in Denver and had plans to visit him again. That relationship was important to hm, and he didn't want to mess it up.

"Here's a brochure. There's a list of bands online who are playing this week. There is one really good jazz band playing down on sixth street."

"Oh yeah?" he said. "I love jazz."

"I read that about you. Why don't you bring your camera and check them out? I can get you backstage. My husband is the drummer. And, well--"

She handed him a card. "Sonja Robbins," it said. "Lead singer, Sonja and the Dropouts."

Nick looked at the card and up at her. "You sing?"

"I play sax, too," she said. "I'd love to hear what you think."

"You're playing tonight?"

"Yep. And it's usually not as crowded on Sunday nights."

"I'll be there," Nick said.

"I look forward to it," she said with a smile.

Nick took his keycard from her hand even though the locks at the hotel were new and would allow him to open the door with his phone and a Bluetooth connection.

By the time he reached his room, he was no longer sweating. He tossed his bag onto the provided suitcase stand, put his camera bag on the desk, and drew a cup of water from the kitchenette faucet. The bed was large and looked comfortable.

He set the brochure on the desk and pulled out his phone. He should make a couple of calls.

He started with Sandra, his girlfriend.

She picked up on the first ring. "Nick, hey! How was the trip?"

"It was good. No bees in the car, no tickets, just heat."

"I bet. Austin isn't known for their mild climate."

"Well, the state of Texas, really. They do have a great music scene here."

"For sure," she said. "I'm actually a bit jealous. Tell me you are going to Franklin's?"

"Wouldn't miss it," he said. The world-famous barbecue joint was top on his list for food, although it was closed for the day, and since the restaurant was closed on Monday as well, he would have to put off his visit until Tuesday.

"I expect a full report, and photos."

"You know it. How are you?"

"The same. Nothing new here. I miss you, Nick. Your life is pretty exciting right now."

"It is. I almost wish I had more downtime, more dull moments, you know." He flipped open the brochure and saw something new to him. An Ax Throwing and Paintball course. Now that looked fun.

"I understand," she said. "I am so excited to come visit and join you soon."

"Me, too. We need to plan for it."

"I hear that. I love you, Nick. Stay safe and focused."

"I will. I think Austin has plenty to do. If I stay busy, I can't get distracted by any mysteries."

"True."

"I love you, too, Sandra."

The call ended, and Nick sighed. Loneliness was another side effect of this type of lifestyle.

But it was only for a year. He could do anything for a year.

He hit the remote for the television and unpacked so he could take a quick shower before dinner and heading down to hear some music. He couldn't wait.

"An unfortunate death has a new Austin business temporarily closed," the newscaster said. "A young man died last night on the paintball course at the just-opened House of Axe. The police are not releasing details, other than at this time, the death is being treated as a homicide."

Nick sighed. Maybe he would skip that attraction after all. "Jared Martin was a session bass player, well known on the Austin music scene," the anchor continued. "He will be missed by many."

"What a tragedy," Nick said aloud. "I wonder if Sonja knew him."

He figured he would ask when he saw her later and offer his condolences.

In the meantime, he needed to clean up and find some food. Not everything would be closed on Sunday night. Would it?

He hoped not. His stomach growled as he headed for the bathroom, and he decided to make the shower a quick one.

2

HIGH NOTE

Τ he smell hit him first.

The venue for the evening, The Culinary Dropout, closed at nine on Sundays, as did many of the restaurants on the strip.

The food looked amazing. The kitchen area was visible when he peered over the bar and Nick saw one cook, a tall young man with a purple mohawk. A chef's hat was perched expertly on top of, and somehow attached to, the spiked hair.

From above, he heard the thump of a bass and the gentle sound of sax drifting down the stairs.

He stepped up to the bar, ordered the Revolver Brewing "Blood and Honey" in a can, the Brussel sprouts appetizer, and a pub burger.

"Headed upstairs?" the bartender asked. He looked up at Nick like nearly everyone did. He wore a band t-shirt, one sporting a saxophone, drums, and a stand-up bass. His hair was shaved on the sides, spiked on the top, and his ears carried oversized studs.

"Yep," Nick said.

"We'll bring your grub up when it's ready. And if you need another brew, a waiter will be around."

"How's the band?" Nick asked out of curiosity.

"Well, I'm a jazz fan myself, so I love them. We get a lot of rock gigs in here, but these guys are my favorite."

"I'm sure I will love them, too."

As he mounted the stairs, shifting his camera bag on his shoulder, the saxophone trilled off, followed by light applause.

"We're going to take a break," he heard a familiar voice say. "But we'll be back in a jiffy."

Nick took the last few steps quickly, hoping to catch Sonja before she left the stage.

When he reached the top of the stairs, he saw her mingling with the crowd, and she waved to him. A man stood behind her. He was tall, but not as tall as she was unless you counted his hair, which puffed out in a large afro. Another shorter, but not much smaller man stood behind him, and stuffed two drumsticks into his back pocket as Nick watched.

The loft area was small, with maybe a dozen tables spaced out with capacity for more if need be. Most of them were full, and Nick found a spot at one near the middle of the room. He set his beer on the table and slid his camera bag from his shoulder as he turned.

"Hi, Nick!" Sonja said and shook his hand. "You came!"

"Well, of course," he said. "What I heard sounded great."

"Just you wait," the man with the large afro said with a booming voice. "Her finale is still coming."

"Oh, stop," she said, turning to him. "Go get us some drinks, would you?"

The man scoffed at her, and headed to flag down the waiter. Sonja turned back to him and gestured to the man Nick guessed to be the drummer. "Dwayne, meet Nick. Nick, meet my husband Dwayne."

Dwayne looked up at him, and Nick shook his offered hand. Sonja's husband wore a gray shirt, a blue bow tie, and a short black jacket covering his broad shoulders. He had a firm grip. His hair appeared to be trimmed closely under the fedora perched on his scalp.

"Pleased to meet you. You the basketball fella she keeps going on about?"

"I suppose," Nick answered. "Basketball fella turned photographer."

"That's swell, man."

"It's good to live your dreams," he said. Not that this was exactly his dream, but he wasn't going to explain how even the best assignment was still work. He was certain a musician understood that.

"Indeed. Shall we?" Dwane gestured at the chairs around the table.

"Sure," Nick answered.

Sonja sat too, and just as she opened her mouth to speak, a man came up behind her and cleared his throat. She turned.

"Hey, Sonja," he said. "Just wanted to say I was sorry to hear about Jared."

"Me, too, Stan," she said. The man who had interrupted them was thin, tall, and pale. His hair was black, but looked dyed, not natural. It was slicked to one side, held in place by some kind of gel. His eyes were close together, guarding a sharp and long nose underlined by a thin-lipped mouth.

"Will we see you at the funeral? Due to the circumstances, it won't be for a couple of weeks at least."

"Not sure I would be welcome," she said quietly. Dwayne stared down at his hands, folded on the table.

"Don't be ridiculous," Stan said. "Of course you would be."

"I'll think about it," Sonja said.

"Fair enough, I'll keep in touch," Stan said and walked away.

Sonja wiped her eyes. "Sorry about that Nick. A former bandmate passed away this weekend, suddenly."

"Not the one who was killed at the ax throwing and paintball place?"

"Yeah. How did you hear about that?"

"The news," Nick said.

"Yes. It is too bad. I left the group under less than ideal circumstances, but Jared was a friend."

"I imagine most of those in the music scene are pretty close," Nick said.

"Yeah. It's a small scene. Jared moved on to playing more rock than jazz. But he was doing well for himself."

"Enough talk of that," Dwayne said. He seemed troubled, but Nick couldn't put his finger on why. He felt there was more to the story than he was being told but didn't want to pry. "Let's hear about this assignment you are on."

Nick took a few moments to explain his trip, his route across the country, and his assignment to photograph every single state capital and capitol building in under a year.

"That sounds amazing," Dwayne said. "And exhausting."

"It is that," Nick said. "It's fun, but sometimes I miss home, you know?"

"I hear that. I did the touring thing for a bit, and we may do it again at some point, but it always felt good to be back home."

By that time, the other band member had returned, the bass player, and Sonja introduced him. "Griffin, this is Nick. Nick, Griffin."

"Do you only play covers, or do you have some original stuff?"

"We have some originals," Sonja said. "Dwane is a songwriter too."

"Aspiring songwriter. I haven't written anything great yet."

"Sure you have. Can we trouble you for something, Nick?" Sonja asked. "We'll pay you, of course."

"Sure."

"Can you get some photos of the band in action? You know, some shots of us performing."

"I did bring my camera," Nick pointed.

"That's wonderful. We also have another show this week. Wednesday, at the Roosevelt Room. It's a decent venue. We could get you tickets, VIP passes, whatever you need."

"That would be great!" Nick said. He'd already scouted a few places to try the famous Austin barbecue, but he wanted to try some other things and see some live music, too. The Roosevelt Room would be a perfect spot.

"Okay. Let us know what you think a fair rate will be. Dwayne will work it out for you."

"Thanks so much," he said. "Will do. I'll take some setup shots tonight and see if you like them."

"Perfect," Sonja said. "We need to get back on stage. If I don't see you after the show, I'll see you at the hotel tomorrow afternoon."

"Sounds good."

The band took the stage, and Nick took his camera from the bag. He took some shots from his seat, but then stood, and moved to one side of the platform. He didn't want to block anyone's view, so he knelt, hearing his knee pop as he focused and clicked the shutter over and over.

First, he got a great shot of the bass player, his hands striking the strings in mid-note. Then he caught Dwayne, his drumstick hovering over one of the cymbals.

He got several shots from that spot, even what he thought was an excellent one of Sonja singing.

Her voice was haunting, sultry and strong. It slid from note to note, and then, as Nick was moving to the other side of the stage for some more photos, she put the saxophone to her lips.

For a few moments, Nick forgot where he was. He forgot his camera, his trip, and the world around him. Note after note of the melody carried him away to another place and time.

Slowly he raised his camera as he came back to reality and took several photos from different angles of the tall, beautiful woman treating her instrument as an extension of herself and her fingers. He was mesmerized. The band was good, but Sonja was the star and the driving force behind it.

Nick found himself smiling as the song ended, and he applauded.

He looked back at his table to see his meal had arrived, and he went back to finally eat. The food was delicious, still warm, and the beer paired with it perfectly.

He polished off the appetizer and the burger as the band played a few more songs. He snapped a couple more photos from his seat, and when he finished his meal, he paid careful attention to what they were doing. The set was cleverly constructed to be an emotional roller coaster.

Each song flowed together, one upbeat and quick, the next slow and melodious. He recognized some of the tunes, but others that seemed familiar to the crowd were brand new to him.

Finally, as closing time approached, the band played one final song. It ended with a really high note on the sax, and a haunting drumroll.

The crowd, now smaller, erupted in applause. As the band packed up, the crowd dispersed, and Nick approached the stage.

"You guys were amazing," he told them.

"Thanks," Sonja said.

"I got some photos. I will go through them and show them to you tomorrow afternoon, okay?"

"Sure. Sounds good."

"Thanks, Nick," Dwayne said. "We do appreciate it."

"My pleasure."

Nick packed up his camera and headed down the stairs and outside. As he did, he checked his phone.

There was a text from Sandra. "How is the evening going?" it said.

Nick pushed the button to call her. He couldn't wait to tell her about the band and the job taking photos of them.

Just before she picked up, he thought of Jared, the man who had been killed.

There was more to the story. He was sure the police were handling it. Still, he was curious about the man's connection with Sonja, and Dwayne's reaction.

Stay out of it Nick and focus on your job. You now have two this week. Isn't that enough?

He decided it was. Sandra picked up and he told her about the show, and they talked as he drove back to the hotel. He ended the call as he entered the parking lot with a simple, "I love you."

It was nearly ten by the time he arrived, and Nick wanted to scout the capitol and get some photos the next morning. He would need to move the band photos off his camera first, so he didn't mix them with the ones for the magazine.

Then he got an idea. He could kill two birds with one stone. He'd run it by Sonja the next day.

His head hit the pillow, and he dreamed of his days of playing basketball for the first time in a long time.

3

PICTURE THIS

Nick woke Monday morning, and made a quick cup of coffee. It was mediocre, one of those packets everyone gets in a hotel room, but it could have been worse. He wanted to get his photos of the band uploaded before he headed out for breakfast or anything else.

His computer took a bit of time to load, and he remembered the trouble he'd had with it earlier on the trip. It might be time for a new one, and he had been eyeballing the new MacBook. Maybe if he made enough from the photos of the band, and threw it in with some of his savings, he could purchase one.

Once the home screen loaded, he logged in and set about moving the band photos from the night before to his hard drive in a folder named "Sonja". He did not want to make the mistake he had in previous cities, uploading these photos to the magazine cloud folder rather than his own.

It took him a bit longer than he thought, as he couldn't resist making some edits as he went. He emailed a few samples to the band and then headed for the lobby, hungry for breakfast. When he exited the hotel, he realized again the thing Austin had in common with Phoenix. It was hot already.

As soon as he walked out the door, he wanted to find food and get back into some air conditioning. He checked his phone and saw a restaurant, Forthright, not far away and close to the Colorado River. It still astounded him that the same river that ran through the Grand Canyon he'd seen just a couple of weeks before also cut through Austin.

It would be a great opportunity to get some photos before focusing on his assignment.

Focusing on his assignment. He cracked himself up.

Either that, or he was losing it with all this alone time on the road. He hoped for the former. He glanced around and saw a few bikes locked in various places, but no Green Bike program like others he'd encountered. A quick Google search revealed a bike rental company that would deliver bikes to you within a certain area. Nick's hotel was within that area, and the rates looked reasonable. He set a reminder to call them after breakfast.

In the meantime, he walked in the general direction of the restaurant. The cafe was down a side street and contained in the bottom floor of a tall building. Nick took a photo from a distance, and one looking up. There was some construction happening out front and one of the workers waved at him.

Nick didn't recognize the man, but perhaps he was simply being friendly. Of course, the longer he traveled the more often people recognized him in each city. He wouldn't call those people fans, although some clearly were. But he was well-known.

The staff was upbeat, smiling as they brought him coffee and something they called a Forthright Benedict. The hollandaise was perfect, just a little tangy but not overly so. It topped perfectly cooked eggs and house biscuits that were to die for.

So little time in each city, Nick thought. *I would love to come back for the biscuits and gravy.*

In smaller places, he had repeated various restaurants, but there was so much to see and do in Austin. He knew he had to try Franklin's Barbecue, an Austin culinary institution, and knew the lines there could be quite long for even a single taste of their famous food.

As he finished his meal, he looked them up on his phone. He saw an option to order ahead to go, provided he selected his chosen food early enough. The quantities were pretty large though.

Why not share? he thought. *I would bet Sonja and the band would help me eat a few pounds of beef.*

He checked the time and decided he would call her later or simply mention it to her at the hotel. It was only Monday. He had plenty of time.

Nick walked to the end of Brazos street and found a green belt area next to the river. It was warm, but a few trees provided shade. He stepped off the path, got close to the shore, and took some photos of the Congress Bridge spanning the river. It was early, he could hit the capitol building in the afternoon and take some interior shots first, so he walked toward the bridge, intending to take some photos of the river despite the heat.

There were few pedestrians this time of day, but all of them seemed friendly. The view from the bridge was different. Both sides of the river were green with vegetation, but large buildings rose on either side, just beyond the water. As he walked across, several cyclists passed him, and the slight ache in his leg made him wish he had one.

As he had the thought, the reminder on his phone dinged, and he called the Austin Bike Rental company he'd found.

"Bike rentals, can I help you?" the voice on the other end said.

"Sure," Nick said. "I'm in town for the week and would love to rent a bike while I am here."

"Perfect. Where are you staying?"

Nick gave him the address of his hotel.

"We can deliver there, or we can meet you if you like."

"Meet me?"

"Sure, if you are out and about."

"Well, I am headed to the capitol building next. Will that work?"

"Sure," the man said. "I'll need your credit card information. I assume you need a helmet rental, too?"

"Yes, I do," Nick said. "Thanks."

"I'll bring a few for you to try. How tall are you?"

"Six-six."

"Whoa. Okay, I have a cruiser that will fit you well. How long do you think before you are at the capitol?"

Nick debated. He could take an Uber from here or walk. A quick check of his phone showed it was under a mile away, and right on Congress Avenue.

"About 20 minutes," he said.

"Okay, see you in a few. I'll be in the blue van with our logo on it."

"Excellent," Nick said.

He walked along Congress Avenue, occasionally stopping to snap a photo, but not dawdling too much. He didn't want to leave his bike rental guy waiting.

The capitol was framed in the center of the street, and it reminded him a lot of the one in Boise, at least from a distance. A blue and yellow bus went by, the words FlyRides.com on the side. "Party bus," it stated underneath.

Nick smiled again. While the day started out warm, it wasn't as hot as he thought. The shade trees along the sidewalk combined with the shade of the buildings sheltered him from the direct sun, although the pavement was warm under his feet.

He took a deep breath. The air was clean, fresh, and dry. Austin got little in the way of rain, and it looked like this week would be no exception. When he reached the capitol grounds, he saw there was indeed a blue van with the words Bike Rentals painted in large letters on the side.

"Thanks for doing this," he said.

"No sweat, it's my job." The man wore a blue shirt nearly the same color as the van with a white name tag with red lettering that said "Rod." Broad-shouldered, he was shorter than Nick but not by much.

Nick threw his leg over the bike at Rod's instruction, and the man took out a pocket tool with various-sized Allen wrenches. He made some adjustments, and Nick took a few quick pedals up and down the street.

"That feels great," Nick said.

"What are you doing here in Austin?" Rod asked, pointing to his camera.

"I'm a freelancer, on assignment to photograph all the state capitol buildings in a single year for *Travel USA* magazine."

"That sounds fantastic," he said. "Are you taking in the sights, too?"

"Yep, and the music scene and the barbecue."

"We have a new attraction," Rod said. "Paintball and ax throwing. I bet you would love it. My brother works there. It's called "House of Axe.' I have a coupon here somewhere."

Rod pulled a card from his pocket. "I probably would," Nick said, looking at the name. "Isn't this where..."

"Yeah," Rod sighed. "There was a murder the other night. Things have been pretty slow this week as a result."

"Do the police have any clues?" Nick asked.

Rod shrugged. "If they do, they aren't saying. The guy was some local musician, but they finished whatever they were doing with the crime scene and okayed the place to open again."

"I may check it out. I have some new, local friends who might enjoy it too."

"You know people in Austin?"

"Well, I met Sonja and the Dropouts the other night."

"Wait, what?"

"Yeah. I took some photos for them, and we will probably get together later in the week."

"You think they would go ax-throwing with you?"

Nick shrugged. "I could ask."

"Hang on a sec." Rod pulled out his phone and stepped a few feet away. Nick could hear him talking excitedly.

Nick saw a parking enforcement officer eyeing the van parked with its flashers on, but he simply waved.

Rod came back a second later. "I talked to my brother. His boss says if you bring Sonja and her band and take photos of them while they are at his place, he'll give you your admission for free, and he'll pay you for them."

"That sounds great!" Nick said, wondering if it was a good idea after all. Taking Sonja and her band to the scene of the crime where their friend had been killed seemed less than ideal.

"I've got another idea, too. Would it be okay if I gave them a call myself?"

"Sure. The number is on the card I gave you. Tell them Rod sent you, and you're the photographer guy."

"Thanks," Nick said, just as the parking enforcement officer started walking their way. "I'll be in touch."

Rod handed him a lock, told him the code, and after making sure Nick had it right, got in the van and drove away. The parking enforcement officer scowled, and crossed the street, checking a hand-held device, apparently to make sure the meters were all paid.

Like many of the other capitol buildings, there was a park surrounding this one. Nick mounted the bike and rode to the east, surveying various photo angles.

On one side of the capitol were the state archives and the library building. He locked the bike to an upside-down, u-shaped rack there, and walked toward the capitol building, snapping photos as he went.

As he approached the north side, he saw something he'd only read about. The state had needed some more room for offices but didn't want to block the view of the capitol, so they had built an addition to the building underground.

The four-story extension included some skylights, which Nick loved. He stopped to take photos of them and walked a little further north. It was there he encountered the inverted rotunda.

He looked down into the circular structure, able to see the first couple of stories and a single, lone star in the center of the round floor below.

He made his way around the outside, snapping several photos from different positions along the railing.

Sweat beaded on his forehead. There was no shade here and no clouds in the sky at all.

So much for interior photos, he thought to himself. Once he'd taken all the photos he thought he would need in that area, at least in daylight, he continued to move around the outside of the building.

Before long, he found himself hungry and in need of some water, so headed back to where he had parked the bike.

He located Cafe Divine, a nearby lunch spot, checked to be sure they were open, and unlocked his bike for the short ride.

As he arrived and locked his bike to a rack nearby, he noted the reason for the name of the cafe.

St. David's Episcopal church was mere feet away. The building was gorgeous, a stone monstrosity clearly older than the other buildings around it. Stained glass windows doubled as the eyes to the soul of the building, and Nick decided to stay and take some photos once he'd satisfied his hunger. It was a great accidental find.

As Nick entered the restaurant, mouth watering, his phone rang. It was a Texas number, and he stepped back outside and answered.

"This is Nick," he said.

"Nick, it's Sonja." The singer sounded out of breath.

"Are you okay?" Nick asked.

"Not really," she said. "Jared's brother has been arrested."

"Jared? The musician who was killed? What for?"

"Murder. I know Phillip well, and he didn't do this. I hate to ask, but you've helped with other investigations in your travels. Do you think you could look into things and maybe help him?"

"I'm not sure how I can, but we can talk about it," Nick said cautiously.

"Great. Where are you?"

"Cafe Divine, grabbing some lunch."

"Is it okay if I meet you?"

"Sure," Nick said, not sure at all.

"Okay. Go ahead and order. I will be there in a few."

Nick shook his head and went back inside.

What are you getting yourself into?

But he already knew, and even with as busy a week as he had, he was almost glad for the distraction of yet another mystery.

4

———————

CHOPPED

Nick ate quickly. He wanted to talk with Sonja for as short a time as he could, get back to his assignment, and make plans for the rest of the week. He didn't know Jared's brother, Phillip, and although he wanted to take Sonja's word for it, he'd found on this trip that not everyone was who they appeared to be.

He thought of Harry and his precarious acquaintanceship with a killer in Helena. He found himself strangely moved by the memory. Not everything in the world was black and white, and Harry had been one example of that.

When he finished eating, he took out the card for the House of Axe Rod had given him. Maybe he could go take a look around himself without the band, at least at first. It would be hard to stay incognito, so to speak, but he could use the excuse of figuring out where the best place to take shots of the band would be.

Meantime, he could follow up with his other thoughts on getting band photos and sticking with his assignment. As he finished the thought, Sonja walked in.

It was clear she had been crying, as the makeup around her eyes had run onto her cheeks.

"Over here," Nick waved, and she headed his way. She smiled when she saw him.

"Thanks for letting me meet you."

"Well, let me start by saying that I don't know what I can do. In the past, I have either seen photos, videos, or other items where I spotted clues others might not have. I don't really have access to any of that here unless there are some photos the paper hasn't yet published. I can go to the crime scene, sort of, but it has probably been pretty well scoured by the police."

"I know, Nick. Can you try? Maybe ask around, and see what you can find out?"

"I suppose," Nick said. "I just don't want to make any promises I can't keep or get your hopes up."

"No worries at all," she said.

"May I ask you something?"

"Sure," she answered.

Nick paused. He wasn't sure how he wanted to ask what he wanted to know, other than straight out, hoping it would not be too offensive.

"What is your interest in this?" he asked. "I mean, I know you knew Jared, but..."

Sonja stayed silent for a moment, staring off into space. Then she looked at him and their eyes met. "Jared and I were bandmates, but we were more than that," she said. "We dated for a long time. The reason I left the band was because of our breakup."

"I see."

"Do you? We were talking about marriage. I met his family. Then a new bass player came along, and that was the end of all of that."

"That sounds painful," Nick said.

"It was. It took me a while to trust Dwayne. But even with the way Jared treated me in the end, I still cared for him as a person. A little while later, the bass player left him, the band, and Austin. But Phillip--well, he wouldn't hurt anyone."

"Why would the police think he did it then?"

"Well, he and Jared had quite a rivalry. You know, brothers."

"A violent one?"

"They fought sometimes, sure. But they always made up afterward."

"What did they fight over?"

"Are you sure you are not a policeman or a detective?" she asked.

"No. Sorry. I'm just trying to understand before I go snooping around where I don't belong."

"Well, I don't know what they fought over. It was often something silly. And Jared was bigger than his brother, and usually won."

"Okay." To himself, Nick thought, *an ax would make an ideal equalizer if Phillip was sick of losing.* "I'll look into it, but I make no promises."

"That's great. I do appreciate you."

"On something off-topic," Nick said. "I had some ideas for band photos for you. How about some at the capitol building, outside on the grounds?"

"Let me talk to the guys. It sounds like a good idea. Listen, I have to head to work, and I work tomorrow night at the hotel too. Then the gig Wednesday I told you about, but maybe we can take photos before that."

The change in subject seemed to calm her, and Nick was glad. He wanted to help her in some ways, but a nagging feeling in the pit of his stomach told him this was a really bad idea.

I'll just go to House of Axe. Take some photos. Tell her I found nothing, and go from there, he thought. *No big deal.*

"Sounds good," he said out loud. "Maybe I will go ax-throwing tonight and see what I can find."

"Thanks, Nick. That makes me feel better."

Sonja got up, Nick paid the bill and followed, his camera bag over his shoulder. He stopped to check on his rental bike.

"This is yours? I thought you drove in?"

"I did. I took up biking in Helena a bit, and it helps my leg," he said. "I'm in better shape, but it is easier on my joints than walking or running."

"You did mention bike riding," she said. "It's a great way to get around the city, and saves you on parking, too."

"Indeed," Nick said. "I'm going to stick around and take some photos of the church for my own collection and some for the magazine too. I'll catch up with you later."

"Sure thing," she said and walked off the other direction.

Nick watched her go and then turned his attention to the church. He walked around the block to get a better view and took a few photos of the exterior from farther away before moving in closer to capture some macro shots.

He focused on a few flowers, some of the intricate stonework that made interesting designs and went inside. There were a few tourists, and he mingled with them, taking photos when he could. He took out his phone and snapped a couple pictures with it and posted them to Instagram using a few Austin hashtags with a status promising more to come.

He exited the building. The day had gotten even warmer, and he checked his map. It would be an easy ride back to the hotel, where he could upload photos, set up his ax throwing appointment, and catch dinner once he was hungry again.

He pedaled down the streets, keeping to the side on the many without dedicated bike lanes. Most drivers were courteous, and the shade of the buildings and trees kept him from sweating too badly.

He arrived at the hotel and locked his bike in a room they had for that purpose.

Walking through the lobby, he saw Sonja, but she was busy checking in a family with a group of small children, so he waved and headed upstairs. As he did, his phone rang.

"Hi Emily," he said, recognizing the number of his editor and contact at *Travel USA* magazine.

"Hey, Nick, how are things?"

"Well, they are good," he said. "The capitol building here is pretty amazing, and I haven't even been inside yet. I intended to today, but I got caught up outside. The reverse rotunda is amazing in person."

"Excellent," she said. "I can't wait to see what you have."

"I'll be uploading them soon."

"How is everything else? Car? Computer? Camera? Everything working okay?"

"So far, so good," he said. "No car trouble to speak of since Boise, although I am due for an oil change again, and a tire rotation. I am thinking of updating my computer if I can."

"That would be nice for you," she said. "What are you thinking about?"

Nick told her about the Mac he had been eyeing. "I am taking some photos of a local jazz band, and that extra cash may be enough to get me where I want to be if I pull a little from savings."

"Well, let me know. You are doing such a good job, the magazine may be able to pay for part of it, as some kind of bonus."

"That would be great," he said as he reached the room and let himself in. "I would appreciate it."

"Sure. No promises, but I will try. Let me know if you need anything from me, as usual."

"You bet," Nick said. "I'll keep you posted."

He ended the call. He didn't want to mention the mystery at all. Emily had made it clear that while a bit of freelancing on the side like band photos would be perfectly acceptable, his name in the news as an amateur sleuth was not.

He worried about that, but only a little.

Nick sat down at his computer, which was already booted up. He reconnected to the internet, connected his camera, and uploaded the photos he'd taken, including the ones at the church, to the magazine folder. He might as well let Emily see those even if the publication did not use them. The church was a lesser-known Austin attraction after all.

He copied those files to his personal folder too. There were some great macro shots he could put on his website. But that would have to wait until the next day. He checked his watch. It was already six local time.

Time flew.

He texted Sandra. "Hope your day is going well. Going out ax throwing and then to find some barbecue."

"Ax throwing?" came the response. "Be careful. And send pictures." She included a smile emoji, and he laughed out loud.

"For sure," he answered. "Wish you were here." He looked at the text before he hit send. He really did wish Sandra was here, and not for the first time.

He sighed. Only fourteen weeks into a year-long assignment, it did no good to get hung up on the facts. They had seen each other only a few weeks before when he was in Denver, but if anything that time together made him miss her more.

He hit send.

"Me, too," came the answer.

He sent a heart emoji, and stood, stretching to his full height, and reaching first for the ceiling and then for his toes.

So far, he hadn't used the hotel gym, but the bike and now an evening of ax throwing would surely make up for it.

He headed downstairs, waving again to Sonja who was busy with yet another customer and went out to his car. He put the address of the House of Axe, a few miles away, into the GPS.

The drive passed quickly, and the place had a dedicated lot, so parking wasn't a problem at all. Once inside, he presented the card he had been given and was issued a wrist band.

"That will admit you to both arenas," the cashier told him. "You can take photos, but not of any of the customers without their permission, and you have to clear them with the owner for commercial use."

"Of course. Can I talk with him really quick?" Nick asked.

"Sure," the cashier said. "He's right over there. He will be giving the safety demonstration."

Nick walked over, head and shoulders above most of the rest of the crowd. He stood to one side and watched as Tony went through the demonstration.

The man threw the ax several ways, underhanded and overhanded, alternating hands like a pro.

Nick wondered how much you had to practice to do that, and how good Jared's killer had been.

No one had mentioned that at all, or whether Phillip was any good with an ax.

Once the demo was over, they were all let loose on the lanes and encouraged to partner up with someone.

Nick approached Tony first. The man was shorter than Nick, but only by an inch or so, had a long, black beard, and clearly worked out.

"Hi, I'm Nick," he said. "I wonder if I might have a minute of your time."

"Are you a reporter?"

"Not exactly," Nick said.

"Because we aren't interested in any stories about what happened here last weekend."

"Not at all. I'm a freelance photographer from Seattle, taking photos at various state capitals," Nick started, not sure why he glossed over the truth of his assignment so quickly. "I'm also photographing other locations, and--"

"Oh, you're Nick. The one Rod's brother told me about. Of course, man, you can take any photos you want. Will you be able to bring the band here for some?"

"I hope so," Nick said. "I figured I would scout out some possible locations first."

"Of course. Look around all you like. Just like our employee probably told you, no pictures of customers, at least not if they are recognizable unless you clear it with them first. If the magazine were to use any photos, we would be grateful for the publicity."

"You bet," Nick said. "No promises, but I'll pass them along."

"I understand," Tony said.

"Can I ask one more question?" Nick said.

"Shoot."

"How long does it take someone to get as accomplished at this as you are?"

"Not long. If you're athletic, it comes pretty naturally."

"Are there any customers of yours who are as good as you are?"

"Yep, and a few surprise me with how good they are. Like that one."

Nick turned to look where he was pointing. There was Stan, the thin man who'd approached Sonja the night before. Next to him was a cute young lady, short, with long black hair.

Stan threw an ax, and it thudded with surprising force into the wooden stump at the end of the lane.

"See what I mean?" said Tony.

Nick nodded, moving in that direction. He figured he'd join the pair and maybe ask a few questions.

A few moments into his investigation, if it could be called that, he had a new potential suspect.

5

ONE STEP FORWARD

"Hi, Stan," Nick said, approaching the couple.

"Hi," Stan said. "You're the guy who was with Sonja the other night?"

"Yes. Nick O'Flannigan, freelance photographer."

"Nice to meet you. This is my--friend, Cathy."

"Hi, Cathy," Nick said and shook her hand.

"She was here the other night, with Jared."

"The bass player who passed away?" Nick asked.

"Yes," Cathy answered. "He was a friend, and I can't believe he's gone."

"It is tragic," Nick said. "I'm surprised you're back here."

"Better to face your demons than run," Stan said. "You know, get back on the horse and all that."

Nick nodded, but Cathy did not seem to be as sure."

"Are you from around here?" Stan asked, changing the subject.

"No. On assignment. I'm from Boston originally. Now from Seattle. I'm traveling the country to take photos of each state capitol building."

"Cool," Cathy said. She wiped her eyes, but her face did seem to brighten when she saw his camera. "Is that an Olympus?"

"Yes," Nick said. "Not the newest, but a pretty good one. Check it out."

Cathy looked it over and whistled. "I'm a bit of a shutterbug myself, but I shoot with an older Nikon."

"Hey, those are nice, too."

"So what are you doing here?" Stan asked, indicating the building they were in.

"Taking photos, and scouting locations to take more," he said. "Sonja's band wants me to shoot some photos of them in various places for some new promotions or something."

"Are you going to do their album cover?"

"I don't know about that. I'm only here for a week, and I have to complete my assignment, too."

"I see," he said. "Want to start with some ax throwing?"

"Sure," Nick said.

He joined the couple and found throwing axes almost therapeutic. It was satisfying when the head stuck in the wood at the end of the lane. Each stump had a crude target drawn on it, and he even got a few "bullseyes." He took photos of axes in the wood and caught a few "action shots" of them flying through the air. He thought they were decent and figured he could share them with Tony just for fun.

He tried throwing with the two-handed overhead method, but that did not work well for him. He tried underhand too, but he kept clunking the ax off the wood and onto the floor.

He tried a few throws underhand, and Cathy laughed when he missed the target entirely.

"We're going to go do paintball next. Want to join us?"

"Sure," Nick said, knowing he would try to go his own way when he could. *But that was the idea, right? To sneak around and not get marked by a paintball?*

Nick waved to Tony as he left the area, and the owner waved back, pointing to his camera.

Tony nodded, and Nick continued to the paintball area. Everyone was issued goggles and a special mask. It took a bit to find one that fit Nick, but they made it happen. Everyone got a Kevlar vest of some sort and some other pads.

"These paintballs won't kill you, but they do hurt sometimes," their instructor explained. "No purposeful headshots, please and respect those around you. This is a game after all and supposed to be fun."

He went on to explain the rules, and that you could continue to play "injured" but just not if you were hit in some vital areas. He explained the boundaries of the course, which were huge, and then outlined where they should go if they were "hit."

Nick smiled and nodded, looking at one area toward the back of the course that had been grayed out on the map they were shown.

I bet that's the crime scene, he thought but did not say. He studied the paths, looking for a way back to that area. *Just a quick look, a few photos, and then I'll tell Sonja I didn't find anything.*

There were monitors, those wearing neon yellow vests, and you were not allowed to shoot them. They would declare you "injured" or "dead" if there was a question.

"Can I keep my camera with me and take photos?" Nick asked one of them. "I'm doing it for Tony."

"Sure, but you should wear a monitor vest. You don't want your camera to get hit and break," the band said.

Nick nodded and thought about it. He could just take pictures with his phone, but that wouldn't be the same, and if he got "shot" early on, he might be pulled out of the arena before he got a chance to see what he wanted to.

So he agreed. He saw Stan and Cathy off to one side getting ready. After putting the vest on, Nick wandered over.

"I'm going to play monitor," he said. "So I can take photos and hopefully keep my camera from being damaged."

"That makes sense," Stan said, looking a little disappointed. "But suit yourself."

"Good luck," Nick said. "Be careful."

Cathy smiled. "You, too." The pair put on their masks and goggles and Nick did the same.

"Ready? Set! Go!" a voice called over the intercom.

Everyone started running. Nick heard squeals of laughter, and then all went quiet as players hid and snuck around.

He walked along calmly, first behind one of the monitors, and then struck out on his own. He stopped to take photos on the way, still able to see the viewfinder through the goggles. It didn't matter too much anyway, as many of the photos were a cover for his real goal. Still, he managed to get some nice ones.

This was in part because the course was pretty cool, with hay bales, fake building walls, and logs to hide behind.

He stopped from time to time to get his bearings. From time to time he heard a shot and sometimes yelling followed. He stuck to the side of the course and saw several players decorated with paint splatters leaving, some with anger on their faces, others laughing. The further he went from the entrance, the quieter things got. For a few minutes, he did not even see another monitor or player. Nick was alone.

Then he saw it. The crime scene tape had been removed, but there were still remnants tied to one side. A bit of yellow tape clung to a wooden stake.

Nick removed his mask and goggles and looked around. He snapped several photos, trying to capture every possible angle.

The scene was larger than he thought it would be and more complicated. There was a tall stump, a vertical log, several bales of hay, and some posts that clearly defined the border of the course.

The area had been cleaned thoroughly, but he could still see what looked like a large, puddle-shaped bloodstain in the center.

Around the backside, Nick stopped. Outside the perimeter of where the tape had been was a clear footprint in some dirt. There was a dark brownish stain right next to it, overlapping the impression.

It had been made by some kind of boot, probably, something with an aggressive tread. Nick was no shoe expert, but it didn't look like those made by his running shoes or any of the other prints in the area.

It might mean something or nothing. He knelt and took a few photos. He placed his own foot next to the print for a size comparison. He put his hand next to it as well and took another perspective photo.

So much for telling Sonja he didn't find anything. But what should he do with it?

Nick had no idea. He had no connection with the media here or the police, and no one to introduce him. His only "friends" were Sonja and the band, and maybe Rod and Tony, although he did not know either of them well enough to ask them for any favors, and he doubted Tony would want to report something new that might disrupt his business.

As he stood and studied the area, he snapped some other quick photos from this angle. He saw a cut like those made when an ax impacted the stump in the lanes up front and focused on it.

He took photos of that from several angles.

He still had seen no one, and the sounds of the game and the players were now distant. It was time to head back.

He turned, put the lens cover on his camera, and stretched his leg a bit. All the kneeling had his old injury aching. He put his goggles and mask back on and bent to touch his toes.

A paintball whistled over his head just as he bent over, and he straightened.

"Hey!" he said. "Monitor here. Don't shoot!"

A second shot came, hitting him in the head. It hurt, and the left lens of his goggles filled with blue paint. He wiped them with one hand, pulled the goggles and mask off so he could see, and looked around. He saw no one, and no more shots came.

Nick rubbed his forehead where the paintball struck him and turned to look more closely at the paint spatter behind him.

Nick walked back to the front more quickly this time. There was no one left in the arena area. When he reached the counter, the instructor was standing there, arms folded.

"Where have you been?" he asked. "Didn't you hear the signal for the end of the game?"

"Uh, no," Nick said. "I was toward the back."

He handed over his mask and goggles and started removing the monitor vest.

"What happened?" the instructor asked, looking at the paint spatters.

"I guess someone shot me before they realized I was off-limits."

"Did you see who did it?"

"No," Nick said. "It happened only a few moments ago."

"Huh. Well, whoever did it should be banned, but if you didn't see anything, I can look into it with the camera footage."

"Camera footage?"

"Yeah. All of the games are monitored, for safety."

"Did you have video of the night the man was killed here?"

"Are you a cop or something?"

"No, but--"

"Media?"

"No, not exactly."

"Tony told us to talk to no one about that night. We've shared everything relevant with the cops."

"Sorry, I was just curious."

"Curious or not, it doesn't matter. It's time for you to leave."

"Okay," Nick said. "I apologize."

The instructor took his gear and simply threw it on a heap behind the counter. "Let's go."

"I can find my way."

"I'll walk you."

The paintball instructor walked behind him all the way to the front door. Nick didn't try to stop, as he didn't think that would be a good idea.

Stan and Cathy were standing by a snack bar, drinking sodas from large cups. Stan waved, but his companion stared at Nick and his escort. Nick noticed Stan's shoes. They had blue paint on them and seemed small for his tiny frame. They were a hiking boot of some kind, with an aggressive tread.

Nick gave them a half-hearted wave and a moment later found himself outside.

It was time to head back to the hotel for the night.

As he fished his keys from his pocket, he thought about the shoes Stan had been wearing and the footprint.

He wanted desperately to take a closer look.

What are you doing, Nick? he thought.

Nothing, he answered himself. *I haven't done anything at all, yet.*

6

———————

SHARK TANK

When Nick walked into the hotel, Sonja was not at the front desk. He didn't know if her shift had ended, or she was somewhere else. No matter, he didn't have anything real to report yet.

Why him? Why shoot a paintball at him rather than someone else? Did it have anything to do with what he'd found?

Nick had discovered on these trips that what people did seldom made a lot of sense. Crimes and the events around them rarely added up at first glance. Most, or so it seemed to him, should be relatively easy to "get away with." But the ones he had seen were either planned poorly or it appeared that the murderer might even want to get caught.

Either way, 99% of the time, the motive was a misguided one at best. Again he thought of Helena. Was that an exception, or did each murderer see themselves as someone doing the right thing? Motives ranged from jealousy to revenge, from anger to even fear. And it could be any of those in this case.

This case.

He got in his hotel room and set his camera carefully on the desk. He didn't even consider calling the police or telling anyone else about the footprint. Especially not Sandra, or any of his friends.

After sending her a good night text, he performed his nightly ritual: teeth brushing, washing his face and hands, and then laid in bed, staring at the ceiling. He did not turn on the television, not tonight, but let his mind wander.

In moments he was asleep. But his dreams were troubled, filled with images from the last few weeks. Giant bees chased kids into swimming pools. A giant, wagging tongue shoved a man in a suit out of a window.

And a noose swayed in the breeze, hanging from a freshly constructed gallows.

When the dreams finally faded, he tossed and turned for what felt like the rest of the night.

He woke to light streaming from the window. So much for getting up early and taking some sunrise photos of the capitol.

Tomorrow, Nick told himself.

He looked at his camera sitting on the small desk in his room, thinking of the footprint and wondering if it meant anything at all.

"Leave it for now," he said. "You have a job to do, Nick."

Twenty minutes later, showered and feeling fresh, he headed down-stairs. Sonja was not there, but he did not expect her to be, as she'd worked last night. Nick collected his bike and headed for breakfast.

Slake Cafe looked excellent from the reviews, and so he biked over to 7th street and locked his rental outside. He was greeted by staff and sat in one of the steel and wood chairs at a square table. The look was a bit industrial with cement floors, red walls, and visible venting for the HVAC system. Various flavorings lined a shelf above the coffee bar.

He ordered a Mexican mocha and had to admit the coffee was good. He justified the sugar because of all of the biking he would be doing.

For food, Nick ordered a kolache and a blueberry muffin. Both arrived within moments and were quite tasty.

As he ate, he considered his plan for the day. First, interior photos of the capitol building. His assignment needed to take precedence, and he needed to upload the photos from the day before as well. Then he would call Sonja, or talk to her at the hotel, whatever came first. Then tonight, he would try some barbecue at Lambert's downtown.

He couldn't wait to pick up his curbside order from Franklin's. He couldn't wait to taste their famed prime rib. As he finished the thought, his phone rang.

"Hi Gerry," he said. "How's it going?" Gerry was one of his best friends and was the social media manager for *Travel USA* magazine. She and her girlfriend had visited him in Denver when his girlfriend Sandra had joined him for a week. They had all gotten along famously, despite Nick's involvement in a mystery that nearly lost him the assignment.

"Good," she said. "How about you?"

"So far so good," Nick said. "I wanted to get some early photos this morning, but I slept in. I'll catch them tomorrow. Today, I'll focus on the capitol interior."

"Sounds like a plan. How is everything else?"

"Well, I know it has only been a few weeks since our visit to Denver, but I miss you, Sandra, and Christina."

"I hear that," she said. "We miss you, too."

"I am keeping busy, though." He told her about ax throwing and paintball, leaving out the part about the mysterious shooting and his discovery. He didn't want to say a thing about the "case."

"Wow, that sounds exciting," she said. "We will have to try that sometime."

"It's fun," Nick said. "I also rented a bike, and I am riding around town."

"Oh, do be careful," she said. "I don't want you to get hurt."

"I'm wearing my helmet and taking care of myself."

"Glad to hear it. Will you and Sandra see each other again soon?"

"Of course," he said. "We haven't set up plans yet, but Oklahoma City might be a little soon. I have no idea."

"Her job seems to offer her some freedom."

"True," Nick said. "I would, of course, love to see her."

"Well, Emily was pleased with what you did in Santa Fe, and what we've seen so far of Austin is pretty cool."

"Just wait. I have an idea for the night photos, one I think you will both love. It will capture the essence of Austin and involves a local band."

"A local band?"

"Emily didn't tell you?" Nick filled her in on his freelance opportunity, and then shared his idea with her. "Don't tell Emily about that part. I want her to be surprised."

"Brilliant, Nick. That is why we picked you for this assignment. Your creativity."

"Thanks."

"As long as you are not too creative. No mysteries this week, right?"

"So far not yet," Nick said noncommittally. His stomach twisted as he said the words.

"Good. Keep it that way, okay?"

"I'll try," Nick said.

"Take care."

"You, too," Nick answered, and ended the call.

He unlocked his bike, rode the short distance to the capitol, and locked it near the state archives again.

He looked at the building and then at the capitol behind him.

Capitol first, he told himself.

Nick often found himself in a zone when he took photos, and today was no exception.

To say the interior of the capitol was impressive would be an understatement. Everything was spotless. He started with the typical shots, up into the rotunda, down at the floor below. In the center of the dome was a large, red "Lone Star" to represent the state's heritage. It was over two hundred feet above the rotunda, according to tourist literature. Just below the dome, thin vertical windows let in the light from outside, and through them, Nick could see the blue skies of the day, dotted with tiny white clouds here and there.

He saw a metal spiral staircase from this angle and snapped several shots of it. There were several similar metal structures left over after the last restoration, and he wanted to document as many as he could. There was another floor above him, and that raised the dilemma. *Where do I start?*

As much as his leg had been getting stronger with all the exercise on this trip, logic dictated that he go up first, and work his way down. It also would help him keep the photos he was taking in order.

So Nick went up first. His photos from the upper level showcased intricate carvings, decorated windows, and more. Once he had exhausted that floor he moved downward. He encountered a group, apparently on a tour, headed up, and remembered he'd read about the tour on his way in.

Tomorrow might be a good day to take that. His time in Austin was already racing by, and as he passed the tour and continued his own process, his stomach growled.

Looking at his watch, Nick saw it was past noon, and he felt like he wasn't even halfway through the large building. He checked his camera to discover he had taken over two hundred photos.

This afternoon was going to be a long sorting session.

Nick smiled. This. This was what he lived for.

Meantime, he wanted to grab something to eat. He walked back toward the tour and waited for the guide to pause.

As the participants moved toward the next area she'd directed them to, she stepped aside and looked up at him. "Do you have a question, sir?" She was short, but not too short, plump, and wore "batwoman" glasses. Her dark hair was tied up in a tight bun at the back of her neck. Nick thought if you Googled "librarian" in the dictionary, you might see her photo. On her left hand, he saw a large diamond and breathed a sigh of relief. At least she wasn't flirting with him.

"I do," Nick said. "I'll be on the tour tomorrow sometime, I hope. In the meantime, is there a spot I can grab some quick lunch nearby?"

She looked at his camera and then back up at him. "Are you the photographer here to take photos this week?"

"I am," he said. "Nick O'Flannigan."

"Maggie," she said. "Nice to meet you. Do you plan to keep taking photos after you eat?"

"A few, before I go do some sorting."

"Then I'd recommend the cafeteria in the extension. It's pretty good, where all the lawmakers and other employees eat too, and you can start your afternoon photo session there."

"Sure," Nick said. "That sounds great."

She reached into a folder she was carrying and pulled out a pamphlet. " Follow these directions. You can't miss it."

"Thanks," Nick said.

"See you around, and see you tomorrow for sure," Maggie said, and hurried to lead the tour.

Nick waved, and found his way to the staircase, walking down to the bottom floor, and then down one more level to the underground extension.

He was completely unprepared for the vastness of the space but made his way to the cafeteria first.

The area below the main capitol and to the North was breathtaking. Nick stopped, despite how hungry he was, turned, and looked back up through the glass windows above. Through them, he could see the capitol building silhouetted against the sky.

It made a great shot, and he smiled at the image on the small screen of his camera.

As he reached the cafeteria, he took a look at the various fare available, pretty standard for the most part, but there was a daily special of prime rib. He walked through the line and opted for that and a side of coleslaw. He grabbed a soda, something he didn't drink much before sitting down.

Nick removed his phone from his pocket and looked at the screen. There were two missed calls, both from Sonja.

I'll call after I eat, he thought. He tried to open his social media apps and check his accounts as he consumed the mix of tangy barbecue sauce and tart cabbage in alternating bites.

They wouldn't load. The reception down here was horrible.

As he was sopping up the leftover sauce with a piece of Texas toast included with the meal, he raised the phone in his hand, seeing if he might get a signal. It was foolish, he knew. As he did, he saw another missed call. His phone hadn't even chirped.

"You done with your tray?" a female voice said from behind him.

Nick stuffed the last bite of toast in his mouth and nodded.

The woman, a brunette with green eyes wearing a hairnet, plastic gloves, and peering at him through wire-rimmed glasses smiled as she gathered his leavings. "Even a guy as tall as you will have to go to the shark tank to get cell signal," she said.

Nick swallowed. "The shark tank?"

She laughed. "It's what we call the reverse rotunda. Cell service is spotty in these corridors, so that's where lobbyists go to use their phones to conduct business."

"I see," Nick said. "Apt name."

"We don't tend to mince our words here in Texas. Hell, we usually don't even chip our beef."

Nick laughed out loud. "That's good! I'll remember that one."

She just nodded. "Have a nice day, sir."

Nick followed the signs to the rotunda and stepped out into the light of the day, squinting. The sky had darkened slightly, and although late fall or winter rains weren't uncommon in Austin, it felt too warm to him for that kind of storm. It might turn into a real thunder boomer.

And he might not want to be riding his bike in it.

Without listening to the voicemail, he hit the button to call Sonja. She answered on the first ring.

"Nick!" she said. "Where have you been?"

"I was in the lower part of the capitol building. The cell service down here is pretty bad I guess."

"Are you still there?"

"Yep. What's going on? Are you okay?"

"Well, I am. But someone was here at the hotel looking for you."

"Looking for me?"

"Nick, it was the Austin police department. They were asking a lot of questions, most I couldn't answer without a warrant, but they want to meet you."

"Why?"

"They didn't say, but it sounded serious. You want the detective's number?"

"Detective? Sure." Nick gulped but kept his thoughts to himself. *Why would they want to talk to me? Am I a suspect or something?*

At the same time, he had another thought. *Here's your in. Your chance to share with them what you found.*

"Sorry, can you repeat that?" he asked. Sonja had given him the number, but he hadn't paid attention while lost in his thoughts.

She gave it to him again, and as he turned to go back inside to decide what to do, a large drop of rain struck the top of his head.

He brushed it away and ducked under an overhang.

So much for being ahead on Tuesday. The reverse rotunda did indeed feel like a shark tank, and he was suddenly uncomfortable like he was being stalked by a predator.

He walked quickly through the lower level of the capitol extension, taking the stairs to the first floor two at a time. His bike was parked on the east side of the building, and so he walked through to another entrance, his camera swinging back and forth on his chest.

The rain wasn't coming down, not yet, but he could feel it in the air, and in his bad leg. So much for a dry week. A few wet spots from early droplets dotted the sidewalk. He put his camera back in the bag and wished he'd brought a poncho or something along against the rain, but he hadn't looked at the forecast.

He raced out to the place where his rental bike was locked.

As he approached, two men exited the door to the state archive building.

"Nick O'Flannigan?" one said. "Can we have a moment of your time?"

7

INTERVIEWED

Nick looked at the bike, and then at the man.

"Mind if I see some I.D.?" he asked.

"Sure," the man said. He fished a leather wallet from his inner pocket and handed it over. As he did, Nick saw a weapon of some sort in a shoulder holster under his jacket.

He was either used to the heat, or he was secretly sweating.

The detective's partner watched the area behind Nick, remaining silent.

"Detective Sergeant Saul Matthews," the badge read.

"How can I help you?" Nick said, handing the badge back. He was more nervous than he had been in quite some time when dealing with police, and he wasn't sure why. Maybe it was the way they approached him or the fact that they had found him at the capitol, although if they knew anything about him, it wasn't a stretch.

But how did they find your bike? he thought.

"Care to step inside?" the cop asked.

A large drop of rain, this time followed by another, and then another, struck his head, rolling off his hair into his eyes. "Sure," he said.

He followed the man and his still silent partner up the steps and inside the archives building. They stood in the lobby. A clap of thunder sounded, and the musty smell of fresh rain reached his nostrils. He turned to face Detective Matthews.

"Sorry for our approach, but this is a matter of some urgency," the cop said.

"Again, how can I help you?" Nick asked.

"You visited House of Axe last night, correct?"

"I did."

"You navigated the paintball course, the one where a body was found this weekend, with a monitor vest on and took photos, yes?"

"Well, yes. I was scouting the location for a photoshoot for a local band."

"I see." The detective stared at him, and his partner, who had been looking out the window as if keeping watch over the two of them also turned his gaze toward Nick.

"I did wander a bit off the beaten track," Nick confessed.

"Did anything unusual happen?"

"Not really," Nick said carefully. "Someone accidentally shot me with a paintball, even though I had a monitor vest on, but it was no big deal."

"Were you near the crime scene at the time?"

"The crime scene?"

"Don't play dumb, O'Flannigan. We know about your past adventures, and we know you were near the crime scene. While the tape is gone, there are remnants."

The cameras, Nick thought. *They looked at the cameras.*

"You seemed to take quite a bit of time photographing the area, and we would like to see those photos."

Nick looked down at his camera and back at the officer.

"Are you working for someone, O'Flannigan?"

"Um, not exactly. Listen, I can explain."

"Just like every other trip, right? Like our friends in Salt Lake? Or Phoenix? Or Santa Fe? I'm starting to wonder if you find trouble, trouble follows you, or you are trouble O'Flannigan. Which is it?"

"Look, am I a suspect or something? I wasn't even in town when your murder happened."

"You're not a suspect."

"And I don't even know the suspect you have in custody, or anyone else directly involved."

"That so?"

"As I said, I can explain."

"I'm listening."

"Can we sit somewhere?"

The detective gestured, and Nick walked with him past a long front desk made of light-colored wood. Both detectives' shoes clicked on the polished marble floor. A woman at the desk looked up, waved at the detective, and went back to what she was doing.

The adjoining room was vast, the floor covered in gray carpet. Drop ceilings with fluorescents provided harsh illumination. Circulation tables lined one side of the room.

In the center were several smaller wooden desks, each with a single, white plastic chair. Nick and the detective each chose one of those. The silent partner stood, facing away from them, seemingly watching the front door and the lobby area.

Nick took a deep breath. He seemed to have little choice, and although he didn't want to get anyone involved who wasn't already or didn't want to be, he decided to share everything he knew.

He started with Sonja, the band, her relationship with Jared, and her belief that his brother was innocent.

"So you agreed to look into it for her?"

Nick nodded.

"Although you are not a detective, have no standing in this jurisdiction, and no friends here to speak of."

Nick nodded again, feeling foolish.

"Do you know the evidence we have on our suspect?"

"No, I don't," Nick said quietly.

"Well, unlike my friends in other cities, I won't share it with you. Instead, you get an overview. Ready?"

"Um, sure," Nick said.

"Means, motive, and opportunity are what we have. Phillip at or near the murder scene. He is known to have a rivalry with his brother. And he had the opportunity to commit the murder. Although we cannot see the murderer clearly in the footage we have been provided, we do have enough to charge him."

"Okay, but..."

"What are you going off, O'Flannigan? Your gut? The thoughts of the suspect's brother's ex-lover, who by the way has no business interfering either. In fact, her current husband could just as easily be a suspect."

"So you aren't even going to look into anyone else?"

"You know what we do here in Texas?" Detective Matthews asked.

Nick shook his head.

"We close cases. That's what we do. We find the suspect, most often a family member, and we investigate. We encourage the DA to bring charges based on evidence, and we close the case, erase it off our board, and move on to the next one. Know how often the guilty party is an immediate family member?"

"No, sir."

"All the time. Hell, half the time they are sitting outside the murder scene, expressing remorse, and we make an arrest on the spot. We have a good track record here in Austin. Let us do our jobs, and you do yours," the Detective said. "Take your photos and move on."

"Yes, sir."

"If I hear from you again this week, and it isn't because you want to take a photo of my regal face in front of the capitol building there in order to highlight the swift justice we offer here in the great state of Texas, I'll arrest you myself for obstruction."

He stood, the tiny plastic chair shooting backward away from him with the motion. He tossed a card onto the table. "My email is on there. I want any of the photos you took in and around our crime scene sent to me. Today. Then delete them from your computer, camera, and anywhere else. I see one of them in the press like your little escapade in Denver, or anywhere on social media, we will be seeing each other again. And I won't be as nice next time."

Like you were nice this time, Nick thought. *Right.*

"Yes, sir," he said out loud.

Clearly, this was a case he would have to back out of. He wasn't sure what he would tell Sonja, but he couldn't risk everything, his assignment and maybe even his freedom, no matter what.

For him, and apparently for the police, this case was closed.

The trio walked past the front desk again and outside, where the rain had subsided from a downpour to a steady drizzle.

"Any chance I can get a ride back to my hotel?" Nick asked.

Detective Matthews turned back to look at him, and simply stared, unblinking.

Nick stared back.

"No," the cop said, and walked away.

Nick wondered if he should go back inside and take the rest of the interior photos of the capitol, or just come back tomorrow.

Sonja would also be wondering what had happened.

Tonight wouldn't be a good night for sunset photos, not unless the rain cleared.

Tomorrow might be a spectacular sunrise, and then he could take the capitol tour.

He didn't want to ride back to the hotel yet, and he didn't want to talk to Sonja either until he had cleared his mind and decided what to do next.

He would love to talk to Sandra, get her advice on this, but he wasn't ready to reveal that he'd gotten drawn into a mystery yet again.

Nick sighed and headed back inside. He'd finish a few more photos, go back to his hotel to edit and sort, and then head to dinner and maybe find some live music again.

He felt isolated and alone, and his best escape was right in front of him.

Photography, and his assignment. At the moment, nothing else mattered.

He walked into the capitol, waved at the tour guide, who was now leaving, a large, closed umbrella under her arm.

He went back up a couple of levels and started where he'd left off before his late lunch and his interruption, but the spark was gone, his photos were normal and pretty lackluster. He decided to give up for now.

He headed back to his hotel through the light rain. The air was cooler at least.

Nick walked through the door and put his bike away in the area provided, feeling his damp clothes against his skin and his hair hanging in his eyes. He kept his gaze lowered as much as he could.

But when he exited the room, Sonja spotted him and called out.

"Nick! What did the police want? How did it go?"

Nick shuffled over. "Not good," he said.

"What happened?" she asked.

Nick sighed and told her the story. The longer he talked, the further her face fell.

8

———————

GOOD CATCH

Nick went to his room, emailed the photos of the crime scene in a zip file to the police detective, but his finger hovered over the delete button. It wouldn't hurt for him to have a look at them more closely before he erased them for good, and besides, he might be able to give at least something to Sonja.

She'd cried when he told her the news he was officially off the case, not because he wanted to be, but because the police had forcibly removed him. The consequences of defying them were too great for someone he'd just met.

She understood.

Nick didn't share his suspicions about Stan or the footprint.

Worry about that later, he thought. He got to work putting together the photos for the magazine and uploading them, complete with labels. As usual, he edited as he went.

By the time he was done, he felt better about leaving the case behind, and also was characteristically hungry. He wanted to go to Lambert's barbecue, but a quick check showed they were closed on Tuesdays. That would have to wait until tomorrow.

Terry Black's was open until nine, so he had a couple of hours, and it was not far away. He looked out the hotel window to find the rain had stopped. He could even walk to the restaurant, and the temperature was milder after the storm.

I mean, it wasn't Seattle mild or Seattle-type rain, but the moisture did remind him a bit more of home.

Home.

He texted Sandra. "Going out to grab some dinner. Will you be around in an hour or so?"

"I should be off work by then," came the rapid reply. "Call whenever you want."

He kept forgetting the time change. He was now in Central Time, she was still on Pacific, so it was much earlier there. "Sounds good," he texted back.

He headed to the lobby and found Sonja still at the front desk. She looked like she had recovered from her disappointment.

"Sorry, Nick," she said as he approached. "I should have never asked you to get involved."

"It's okay," he said. "I didn't have to say yes."

"Well, thanks for trying," she said.

"Remember, I still want to get some photos of you and the band if you are still interested," Nick said. "Maybe we can take some at the capitol building. I can kill two birds with one stone."

"That would be great," she said. "You're a good guy, Nick. We will pay you, of course."

"Of course," Nick said. "But I promise to be very reasonable. You have a show tomorrow night?"

"We do."

"What time?"

"We start at 9. We need to be there at 8-ish to set up."

"Okay. Can we meet at the capitol before that? I'll see if I can get permission for you to set up outside, even for just a few moments."

"That would work. How about six or six-thirty?"

"Perfect. And Sonja?"

"Yes?"

"I am sorry I couldn't help more."

She put her hand on his arm. "See you later, Nick."

"For sure," he said. It would be at least nearing dusk at the time they met for the photos, and if he was lucky he would catch the sunset or the lights coming on in the capital at least.

Emily and Gerry would love it.

He left, walking toward Terry Black's. Once inside, he ordered a chopped beef sandwich combo, and then a peach cobbler for dessert. He ordered a beer in substitute for the soda, a local porter that he found pretty good.

As he sat and ate, he thought more about the footprint, Stan, and the murdered bass player. There had to be a connection, something he was missing, and as much as he wanted to put it out of his mind, he couldn't.

Maybe a phone call to his parents. Nick glanced at his watch. They would likely be in bed by now, so he would call them tomorrow, too. It would be a busy day.

I'll start early, with sunrise photos. Sunset with the band and after they have to leave, music tomorrow night. Then Thursday, I'll top it off with a few more outside and a final of the interior. Friday, I'll finish up anything I missed.

Even his assignment kept him busy this week. Band photos and concert on Wednesday and he'd need to edit and polish those quickly. Then he could complete his assignment, and get ready to head north again, to Oklahoma City.

No rest for the wicked, he thought as he finished up and paid his bill. He hurried back to the hotel, waved to Sonja, and headed upstairs.

Once in his room, he stared at his phone. It was time to talk to Sandra about what was going on.

Don't shut me out, she'd told him in Denver, and even since. *If you are involved in something, let me help you.*

She was right of course. If they were going to make this work, he needed to be open with her, and Santa Fe hadn't been that bad. Despite the mystery, he'd gotten some of the best photos of the trip and stayed clear of trouble.

He could do the same here, but he wanted her advice. Nick wanted to make sure he was doing the right thing.

The phone only rang once, and then he heard her voice.

"Nick, how are things?"

"Well, good, but interesting," he told her. "I need your advice."

"Another mystery?" she asked, her voice low. He could hear her disappointment.

"Well, sort of. Let me explain."

As he told Sandra the tale of his involvement so far, he opened his laptop and the file with the photos he was supposed to delete. He scrolled through them until he got to the footprint.

"So, wait," she said. "You saw a footprint that may or may not be related, similar to the shoes of someone you think might be a better suspect than the one the police have?"

"Yes."

"You did include that in your photos you sent to the police?"

"Yes, but they may not see why it's significant. But I don't think it would help matters to offer help after they told me to get lost."

"You're right."

"I wish I wasn't. I think if I passed anything to the media, I would get crucified."

"You didn't delete the photos like they asked?"

"Not all of them," Nick said. "What do you think I should do?"

"Delete them. Leave it. You shared the photo with them, just without commentary. Let them handle the case from here. You've done your part. You don't want to get in trouble with the magazine do you?"

"No," he said. "You're right."

"Of course I am, Nick. You should know better."

"Thanks for setting me straight."

"Hey, I am here for you."

"Thanks, Sandra."

"I love you."

"I love you, too."

"How are your parents?"

"I'll check on them tomorrow." Their conversation descended into the normal talk about her work, his family, and what he had planned for the next day.

He ended the call, deciding to glance through the photos one last time before deleting them.

In one photo he spotted a figure in the background. He'd been trying to capture where the footprint he'd seen was, a footprint that the more he thought about it, the less significance it might have. I mean, it could have been made any time before or after the murder, by anyone.

As he scrolled through a few more photos, he looked at the footprint again. The tread looked odd, and he zoomed in.

Right across where the ball of the foot would be, a line crossed the entire heavy-duty sole. It looked like the material must have been cut, as it did not match the rest of the tread.

That flaw, whatever had caused it, would identify the boot wearer.

His computer dinged, and he looked at his email. There was a message from the detective. "Got the photos. Thanks."

Nick resisted the urge to reply, to tell him to check the print carefully.

He wondered what size of shoes the suspect they had in custody wore, what kind of soles they had, and if the soles had this particular mark.

Of course, the killer could have ditched the shoes, even if that person made the print.

I may not be able to dunk a basketball anymore, Nick thought. *But I sure can jump to conclusions.*

Still, he opened a browser online and found all the news photos of the suspect he could find. There were only a few, mostly mugshots, and not one showed the suspect's shoes.

Why would they?

Nick gave up and went to bed. Before he did, he set his alarm for early the next morning.

His assignment would consume his day, and he couldn't wait to play with light and shadow, take the typical capitol tour, and finish a large portion of his photos.

He closed the window with the paintball photos, but he didn't delete the rest of them.

Not yet.

9

____

CASE CLOSED

The alarm went off early, and Nick grabbed coffee and a bagel on the way out the door. He mounted his bike and found the air almost chilly after the last few days of heat. He started to see how people could adjust to this weather but was glad he would not have to long term.

The bike had a light mounted on it, and he was glad of it as he made his way through the gray dawn to the north side of the capitol building.

The sun was slightly to the south and the east, and he set himself up just to the west of the "shark tank" on the ground level. As he'd suspected, clouds dotted the sky, remnants from the storm and rain the night before. As the sun rose, it turned them a mix of orange, red, and yellow. He moved a few times, catching the best angles he could.

As he sorted through the photos, his stomach growled. Finding a quick breakfast became a priority, as he wanted to be on one of the early tours of the capitol.

He left his bike locked in what had become his usual spot. He stretched first for the sky, and then reached for his toes, then started walking the direction of Cisco's, a popular spot he'd seen advertised on social media. It promised affordable Tex-Mex fare, just what he needed.

As he walked, he took in the smells of the remains of the rain from the night before. The air smelled cleaner, and while he could feel the promised heat of the coming day, at the moment it was cool and calm.

A chirp from his phone interrupted his reverie and he saw his mom's name on the screen. He stopped walking and leaned against a nearby brick wall next to a glass doorway.

"Hi, mom. I was going to call you guys this morning."

"Hi, Nick. You're in Austin still, right?"

"Yes, mom." His parents struggled with this assignment and keeping track of where he was and what he was doing. Hell, it was hard for him to keep track himself sometimes.

"How are things?"

"Warm," he said. "Although it rained last night. It is nice here though. Lots of trees, shade, and the city is pretty clean. The capitol is huge and elegant."

"That is fantastic, Nick."

"How are you and dad?" His dad had suffered a stroke not long ago and was still recovering.

"Good. Your father gets stronger every day."

"Where is he?" Usually his dad would have interrupted by now, and loudly, due to his deafness.

"I can hear you!" his dad shouted. "How is that girl?"

"Sandra," Nick and his mom said at the same time, his mom's voice much louder than his.

"She is good," he said. "She will probably come see me again soon."

"Very good!" his dad yelled. "Are you going to marry her?"

This was a topic Nick actively worked to avoid. "We will see, Dad," he said out loud. "Give it some time."

"Ha! Time! Your mother and I married right away!"

"And look how that turned out," his mother muttered. Nick stopped himself from laughing.

"I am sure either way, things will work out," Nick said. He'd been married before, briefly to his college sweetheart, and Marriage was not first on his agenda. This trip had not raised its priority level, although he did love Sandra.

"Well, don't wait too long. You don't want her to get away," Nick's dad said.

"He's right," his mom said gently. "But you know we love you Nick, no matter what you do."

"I love you, too," Nick smiled as he said it.

"We're glad you are doing well," his mom said.

"You, too. I'm headed to breakfast, but I will talk to you soon, okay?"

"Sounds good."

His mom ended the call, and Nick studied his phone. He worries about them all the time, but there was little he could do while on assignment.

He didn't always like it, but he could endure. He'd moved away from Boston a long time ago, and nothing other than his parents would ever draw him back. In fact, he would prefer that they move near him when the inevitable "time" came that they could not care for themselves.

He put it out of his mind, pushed off the wall, and headed to breakfast. As he straightened, he got a text notification.

"Your curbside order is ready at Franklin's. You can pick it up anytime between 11 and 2."

Light breakfast, then. He couldn't wait to try the famous barbecue.

He'd go right after the capitol tour and whatever other photos he could take by noon.

Only a moment later, he walked up to Cisco's. A short ramp with red rails led to the front door, and when he stepped inside, he could see the place was small and nearly full. There were several red stools along the bar and a few tables scattered around.

He took one of the open stools, sat down, and looked at a menu. As he did, he glanced up at the television too.

A newscaster stood in front of an official-looking building, maybe a courthouse or police station.

"Phillip Buck, the brother of deceased Jared Buck, a local bass player on the Austin music scene, had an arraignment hearing this morning. He's been charged with murder, and the judge remanded him without bail. We heard from his defense attorney as he left the courthouse." The view switched.

"This is a ridiculous charge," a man in a suit told several microphones. "My client is innocent, has an alibi, and there is evidence he did not commit this crime. We look forward to a trial where he will be cleared of all charges."

"Here is the video of him leaving the courthouse," the reporter said as a new video appeared. Surrounded by uniformed officers, a short, somewhat thin man with dark hair was led from the courthouse towards a waiting van. Nick concentrated on one thing: his feet.

They looked big, too big to fit the footprint he'd photographed, but it was hard to tell from this distance. He wore what Nick assumed were prison shoes to go with his orange jumpsuit. He wondered again what shoes he'd been wearing at the time of his arrest. It was, of course, impossible to know.

The case was closed, though. Phillip had been indicted, and even if he was the wrong guy, there was nothing Nick could do about it. And that was a big if. The DA would not press charges unless they had something pretty solid.

He placed his order and watched the rest of the local news without comment. The weather was supposed to clear up today, but some clouds would move in late tonight. That might be good for his photos later on.

He ordered the huevos ranchero with fajita, another cup of coffee, and looked through the photos on his camera while he waited.

The ones from this morning were decent. He deleted some duplicates on the spot and then dove into his food when it arrived.

By the time he was finished, he was full, but he knew he needed to get moving. Time was flying, and there was only so much morning remaining.

He paid and left, making the walk of just over a mile quickly. He arrived right on time for the nine-thirty capitol tour.

As he joined it, he saw a young woman walk in the opposite direction, headed outside. She wore a brown dress, a light leather jacket, and on her feet, she wore short socks and boots.

A hiking-type boot, with aggressive tread.

Nick stopped for one second, his brain shifting into a different gear entirely.

Maybe the maker of the boot print had been a woman and had nothing to do with the crime at all. Or maybe, just maybe, it was a woman who was good at throwing axes. Like Cathy?

He tried to think back to what she'd been wearing, specifically footwear, but he could not remember for the life of him. He wondered if she would be at the music set tonight.

"Are we ready?" Maggie said.

Nick joined the tour and started taking photos and making mental notes of facts as he went, just like any other tourist. Except every now and then, thoughts entered his head.

Thoughts about the mystery, and how Phillip did not fit the profile of the murderer. At least not in his mind, and certainly not Sonja's.

These were far from normal tourist thoughts, but as hard a Nick tried to push them aside, they persisted.

When the tour ended, he looked at his watch. It was 11:00. He could either stay and take some more photos, or he could go to Franklin's and come back.

He decided to stay. Checking his own notes, he started where he'd ended the day before, backtracking to cover those areas where he'd felt his photos were sub-par.

After about ninety minutes, he ended up back where the tours started as Maggie was finishing one up.

"Hi, Mr. O'Flannigan. Getting everything you need?"

"Yes," Nick said. "Sometimes I wish I had more time in each city. Of course, an interview with the governor never hurts."

"I might be able to arrange that. Do you have lunch plans?"

"I do," Nick said. "I'm picking up barbecue from Franklin's."

"Oh, I'm jealous."

"Well, come along. I am sure it will be more than I can eat by myself."

"Are you sure?"

"Positive. Consider it a bribe to get me in with the governor."

"Sounds good to me," he said.

They walked out into the warmth of the day. Nick set off, trying to remember to shorten his strides.

"Are we walking?" she asked.

"Oh, um," he said. "I actually rode a rental bike."

"Let's take my car," she said. "I'll let you run up and get your food while I circle the block. We can bring it back here and chat about the governor."

"Okay," Nick said.

He followed her in the opposite direction of the state archives, and as he did, he saw a large man in a suit approaching that building. It looked like the detective he'd met before. Matthews?

But it couldn't be. Why would he want to talk to Nick again?

He shrugged it off. He was hungry again from all the walking, and his mouth watered.

10

A LARGE PROBLEM

M aggie led Nick to a Tesla, one of the newer models, and the door opened smoothly. He slid into the passenger seat, finding that there was plenty of legroom even for someone of his height. The dash looked like one from a spaceship of some sort, and the leather seats wrapped him in comfort. He didn't even hear the car start as much as feel it.

The seat immediately got cooler.

"I've never ridden in one of these before," Nick said. "This is nice."

"It is. And no more gas stations. Just a charging station at home. There are some here at work too, if I need one."

She pointed, and Nick saw four charging stations across from them. Another Tesla sat in one space, a Nissan in another, and a BMW in the third. The fourth was empty.

"That is too cool," he said.

"You should have one of these for your trip across the country," she said. Nick glanced over at her and saw the seat pulled forward nearly all the way and apparently higher than his seat position, and the small woman perched on the edge looking out the massive front window.

His image of a typical Tesla owner did not include her.

"I'd love to try one," he said. "But I was concerned about finding charging stations along the way."

"Most major hotels have them," she said. "Sometimes Costco and other retailers too. They are everywhere, even at truck stops. Of course, you will need to stop at something other than a fast charger every now and then."

"You sound passionate."

"I'm a big environmentalist. You'll see a lot of these in Austin, especially since Elon Musk moved here."

"I'll have to look into it."

"I bet if you look at your route, you'll find it's doable. And your magazine might like the money savings."

Nick nodded and looked around the car and then outside. The ride was a short one, and he could have walked, but he was glad he hadn't. Then he spotted Franklin's. Just like he'd seen on television, there was a huge line of people outside on the front sidewalk and a shorter line on the other side.

"Curbside pickup," a sign over that group read.

"I'll drop you here," Maggie said. "And circle the block until you come out."

"Thanks," Nick said. It took him a moment to figure out how to exit the car. Once he did, he stood to his full height, and Maggie silently glided away. He joined the line, which moved quickly.

"Nick O'Flannigan," he said when he got to the front. "I have an order."

"You bet!" the enthusiastic person behind the counter said. The smell in the area overwhelmed his other senses, a mix of smoke, meat, and underlying tang that had to be the smell of the restaurant's famous sauce.

When he did manage to look beyond the end of his nose, he could see the restaurant was a humble one, the structure pretty normal, a few tables scattered in a courtyard to one side. They were all full, and most people were taking their food and either walking away or getting into cars. There seemed to be a group circling the block, just like Maggie.

The employee returned and handed Nick a heavy bag. Heavier than he thought it would be. "There's sauce in there if you want it," the young man told him.

"Thanks."

"Anything else?"

"This will do, thanks."

He turned and saw Maggie almost opposite him. He jogged over lightly, his leg feeling pretty good, and slid into her car holding the bag.

"Oh, that smells heavenly. Let's go back and torture everyone in the shark tank by eating there."

"Sure," Nick said.

They parked the Tesla in the spot she'd left before, and Nick admired it as he walked away. He really would have to look into getting one.

He grabbed his camera bag and the food, and he and Maggie walked toward the capitol. She pointed out a few things along the way, and they chatted about the city, the capitol grounds, and Nick made some mental notes for himself to use later.

Once they were inside and had walked down to the "shark tank" area, they sat on a bench with a table between them.

"So how long have you lived in Austin?" Nick asked, taking a large bite of prime rib using a plastic fork.

"Pretty much my whole life, except for a short stint in the Army, and a few years in college," Maggie answered. She chased her answer with a bite of her own, humming in satisfaction as she chewed.

"The Army?" Everything about her surprised him.

"Yep. Met my husband while I served. I got pregnant and got out, then went to college. He stayed in for another few years, we traveled around, and then he got hurt and the Army chaptered him out too, with disability pay, and we moved back here."

"How long have you worked at the capitol?"

She laughed. "Depends on what you mean. I graduated with a degree in criminal justice, got my master's, joined the capitol security team, and worked here for a number of years."

"Wow."

"I retired, but I don't do well sitting around, and my husband is still working, so I took on this job, as I already had pretty intimate knowledge of the capitol building and grounds."

"Thus your in with the governor."

"Indeed," she said. "Would you like to meet him?"

"Absolutely," Nick said.

"How about tomorrow? I'll check his schedule and shoot you a time."

"Sounds great."

They both dug in. The smokey smell of the barbecue nearly overwhelmed his senses. They ate in silence for a few moments, each going through a series of napkins. Finally, Nick licked his fingers and sat back.

"You know, this food never gets old," she said. "No matter how long I live here, or how much of it I eat, it never changes for me."

"It is good," Nick replied.

"Do you really think so? I've had people not from Texas tell me barbecue from other place is better."

"Well, not so far on this trip," Nick said. "But I haven't been to Kansas City yet."

Maggie laughed. "You haven't missed anything. However, when you get down south, that might change."

"So I have been told. This will be my first time to many of the fifty states."

"That's great. You really do have a neat assignment."

"I do." He stared at the sky. There were still wisps of clouds, and it had warmed up considerably. The smell of the rain had been replaced by some sort of pollen, drifting into the open area on a light breeze.

"It's a nice weather day in Austin," she said. "You hit this one perfectly. What's on your agenda for this afternoon?"

"A few more photos here, and then I am meeting up with a local band to take photos on the capitol grounds."

"Which one?"

"Sonja and the Dropouts."

"Really? I love them!"

"Well, you can meet them this evening. We're going to try to get some night shots before they play a gig tonight."

"Can you introduce me?"

"Sure," he said. "They will be here at six or so."

"I'll stick around after work. I may even bring my husband along."

"Perfect," Nick said.

Maggie looked at her watch. "Goodness, I have to go. I am late for the next tour."

"Oh, man. Go," Nick said. "I'll see you later."

Nick cleaned up the mess from their lunch and tossed it in a nearby receptacle. There were several men wearing suit coats and ties standing around the perimeter, usually several feet apart, each talking excitedly into a phone.

"The lobbyists," Nick said out loud. "Must be a big vote coming up."

But he had no way of knowing that. Maybe these lobbyists were always here like this.

He turned and walked back through the tunnel, and unable to help himself took another photo of the capitol through the glass roof. He might never get over the awe of that view.

He made his way into the capitol and snapped a few photos of things he thought he might have missed. Then Nick made his way outside but found the air to be pretty warm and humid. Even though it was not the heat of summer, sweat turned his torso damp.

I'll just head back to the hotel and sort what I have before tonight," he said aloud.

"What was that O'Flannigan?"

Nick turned. Detective Matthews stood behind him. "Oh, nothing. How can I help you, Detective?"

"Well, O'Flannigan, we have a large problem."

"What is that?"

"Our suspect didn't commit the crime. He couldn't have."

"Good news for him, I guess."

"And bad news for us. We had to let him go, but we haven't released that information to the press yet, because we want to have another suspect first."

"But you let Phillip go?" Nick asked. As he did, his phone chirped. He didn't look at it, but it chirped from his pocket again.

"You need to get that?" Detective Matthews asked.

"No, I'm good," Nick said as another chirp pierced the air.

"Go ahead, I'll wait."

Nick slid the phone from his pocket to find a message from Sonja. "Phillip is free," it said. "Call me," the next one read. "URGENT," the last one said.

"One minute," Nick texted back.

"Who's that?" Detective Matthews asked.

"Sonja," Nick said, thinking it would be a bad idea to lie. "She's happy. She wants me to call her."

"Well, I'll only take up another minute of your time. We, as the police, have an issue. We want to solve this case, but our number one suspect turned out to be a dud. And the leads we have might be in the photos you took."

"Why is that a problem?"

"Because we want to make sure you keep your mouth shut. No leaked photos, no chats with your little friend--" Matthews nodded at the phone "--about them, or anything you might suspect. You did delete your copies, yes?"

"I thought we talked about this."

"Maybe we did. Just making sure you got the message."

"Loud and clear. I've been through this before, remember?"

"Good."

"One more thing, Detective."

"What, O'Flannigan?"

"I did notice something in the photos. It might help. The shoe print from the paintball arena. There is a flaw in one of the soles like it has been cut or something. You can see it clearly if you look closely."

"Which may not even belong to the killer. Could be totally random."

"You're right. Just wanted to let you know what I saw."

"Well, thanks, Agatha Christie. Or whoever you think you are. We have photo experts. We'll decide what's relevant. You just keep your mouth shut, okay?"

"Yes, sir," Nick said.

The detective spun and walked away, and Nick made his way to his bike. He'd need another shower before the photoshoot, and he could get the photos from today uploaded in the meantime.

But the detective's attitude bothered him. What if the footprint did mean something?

Then it's not your business anymore, Nick thought.

His phone rang.

"Hi, Sonja," he said.

"Hi, Nick. I just wanted to say thanks. I don't know how you did it, but Phillip is free, and has been cleared of all charges."

"I know, but--"

"He said the police told him new evidence had come to light. That must have been from you, right?"

"No, actually. I've been warned off by the detective in charge of the case."

"What?"

"They must have some other evidence. It has nothing to do with what I gave them."

"Are you sure?"

"Yes." But the more Nick thought about it, the less sure he was. Why was Detective Matthews so keen to keep him away from the case? Why seek him out?

"Well, that is weird. But thanks anyway for helping us out. We're still on for tonight, right?"

"Yep," Nick said. "I'm headed back to the hotel to do some file uploads, but I will see you around six or so."

"Perfect," she said.

Nick ended the call and swung his leg over his bike. As he pedaled back to the hotel, he couldn't shake the feeling that they were all missing a critical clue.

11

BAND TOGETHER

Nick went about his work with his usual precision. He edited photos first, and then uploaded them to the shared cloud drive the magazine had provided him. Sometimes, when hotel WIFI was slow, he would use data on his phone as a hotspot but doing this during the day meant fewer people were on the network.

He tried not to become mechanical. On state capital number 14, he knew the risk. Many of the buildings looked similar, so he had to focus on the differences, the history, and what made the capitol building and the city unique.

In this case, the inverted rotunda, or the "shark tank" as it was called, was a major feature, along with the glass ceiling corridor that led to it. The grounds were gorgeous as well, and definitely different than the others he had seen.

But his ace in the hole was the band. He could combine the Austin music scene with the capitol building, and he'd be offering something truly out of the ordinary.

Still, the mystery nagged at the back of his mind. He wished, as he often did when on the road, that he had multiple monitors and a larger screen.

The idea of a new Mac, and some of the detachable monitors that traveled well, excited him.

Wow, Nick. You're quick to spend money you don't have yet, he thought. *A new camera, a new car, a new computer? You'd think you're Rockefeller or something.*

He smiled at his own foolishness. His assignment was a lucrative one: he got paid by the mile, got his hotel rooms and meals comped, and what he didn't have the magazine pay for became a deduction on his taxes. But he certainly wasn't wealthy.

Hell, the best a freelancer could hope for is a story to go viral or a photo to get optioned by the AP or another media outlet, similar to what he'd been doing in Denver. In that case, things had not ended well, or with a huge payday. Instead, it had nearly gotten him fired from the job that did pay the bills.

In the case in Denver, he'd been able to use the app he'd gotten in Carson City to zoom in on the photo and enhance it enough to catch the killer, placate the media, and satisfy his editor enough not to fire him. In this case, an app that removed filtered layers would do him no good.

He wondered if the footprint was even relevant or if his hunches were just that and nothing more. Or if there might be something else in his photos the police had spotted that he hadn't.

There was no way to be sure, and he should just let it go.

He pushed the case from his mind as he uploaded the last of the photos and closed his editing app. He opened his website and uploaded a couple of photos he'd saved for that purpose, tiny macro things. As he did, he looked at the folder where the photos he'd taken of the crime scene were.

"What if--?" he stopped himself. Uploading them to social media could be big trouble or to his website. The likelihood of him getting caught was--huge.

He'd already bounced ideas off of Sandra once, but she'd been right. The case was closed, and even with the police reopening it, this was none of his business.

Just then his phone rang.

"Hi, Emily," he said. "How are you?" His editor at *Travel USA* knew about his side job taking photos of the band, but he'd carefully hidden his idea for this evening from her.

"The question is, how are you?" she asked. "How is Austin?"

"It's fun," he said.

"I bet. How's the side gig going? No surprises?"

"None so far," he said. And it was kind of true. The surprises were not related to the side gig, other than the ones he had planned tonight. "I do have a meeting with the governor sometime tomorrow. I plan to get some more night photos this evening, and I should finish up with the major work tomorrow."

"Sounds good, Nick. I like what I have seen so far. That underground addition is something, isn't it?"

"Indeed," he said. "This is a great town. I went to Franklin's, too. The food here is as good as they say, maybe better."

"That is good to hear. Well, let me know if you need anything."

Nick ended the call. He didn't mention a Tesla, and some extra screens, or a new camera. He'd already mentioned the new computer, and he didn't want to overwhelm her by sharing his entire wish list.

He checked the time. Ten after five. He could grab some quick food on the way, and then set up at the capitol. He needed to inform security that the band would be setting up, only temporarily, for the photoshoot. He was sure Maggie cleared the way for him as a former member of the security team and a fan of the band.

He quickly walked down the stairs and made the decision to take an Uber, at least initially. That way he wouldn't have to worry about his bike at night and could just make his way back to the hotel after he followed the band to listen to at least a set or two.

He waved to the desk clerk, one he hadn't seen before.

When he arrived at the Capitol, he ran across the street, and grabbed a sandwich at a local shop, adding an energy drink to go with it. He'd need the extra caffeine later. After devouring the food, he headed back to the capitol building, where he saw Sonja and the band setting up. Maggie stood to one side, watching. A tall man stood next to her, not as tall as Nick, but not short either.

He wore dark-rimmed glasses, a bowler-type hat, and a sport jacket. Nick thought he must be sweltering.

The pair turned to look at him as he walked up.

"Hi, Maggie," he said. "You made it."

"I did. This is my husband, Albert."

"Nice to meet you," Nick said, shaking his hand. "Are you a jazz fan?"

"Have been since college," he said. "And thanks to Maggie, I hear all about the rising local talent."

"It's great that the two of you share that." Nick glanced down and saw a cane in his right hand, remembering that Maggie said he'd been discharged from the military after an injury.

Albert followed his gaze. "Maggie must have told you. Really, it's no big deal. Just a limp."

"I hear you," Nick said. The ache in his leg was likely mild compared to the pain this man must experience all the time.

"Let me go say hi to the band," Nick said. "You want to be introduced?"

"Sure. Are they playing elsewhere this evening?"

"Yep," Nick said. "I plan to follow them over when we finish the photo-shoot and take a few more photos of their performance tonight. It works for them, and it works for my assignment, too."

"Maggie told me about that. We'll have to chat more about what you're doing later."

"For sure." They walked slowly toward the band, Albert limping along. and as Sonja spotted them, she stopped her setup and turned toward them.

"Sonja," Nick said. "This is my new friend Maggie, and her husband Albert."

"So pleased to meet you," Maggie said. "I'm a huge fan."

"I didn't know we had huge fans," Sonja answered. "But I am flattered."

"I, too, am a fan," Albert told her, holding out his hand. "Pleased to meet you."

Sonja took it, and then shook Maggie's hand as well. "I am pleased to meet both of you."

"How did the two of you meet?" Maggie asked.

"Sonja works--"

"I work at a hotel front desk for my day job at the moment," Sonja said. "But I hope to at some point be doing music full time."

"That would be amazing," Maggie said. "It's awesome to be able to do what you love for a living."

"It sure is," Nick and Albert said at the same time.

"Shall we?" Sonja asked.

"You bet," Nick said. "The two of you are welcome to watch the photo-shoot and join us afterward."

"That sounds great," Albert answered. The pair headed for a bench nearby.

The band, without plugging in, played their instruments and Sonja stepped up to the mic. Dwayne played a few beats on the drum, and Nick caught him in several action shots. He zoomed in on his feet, moving closer to the band and lowering himself to the ground. As he watched, he marveled at Dwayne's ease with his instrument. The drums seemed simply to be an extension of him.

The band laughed as he moved around them, snapping photo after photo, making sure to back up so he got the capitol building behind them more than once. As he was finishing up, sweating and more than a little out of breath, but exhilarated by the shots he'd gotten, Sonja motioned for the others to be quiet. There were a few people milling around the plaza, and a few had looked their way, but the sudden silence drew their attention. She moved the mic aside and started to sing.

> *"We will march through the streets of the city*
> *With our loved ones (that's) gone before*
> *We will sit on the banks of the river*
> *Where we'll meet to part no more."*

The familiar words of the hymn made popular by George Lewis rang off the stone of the nearby buildings. Movement in the plaza stopped as she continued the song.

Partway through, Dwayne added a little rhythm, some light cymbals. He ran down as Sonja finished the final note.

A scattering of applause came from those around, and Nick caught Sonja just as she smiled and looked up into the sky. It was orange streaked with some shades of purple, and the north side of the capitol building was framed perfectly behind her. She blew a kiss, as if to heaven, and Nick found himself fighting back tears.

A quick glance around showed others doing the same, some openly crying. She had moved all of them.

He wondered if the song had been for Jared or some other spontaneous reason. Either way, the beauty of the moment eclipsed everything else for a little while.

The band packed up as Nick did. He spotted Maggie and Albert talking to Sonja briefly, and then the couple disappeared.

"I'll follow you guys over," Nick told her. "I can't wait to show you the photos I got. I'll share them with you tomorrow."

"Sounds great, Nick. Want to meet up in the afternoon?"

"Sure. Can I text you a time? I'm supposed to meet with the governor tomorrow, too."

"Exciting," she said. "Yes, just let me know."

Her voice betrayed sadness. He understood. She celebrated Phillip's freedom, but still mourned Jared, and still not knowing who killed him must be taking a toll.

Nick had no idea what to say to her. Nothing he could say or do would make it better.

He could only hope the police did their jobs.

He took an Uber to the Roosevelt room. His leg was tired from all the walking and biking over the last few days, but truth be told he felt in better shape than he had in a long time.

When he walked inside, he spotted Maggie and Albert and joined them. While they waited for the music to start, he texted Sandra a few pics of the band from the capitol building shoot he'd taken with his phone.

As he sat with the couple so clearly in love with each other after all these years, he added to his message: "I love you. I know it is a cliche, but I really do wish you were here."

"I love you, too," came back the immediate reply. "I miss you."

He smiled and watched the band. He pulled out his camera and took some more photos, but nothing matched what he'd caught that afternoon, and so he stopped and put it away.

For the rest of the night, he just enjoyed the great jazz, Maggie and Albert's company, and a few delightful drinks. When the last set was over, he took an Uber back to his hotel.

He would finish tomorrow, topping the day off with a meeting with the governor. That left Friday to fill in any photo gaps he found, listen to some more music, eat some more great food, and prepare to move on.

If you didn't count the murder, it had been a pretty good week, and the case hadn't been that disruptive after all.

It was beyond time to let his suspicions go and move on. Nick fell asleep quickly and didn't dream at all.

12

THE SHOE FITS

Nick woke after a fitful and dreamless sleep. The sun streamed through the hotel window, and he welcomed it. Today, he would try to wrap things up, but much of his timeline hinged on Maggie's promised meeting with the governor.

He checked his phone as he headed for the shower, found a good morning text from Sandra, a text from Maggie that said simply, "How about 11?"

Nick rubbed his eyes and stared at the screen. It was 8:30 now, a little late, but not oversleeping. He'd go through the capitol photos he'd taken yesterday quickly, and see what he was missing, if anything.

Meantime, his stomach growled, and he needed a shower. He sighed.

He felt pressed for time even though it appeared he would have a free day tomorrow. He hated to settle for the hotel breakfast, but in this case, the moments he saved would help him prepare for his appointment.

A shower, a quick run of a razor over his face, and a dash downstairs earned him a decent bagel, a banana, orange juice, and passable coffee, although he would need to find something better shortly.

Once settled at the little hotel desk, he opened his laptop, uploaded the band photos, and put them in a separate file. He would surprise Emily with those tomorrow, once he had everything else uploaded.

He then took the rest of the capitol photos and looked through them by opening the entire folder in Photoshop and scrolling through the gallery view. He'd prefer to be doing this in Lightroom, but this software was the best he had at the moment.

There was always something new he could use, if he were able to afford it.

Soon, he told himself. *Soon.*

He saw that he could use a few more photos of the various floors and the art in the capitol. He'd focused almost too much on the shark tank and the underground extension, and he'd have to eliminate some of those photos. Still, it wouldn't hurt to give Emily and the book editors choices.

A reminder on his phone chimed, and he determined it was time to go. A dash to the capitol building on his bike, a second dash to a coffee shop, and a few photos would put him right on schedule. He could gather the rest after his interview.

The ride went smoothly. It would be warm again today, but it felt like the temperature wouldn't reach the sweltering heights of the day before, and the humidity was definitely lower.

He found coffee at a stand across from the capitol plaza, purchased a cup, and sipped it as he made one more round of the outside of the building. As much as he was drawn to the north side, he made sure to balance that with shots from every angle he could think of.

Ducking inside, he spotted Maggie finishing up a tour, and he waved and then waited for her.

"You made it," she said when she was done. "Come with me."

"Aren't we a few minutes early?" Nick asked.

"No worries. The governor is a friend of mine, you know."

"Thanks again for this," Nick said.

"Anytime," she said. He followed her up to the second floor of the capitol building and to an ordinary-looking door like many others he'd found in capitol buildings before this one.

Maggie knocked once and went in. Nick followed the shorter woman inside.

"Hello, Governor," Maggie said. "This is the photographer, Nick, I was telling you about."

"Pleased to meet you," Nick said, holding out his hand. The governor wore a dark blazer, a red tie, and a white shirt. His salt and pepper hair was combed immaculately. Even though Nick was taller than him, he felt slightly intimidated.

"Nice to meet you, too, Nick. I hear you are on quite the assignment."

"I am," Nick answered.

"Well, let's chat a bit, shall we? I'm sure you have some questions, and I have a nice break for a little while."

They moved to a secondary office with a large desk, and Nick sat in a chair in front while the governor made his way behind it, where he was flanked by both an American flag and a Texas state flag.

"Mind if I take some photos, and record this?" Nick asked.

"No problem," the governor said. "What would you like to know about the great state of Texas?"

Nick started with questions about the capitol itself and then moved to questions about the state, and how the governor saw the future of Texas and the huge tech startup culture emerging in Austin.

He found the governor to be quite forthright and charming.

"That's about all I have," Nick said when he finished his scripted questions.

"Well, I have some questions for you," the governor said.

"Really?" Nick said. "Ask away."

"So this is a year-long assignment you're on, and we are state number fourteen?"

"Yes, sir."

"What is your favorite state so far?"

"That one is hard to answer. I like things about each, and I loved Colorado, because friends came to visit me there, but there were also--" Nick hesitated. "Issues."

"I hear you've had some adventures along the way. How do you like our barbecue here?"

"Well, this is some of the best food so far." Nick patted his stomach. "And I love the music scene, although that has limited the time I have to sleep."

"Understandable. Ah, to be young again," the governor said.

"Nick even photographed a band here at the capitol last night," Maggie interjected.

"Very creative," the governor said. "You'll have to share those photos with my office. We may use them. We'll give you credit of course."

"That would be great," Nick answered. "I can email them over this afternoon."

"Sounds perfect," the governor told him, glancing at his watch. "I do have another appointment, but if you need anything else while you are here, even over the next couple of days, let my office know."

"Of course."

"Maggie, thanks for this pleasant interlude to my day."

"Anytime, sir," she answered.

Nick and the governor shook hands, and Nick had Maggie take some photos of the two of them together. Nick asked for and got a couple of posed shots before he left.

"Thanks again," Nick said.

"Anytime. Have a pleasant rest of your trip, young man."

Nick followed Maggie out the door.

"That was exciting," she said once they were in the hall. "I think that went well."

"It did. I appreciate it."

"I'll see you around?" she asked.

"Yep. I plan to finish today and use tomorrow as a relaxation day before I move on."

"I bet you only get a few of those," she said.

"Not enough, for sure," Nick answered.

"Well, take some time for you. Take care, Nick."

He held out his hand for her to shake, but Maggie moved in and gave him a quick hug. "It was great meeting you," she told him.

Then she left. Nick stood there a moment longer, feeling a little lost. He looked down at his camera.

His light breakfast left him hungry. He'd eat, edit photos, and maybe take in some of the rest of the Austin music scene tonight. He'd really only seen Sonja and her band, and as much as he liked jazz and them, he longed for some good, live rock music.

There was a chain, one he'd seen in Boise too, called Eureka! He ducked inside.

Nick ordered the Brussel sprouts as an appetizer and a burger for his meal. It turned out to be a lot of food, but it was excellent, and the restaurant had local beers on tap, so he grabbed a stout, but opted for the smaller offering, 16 ounces over 20 ounces, knowing he would likely have another couple later in the evening.

By the time he finished eating, he was stuffed, making the ride back to his hotel a heavy one. Sonja was not at the front desk, and he thought they had a gig tonight that she'd mentioned earlier.

He had her phone number and email for sending the photos he'd taken, and he'd get them over either this afternoon or tomorrow. Tomorrow.

A day off. It would feel so nice to not have to go out and take photos, although he probably would for his own collection, but being done with his assignment meant he could do whatever he wanted.

He sat down at his laptop and opened his photo editing software. He went through the last of the capitol photos quickly. He had everything covered, and then some. He deleted duplicates, even going into the magazine cloud file and removing extras he'd uploaded.

Everything was in the cloud except for the few band photos he would share with the magazine. Nick made sure to email the photos of the governor and a couple of the band photos to the email address he'd been given. It would be great to see some of his photos in their advertising.

Then he opened the folder with the photos of the band, and went through them, starting with the long shots that included the capitol in the background. He included a few close ups, including a great one he got of Sonja singing.

Once the upload for the magazine was complete, he decided to go grab something to drink before he uploaded the band photos. For some reason, he craved something other than water.

There were drinks in the hotel lounge downstairs, and he could bring back flavored water and maybe a small snack to tide him over to dinner, and then finish the band photos.

Nick was on a roll, and getting things done felt really good.

As he stepped out of the elevator on the ground floor, his phone rang.

"Nick!" his editor Emily said before he could say hello. "You're brilliant!"

"Um, thanks," Nick said. I'm glad you think so. But what did I do?"

"Two things. I just went through your photos. Fabulous shots with the governor by the way. I'd love the text of that interview."

"I'll write it up for you tomorrow," he answered. "I'm about done, so I'm going to take a day off and act like a tourist."

"Good idea. I know you could use a break."

"It has been a harrowing few weeks," he said. More than a few. Starting in Denver, things had been more exciting than he would prefer. From nearly being poisoned himself in Phoenix to being stung by a bee in Santa Fe and determining he had a serious allergy, he could do without any more adventure in his life, and a day off was exactly what the doctor ordered.

"Second," she said, bringing him back from his reverie. "Nice shots of the band! That was a great idea to include people and a flavor of Austin in your photos."

"I thought so. Since I was photographing them anyway, I thought it would be a good idea to share some of them for the book."

"It's brilliant. This book will be amazing," she said.

"I do appreciate that," he said.

"Anyway, just wanted to congratulate you. Do you need anything from us, or do you have everything you need?"

"No, I'm good," he said.

"Good," she said. As he ended the call, Nick headed to the small lounge and "store" area in the hotel lobby. Things would be more expensive there, but it didn't matter to him. He just wanted a quick break and then to go finish his work.

He glanced over and saw Sonja at the front desk. He smiled and walked over.

"What are you doing here?" he asked.

"I stopped by to grab some things I left in my locker. How are things going?"

"I'm done with my assignment, pretty much. I'll be going through your photos next, and I'll have them for you later this evening or first thing tomorrow."

"Sounds great."

"How is Phillip?"

"He's good. Glad to be free. I wish we had some resolution for him about his brother."

"Me, too. I am sorry I can't help more."

"I know, Nick. You did what you could."

"Don't you guys have a gig tonight?"

"Yeah. We are playing a couple of sets. It should be fun."

"Good," Nick said. "I'll talk to you later."

"You can just send the photos in the morning if you need some down-time," Sonja said. "We won't be able to look through them tonight anyway. Then invoice me what we agreed on. We'll be sure you're paid before you leave."

"Sounds perfect," Nick said. "Thank you. It's been great getting to know you and the band. You're all very talented, and I'm sure you'll go far."

"Thanks, Nick." He saw a tear roll down her cheek, and she quickly wiped it away. "You really are a gem."

Nick smiled. "Take care."

He walked away, grabbing a Diet Coke and a large pack of peanuts. He paid way too much for them with his debit card and headed back upstairs.

When he got there, he sat and tapped the trackpad to stop the screen saver on his laptop. On the screen was one of the photos he'd taken of Dwayne drumming, a close-up of his feet working the drum pedals. He scrolled forward through them, rather proud of how well he'd captured the motion. The photos almost seemed to move.

He spun the cap off the soda, and then stopped mid-drink. That photo.

It showed the sole of Dwayne's foot, mid-air as it switched between two pedals.

A perfect shot.

And across the bottom of the sole of his shoe, a hiking boot really, was a line, what must be a crack. Maybe caused by pressure on that point of his foot by the drum pedal. On his feet were hiking boots, with an aggressive tread.

It looked like--but it couldn't be...

Nick brought up the photo of the shoe print he'd sent to the police and flipped it until it was at the same angle as the drum photo.

He placed it on one side of the screen, and the photo of Dwayne's foot on the other.

They were identical, and unless he missed his bet, the feet were the same size.

Dwayne made that footprint.

Even if he wasn't the killer it placed him at the scene of the murder.

Nick sat back, not knowing what to do next.

Should he ask Dwayne about this, and confront him first, or should he take this to the police, who might not listen to him anyway?

For a few moments, he froze, running the events of the week back through his head.

He remembered Dwayne's reaction to the news about Jared.

He'd looked troubled, upset at the mention of his name.

Troubled enough to kill him?

He didn't want to think so, but it seemed an unlikely coincidence.

Then it came to him in a flash. He knew what to do. He went over the plan in his head, and then called Sandra.

"Hi, Nick," she said. "What's up?"

"Got a minute for me to run something by you?"

13

———————

TYING THINGS UP

"That sounds like a plan, Nick, but why not just give the information to the police anonymously?" He could hear the concern in Sandra's voice.

"Because the cops and the band will know it came from me. They haven't released any information about the footprint, probably because it might really be a coincidence."

"Okay. Are you sure, Nick? Maybe the police will find this out some other way."

"Look, if it turns out to be nothing, Dwayne won't do anything. If he does something suspicious, the police will know. Then they can take it from there."

"How will Sonja and the band react?"

"I'm not sure. I don't want to betray them and their friendship, but I can't just ignore this."

He heard her sigh. "Okay, I know you can't. Be careful, Nick."

"Will do."

He ended the call, and then looked at the card Detective Matthews gave him. On more thing to do before he made that call.

Nick dialed Sonja's number. She answered on the first ring. "What's up, Nick?"

"Hey, I just wanted to let you know the police have something new, something that might help solve the case." Nick heard Dwayne in the background.

"Who is that?" he asked.

"It's Nick. With new information about the case."

"Put him on speaker," he heard Dwayne say. He heard the beep of a button.

"Sorry, I'm back and you are on speaker. What do they have?"

"A footprint at the scene. There is an odd mark in the sole of the shoe they think belonged to the killer."

"A mark?"

"A flaw. Should make it easy for them to identify him."

"That's exciting! Do they have a suspect?"

"Not yet, but they are looking through the photos I took and some other camera footage. Just thought you would want to know."

"Thanks for sharing, Nick."

"You bet. I'll be sending the rest of the photos to you shortly."

"We're looking forward to it," Dwayne said, his voice sounding far away.

"Of course," Nick said, and ended the call.

After a deep breath, he looked at the detective's card again, and dialed the number that said "cell."

"Matthews." The detective's deep voice answered, the single word causing Nick to gulp. He almost hung up but knew the detective would be able to see that he called, and simply call him right back.

"Hello?" The detective said. Nick realized he'd hesitated, waited too long to answer.

"Hello, detective," Nick said.

"O'Flannigan? What do you want?"

"I-I-I have something for you." Nick stumbled over his words, suddenly afraid that he was doing the wrong thing.

"Oh really? What is this, some kind of plea for attention?"

"I know who the footprint I photographed belongs to. The one with the odd mark in the sole I told you about."

Silence followed. Nick waited.

"Hello?" he said, mimicking the detective's earlier dialogue without thinking about it.

"I'm here. Who do you think it belongs to?"

"I know who it belongs to, and I have proof." Nick made the statement with much more confidence than he actually had. "I have an idea of how to catch him if you want to hear it."

"Spill it, O'Flannigan. I don't have time for games."

"It belongs to Dwayne Robbins, Sonja--"

"Sonja Robbins husband." A statement, not a question. Nick might not even need to use his plan after all.

"How do you know?"

"You think he wouldn't be a suspect? C'mon O'Flannigan, even an amateur like you should know the killer is almost always someone related to the victim or who knows them."

"But Phillip--"

"Estranged brother, with a rock-solid alibi. There were others. Dwayne was top on our list. Until now, we had nothing. In fact, we still don't."

"What do you mean?"

"We have your suspicions. I want to see your so-called proof."

"If you use it, he will know where it came from. I called Sonja--"

"You what?"

"I told her about the photo, but not whose footprint it might be. Dwayne was listening."

"Why?"

"If he tries to get rid of the boots or shoes right now, it will look funny. But you will be able to find them, if you hurry and act on this."

"So you set a clock for us."

"I did. I had to know you would take this seriously."

"We'll have to reveal where this evidence came from."

"I'd rather you didn't."

"Not my problem, O'Flannigan. You want to do the right thing or not?"

Nick hesitated. He did want to do the right thing, whatever that was. He just second-guessed himself, as he'd done already on this trip. In other cities.

He realized it then. Detectives and cops often seemed cold not because they were heartless and not real people, but they couldn't let any personal feelings get in the way of their investigations. The Truth, with a capital "T", was the truth, like it or not.

A capital "T". Nick snorted at the unintentional pun.

"Something funny, O'Flannigan? You trying to make a fool out of me?"

"No, sir."

"Look," the voice on the other end of the line softened. "I know this is hard. And I'm sorry that you're involved at all. Don't you see what you're doing to yourself?

"Doing to myself?"

"Every city you are traveling to, or at least several I know of, you're involving yourself in some kind of local case, intentionally or not. You're taking an assignment that could double as a vacation and turning it into not just one job, but two."

"I don't mean to."

"Doesn't matter. Listen, if you have some kind of aspirations of being a detective of some sort, some kind of forensics photographer figuring out puzzles all the time, give it up."

"I don't really--"

"Don't lie to me O'Flannigan. I saw you light up when you gave us your photos. You were like a kid putting the final piece in a giant jig-saw puzzle. Walk away. This is the kind of career that can ruin your life. Go back to taking photos of flowers, bees, and all that stuff."

"I don't know what to say. Thanks, I guess?"

"You're welcome. Now, give me the evidence you have."

"Do you want to meet?"

"No. Email it. I'll take a look."

"Um, okay."

"Do you want to be more involved?"

Nick stayed silent.

"I didn't think so. I'll do my best to keep your name out of it. Now, O'Flannigan."

The call ended.

Nick opened his laptop without thinking, clicked on his email, typed in the detective's address, attached the photos of Dwane's foot, and hit send.

Then he closed it.

His phone dinged, and he looked to see a message from Sonja containing an address.

"Here's where we're playing tonight if you want to come," a second message read.

Nick wanted to find some music, some food, and now something to drink. Something stronger than beer.

"Maybe tomorrow," he typed back. "Thanks for the offer!"

He stared at the exclamation point, but only for a second. A change of clothes, and of scenery was in order.

The Hole in the Wall sounded about perfect, if he wanted some head-banging rock. But then he saw an interesting band playing at Tellers. Nick set up an Uber on his phone and walked downstairs.

Tonight, he just wanted to get lost in the music.

But the things the detective said to him haunted him all through the evening. He drank too much, hoping to shut them out.

But it didn't work.

By the time he got back to his hotel, he collapsed on the bed without undressing.

14

ADIOS, AUSTIN

The sun pierced the room, and Nick rose slowly. His head hurt.

Today was his day off, technically the first one he'd taken in quite some time.

Rising slowly, he checked the time on his cell. Nine.

Nick rarely slept this late. He needed to return his bike rental and take care of some simple things, but other than that, his time was free. He had no idea what to do with it.

He decided to take his camera down near the Colorado river. There were some beautiful parks there. He stretched his leg. It felt good. Limber.

He opened his browser and looked for a short hike. One listed was Sculpture Falls, a little over a mile and a half long that led to what would normally be a swimming hole. A quick check of the temperature told him it would likely be a little cold for a swim, even for locals, but he could get some great photos for his website, and some exercise at the same time.

Nick dialed the bike rental company and told Rod he was ready for him to pick up the bike and gave him the address of the hotel.

"I'll be there shortly," he said. "How did it work out for you?"

"I rode all over the place," Nick told him. "It worked out perfectly. Saved me a lot of parking woes."

"Good to hear it," Rod said.

Nick ended the call, and then looked at his open laptop. Damn.

He'd forgotten to send the photos to Sonja and the band after his discovery and his conversation with the detective. He'd need to do that before he went out.

For his first step, he headed downstairs to turn over his rental bike. Just as he arrived in the lobby, Rod walked in.

"Hey man, thanks for the ride for the week," Nick said as he retrieved it from the locker.

"Anytime. Did you have any problems?"

"No," Nick answered. Everything went well, but I really didn't ride far."

"Good to hear. What did you think of Austin?"

"Loved it."

"Are you going to come back our way?"

"Sometime, for sure," Nick said. It may be a while though."

"Oh, yeah. Your assignment. Did you get everything you needed?"

"And then some," Nick smiled. "Thanks."

He and Rod shook hands, and Nick followed him out to his van to get his receipt. Then he headed back inside. Far from ideal, the hotel breakfast area was just barely open, and there wasn't much left, but he grabbed a banana, a granola bar, and a small glass of orange juice, along with a cup of what was clearly old coffee.

"Just a snack," he told himself. "I'll fuel up before the hike."

When he got back to his room, he woke his laptop, finding the band photos still up on his screen. He clicked on the close up of Dwayne's shoe, and his finger hovered over the delete button.

Making a quick decision, he deleted the photo entirely, and then put the rest into a ZIP file. He then emailed it to Sonja with a stock invoice.

Nick way underbid the job. As he hit send, he remembered the jazz singers words.

"Just let us know how much you'll charge. Dwayne will settle up with you."

Nick hadn't seen any news. He had no idea if the police had acted on the information he gave them yet or not.

It was out of his hands now.

Nick closed the computer and shut it down.

It was time to find a good coffee, grab a water bottle, and get hiking.

The sun warmed his skin. A slight breeze ruffled his hair, reminding him he was due for a haircut. Maybe he could get one this afternoon before heading out of town tomorrow. Or he could stay one more day, and head for Oklahoma on Sunday.

Then he remembered how far it was. An overnight stay in Dallas might be in order and give him time to see some sights there. A quick stop at a convenience store got him what he needed.

When he reached the Barton Creek Greenbelt entrance, he grabbed a bottle of water, stuffed a couple of granola bars in his pockets, and hung his camera bag over his shoulder. He might want more than one lens for this hike.

He locked the car, walking toward a sign describing the park area and the route.

He stepped back and snapped a photo. The descent to the water went smoothly. The trail was surrounded by greenery, and he passed a few people coming back up the hill. He waved or said "hi" to each group.

When he reached the falls, he understood why this was such a popular spot.

The water was clear and beautiful. The falls was short, and water cascaded over a small group of rocks. It was nothing like some of the falls he'd seen in the northwest, but still beautiful in its own right.

It was hard to believe that miles later, this same river raced through the Grand Canyon. Although there was a light ache in his leg, Nick knelt and took several photos, capturing small eddy's in the water.

Moments like this reminded him of how much he loved photography and what he did.

Once he had several dozen photos, he pulled out his phone and took a few with it too. He then sent one to Sandra. "Day off. Wish you were here."

"Me, too," came the quick answer.

God he was lonely.

"You're only fourteen weeks in," he told himself. "Get it together."

"What's that?" a voice said from behind him.

"Just talking to myself," he answered, turning to see a young woman standing there. She was tall, thin, and blonde. She wore running shoes, loose athletic shorts, and a zippered sweatshirt.

"Ah," she said. "You know, loneliness is not a bad thing. You can be much more comfortable with someone else once you're comfortable with yourself."

"I know," Nick said. "At least intellectually. But some days are harder than others."

"What's her name?" she asked.

"Whose name?"

"The woman you are missing."

"Sandra."

"Do you love her?"

Nick stared at her for a moment. *Why are you having this conversation with a total stranger?*

But he answered anyway. "I do. At least-- Our relationship is young."

The woman just smiled. "You think she loves you, right?"

"I do."

"Then be patient. You'll be together soon enough."

With that, she turned, and jogged back up the trail.

What the hell was that? Nick thought. *But she isn't wrong.*

He took one final look around and headed back up the trail himself.

Coming down had been pretty easy. Heading back up was a little harder. What had seemed like a gentle hill coming down caused him to break a sweat going up. His bad leg ached even at the halfway point, but he pushed through. By the time he got back to his car, he was sweaty and exhausted.

And he felt great.

He took a selfie and sent it to Sandra. She replied with a "shocked" emoji.

Nick used his phone to search for lunch nearby, found a spot within walking distance, and decided to grab a pulled pork sandwich to go and eat it in the park.

It took only a few moments for his food to be ready and headed back to the park right away. He found a bench to sit on and started eating.

Just as he did, his phone rang. The name on the screen said, "Sonja."

"This is Nick."

"Hey, Nick, I got your photos and they're great."

"Thanks," he replied.

"I also got your invoice. It seems a little low. Is this amount right?"

"I gave you the good guy discount," Nick said. "I feel like I know you."

"Thanks," she said. "We'll send your payment over today."

"I do appreciate that," he said.

"On another note, a Detective Matthews called Dwayne today."

"He did?" Nick did his best to inject surprise into his voice.

"Yes, he did. He says he has some questions and has some new evidence. Do you know anything about that?"

"No, I don't," Nick said. He tried on confidence but felt like it fell flat.

"Okay," she said. "I know your ideas really didn't go anywhere with them, but I wanted to check. So Dwayne could be prepared."

"I understand," Nick said. "I wish I could be more helpful."

"That's okay, Nick. I'm off tonight. We've got another gig. So if I don't see you, so long."

"So long," Nick repeated.

She hung up. He looked at what was left of his lunch, but his appetite had vanished.

He glanced around at the area around him. Like many other cities he'd visited, his leaving would be bittersweet. But he also felt bad.

He'd just lied to someone he would like to think of as a friend.

His loneliness came not just from being alone, but from having to isolate the truth from some of those around him.

Detective Matthews was right. He should run from this, quickly. Never become involved in another mystery again.

Even if he saw something, he should just let it go.

Nick resolved to do just that.

He headed back to his car. He'd go out again tonight but turn in early. Tomorrow, it was time for him to say goodbye to this beautiful place.

And he couldn't say he'd be sad to do so.

15

____

OFF TO OKC

The trip would only take six hours, but Nick wanted to take his time. His head was a mess.

The girl on the trail was right. He needed to learn to like being alone. He thought he was better at it than he really turned out to be.

And the Detective was right, too. These mysteries were not great for his mental health. He needed to stick with what he loved: taking photos, traveling, and spending time with cool people, friends even, when possible.

He didn't need to solve every mystery he came across, and he certainly didn't need to lie to those involved. It felt like a stain on his soul.

After checking out, Nick climbed in his car, and set the GPS for Killeen, Texas. He wanted to stop briefly and see Ft. Hood, the largest military base in the continental United States, with a full two divisions of troops stationed there.

He'd then move on to Dallas, leaving himself only a short drive on Sunday.

He started the car, and a local news station came through the speakers.

"Local man arrested on suspicion of murder," he heard. "The drummer of local band Sonja and the Dropouts Dwayne Robinson has been arrested for the murder of a local bassist killed last weekend. Police refused to comment--"

Nick shut the radio off. He didn't need to hear more.

His phone rang, and he saw it was Sonja.

Instead of answering, he let it go to voicemail. He turned onto I-35 North, got up to speed, and set the cruise control. He'd arrive in just over an hour if he took the shorter route using Texas 195. Killeen had to have some decent lunch spots.

He left the radio off and let himself get lost in his own head for the next hour. The phone chimed, and he saw his mother was calling. Whatever she needed, he would call her back.

She always left a voicemail.

The miles raced under his tires, and Nick thought of how far he'd come, and how far he still had to go.

Before he knew it, he topped a rise. Miles and miles of desert stretched out in front of him, and in the distance he saw a helicopter rise from the desolation, turn and head northwest. The same direction he was going.

A new excitement rose from his gut to his throat, and his frowning concentration broke into a grin.

Today was going to be a good day. He just knew it.

FACTS ABOUT AUSTIN, TEXAS

While Austin, Texas is considered to be the Live Music Capital of the World among other things, and despite the fact that Texas is conservative overall, Austin tries to keep it weird, much like Portland, and is a bit more liberal.

In fact, Austin has the only clothing optional beach in the state, even though there is no Texas state law prohibiting women from going topless.

Austin also has the largest urban bat colony in North America, with over 1.5 million bats inhabiting areas of the city during the summer migration from Mexico.

Austin is also the sunniest city in the country, with 300 out of 365 days being sunny. Once when I was visiting Austin (in August, one of the hottest times of the year) it had been over 100 days since they had rain, and it started to rain that evening. People came out of the hotel where I was staying and stood outside in the rain. It was amazing to see, and the rain was almost as warm as the water in the shower.

The Capitol building in Austin is the second largest in the country as well, only second to the national capitol in Washington, D.C.

There are also a ton of museums in Austin you should visit when you can. Especially the Cathedral of Junk, dedicated to, you guessed it, junk.

And while you might think of barbecue (I LOVE Franklin's and had to include it in the book), the food Austin is most known for is breakfast tacos.

If you get the chance to visit Austin, do it. And look around. If you see a tall red-head taking photos, give Nick a shout, would you?

OFFERED IN OKLAHOMA CITY

BOOK #15

KICKED OFF

Myssi took the piece of fingernail from between her teeth and stared at it. Even when she bent it between her pointer and her thumb, the polish stayed in place, and for some reason, she found that fascinating.

She rubbed her nose, the metal ring in her left nostril cold against the back of her hand, and glanced at the sign overhead, the one with the gas prices on it. $3.94, it read. Most times with Jeb's Convenience and Curiosity, you couldn't count on the sign to be accurate.

She sat astride a red moped, her main means of transportation. Less than four bucks would keep it motoring for more than a week at the steady sixty miles to the gallon the tiny engine sipped. The worn Honda was a little worse for the wear, but every mechanic she met told her the bike would run forever if she kept the oil changed, the gas fresh, and the spark plugs good. She did all three. Religiously.

Religiously. That was about the only thing she had to do with organized religion, besides an occasional Black Mass or similar ceremony at the Church of Ahriman. Most people thought it was a place to worship Satan, but she didn't. She found the ceremonies and rituals freeing.

She shivered, the wind biting through her short, sleeveless leather vest. Under it, she wore only a Thin Lizzy t-shirt that lived up to the band's fabric-descriptive name. Black jeans covered her legs --riding in shorts was for crazy people, and calf-high boots with silver buckles protected her feet.

It wasn't that cold for the outskirts of Oklahoma City, but the wind certainly didn't help this time of year, not that it ever stopped for long. A greasy fast-food bag drifted across the cracked pavement, and she watched it drift into one of the two lanes stretching into the distance. As she puffed on her vape, the bag crossed the center line, and an older Ford F-150 that had once been yellow crushed it under its balding tire before it continued to the freeway a few hundred yards behind her.

Myssi was 18, but people rarely believed her, and she got carded all the time. Jeb knew her, as well as he knew those boys goofing off on the other side of the parking lot, and he didn't hassle her, so she'd become a regular at this odd convenience store, buying her vaping supplies from the wide selection on the wall behind the counter.

For some reason she could not identify, today felt different. The lot *looked* different. The four pumps protruded from the parking lot like four broken teeth from an addict's gums, and an "Out of Order" sign on one of them fluttered in the wind like the American flag on top of the building.

Her martial arts instructor always told her to trust her instincts.

"If something feels off, it is. The key is to pay attention," he'd told her. "Attention is something everyone can afford."

As Myssi reached the front door, a late model sedan of some sort pulled up to the pumps. A quick glance revealed Washington plates, and a tall red-haired man exited the driver's door, stood, and stretched.

She smiled. Tourists. They were down here by both the convenience and the curiosity part of the name, both declared on a big sign beside the freeway.

The bell over the door dinged as she entered. Jeb's Convenience and Curiosity was aptly named. The front of the store looked typical: aisles of junk food, drink coolers filled with soda and energy drinks, and a giant sign that read, "Restrooms This Way." Underneath, in smaller letters, the declaration "For Paying Customers Only" reinforced the message that even if this was a bathroom stop, you needed to buy something.

Jeb himself was a curiosity. He stood behind the register. Over the counter hung the old-fashioned racks of cigarettes, although he'd told her he might get rid of them at some point.

"All this healthy living stuff people are doing, I might put some Keto snacks up there instead," he'd told her with a crooked smile.

Behind him was a wall of vaping supplies, something a lot more popular than smoking now, at least in Oklahoma. Jeb stood nearly seven feet tall., his head covered by long, black hair, and was a former basketball star, although "Long before the Oklahoma City Thunder existed," he would tell anyone who would listen.

His nose protruded from his face and hooked downward, toward his mouth. His lips were thin, nearly non-existent, but his teeth were straight, white, and large. A sharp chin protruded from an angular face, what some would have called a fox's face.

He always wore nearly the same thing-- a pale leather top it could be assumed he purchased from a local tribe, usually with some kind of bead work and open over his thin chest. Jeans covered his legs, which made up a good portion of his height, which was amplified by the low ceilings. She didn't know what the building used to be, but her guess was a bar or something. Unlike more modern places, the tallest walls here were somewhere around eight feet high.

The roof actually sloped downward toward the back of the store and became even shorter. She'd seen Jeb duck the few times he'd been back there when she came in.

Myssi headed to the cooler, where Red Bulls were marked down to two for five bucks. She grabbed a couple to go with her gas and vape juice.

As she closed the door to head back up front, the not nearly as tall as Jeb but taller than normal red-haired man came through the front door. If she hadn't seen his out-of-state plates, Myssi might have mistaken him for a member of the Thunder himself. An expensive-looking camera hung from a strap around his neck. She walked up behind him.

"Hi there," the man addressed Jeb. "This is a cool place you have here. I'm Nick O'Flannigan."

"I'm Jeb, the owner."

"Nice to meet you. I'm on a freelance assignment from *Travel USA* magazine, and I'd love to take a few photos and ask you some questions about your place if that's okay."

"For most people, the answer would be no," Jeb said. "What are you going to do with them?"

"The magazine is putting together a book on all the state capitals, including the area around the Capitol building and local attractions," he said. "It will provide some free publicity for your place. I'll share on my social media channels, too.

"Okay," Jeb told him. "Just be sure if you take any of the art you find, you give credit to the artist, okay? And let me review any of the photos you want to publish before you submit them."

"Thanks. I'll let you get to your customer," the photographer indicated Myssi. "I'll come back to interview you in a bit."

"Sounds good," Jeb said. As the man walked away, Myssi stepped forward.

"How are you today?" he asked her. "What can I do for you?"

"My usual juice," she said. "And a pack of batteries."

"Triple-A, right?"

"Yeah."

"Why don't you get one of these new rechargeable jobs?" He said, pointing to one hanging on a hook. "I'll give you a deal. It will save you on these for sure." He waved the pack of batteries in front of her face.

"Maybe next week," she said, looking at the meager cash in her wallet. "And can I get three bucks on pump three?"

"You bet," he said, putting the juice next to her Red Bull. "That'll be $18.50."

Clearly, he had given her a discount of sorts, but she didn't say anything. She handed him a twenty.

As Jeb took it, the front door banged open, the bell above it violently ringing.

"Everybody back!" The male figure said. "They're coming."

"Who's coming?" she asked.

"They!" he said. The mask over his face puffed in and out with his clearly rapid breathing.

Myssi didn't see anyone through the dusty, poster-laden front window behind him.

"Just calm down," Jeb said. "Tell us what is going on."

"You! You're one of them!"

"What?"

The man's eyes darted back and forth nervously. "Who else is here?"

"No one," Jeb said, glancing toward the back room.

The intruder pulled a small pistol. "There is, too. Come out, whoever you are!"

The tall redhead appeared from the back. "What is--?"

"Put the gun down," Myssi focused on the black-clad figure.

"I can't do that."

"You can. You will," she said the last word forcefully.

The gun moved from Jeb to the stranger, and then back to her. Time slowed down.

Sweat stood out on the robber's forehead despite the cool interior of the store. But his eyes. They bothered her the most. They were glazed as if he wasn't seeing her, or his surroundings. He was somewhere else. Whoever he was, he was high. Really high.

"Look, stay calm," she said, her words seeming to come from far away. "Give me the gun."

From the corner of her right eye, she saw movement, and her eyes darted that way. Jeb had stretched his full height across the counter, had a baseball bat in his hand, and swung it downward.

Both Myssi and the armed newcomer stepped back, and the swing missed, the bat falling to the floor with a clatter. Jeb quickly ducked behind the counter as the gunman turned his weapon his way.

A gloved finger inside the trigger guard twitched.

The martial arts training her now absent father had insisted on kicked in. Literally.

He must have seen her movement because her first kick knocked his arm to the side. The gun went off, followed by a shout.

She didn't grab for his wrist. That would be a fatal mistake. Instead, she brought a knee up into his gut, wanting to disable him but not really hurt him.

He doubled over, and the small pistol dropped from his hand, landing next to the baseball bat on the dull, seldom waxed floor.

Then she simply pushed him backwards.

The shooter straightened and stumbled. He lunged forward.

So Myssi kicked him in the center of his chest. His face went slack, and he fell further back. His head hit the floor with a giant "thwack" that sounded like a discarded bat connecting with a pitch for a homer.

Time raced to catch up with her. Blood poured from the shooter's head into a pool on the floor.

"Myssi!" Jeb said.

She turned. The redhead lay face down. Blood flowed from the side of his head into a second crimson pool.

"He's been shot," Jeb said.

In the distance, sirens wailed.

"I activated the robbery alarm," the store owner explained.

She stood paralyzed, shaking, and studied one downed stranger and then the other. The red-head and the man were lying on the floor bleeding.

Jeb was assisting the photographer, so she went to the shooter, and knelt beside him. She checked for a pulse. Nothing. His mask wasn't moving, and he didn't appear to be breathing.

She pulled the cloth away.

"Toby?" she said, recognizing not the man who was the shooter, but the young man her age. Her friend.

The door to Jeb's burst open.

"Police!" she heard. "Nobody move!"

There was no danger of that. Toby wasn't moving. He wasn't breathing.

"Help!" she screamed. "Help!"

A moment later, after a few officers moved toward the back of the store and she heard shouts of "Clear!" echoing back to her, another police officer moved her away. He checked for a pulse and breathing, just as she had, and started CPR. A moment later, a second officer joined him.

Another officer wrapped a blanket around her shoulders and led her outside.

"What happened?" he asked.

"He-he came in with a gun. Is he okay?"

"We'll see," he said. "We're doing all we can, and the paramedics are on the way." He helped her take a seat on the curb. "Stay here," he said. "Don't go anywhere."

Soon the parking lot was full and contained two ambulances, a fire engine, and several police cars.

Suddenly Myssi felt very cold and tired. She looked up to the sky, then down at her hands, and wept.

2

AWAKENING

Nick's eyes fluttered open. He heard voices, some distant, a couple closer, what sounded like a man and a woman. He was lying on his back. The last thing he remembered was--what?

He'd been almost to Oklahoma City, stopped to fill his gas tank, and decided to take some photos in an unusual shop.

Bright lights over his head betrayed the fact that he was no longer in that shop, and he couldn't remember the name. Joe's something? He tried to sit up.

"Whoa, there," a soft, male voice said. "Easy. We're glad you're awake."

"What happened?" He felt cool sheets under him and tried to clear his vision, but everything still seemed a little blurry. His head hurt, his body ached, and he tried to reach up and rub his eyes, but he couldn't lift his hands.

"You don't remember? You were shot. Well, a bullet grazed your head at least."

"You mean--what?"

"There was a robbery. Out at Jeb's Convenience and Curiosity. Do you remember anything?"

Nick nodded, but he tried to piece together the fragments of his memory. He'd been taking photos, and heard some noise, went out front, and then--

Nothing.

"My camera. My phone. My car. What's going on?"

"You're in the hospital. I'm your nurse, and my name is Marc. I'll let the doctor know you're awake. And a young lady is waiting in the lobby who's anxious to see you."

"A young lady?"

A fuzzy head, all he could make out, nodded and this disappeared.

Nick closed his eyes, shook his head, and then blinked several times. He needed to figure out what was going on, and where his stuff was. He needed to make some phone calls, let his girlfriend Sandra know what was happening, his parents, his editor Emily, and his friends.

His vision cleared some more, and he finally became aware of the room around him. An IV stand with two bags of something hanging on it hung on one of those metal trees. Two tubes came together at one point and then ran into his arm.

A simple black and white clock on one of the beige walls told him it was eight o'clock. Thick drapes over the single window and the meager light in the room didn't reveal if that was a.m. or p.m. The usual medical cupboards hung on the walls, accompanied by a sink and two doors. He assumed the one to his left led to a hallway, and the one on his right, behind the single chair in the room, for visitors, led to a bathroom.

Bathroom, he thought. Suddenly he really needed to pee.

I wonder how late I was out.

A television hung dark in one corner, and he almost wished it was on, but at the same time the ache in his head and behind his eyes made him suspect he wouldn't be able to take much of that.

Turning his head back and forth revealed that it must be wrapped in some kind of bandage, and the left side hurt more than the right.

Then the nurse's words caught up to him. "Wait, shot?" he said aloud. "I was shot?"

Again, he tried to move his hands, wanting to use them to explore his head and check for other injuries but they were restrained somehow.

This was a nightmare. He was on a dream assignment, traveling the country to photograph every state capitol building and the surrounding areas, and in every city, there had either been a mystery or some other kind of trouble. He'd managed to stay on schedule despite those things, but now he again found himself in a hospital.

The only thing he could do at this point was wait, and everything felt better when he closed his eyes. His urge to use the restroom lessened. He would rest until the nurse came back and freed him.

He must have dozed.

"Mr. O'Flannigan," a booming voice said, and Nick would have jumped from the bed had he been able. "Dr. Radon here. Nice to meet you."

Nick looked up at the looming man. Broad-shouldered but with an ample middle as well, the doctor had chocolate skin, what was clearly a shaven head, smile lines around eyes that were nearly black, and a too-small-for-his-face nose over a salt and pepper goatee. The facial hair both circled and highlighted an infectious smile.

"Hi," Nick said. "Can I--I have to go to the bathroom."

"That's a good sign. And I'm glad you're awake. I'll have a nurse come help you with that in a moment. Can you wait for a few moments longer?"

Nick nodded, and a sharp pain radiated down into his left eye socket like lightning.

"Easy," the doc said. "You'll want to keep those head movements to a minimum."

Nick sucked a breath in between his teeth. "I suppose so."

"You were shot during a robbery," the doc began. "The police will have some questions for you. I'll hold them off for a while. The bullet grazed the left side of your head, and basically cut your skin open and ruined your hairdo for a while, at least until the stitches heal and the hair grows back."

"How long will that take?"

"One thing at a time, tiger. You've got a concussion, too. We're going to have to watch that. We'll want to keep you under observation for a couple of days, less if you progress well."

"Another concussion?" Nick muttered. "Great."

"Another? You've had other concussions."

Nick forgot the earlier pain, and nodded, getting another shot of agony as a reward.

"Recently?"

"Yes," Nick said. "Two within the last several weeks."

"That's not good news."

"Any chance, anything I can do to speed up getting out of here? I'm on an assignment--"

"Do you have anyone at home who can keep an eye on you?"

"Not exactly. I'm traveling alone, working for Travel USA magazine." Nick found that just talking, trying to explain things to the doctor, was exhausting.

"Not a chance. Until I am sure you are ready, you can't leave here Mr. O'Flannigan. No matter what your assignment is, or what it involves, you have to stay put."

Nick sighed and closed his eyes. Better. The doctor was right, he needed to rest and heal. He didn't have another option. He only hoped this was not the final straw, the one that would end his assignment.

The doctor left with a smile and a nod, and Nick laid still until a stocky female nurse came in.

"You need to use the restroom, Mr. O'Flannigan?"

"Nick, please," he said. "If you're going to help me to the bathroom, you might as well use my first name."

"Well, okay Nick. We'd like you not to be up walking around yet, so I'll find you a urinal and free your hands, okay?"

"Okay."

The nurse opened a cupboard, pulled out an odd-looking device, but its use and how it worked were obvious.

She unbuckled his hands from some padded leather restraints, ones that looked like those he'd seen on a dentist chair in Salt Lake. Nick shuddered. He flexed his arms, making sure they were working again, and even that action sent a stab of pain through his brain.

Then he took the urinal from her and prepared to do his thing. By now, his need was more urgent. She turned her back to give him privacy, and a moment later a stream of relief followed.

He sighed loudly and was just about to finish up when he heard loud voices from the hallway.

"Is he awake? Let me in!" a male voice shouted.

"He isn't ready for visitors yet. He needs rest." This was another forceful male voice, a bit softer. The nurse from earlier?

"I don't care. I have questions and I want answers."

"Here's one," Nick heard the male voice say. "No. You can't go in yet. You need to talk to the police. We've told you this."

The stocky nurse clicked her tongue. "Just a minute, Mr. O'Flannigan. I'll be back."

Noises of a scuffle in the hallway came through the door as the nurse headed that way. Nick turned his head to see what was going on.

Ouch, that really did hurt.

The door burst open and a bulky man pushed his way in. He was barely over six feet tall, shorter than Nick's six-foot-six frame, but clearly not a former basketball player. Maybe football, with his thick shoulders and forearms, but age had given him a gut that had suppressed the circumference of his chest.

He wore a red tie over a white shirt, an unbuttoned fray suit jacket, and matching pants.

"What happened to my son?" he shouted.

It took Nick a moment to connect the dots. His son? This must be the father of the boy who'd been shot.

"Reverend Ayunda," the nurse said, stepping in his way. "You cannot question Mr. O'Flannigan. He's had a concussion, and we have told you to direct questions to the police."

Though the woman's head only came up to the bridge of his nose, she clearly had the upper hand over the new arrival.

Nick still wasn't sure exactly what was going on.

"He saw that--that girl kill my son, and I want to ask him some questions. Now."

"I don't care," the nurse told him. "I know who you are and what your church means in this town, but that has nothing to do with what is happening now. Get out."

"But--"

Behind him, two uniformed security personnel appeared.

"You can go now," the nurse said. "With help, or without. I know how devastated you must be. But this isn't the way to deal with it. Talk to the police, Reverend. Please."

The intruder did not answer. Instead, he spun on his heels and left the room, a security officer slowly closing the door behind him.

Nick looked at the nurse with fresh eyes and found her name tag. "Nancy," he said. "Thanks so much."

"You're welcome, Mr. O'Flannigan."

Nick sighed. His head hurt, and his eyes were much more tired than they should be.

"You get some rest, now," she said, adjusting the I.V. bag above his shoulder. "I'll let the young lady waiting to see you that it might be a little longer."

"Young lady?" he said again. The nurse earlier had said something about a young lady too. But before he could reason for himself who it might be, he fell into a deep sleep.

3

———————————————

HELP FROM AN ANGEL

Nick woke again and looked at the clock. A few hours had passed, and he felt better. He turned his head and found that the pain from earlier had moved further away.

But he also had to pee again and pressed the call button. Maybe they would let him get up now.

The door clicked open, and Nancy reappeared.

"Welcome back," she said. "Glad you're awake. How do you feel?"

"Well, I have to use the bathroom again," he said. "But the pain is better."

"Good. Let me get the urinal for you."

"Thanks," Nick said.

They repeated the process from earlier, and as Nick was finishing up, a tapping sounded at the door.

"Knock-knock," said a familiar male voice. "You have a visitor."

"Just a minute," Nancy said. He saw her move toward the door as it opened, but she was too late.

Nick was finished but still exposed, the now full plastic bed urinal in one hand.

"Right this way, ma'am," he heard.

"Hello, Nick," a familiar voice said, and then she was in the room. "I came as fast as I could."

"Sandra?" he said.

"Yep," she said. "Coming to your rescue again. And I can see I'm just in time." She indicated the urinal.

Nick turned as red as his Irish locks of hair, and stared at the container, unsure what to do with it.

"We'll give you two some privacy," the female nurse declared. She plucked the urinal from his hand with blue gloved hands of her own and left.

As soon as the door closed behind her, Sandra burst out laughing.

Nick tried to join her and groaned as soon as the laughter started.

"Don't," he said. "Hurts."

"Oh, Nick," she said. Her warm hand was in his a moment later. "What did you do this time?"

Nick couldn't believe she was here. Her dark hair, green eyes, and fair skin all blended into the most welcome face he'd seen in a long time. Since he saw her in Denver as a matter of fact.

"I can't believe you're here," he said. "How did you know what happened?"

"I'm in the health app link on your phone. When they couldn't unlock it, the paramedics used the SOS feature, and it texted me your location. I called them, got the story, and hopped on a plane. Tell me more about what happened to you."

For the next few moments, she stroked his arm as he told her the little he knew of the story, from stopping at Jeb's to the robbery, and the young lady taking down the attacker.

As the story wound down, she smiled at him.

"I love you," she said. "I had to come. You may need my help for a couple of weeks."

"I may at that," Nick said. "I don't know how long I will have to keep this bandage on my skull."

"Until the stitches come out. Even after that, you'll have to be careful, and you'll probably want to wear a hat for a while."

"I'm okay with that. Can I see what I look like?"

Sandra smiled. "If you insist." She closed her laptop, pushed the table aside, stood, and pulled out her phone. "Ready?"

Nick smiled while she took a quick photo. She turned it around and showed it to him.

Starting over his left eye, a bandage started and weaved its way around his head. On the right side, a lock of red hair stood stubbornly outside the bandage. The left was entirely covered in white wrapping over what appeared to be gauze.

"That's enough of that," he said. "I need to call mom and dad, and Emily too. I need to tell her I might be delayed."

"You won't be delayed."

"Well, I can't go take photos like this."

"I know," Sandra said. "I'm going to take some of them for you. I already cleared it with Emily. You can give me direction on what you like and don't like, and as soon as you get out of here, I'll take you to the capitol itself, even if I have to push you around in a wheelchair."

"I don't think that will be necessary."

"It might. You need help so I'm here for you."

"What about mom and dad? Did you call them?"

"Done. Your mom is worried, but not overly so. Your dad is--well, loud."

"And Gerry?"

"Talked to her, too. She's fine."

"Seems like you have it all covered."

"I do, until you are better."

"But if I need a couple of weeks..."

"We'll get you cleared for travel, and I'll go with you to Topeka and beyond if needed."

"But what about your job?"

She gestured to the laptop. "Got it. Most stuff I can handle remotely and the rest is taken care of for me."

"Okay. Again, thanks."

"Of course, Nick."

"I love you," he mumbled. She leaned over and gave him a kiss on the lips, and he lifted his hands, wrapping her in a weak hug.

Another knock came at the door.

"Hey guys," a voice said. "I'm Randy, from the imaging department. The doc ordered us to check inside your head."

"What?" Nick responded.

"I'm taking you for an MRI."

"Oh, okay."

"He wants to be sure about your brain after all those concussions."

"Makes sense. Will you be here when I get back?" he asked Sandra.

"I don't plan on going back to the hotel until very late, if at all," she said. "I'll be here."

Nick waved as he was wheeled away, still trying to work out in his head what had really happened to land him in this position.

4

SHARING AND CARING

When Nick arrived back in his hospital room, Sandra was typing intently on her laptop.

Randy set the brakes on the bed. "We'll have the results later when the doc reads the data," he said. "Take care, Mr. O'Flannigan."

Sandra smiled. "Thank you. We do appreciate it."

While in the MRI tube, Nick's mind had been racing. When Randy had gone, he turned to Sandra.

"I really do want to thank you for being here."

"Of course, It's my pleasure."

"Has anyone told you more about what happened to me?" he gestured at his head. "What about the girl who was at the scene of the--whatever happened? What did happen?"

"It's probably easier to show you than tell you," Sandra said.

She reached for a remote by his side and turned on the television on the wall.

Just then Nancy, the nurse from earlier, poked her head in the door. "Hey there," he said. "Everything okay?"

"Better," Sandra said. "Look who's awake!"

Nick smiled, and Sandra muted the television while she checked his vitals, and he was given a thumbs up. "You're doing fine," the nurse said. "You'll be out of here in no time."

"Good," Nick said.

"Dinner service in about 20 minutes."

As he left, the news started, and Sandra unmuted the sound.

"Jeb's Curiosity and Convenience, an OKC icon, was the scene of a grisly crime yesterday. One man, a photographer from out of town was shot and is stable in the hospital. A local woman, Myssi Renata, over-powered the potential robber. However, he died at the scene as a result. According to our sources, she is being questioned about how, exactly she overpowered him, and prosecutors declined to comment about whether any charges will be made in the case.

"The intruder was Toby Ayunda, the son of mega-church pastor and televangelist Adam Ayunda of Faith Light Church, who is demanding that his son's killer see justice."

The screen changed, and the man who had charged into his room earlier appeared on the screen. "The woman in the store and the owner used excessive force to stop my son," the man said. "He was in the wrong, but so were they, and I will not rest until justice is done in this case."

"The investigation of what actually happened is underway," a uniformed officer appeared on the screen. "We'll keep you posted with any updates."

"Reports say the father and son were estranged, as the deceased had been involved at the Church of Ahriman and had not been living at home for some time now."

"Thanks," the anchor took over the screen. "This is of course a developing story, and we will keep you up to date with any new developments."

The report ended, and the weather came on, predicting warmer than normal temperatures over the next week.

Sandra shut it off.

"Do you remember what happened?" she asked.

"Not really. I heard shouts, so I came out of the back. That's when I saw the girl struggling with a guy with a gun. It went off, and then I don't remember anything after that."

But there was something. Nick couldn't put his finger on it yet, a flash of an image he remembered.

"Well, the police want to talk to you. We can probably hold them off until morning," Sandra told him. "The media I am sure will want something, but I'll try to find a way to keep them away, too."

"Hopefully they will keep that pastor guy under control. What is he thinking?"

"I don't know," she said. "But I'm glad she was there, and that she acted when she did. It probably saved your life."

"Probably. Maybe there is video footage or something that will show what happened."

"Which you will never see if I have my choice."

Someone knocked. "Come in," he and Sandra said at the same time.

A woman in pink scrubs came in with a tray, a brown, covered plate on it, and a juice to one side.

"Your dinner is here," Sandra said.

"Indeed," the young lady told him. "The best our kitchen has to offer. Let me know if you need anything else, and if you get hungry later, don't hesitate to call a nurse or give us a ring. The number is on the phone next to your bed."

Sandra helped him eat, and Nick took in as much as he could before he felt sleepy and full.

"Thanks, hon," he told her. "I do appreciate your help."

"Anytime," she said. "I should let you sleep."

"You have a hotel booked?" he asked.

"I took your room," she told him. "It was a bit tricky, but they let me check in when I explained the situation."

"You have any plans for the evening?"

Sandra smiled and held up his camera bag.

"I'm going to get a jump on some night shots of the capitol building for you."

"Oh, man. You're amazing."

"I try. See you tomorrow?"

"You bet," Nick said. "Hopefully they will let me leave since you are here to keep an eye on me."

"I hope so," she said and kissed his forehead.

Nick turned the channel on to a mindless reality show and watched until he couldn't keep his eyes open anymore. As he drifted into sleep, he dreamed, of odd convenience stores, rickety gas pumps, and a large, hand-drawn pentagram.

He woke the next morning with a dry mouth, parched lips, and an overwhelming need for the bathroom.

5

—————

QUESTIONS

Nick woke to find Sandra already by his bedside in that same chair. She was typing away on her keyboard and kept typing until he cleared his throat.

"Good Morning," he said. "You're here early."

"Actually, you slept a little late," she said. She clicked a couple of keys on her laptop. "But I did bring you something."

She spun the laptop around, and Nick's breath caught in his throat. There was a gorgeous night shot of the capitol, the moon overhead, but something odd dominated the foreground, a tower-like structure. "What is that?" he asked.

"An oil derrick. One of several around the state capitol. It is such a cool place, Nick, I can't wait to take you there. And to get inside."

"Wait, oil derrick?"

"Yeah. The building itself sits on over 100 acres of land, and there are a bunch of active wells around it."

"Wow. I thought I read something about those," Nick said, "But it's different actually seeing one."

"I thought the same thing," she said, and then advanced to another photo. It was a sunrise shot, taken this morning. The sky was orange behind the capitol building, and the dome looked like it had been lit by a Hollywood director.

"Another gorgeous shot," he said quietly. Sandra had an excellent eye. Her photos were brilliant. She could easily replace him on this assignment. They were even better than what she'd helped him with in Sacramento.

"I really loved taking them," she said. "I'll need your help uploading them, but Emily says she will give me a login and my own folder in case you are incapacitated again."

"God, I hope not," Nick said. As she said it, he thought again of how he had gotten here. A moment later, a knock came at the door, and Marc, the male nurse from the morning before, entered.

"Mr. O'Flannigan?" he asked. "How are you feeling?"

"Better, I think," he said.

"Listen, I have held them off as long as possible, but the police are here and would like to talk to you. They want to take a statement at least."

"Sure, I think I'm up to that." He wasn't really sure, but maybe he could talk to them only once and get this done

"Okay. If you get too tired or overwhelmed, hit the call button, and I'll come in and shoo them out.

"Thank you."

"I'll keep an eye on him, too," Sandra told him. "I won't let them overstay their welcome."

"If it is any comfort, I think we'll spring you this afternoon," Marc said. "As much as we love your company, with your wife here to watch you, I am sure we can set you free into her capable hands."

"My--" Sandra caught his eye and put a finger to her lips. "I mean, of course. I would love that."

"I knew you would. I'll send the cops in right away."

Marc wasn't kidding. He disappeared for only a second, and a man and a woman entered the room. Both had badges on their belts, guns on their hips, and both wore similar button-down shirts.

"I'm Sergeant Peabody," the woman said, extending her hand. She was taller than her partner, had broad shoulders and a strong grip. Long black hair descended her back, woven into a thick braid. "And this is my associate, Detective Jenkins."

Nick shook the woman's hand first, and then the clearly younger and smaller man shook as well. His blond hair was cut military style, and green eyes set behind his wide nose studied the room. He looked like a typical marine with a barrel-shaped chest and a narrow waist. A tattoo on his forearm poked out of his sleeve.

"This is my girl--my wife, Sandra," Nick said awkwardly, and Sandra laughed.

"Girlfriend, but I wasn't sure if the hospital would let me in, so I put wife on the form. I've since cleared it up, but some staff members remain confused."

Both officers shared a smile, and Nick glanced at Sandra. She smiled back and him and winked.

"Are you feeling better, Mr. O'Flannigan?"

"Please, call me Nick. And yes, I am. My head still hurts from time to time, but I imagine that will take a bit to go away."

"More than likely," Sergeant Peabody said. "You'll have headaches for at least a few days. I hear they are going to let you out soon?"

"Hope so," he said.

"Where will you be staying once you leave?"

He noticed the younger detective had pulled out a notebook. The interrogation had officially begun and in a subtle way. Nick sighed.

"The Marriott downtown. I'm sure Sandra can give you the address."

"No need," Jenkins said. "But thanks."

"As I am sure you know," Peabody began again. "You are a material witness to--well, potentially a couple of crimes."

"A couple of crimes?"

"Yes. There is the attempted robbery," she said. "But possibly manslaughter as well."

"Manslaughter?"

"There are--extenuating circumstances."

"What are those?"

"Let's start with what you can remember about what happened at the convenience store," Jenkins said.

"Uh, okay. I saw the sign on the highway for Jeb's Convenience and Curiosity, and I was, well--"

"Curious?" Peabody said with a grin.

"Yes," Nick said. "I needed gas and a stretch anyway, and so I pulled off, parked by the pumps, and went inside. That's when I saw the back room. If you're familiar with the place, you know the one. There is a lot of interesting stuff back there, I asked the guy behind the counter if I could take some photos of the curiosities, and he said yes. Just no photography of the art and I was to get any shots approved by him before I published them."

"Jeb, you mean. How did you get him to agree?" Jenkins interrupted. "I know he has been touchy in the past."

"He must've thought it would be good publicity."

"Not a bad reason at all," the detective mumbled. "Go ahead."

"Well, I heard a commotion up front. Someone yelling."

"Yelling what?"

"Something about 'they're coming,' or something."

"Any idea who 'they' might be?"

"No. I think Jeb was trying to protect me. He told what turned out to be the man with the gun that no one was in the back. But he must have been the one I saw outside before I went in, because somehow he knew I was there."

"Saw before you went in?"

"Yeah, there was a young guy sitting on a picnic table outside. He had something in his hand, but I couldn't see what it was. There were a couple of other kids to one side, goofing around."

"Was the item in his hand a weapon?" Peabody took over the questions.

"I don't think so," Nick said. "But I can't be sure. I thought was a pill bottle or something."

"What happened next?"

"The guy yelled at me to come out, and I did. As I did, the girl, Myssi, I guess her name is, told him to drop the gun. Jeb tried to hit it out of his hand with a baseball bat, the gunman turned on him, and she jumped him."

"Jumped him?"

"Looked like some kind of martial arts move," Nick said. "I heard a loud pop, felt pain in my head, and I don't remember a thing after that until I woke up here."

"Okay. That's pretty helpful, Mr. O'Flannigan," Jenkins said. "It lines up with what the video shows, and with what Jeb said too. Except for one thing."

"What's that?"

"When you arrived, was the girl already inside?"

"Yeah, I mean, I assume so. I saw her as soon as I walked through the door."

"You're positive? Any way you could describe the guy outside?"

"No. Just a got a glimpse really."

"Did you notice this tattoo on his forearm by any chance?" Peabody asked. "Either when you saw him before you went inside, or before you were shot?" She held out a phone and turned it toward him. The photo showed a crudely drawn pentagram with a candle in the middle.

"No," Nick said. "I think I would remember that, but you know," he pointed to his head. "At this point, I can't be sure what I forgot or missed."

"I understand," the detective sighed. "Do you recall the girl saying anything particular or peculiar to him? Did she call him by name or anything?"

Nick searched his memory. She hadn't, not that he could think of.

"No, why?"

"Well, it appears they knew each other. And while her takedown of him was clean, and clearly self-defense, that isn't what killed him."

"What?"

"Look, not a word of this to anyone, especially not the media, because they will turn this into a circus."

"Word of what?"

"The robber was drugged. And he and Myssi hung out the same places."

"Really?"

"We're certain of that."

"There was a scooter out by the gas pumps," he told them.

"Myssi's. But it is possible the victim, Toby, rode to the station with her."

Nick searched his memory again. Something else nagged at his mind. An image he couldn't quite retrieve.

"Toby was likely hallucinating when he came into the store. And we're reasonably sure the drugs that caused that also killed him."

"Was he a known drug user?" Sandra asked quietly, and everyone turned to look at her.

"Um, no ma'am," Jenkins said. "He was the son of a prominent local pastor."

"Although he was on the outs with his dad," Peabody added. "Probably the reason for the pentagram tattoo."

"And where he hung out with Myssi," Jenkins said.

"Where was that?" Sandra asked.

"The Church of Ahriman," Peabody answered. "A Satanic cult."

Marc appeared at the door. "Hey, detectives. Sorry to interrupt, but the doctor wants to chat with Mr. O'Flannigan before we release him."

"We were just finishing," Jenkins said. "Thanks for your time, Mr. O'Flannigan. And Miss--"

"Call me Sandra," she said.

"Sandra then. We'll be in touch. And Mr. O'Flannigan?"

"Yes?"

"Your reputation precedes you. You're in no shape to be investigating anything, and these Satanists are bad news. Stay away from this, okay?"

"Don't worry," Sandra said. "I'll keep him out of trouble."

They left, and the nurse stayed. "You alright for now?" he asked.

"I could use some water," Nick said.

"Right away." Marc disappeared.

"You ready to get out of here?" Sandra asked.

"You bet," Nick said. But he could see by her face, and by the expression behind her eyes, she was troubled about something. He was sure they would talk about it later.

The doc came in a moment later, briefed him on the MRI results, and provided the couple with some discharge instructions.

"Just sign here, and I will get the nurses started on your release papers."

Nick scribbled his name, and as he did his stomach growled.

He was starving, and he couldn't wait to leave and find a great burger somewhere.

6

GOTTA GET OUT OF THIS PLACE

The door to the hospital whooshed open, and Sandra rushed to his side. He was being pushed in a wheelchair by his nurse, Marc, flanked by Nancy, who had just come on shift.

As she met them between the two sets of exit doors, she leaned down.

"Nick, there are reporters. Lots--"

"Mr. O'Flannigan!" an excited voice said. "Can we get a comment?"

"Comment on what?" he said, shielding his face from a flash, followed by a bright light mounted to a video camera.

"On the crime you witnessed," the voice said.

"Listen, there--"

"The robber's father was here earlier. Did you talk to him?"

"What about the connection between the victim and the assailant? Did it seem like they knew each other?"

"We aren't going to comment or answer questions at this--" Sandra began, but Nick put his hand on her arm.

"I don't know the girl, Myssi, did anything wrong," he said. "The two people I saw didn't appear to know each other, but I only got a quick glimpse before I was shot. I've shared everything I witnessed with the police, and I'll be cooperating fully with their investigation." As he finished the statement, his voice faded. He felt tired already and wondered if he was actually ready to leave the hospital after all.

"Now," Sandra said. "Can you let Mr. O'Flannigan and I pass?"

"Mr. O'Flannigan, can you tell us more about your involvement in other mysteries on your trip?" The voice was feminine in nature, and when Nick turned to look, he saw a tall, slim redhead with sharp features and a freckled complexion. She wore a sand-colored business blazer over a white blouse tucked into a similarly colored pencil skirt.

He opened his mouth to speak, but Sandra, mimicking his earlier action, put her hand on his arm.

"No comment," she said.

"Could any of the mysteries you've been involved with before be connected in any way?" the reporter asked.

Nick didn't think so, but he asked himself the question anyway. Ticking the past cities in his trip off his fingers, he couldn't see any connection at all...

Except that he was the one common denominator. He was present in each city, he found himself in the middle of mystery after mystery, and even though had kept most of them out of the news, it wouldn't take a genius detective to make some assumptions.

A genius detective. Something he was not. He'd gotten lucky in some cases, unlucky in others. He couldn't deny his involvement, but he tried to think of what situations he could have avoided.

And about his actual assignment. Maybe that was, at least in part, why Sandra was here. To keep him on track, focused, and away from another case. More, if she really stayed with him for a couple of weeks.

It would be great if she did. Staying out of trouble was something Nick seemed unable to do on his own.

Including this week, he told himself. Already, it's a media circus and they know who I am.

Well, just because he'd been shot at the scene of the crime didn't mean they needed to find out any more about him.

"No comment, as my girlfriend said," he responded. Marc gave her a knowing look, and Nick swallowed hard. "I'm here on a freelance photography assignment, and I plan to focus on that, and only that."

"Okay, Mr. O'Flannigan," the reporter said.

The group parted as he, Sandra, and Marc moved forward. A few camera shutters clicked, but other than that, the questions stopped.

Then he glimpsed his car and the man next to it.

The man appeared to be in his early to mid-thirties. He reached nearly Nick's height, but rather than being thin, he sported a round chest and a rounder belly, but not an overly large one.

His clothing, not his size, is what made him stand out. He wore a crimson robe, or that was the best description Nick had for it, with intricate gold weaving around the waist, almost like a sewn-in belt. The same pattern stretched in a wide line up his chest to where the cloth met his chin. Overlaying his intricate clothing, a gold necklace with what must be a heavy pendant decorated with a couple of odd symbols Nick did not recognize hung.

In contrast to the crimson of the robe, the man wore a black hat, plain save for a single yellow flower. Troubled green eyes stared at him from over a salt and pepper goatee with a bit of extra salt.

"Mr. O'Flannigan," he said, his voice nasally, but not unpleasant. "Pleased to meet you. I'm Adrial Finbar."

7

———

THE PRIEST

Adrial held out his hand, revealing a heavily tattooed forearm, and Nick heard Sandra suck in a breath between her teeth.

"We said we have no--"

Nick interrupted her and took the man's hand carefully. "Hi." His voice sounded weak to his own ears, and he could feel Sandra's eyes on him. "I'm sorry I can't talk now."

"That's okay, Mr. O'Flannigan. I'm the high priest at the Church of Ahriman. Where Toby and Myssi were--members."

"We have to go," Sandra told him coldly. "My boyfriend needs rest. And we have a lot of work to do still this week."

"No, I get that. I just wanted to let you know I'm here to help with any investigation you may be a part of, or if you have questions or want to talk."

"Investigation?" Sandra said. "He isn't a detective. Nick is a victim."

"I'm sure he is, ma'am. And I'm not trying at all to be rude."

"We're not either," Nick said, trying to move things along. "We really do need to get moving."

"I understand," he said, moving to the side. Nick noted none of the media approached as they talked. *Ad occursum futurum.*

Adrial stepped aside, and Sandra helped Nick into the passenger side of his car. When he turned to look back, the large man was gone, and a few reporters stared after him. In the parking lot in the opposite direction the priest walked, Nick saw an older truck that seemed out of place but looked oddly familiar. Someone sat in the driver's seat, but he couldn't make out who it was.

Sandra slid in behind the wheel. "Do you know who he is, Nick?"

"No. Other than his introduction."

"The Church of Ahriman is a world-famous Satanic temple."

"The place the police said the Myssi and Toby hung out," Nick rubbed his head, but on the opposite side from his wound. "It's a church?"

"Don't call it a church. Don't--"

"Okay, whatever you want me to call it. But a kid who was a Satanist? His dad is a pastor. I wonder where Toby got his drugs?"

"Probably the Satanist church. Pastor's kids rebel all the time."

"I wonder what his father thought. He clearly didn't like Myssi."

"I know you care about others a lot, Nick, but it doesn't matter the way you getting better does. We need to stay away from him, and out of this whole mess. The police will handle it."

"I think we already agreed on that."

"You've made your statement. From here on out, say only' no comment' if anyone approaches you, understood?"

Nick turned to look at her. Her narrowed eyes and pursed lips told him she was angry, and not a little either. Perhaps furious would be a better word.

"What's going on?" he asked.

"I've had a bad experience with a group like this before," she replied simply. "I don't need to have another one."

Nick gave in. He wanted to go see the capitol building, to get a sense of what this assignment was all about, but his head throbbed, and after the encounter this morning, he could use a little quiet rest.

First, the police warning him off, members of the media who apparently knew who he was somehow, and an odd--church? No, Sandra had said not to call it that and called it a temple, a Satanic one.

Whatever it was. Things were already complicated, and it was hard enough to stay under the radar without a giant bandage on his head.

"Anyway, you wanted a burger, mister?"

"I would love one," Nick said. Despite the pain in his head, which medication had reduced to a dull throb, his hunger was even greater.

"Excellent. We'll head to S&B's. You've never had a burger quite like this one."

They entered to find simple black chairs at wooden tables. Nick ordered a 1/2-pound Jalapeño burger with the smothered fries called "Fire" and Sandra ordered a smaller one, the Frenchman, and some sweet potato fries.

The portions were huge, and they talked as they dug in.

"Did I tell you already how much I appreciate you being here?" Nick asked. He sipped from an icy glass of water. He wanted a beer, but the doc had told him to avoid alcohol, partly due to pain meds, partly due to his concussion.

"I'm glad I am here," Sandra said. "I really do love what you do."

"Me, too, mostly."

"I understand. No matter how enjoyable, there is always work involved in any job."

"True," Nick paused. "Can I ask you something if you are ready?"

"Sure."

"What experience did you have with--Satanism, I guess?"

Sandra sighed, popped a fry in her mouth, and chewed while Nick waited. "I knew you'd ask. Listen, I'm not a religious person, but I do believe in a spiritual realm. And I don't think messing around with it is a great idea."

"Okay. Me either."

"That being said, I've encountered some Satanists before. Most of them were either going for shock value or using their 'religion' to justify mischief."

"Sounds like most other religions," Nick answered, thinking back to his own catholic upbringing. "You mentioned you had a bad experience."

"That's a story for another time."

"I see," Nick said. "It's just odd anyone from the church would show up and talk to me. I mean, why?"

"Who knows, Nick, but it is not something you want any part of."

"None of this is," he agreed. As he finished his last fry, he realized he was full and exhausted.

Sandra appeared to be done, too. "Can we head back to the hotel?" he asked. "Maybe we can visit the capitol later tonight?"

"How about in the morning?" Sandra said. "With me helping you with photos, we should be able to get some great stuff, and still allow you to rest."

"Of course."

"And besides, we can take some quality time to relax together. The hospital was no good for that." Nick looked over, she winked at him, and he blushed.

She was right. Tomorrow would be a new day.

8

QUESTION EVERYTHING

The sun woke him, and Nick felt quite refreshed. When he moved his head, a dull ache reminded him to take it easy.

He sat up slowly and looked around. Sandra stood by a small counter in the hotel room, fiddling with the coffee maker.

"Hi sleepyhead," she said, turning around. "How are you feeling?"

"Better," he told her. "Are you making coffee?"

"It's not great, but it will get us by until we can head to the capital. How's your energy level?"

"I'll know when I am up and moving. A shower might help."

"You can do that. We just have to be careful of the bandage on your head. Think you are up to taking some photos?"

"You bet," he replied.

His phone rang, and he winced at the sound. He'd have to remember to turn the ringer volume down. It was his mom, and so he answered and put her on speaker.

"Hey, Nick," she said. "How are you doing?"

"Yes, how is he?" he heard his dad shout from the background. It was good to hear his dad be this vocal, the most Nick had heard from him since he'd suffered a stroke earlier in the trip. Nick had almost left his assignment to go help him, but his mother had discouraged him from doing so.

"I'm okay," he told her. "I'm going to try to go take some photos today."

"Well, be careful. You were shot, you know."

"Just a graze, mom. More like getting hit with something."

"Still, Sandra said you have a concussion."

"I do, mom, and some stitches that need to heal. She is here with me and will keep an eye on me over the next couple of weeks. She'll be helping too."

"That's great," she said. Nick could hear the pleasure in her voice but dismissed it. "I just want you to be happy and safe."

"What did he say?" Nick's father yelled.

"Sandra is helping him," his mom explained. "He is doing fine."

"She is good for you, Nick!" his dad shouted.

"Tell him I know, mom, and I love you both. I'll stay in touch, I promise."

"Well, I have Sandra's number now, so even if you don't, I know who to call."

Nick glanced at Sandra, who simply smiled. "I'm glad," he said into the phone. "We'll talk later, okay?"

"Okay. We love you."

He ended the call and rubbed his eyes. He stood, testing his balance. His head felt okay. Maybe he would recover faster than he thought.

Sandra moved to his side. "Are you alright?"

"Yep. I'll be careful in the shower."

"I'll come with you to make sure."

A half an hour later they were both clean, dressed, and smiling. "Want to grab some breakfast?" Sandra asked. "I've made a schedule for us I hope will get us all the photos we need. We can go over it while we eat."

"Have I told you lately that I love you?"

"Not enough," she said with a smile.

"Well, I do, and thank you again. I couldn't do this without you."

"I know," she said with a wink. "Now, I have a breakfast spot picked out. It's a few minutes away, but it is near another place where we should photograph while we are here."

"What is that?"

"The memorial near the 1995 bombing of the Murrah building."

"The National Memorial and Museum? I was planning on visiting as part of this trip."

"You laid up gave me a bit to do some research."

"And it is Wednesday. We have to get moving for sure."

"Don't worry mister. We have a head start."

"Again, thanks to you."

Sandra headed downstairs, almost leading him, and making sure he was okay along the way. Nick couldn't believe she was here, and quite honestly didn't feel like he deserved her.

"Wait here," she told him when they reached the lobby. "I'll fetch the car."

While he waited, Nick glanced up at the television. The news didn't show anything about the story. Maybe it would fade from the headlines and be seen for what it was: an attempted robbery and an accidental, and unfortunate death.

"Mr. O'Flannigan?" The voice interrupted his thoughts as he saw Sandra pull up outside the front doors.

"Yes?" he said, looking down. There, standing in front of him was the young woman from the store, Myssi. "Um--uh--what are you doing here?"

"I need your help."

"I don't know if I can help you," he answered. Her soft brown eyes pleaded with him, and he tried to return her smile.

He noted her pierced nose, her wolf-like earrings, and a pendant with a pentagram around her neck. He'd been raised a good Catholic, although he would call himself non-practicing if asked, and wasn't sure what he believed anymore. Her wearing the symbols he'd always associated with evil threw him off.

So did the t-shirt she wore--something from a heavy metal band he hadn't heard of. But he tried to keep an open mind.

From the corner of his eye, he saw Sandra come through the doors and stopped.

Myssi turned and saw her, too, then burst into tears.

Nick stood still. He didn't know whether to open his arms and offer a hug to the crying young lady, and truth be told he felt a little dizzy.

"What is going on?" Sandra asked.

"She just came up to me. I'm not really sure."

Sandra moved to the girl's side and wrapped an arm around her. "There, there. What's going on?"

"I need help," she said. "I'm in serious trouble, and I thought--" She stopped and pointed at Nick. "You know, maybe he could help."

"Help with what?" Sandra asked.

"The police are accusing me of killing Toby."

"Someone said something about that yesterday as we were leaving the hospital, but it makes no sense," Nick said. "You acted in self-defense."

"I have a question," Sandra said. "Since you know his name, you knew Toby before the robbery, true?"

"He was my friend. But I didn't recognize him until after--"

She stopped again, sobs wracking her body, and Sandra patted her shoulder, but looked at Nick and shook her head.

"I'm sorry," Sandra said. "We can't help you. Nick has a job to do, and I'm here to help him. Maybe your--church person has some options for you."

"High Priest Adrial has been very helpful, but you were there," she said, looking at Nick. "You can tell them what happened."

"Well, I was kind of out of it," Nick said. He still had the nagging suspicion he did know something. An image and idea he could not get out of his head.

"I didn't kill him."

"Who gave him the drugs that killed him?" Sandra seemed tense, suspicious.

"Not me," Myssi said. "I'm clean and have been for a while. Someone gave him something that set him off, and he overdosed."

"And the police think you gave him the drugs?"

The girl shrugged. "Before we found the church, we partied together. But we were both clean now. He hadn't done anything in a long time."

"The police and the evidence say otherwise. Could it have been one of the kids he was with outside before you went in?"

"No, they were clean, too. And they were leaving as I opened the door."

"Just Toby, or all of them?" Nick asked.

Myssi nodded and her shoulders shook. "Toby must have come back. When he came through the door, he was clearly hallucinating, and he died before he hit his head or the ground."

"He was dead when you kicked him?"

"That's what the police say. And they think I gave him the drugs that caused it."

"What motive would you have to do that?" Sandra asked.

She shrugged. "We were dating. We broke up a while back, but we were still friends."

"Who broke up with who?" Sandra asked.

"He broke up with me," Myssi said, her face reddening.

"So, you did have a motive at least," Sandra said coldly. "And means and opportunity. What if the police are right?"

"I loved him!" Myssi yelled. Nick stepped back.

He'd never seen Sandra look so angry, and never heard her talk like this, and Myssi's fury seemed to match hers.

The two women faced off, and Nick was sure for a moment a fistfight would break out, but then Myssi dropped her gaze and mumbled something.

"What was that?" Sandra said.

"I didn't do this. But no one, not even you believe me."

"I'm sorry you have all this going on," Sandra told her. "But we can't help you. We have our own things to deal with."

"I'm sorry," Nick said. "I do wish we could do more."

"Let's go." Sandra grabbed his hand and led him to the car. When he looked back, Myssi had disappeared.

Still, there was something about what she'd said. Toby died before he hit the ground. The cops said the same thing. And Nick knew that at least before he'd been shot and blacked out, she hadn't seemed to recognize the robber. What was going on here?

Nick had a lot of questions, but Sandra was right. This was none of his business.

He climbed into the passenger seat of his car, minding his head, and Sandra slid in behind the wheel. She stared straight ahead for a second, the anger on her face slowly fading.

"Should we go?" Nick asked quietly.

Sandra faced him, and her face dissolved into tears. "Oh, Nick," she said through choking sobs. "We have to help that poor girl."

9

———————

GOING BACK

"What is going on?" Nick asked, staring at her.

"We can talk about it over breakfast," Sandra said. She sniffed, and her emotions seemed to be back under control. Nick had seen her angry, albeit mildly, frustrated, upset, and happy. But this? This was something else entirely. First, she'd been upset and then dissolved into tears a few moments later.

The ride to the restaurant took under 10 minutes and passed in silence.

When they arrived, Sandra sat across from him. Nick didn't want to speak first. His head ached slightly, so he waited for her to speak.

They ordered coffee, and when he couldn't stand it anymore, Nick broke the silence. "Are you okay?" he asked. "I don't think I've ever seen you like this before, even in Denver."

"There's something I need to tell you, and I don't know how."

"Nothing you can tell me will change how I feel about you," Nick said, but as soon as he uttered the words, he knew it wasn't true. Everyone's love had limits, and theirs was new, fragile. There was no way to predict how what she said next would affect him.

"Do you know what I do for a living?" she asked.

"Something in your family business," he replied, unsure. What had she told him before? How could he be dating someone this long, and not really know what she did for a living? "Photography related?"

"Sort of," she said. "But my family started a foundation after my brother passed away, and my primary job is to run that part of the business. Fortunately, I have good administrators and managers who make it possible for me to do things like this." She indicated the diner and Nick.

"I'm sorry about your brother. I had no idea."

"It was a long time ago."

"What does your foundation do?" he asked.

"We run a rehab for kids who can't afford it and whose families either can't or won't help. When we are at capacity, we pay to send them to other facilities. Part of the rehabilitation process helps them to find hobbies they can engage in to help them prevent relapse."

"That sounds noble and good!"

"There's more. You might not feel the same way after you hear it."

"Why would I not want you to do great work like that?"

"Because," she said, studying her hands. "One of the first kids my family helped was me. For my brother, it was too late."

"Too late?"

"He died because of me, Nick. I gave him the drugs that killed him. An overdose."

"I'm so sorry," he said, unsure what else to say. "I would never have guessed. You don't look like you used to be an addict."

"I am an addict. My addiction is under control."

He needed to tread carefully. "I'm sorry,"

"What does an addict look like, Nick?"

He looked at her silently, knowing she wanted an answer, but unable to give her one. Was it a masked man in a convenience store? A girl who dressed in black and was associated with a Satanist church? Or was it...

His hands suddenly became very interesting to him and took up all his focus. "I--I guess I don't know."

"Let me tell you a story. My younger brother Travis kind of rebelled against my family. My mom and dad were uber-religious, and so he went his own way as soon as he was old enough. Well, both of us did. We got into drugs, pot at first, which was pretty harmless. Someone exposed him to meth and other stuff, and things got a little ugly for a while. I stayed with more mellow substances but dropped acid and played with mushrooms from time to time."

Nick nodded as she took a breath but chose to just listen. He had no idea what to say anyway. This was a side of her he hadn't known up to this point, and he wasn't sure how to react to it.

"He cleaned up, not because of anything we did, but because he went to rehab and met some people he identified with. They were part of a small branch of the Church of Ahriman, essentially a church that worshipped Satan. My parents flipped out.

"My dad, an attorney, hired one of those intervention people, someone from his and my mom's church, to go get him. They locked my brother up. He came out a different kid.

"By then, I was living on my own. He snuck out and came to my place. He was clean, Nick, but depressed. I thought some acid, might help him see things differently. It always worked for me, and just one time couldn't hurt."

She took a deep breath, and Nick saw their waitress was standing by, waiting for an opening. He simply waved his hand, she nodded and went to take care of other tables.

He sipped his coffee. "What happened?"

"He had a bad trip, you could say. He'd been clean so long that even a small tab hit him hard. He went nuts and left my place, hallucinating. I followed him, but if I got too close, he thought I was someone else chasing him.

"I called his best friend, who was still in the Satanic church my parents had pulled him out of. He showed up and tried to talk my brother into sobering up.

It didn't work. Travis resisted him and ran out into the street in front of a semi-truck. The driver tried to stop, but--"

"I'm so sorry."

"No one blamed me, but me. I never forgave myself. I haven't touched any drug stronger than aspirin since, unless absolutely essential. I drink, but only socially. And I help kids from all backgrounds find a better way."

"And you help them find hobbies, things to help them stay clean?"

"Yeah. And some end up turning to unconventional places. My brother found support in that Satanic church, no matter what my parents thought of them. I blamed them for his death for a long time, but they were the ones who helped him get clean. I was just trying to blame anyone but myself. I gave him drugs to 'help' him cope with being taken away from his support system by my parents, and it got him killed instead."

Nick sat quietly. He finally said, "I had no idea."

"I don't talk much about it. He could have turned to anything, but he turned to that church like Myssi and Toby have. There is better stuff out there for them."

"You're right, and I admire what you do."

"Thanks, Nick. My older brother and I run the charity. My mom and dad never left the church, but they have changed their attitude about a lot of things."

"I can imagine."

"I never plan to go back to that life. I encourage kids to take up photography, and you could probably be a huge help in that area when your assignment is over. But right now, we need to help this girl. She didn't do anything wrong, or so it seems, and if someone else gave the kid the drugs that killed him, they need to be held responsible. The group they were a part of may seem evil to some, but I doubt they had anything to do with this."

"I think you're right. So, what can we do?"

"Well, first, we have to take care of your assignment. At the same time, we're going to help this girl at least prove her innocence."

"One question," he said. "Why did you tell her we couldn't help her?"

"Because I don't want to, Nick. But she doesn't have anyone else."

"What about Adrial?"

"She needs better help than that."

"Okay. Do you want to contact her or should I?"

"I think you should. But not until I know what we have to offer exactly."

"Okay. First though, breakfast."

"Nick, do you still love me?"

"I don't have a perfect past myself. My own experience in Phoenix must have triggered you in a big way."

"More than your other adventures," she said with a nod. "But I didn't want to say anything then. This--this is different."

"So, you are saying you want me to get involved in a mystery?"

"Only this one time. Don't get used to it, Mr. O'Flannigan."

"Yes, ma'am," he said, and signaled their waitress, who came over and took their order.

When she was done, Nick turned to Sandra and grasped both her hands. "So, it is Wednesday already. Tell me, how are we going to take all the photos we need and still help Myssi?"

She smiled. "You're going to handle a lot of that, and I can help."

Sandra opened an app on her phone, some kind of project management thing, and showed him what she had in mind.

Nick wondered to himself why he hadn't used a similar planner all along on this trip, but he knew he would be going forward.

When their food arrived, they dug in with enthusiasm, and as he studied Sandra, he found her even more amazing after her revelation. He wondered what else he didn't know about her. He felt like he'd only just scratched the surface.

10

THE NATIONAL MUSEUM

They arrived at the National Memorial and Museum and parked quickly.

"I've already got our tickets waiting," Sandra told him, and she helped him out of the car. "And the photography permit. Wait here."

She disappeared inside the building, and Nick waited outside, looking around while Sandra checked them in.

The site of the bombing of the Alfred P. Murrah building on April 19, 1995, the memorial consisted of three manicured acres, including a reflecting pond and educational exhibits.

As he entered the grounds, the atmosphere changed. The first thing he noticed was the field of empty chairs put there to symbolize those who died in the tragedy. Sandra gestured for him to follow her.

"There's a walking tour," she said. "It starts over here, at the survivor tree."

Nick followed.

"This tree was damaged during the attack," Sandra told him. "Even with metal in its bark and leaves sheared off by the blast, it has lasted and grown more since that time."

He paused, taking some photos of the tree from various angles. The air around them was quiet and still, and it wasn't yet overly warm. He felt a certain peace here. Terraces surrounded the tree, and while the area wasn't crowded on a weekday, a few people strolled around and a few others sat on blankets on the ground.

They moved on to the field of empty chairs he had noticed first. It was almost difficult to photograph them. He could feel the presence of other souls, restless, with unfinished business, and it made him consider for a moment how many close calls the last few months had brought for him.

"We're all lucky to be alive," he mumbled.

"What's that?" Sandra asked.

"We're all lucky to be alive," he said again. "Being here makes me all the more thankful for that."

"It is an amazing place," she said quietly.

"You've been here before?" he asked.

"Once," she said. "A long time ago."

Nick knelt and took a shot, an angled view along the lined-up seats of one of the rows of chairs.

"Do you feel them?" he asked her. "I can almost feel their presence here."

"Their memories, yes," she said. "I think for those who died here, their souls will always leave a shadow on this field."

"Each chair is unique," he said. "Look at the patterns on the panels."

"Yes," she said. "And some of the chairs are smaller than others. Those represent the children who were killed, most in a daycare center on the second floor of the building."

Nick wandered, taking some more photos. His head started to throb, and he knew he would need some more medicine soon, but he didn't want to stop their tour to do so. This place was truly special.

"See all these trees?" Sandra asked. "Those mark the boundaries where the building once stood."

"The designers did such a great job on this," he told her. The experience made him think of visiting the Holocaust Museum in Washington, D.C., and the feelings that evoked.

"Let's go to the reflecting pool," she said.

The pool filled with peaceful water dominated the center of the site. As they got closer, he heard running water, but he couldn't spot where it was coming from. The pool itself looked still and quiet.

It looked deep, but a closer examination revealed the water couldn't be more than an inch or two deep.

"I do want to come back," he said. "If we can fit another visit into your plan. I would love to take some night photos of this pool and the gates over there," he said.

"We will see," she said. "We can try, and if not we can visit Oklahoma City again when your assignment is over."

"I would love that," he told her.

He walked over to the gates, two four-story structures with a space, or a vestibule in between. The one had the numbers 9:01 in large numbers on it representing the minute before the attack. and Nick snapped a couple of photos of that, along with the other gate, which read 9:03.

"They say the 9:03 represents the moment after the attack, and when the healing began," Sandra told him.

Nick stood in awe for a moment and then moved around to the part of the memorial called the survivor's wall.

This consisted of two surviving walls of the structure, ones on the east end of the building that had not been completely destroyed. Etched into them were the names of those people who had also survived the attack, but whose lives had been forever changed.

Nick moved around the 9:01 gate to the west side of the memorial and the area where a section of fence that had been constructed around the site had been preserved. Some mementos appeared to have been left on the fence long ago, but others appeared to be new.

"People still leave messages of hope here," Sandra said quietly from beside him. She had been taking photos as well, and wiped a tear from her cheek.

He turned to face her, intending to take her into his arms, but instead almost leaning on her instead.

"I love you," he said again. For some reason, he found he couldn't say it enough. "Coming here first was a great idea."

"Thanks," she said. "Should we head to the rescuer's grove?"

He followed her to a group of fruit trees, and he saw a perfectly framed shot. Through the branches of one tree, he could see the 9:03 gate and took a couple of photos with the limbs like a frame surrounding it.

The trees were neatly arranged in rows, and each had red blooms on them, a splash of color in the middle of the green of the park area.

Once he had taken several photos, they moved toward the entrance to the actual museum, where just before going inside, they reached the children's area. There were chalkboards where kids were encouraged to write about their feelings.

Nick stood back as Sandra photographed several of the messages printed there, and then they went inside.

"Good morning again," the person at the front desk said. "You're just in time for your reservation."

Nick had not been watching the time, but apparently, Sandra had planned things well once again. "We're about five minutes early, though,"

Sandra said. "We'll probably take fewer photos inside than we did outside."

"That's okay, we can get you started," the woman said. "Just remember, we need to approve any photos taken inside before they are published for commercial use." She explained the flow of the museum, pointed out where you could listen to first-hand accounts of the tragedy, and where the interactive exhibits were.

Nick, already tired, perked up a bit for the tour, finding a second wind. He let Sandra lead him from exhibit to exhibit, but he saw there was no way they would have time for them all. He should have planned a whole day here.

"Let's get you some lunch and a chance to sit down before you work on the capitol building this afternoon."

Nick smiled again and checked his watch. One o'clock already. Time was flying, and they had so much to do.

And he wanted to add one thing to the list, but he kept it to himself. At least for now.

11

ART AND CRITICAL THINKING

After lunch, Nick got his first look at the inside of the capitol building. He found himself tiring even though he'd only been wandering the lower floor for about an hour.

Like other state capitols, he found the Oklahoma State Capitol building had an extensive and varied art collection. One of the most fascinating to him was a bronze statue of Kate Bernard, the first woman to be elected to state office, and the first commissioner of charities and corrections. Although women could not vote at the time, she got more votes than the first governor of Oklahoma and was affectionally known as Miss Kate.

The statue, created by Sandra Van Zandt, was a part of a bench also made of bronze, and between Nick taking photos, a few tourists, mostly children, posed for photos sitting next to her.

There was also a portrait of Micky Mantle, who Nick never realized was an Oklahoma native.

Despite his weariness, when he checked his camera, he found several of the shots were decent ones, and he moved to the second floor, determined to cover a good part of the interior. He would have to do stay on schedule for Sandra's plan.

He had to admit it was solid, thoroughly organized. Even though she had taken some sunrise photos already, he wanted to try to get some sunset and night shots this evening if he could.

On the second floor, Nick captured several bronze busts portraying some of the historical figures of the state. He learned a lot by reading the plaques and information under them, and he got lost in the history of it all.

He felt a tap on his shoulder.

A uniformed security officer entered his vision as he turned. "Are you okay, sir?" The officer asked.

Nick realized then how he must look to this man. A tall, red-haired guy with a large camera and an even larger bandage on his head wandering the capitol building slowly taking photos.

Usually, he would have introduced himself to someone right away, but he hadn't this time.

"Yes, I am," he said, putting on a smile. "I'm Nick O'Flannigan, here on a freelance assignment--"

"You're the guy from the news who got shot."

"A graze, really," he said. "I'm doing fine."

"Okay, if you need anything, do let me know. I'm here for you, and I am a huge fan. You have taken so many great photos around the country. I was surprised I hadn't seen you yet this week."

"I was a little tied up," Nick joked, thinking of how literal his answer was.

"Well, you're here now. I'll see you around. Be careful and let me know if you need anything."

"Will do," Nick said.

He went back to studying and photographing the art.

Two of his favorite paintings on the floor were by Wilson Hurley, part of his *Visions of the Land: The Centennial Suite* series on display. The first was titled *A Storm Passing Northwest of Anadarko* and the second was titled *Spring Morning Along the Muddy Boggy*. Both depicted the sun shining through dark clouds, and they matched Nick's hopeful attitude about this week, having Sandra here, and now her desire to help Myssi.

Myssi. His mind wandered again. She seemed nice, kind, not like any picture he had of a Satanist or even a goth girl. In fact, she seemed like the opposite, and certainly not someone who was an addict or even had been.

Maybe she wasn't. Maybe Toby had been, and she was trying to help him. But if she didn't give him the drugs, who did? Was it his father, like Myssi said, or did he buy them himself and just overdose? If his father did give his own son drugs, why?

There had to be some evidence somewhere, something that would reveal to the police, and him, what actually happened.

"He was dead before he hit his head or the ground," she'd told them.

And Nick closed his eyes for a moment, thinking. What had he seen?

The boy, the flash of the gun, the pain, and the masked stranger swaying, his eyes...

His eyes.

Nick snapped his own eyes open. That was the key. He needed to see the footage of the boy and his fall to determine if...

If what? He wasn't sure if what he saw would mean a thing. There had to be something, someone who had seen something outside.

Had to be.

He moved down the stairs and back to the first floor, looking at his watch.

It would be another half an hour before Sandra picked him up. He went through the photos on his camera while he waited, deleting some, keeping others, all the while his mind struggling to process what exactly he had witnessed before he was shot.

To find the truth, he needed more information.

12

MY MARRY WAY

"You need some rest," Sandra told him when he got in the car.

"I need to take some night photos of the capitol," he answered.

"Well, I have some and we can get some more tomorrow evening. How about instead we have dinner, turn in early, and take some sunrise photos first thing tomorrow instead?"

Nick evaluated his body, something Sandra must already have done. After their time at Jeb's place, his head did hurt a bit more, and he was probably overdue for his pain meds.

And he didn't want to take them without eating.

But he also wanted to get the photo he took at the crime scene to the police somehow. He checked to see if the Oklahoma City Police Department had a text tip line. They didn't, but they had a 'Crime Stoppers' website where he could upload his photo. He started typing an explanation to go with it.

"Nick?" Sandra snapped him out of the search on his phone. "How does that sound?"

"Good, good," he said.

"What are you doing?"

He showed her the website and the upload, clicked the send button and closed the app.

"We've done our civic duty," he said.

"Besides looking at the video footage later."

"Well, that too," Nick said. "Of course."

"So where do you want to eat? What are you in the mood for?"

Nick smiled. "My dad told me when I was younger that marriage was thirty years of two people deciding what they wanted to eat."

Sandra laughed, but it was a little forced. "Marriage?" she said.

"Um, I meant--" Nick glanced over and glimpsed a smile at the corner of her mouth.

"What did you mean, Mr. O'Flannigan? You are not proposing to me in your car outside the state capitol building in Oklahoma with a big bandage on your head, are you?"

"Well, no. Not exactly. I mean, not that I don't want to marry you. Some-day. Not now."

Sandra just stared at him with a smirk.

"I mean, not that now is a bad time. There would be no bad time to marry you. If we were--you know, if you wanted," Nick stumbled over his words, realizing that he was only making things worse the longer he talked, but unable to stop himself.

"But we would have to talk about it, and I would have to ask properly. And there is a lot to talk about. Not that I am nervous, or don't trust you or anything, but yeah." He stopped and looked over at Sandra.

She clearly struggled to keep a straight face. Then she burst into laugh-ter. "Oh, Nick. No pressure. I am just giving you a hard time. But I think you are tired, hungry, and may have hit your head harder than you think."

He laughed at her mirroring of his unspoken thoughts, but the very act hurt.

"Okay. I'll stop talking now. Did you mention dinner?"

"I did. We aren't really dressed for Cheever's. We will go there tomorrow. My treat. How about Red Rock Canyon Grill, and a nice steak?"

"I'll take it," Nick said, and his stomach grumbled. He pulled the pain pills from his pocket as they drove, and dry-swallowed two, knowing he was about to add food to his stomach.

As he moved to put them away, he noticed the lid. It was the same type, the letters the same color as the one he had seen on the ground at Jeb's.

And this had come from the hospital pharmacy.

They all use the same pill bottles, he told himself. *Right? From Walgreens to Rite Aid, there really isn't any difference in packaging.*

Maybe. But he thought about the piece of paper. FA, LIG, CH. The corner of something from Faith Light Church.

And the boy and his father did not get along.

The reverend couldn't be a suspect, could he?

But then Nick remembered what other detectives had told him along the way. The killer is almost always someone familiar, a family member, and often they are remorseful and confess right away.

Or they get angry, putting on false anger to hide their real emotion.

Guilt.

But why would a father, even an angry one, give drugs to his son?

Nick shook his head.

"You're thinking about who might have drugged that kid, right?" Sandra asked.

"Yes," he said. "Myssi said they had both been clean since they started hanging out at the Satanic temple, right? But she has every reason to lie, especially if she gave her friend the drugs he overdosed on."

"I don't get the sense she is lying."

"Me either," Nick said. "But someone is."

"Who?" Sandra asked. "If you run down the list of people who knew one or both of them, it is pretty short, at least as far as we know."

"Yep," Nick said, steadying himself as they took a sharp right turn. "Jeb, store owner, not likely. Toby's father. Adrial, the priest. Myssi. And two of those were not at the crime scene."

"As far as we know."

"As far as we know," he corrected himself, looking up. He saw the front of the restaurant and the now dark lake behind.

"Oh, I didn't realize we were this close to Lake Hefner," he said.

"We'll have to come back and capture some photos leter if we can," Sandra said. "It is beautiful, day and night."

"It amazes me how much I am drawn to the water," Nick told her. "In Austin, it was the Colorado River. In Salt Lake, well, there is the huge lake. The rivers in Boise and Sacramento drew me too."

"Maybe that is why you call Seattle your home?" she said. "But I thought Sacramento might be your favorite for another reason."

"Oh, yes," Nick said. "My time with you there changed my life."

And he thought about it. It had.

"Well, let's eat," she said. "Then, you can take me back to your hotel, and tell me all about how great I am for you."

Nick smiled, and she winked. "Sounds like a plan," he said.

13

ALL HAIL

Nick woke to the smell of coffee again and thought he could really get used to this. The impromptu conversation about marriage the night before scared him just a little though. He'd been married once before, and things had not ended well.

He wasn't sure he was ready, but he did love Sandra and she seemed to love him. But it was early days yet, and they had spent more time apart than together. Over the next couple of weeks, that would change.

"Good morning," she said, turning around. She was dressed for the day, or so it appeared, in a loose-fitting blouse and a simple pair of blue jeans. "Coffee to carry you over?"

"Sure," he said, glancing at the time and at the darkness outside the window. Then he remembered. Sunrise photos. "Let me take a shower, and we can get going."

He hurried through his shower. Although they were not far from the capitol building, he wanted to get there and pick his angles. He was also hoping Sandra would help him take some more shots of the oil wells too.

Two for one. This was working out well. They needed to take some time this afternoon to do some major sorting and uploading.

As soon as he came out of the bathroom, he saw Sandra ready, her camera bag over one shoulder, Nick's dangling in her hand.

"Let's get moving, mister." She kissed him on the cheek and they left. On the way, Nick outlined his ideas, and Sandra agreed. It only took a couple of moments for them to reach the capitol, and Nick walked as fast as his healing head and his chronically injured leg would allow to the west side of the building. He tried a couple of different angles as the sky lightened. A few low lying clouds would enhance the beauty the rising sun was sure to bring.

The sun would come over the horizon first, and he could catch it beside the capitol dome and illuminating the area. Then, if he took a couple of strategic steps to his right, he could catch the light coming over the building itself. Maybe.

Either way, he wanted to try. His head felt clearer, better, his body more flexible and alert.

As the sun rose, Nick snapped photo after photo. From where he stood, he couldn't see Sandra, but he assumed she was doing the same.

Even in the small viewfinder on his camera, these shots looked great.

Once the sun was high in the sky, Nick found himself hungry and in need of coffee. The doctors had warned him he would tire quickly, but he knew he still had a lot of work to do.

Miles to go before I sleep, he thought.

"C'mon, Nick," Sandra said, walking his way. "Let's grab breakfast and coffee, and we can come back to finish covering the inside."

"Where should we go?"

"Waffle Champion is only a couple of miles away, and they are well-rated online."

The restaurant was not far, and Nick ordered coffee and the chicken and waffles. Sandra ordered the same, and their food arrived quickly.

"I was thinking we would take photos this morning, and this afternoon, we can upload them for Emily and determine what we have missed. We can also look over the footage we got from Jeb."

"Yeah, I would like that," Nick said. "I'd love to give the police something more than my photo if we can and put this mystery behind us."

"Same," Sandra said, taking a sip of her coffee. "I want to help Myssi, but we do have a job to do, too. Anything we miss, we have to get tomorrow."

"True. You are coming with me to Topeka?"

"At least. You shouldn't be driving until they remove the stitches out of your head and get checked out, and I want to keep an eye on you in case of any long-term effects."

"I like that," Nick said. "How long can you be away from work with your family foundation, though?"

"I have as long as I need," she said.

Nick smiled. The company would be good, and he honestly could use the help. Also, this mystery aside, he would love someone with him to keep out of these things. The concussion might be part of the problem, but the truth was he was tired anyway.

This trip, 15 weeks in, had been more exhausting than he ever imagined, and certainly a part of that was encountering some kind of trouble in every single city.

His phone rang, interrupting his inner monologue.

"Hey, Emily," he answered.

"HI there. I almost expected Sandra to answer. How are you?"

"Improving," he said. "We are also getting some work done."

"That's good to hear. Are you going to finish this week on time?"

Nick thought about telling her no, and buying them some time, but he knew the deadlines everyone was under, all of them dependent on him finishing his assignment on time. One year was a quick turnaround for visiting every state capital, and he might need to accelerate the photo taking, but if he stayed healthy and focused, he could take a few days off here and there, and still make it.

That appeared to be a big if.

"We will, no problem at all. Sandra is a huge help, and a talented photographer."

"She definitely adds a new perspective," Emily said. "I like it, and you are lucky to have her."

"I am," he said. "We plan to upload a bunch of photos this afternoon, once we have sorted through them."

"Glad to hear it. Don't overdo it. You need to take time to recover."

"Sandra is keeping me in check."

"I knew she would. Can I talk to her for a second?"

"Sure," he said. "Talk to you soon."

He handed the phone to Sandra, and she stood as he did. "Hi, Emily, how are you?"

Sandra walked away from the table toward the door, and Nick took the hint to stay put. He could see Sandra shielding her mouth as she spoke into the phone.

He had the distinct feeling a part of his life was being planned for him, without his knowledge.

For the first time in a long time, he didn't mind the idea at all.

He looked around for the waitress, thinking he would take care of the check while Sandra talked, and then he spotted him.

The large man was unmistakable. Nearly Nick's height, sporting a bushy salt and pepper beard, he wore black jeans, a red shirt, and a maroon ball cap, but such simple changes didn't hide his identity.

The priest from the Church of Ahriman. People in the diner stared as he approached Nick's table.

"Good morning," he said. "May I?" He indicated Sandra's seat.

"For a moment. My--girlfriend will be right back."

"I'll only take a minute of your time."

"Okay," Nick said, as the man lowered himself into the chair, but sat forward and stiff, not relaxing at all. "How can I help you?"

"Help me? Perhaps I just came to chat and see how you are doing."

"I doubt it," Nick glanced up and saw Sandra from the corner of his eye. She was right outside the door, still on the phone. He felt a heaviness settle on his chest, and he had difficulty taking a deep breath.

"You are perceptive, Mr. O'Flannigan, and I am sure the police and others know that as well. Have you been investigating this--event on your own?"

"Not really," Nick said. It wasn't exactly a lie. He had gone to the scene of the crime, but not learned much, not that he wanted to share. And he did have video footage to study, but this man didn't need to know that. "How do you happen to be here at the same time we are?"

"This is one of my favorite breakfast spots," he said, looking around. A few patrons still stared at him, but most had gone back to eating. "I don't come often though, as people everywhere tend to know who I am."

"You have had some national exposure."

"International, actually, but that is neither here nor there. The reason I am here is to give you information the police may need but won't take from me."

"Why not?"

The priest scoffed. "We are in the middle of the Bible Belt. That answer should be obvious, even to you."

"What makes you think I'll share it with them?"

"You are a truth crusader, Mr. O'Flannigan. Every one of your little escapades, for which you are getting a lot of attention by the way, involved you trying to find the truth regardless of who it came from or how it affected people around you."

"Thanks, I think," Nick said.

"Hey, people give our church a bad rap. In fact, they don't like to call it a church. But it saved my life and offered me comfort when no other religion would."

"I've read your story."

"I'm sure you have. But our beliefs are not what people think they are. We have the highest respect for anyone, regardless of race, sexual orientation, and we value women greatly."

"Okay."

"I know you hardly want a lesson in Satanism or our Bible, but I wanted to make it clear we do not condone the use of drugs by any of our members. Quite the opposite. The only time we sanction drug use is for medicinal or mental health reasons, and always supervised by someone who knows what they are doing: a doctor, a shaman, even those who practice Wicca."

"Were Toby and Myssi taking any drugs you're aware of?"

"That's just it, Mr. O'Flannigan. No. Toby's family had him on antipsychotics and he was taking other drugs on his own before he came to us, but when he joined our small group, he quit."

"How?"

"Faith, Mr. O'Flannigan. You may think we are heathens and worship a monster, and perhaps we do. Maybe we are wrong, but we have standards, morals if you will. They may differ from yours, and definitely differ from those of Toby's family, but if anything, we are more adamant about obedience than others are."

"Look, Mr. --"

"Finbar. Adrial Finbar."

"Mr. Finbar, I can't agree with your 'church' if you want to call it that. But I appreciate you sharing this with me. But if your church does not condone the use of drugs, and Myssi and Toby were both clean, where did Toby get them?"

"*Cui bono*. Who benefits from him being addicted? Think about it Mr. O'Flannigan."

"I do have one question. Where were you on Sunday afternoon, when the robbery took place?"

"Home, with my wife and children."

"Did you see Toby or Myssi that day?"

"No, Mr. O'Flannigan, I did not. Your police friends already checked, but you are welcome to do the same."

"That won't be necessary."

Beside him, Sandra cleared her throat.

"Oh, hello Miss. I was just leaving," the priest said.

"Good," Sandra said. "Please leave me and Nick here alone. I really--I'd really appreciate it."

"Absolutely. *Ad occursum futurum*, Mr. O'Flannigan. Truly."

The man stood, and as he did, Nick felt a heaviness leave his chest, and he could breathe again.

"What was that about?" Sandra said.

"He said the same thing Myssi did. That Toby and Myssi were not doing drugs, and that in fact, his church helped the young man get clean."

Sandra frowned. "That story sounds familiar. A lot like my brother's."

"It's odd, but matches with what Myssi told us."

"I hate what he stands for. I almost feel a dark presence around him."

"Me, too. But I do know one thing."

"What's that?"

"Either he is telling the truth, or he believes he is."

"Are you crossing him off your suspect list?" she asked, a twinkle in her eye.

"Not yet. But I'm leaning that way."

Sandra shook her head. "He still gives me the creeps. I'm going to reserve judgment until we see the video."

Nick nodded. "Sounds fair. First, let's go finish up at the capitol."

"Deal," she said. The waitress came over and gave Nick a funny look, but he ignored it, paid the bill and they left.

In the back of his mind, he ran through what he had seen just before being knocked out, and their find at the scene--the pill bottle cap and the small scrap of paper.

There was a connection, he just couldn't make it out quite yet.

14

NEW MEMORY

The photos at the capitol went quickly. Nick took a few of the hallways, and Sandra, who was moving faster than he was, took the rest.

A couple of hours passed quickly, and they met on the second floor, both looking up first and taking photos of the rotunda, and they looked down, taking the almost obligatory photo of the floor from above.

When they were done, Nick turned to Sandra. "I think we covered it all."

"Me, too. I hope so."

"Yeah. It would be nice to have just a few things to clean up tomorrow. I could use the rest for sure."

"Me, too," she said. "This assignment is pretty exhausting."

"It can be," he agreed.

They drove back to the hotel and went up to his room, and Nick opened his laptop. The screen flashed the login for a moment and then went blank.

"Shit," he muttered.

"What?" Sandra asked and looked over his shoulder. He powered the computer down and turned it on again. Instead of a clear screen, it was black.

"What's happening?" Sandra asked.

"This happened to me in Carson City. I was able to get it fixed because it was a battery problem. But this is not the same."

"No, it's not. Have you considered getting a new one?"

"I have."

"Do you think Emily and the magazine would pay for it?"

"They might help, but I've actually been saving up."

"What are you thinking?"

"A new Mac, with Lightroom and Photoshop both."

"Oh, nice. That would be awesome for the rest of your assignment."

"Faster too. I already have an iPhone and everyone tells me I should make the switch."

"Well," Sandra said, tapping on her phone. "There's an Apple store at the Penn Square Mall. I have been thinking about upgrading my older Mac as well. You want to go now, or upload photos using my computer first?"

"Let's go now."

"Sounds good."

They made the short trek to the mall and wandered into the Apple store, where they were greeted by a long-haired salesman, who asked how he could help.

They wandered over to the laptop table, where they were shown the different options the store had in stock, and what they could order. Nick went for a larger screen, more power, and a package that included Lightroom as part of the deal.

"You'll save a little bit if you order online, and if you apply for an Apple Card even if you pay it off right away."

"Oh, cool."

"Just select pick up in store since we know the model you want is in stock, and choose this location," he said. He turned to Sandra, who chose a different bundle than Nick's, but one that was similar and included the software she wanted.

When Nick saw the total for both, he took a deep breath and paid for them with his new card.

"It will be just a few minutes," the Apple employee told them. "We'll text when your order is ready, and then we can help you set things up."

"Cool," they said together.

"Is there anywhere to get a coffee and have a seat while we wait?" Sandra asked.

"There's a food court," he told them. "You'll find a Starbucks and an Orange Julius, along with the other typical places."

"Thanks again," Nick said.

As they left, he pulled out his phone and called his friend Gerry, the social media manager for *Travel USA* magazine, and the reason he had this job in the first place.

"Hey there," she answered. "How are you feeling, Nick?"

"Recovering. But I just bought a new computer."

"It's about time. What happened?"

"My old one died. We are at Apple. Sandra got an upgrade too."

"Very nice. I'm so glad she's there to help you."

"Me, too. Do you think Emily will contribute to my computer fund?"

"Probably. You should definitely ask."

"Will do, thanks. How are you?"

"Things are going well, and Christina and I are settling in."

"I'm happy for you. I love you guys."

"We miss you, Nick. I wish we could have come with Sandra, but she really is the best."

"I am. Thanks."

"Take care, Nick, and do ask Emily about your computer. I will put a good word in for you."

"Thanks." Nick hung up as they headed for the food court, ordered a couple of drinks, and sat down to wait.

"Nick, look," Sandra said.

Nick turned his head. He saw Myssi, and next to her saw Reverend Ayunda. They were arguing, and as they watched Myssi flipped him off and stomped toward them, looking down at her phone. The pastor fled down the escalator.

"Myssi?" Sandra said. "Are you okay?"

The girl came over slowly. She wore a different band shirt, but essentially the same jewelry as the last time he had seen her. She stopped a few feet away and stared.

"Are you okay?" Sandra repeated.

"What do you care?" she said. "I thought you didn't want to help me."

"I--we changed our minds," Sandra said.

"I heard you went out to see Jeb."

"We did. What was going on with Toby's dad?"

"He still blames me, although I've told him I didn't give his son anything. He's mad that the cops haven't put me behind bars yet."

Nick looked at Sandra, and she met his gaze. "I also ran into Mr. Finbar this morning," Nick offered.

"You mean High Priest Finbar."

"Sure," Nick said. "Although I didn't call him that."

"You wouldn't," Myssi said.

"Either way," Nick said. "He believes you are innocent and claims he is, too."

"I told you, he helped Toby get clean."

"That's what he said. What neither of you has offered me is any kind of clue as to who might have given Toby drugs. Would he have gone to score them on his own? Would his friends have given him any?"

"No. He really was changed."

"Any chance he had a prescription?" Nick asked, thinking of the lid they had seen.

"Not that I know of."

"But he did take prescription drugs before."

"Yeah. The ones his father put him on. But he stopped taking them."

"Any chance he would have had them with him Sunday?"

"No. I don't think so."

"Did you see him before you went in the store?"

"Yes. He and some other kids were at picnic tables but they were all leaving as I went inside."

"Did you see any other cars leave the parking lot before I arrived?"

"Nope. I saw you pull up just before I went inside."

"What about an old Ford truck?" Nick said, remembering the vehicle that passed him going the opposite direction when he pulled off the freeway.

"I saw one go by," she said. "But it didn't come from Jeb's."

Toby was there with friends when she pulled up. Nick swore he had seen only him, or someone in a dark hoodie before he went inside, and the other kids off to one side, not interacting with him at all.

The time between the two events was small.

Cui bono, the priest had said. *Who benefits?*

Nick spaced out for a second, thinking.

The priest and Myssi both benefitted from a sober Toby. It enhanced the reputation of the so-called church, and made Myssi's friend more pleasant too, especially since she was clean herself, or appeared to be.

Jeb did not seem like a drug dealer, so there would be no benefit to him. Besides, the prescription lid made Nick think the drugs he took were not of the illicit variety.

There was also the scrap of paper.

Cui bono?

His father, the pastor? Sure, if his son was addicted, he could blame his "opposition" and win his son back. And the boy would be back under his control, especially if...

He heard Sandra ask him something and snapped out of his thoughts.

"Don't you think that is a good idea, Nick?"

"Sorry, what?"

"Once we set up our computers, Myssi can help us look at the footage Jeb sent us. She knows the place better than we do. Maybe she will see something we're missing."

"Um, sure," he said, not entirely sure at all.

His phone beeped. "Alright, our stuff is ready," he said. "Let's go. I want to see if they can recover some of what is on my hard drive."

"Okay," Sandra said. "Can we call you when we're done, Myssi? You can meet us at our hotel."

"Sure," the girl said without much enthusiasm. She and Sandra exchanged numbers, and she walked away.

Sandra and Nick walked toward the Apple store together, but Nick couldn't help but repeat the question to himself.

Cui bono?

And who was the owner of that old Ford truck he and Myssi had seen? Did it even matter?

He had a feeling it did, and that the answers might just be a file in the cloud away.

15

PHOTOS AND STORE VIDEO

By the time they headed back to the hotel, Nick was ready for a large burger and a nap, probably in that order. The setup of his new computer had taken some time, as the techs were able to save some of the information from his old hard drive but had to use a special machine for the transfer.

Sandra's was easy. As a Mac user already, she signed in with her Apple ID, and everything transferred easily. It took time, but the store WIFI was reasonably fast.

By the time Nick finished, she had already logged in and appeared to be doing some research on the web. Luckily, Nick's new laptop fit in his old bag, and he bought a couple of extra cables to enable him to connect to a television or larger screens.

They stopped and grabbed a burger to go from Iron Star Barbecue. They called Myssi while they waited, and then took their food, including a huge order of fries, back to their hotel.

Nick opened his new machine and connected his camera to Lightroom. The program was so fast, he almost clapped as it clipped along while he devoured his food.

Sandra set up her new computer next to his, and they worked their way through capitol building photos, deleting some, uploading others. A few moments later, a timid knock sounded at the door.

Sandra stood, walked over, and opened it, and Myssi came in a second later. There were only two chairs in the suite that really worked at the desk, but there was a comfortable leather chair in one corner, and Sandra pulled it over.

"Give us a minute," she told the girl. "We have to finish some work. You want some fries?"

"Sure," Myssi said, with little more enthusiasm than she had shown before. She took a handful fand ate them slowly.

Nick hurried, sorting some photos into his personal cloud folder, and making sure everything was still there. Fortunately switching computers hadn't messed with his cloud files at all.

He and Sandra finished around the same time and gave each other a quick high five and a kiss. Myssi looked up and smiled at them.

"You two are cute," she said.

Nick smiled. "Thanks. We do pretty well together."

Sandra grinned too. "Okay, let's pull up this video, and have a look."

Nick opened the email from Jeb and downloaded the video file. In some ways, he didn't want to see another perspective of his injury, but he hoped he was out of the picture for the most part. The camera had been pointing toward the door and the counter after all.

But he did want to see what happened.

Something still nagged at him, and he found it impossible to shake the feeling he'd missed something.

It had to be in the video, or they were out of hope.

Myssi joined them on one side of the desk, and Nick hit play.

The images were a little grainy, black and white, and stuttered in a couple of places. The video was long, around 90 minutes, so he scrolled through quickly. There were a few customers in and out, and they darted through the frame on fast forward. Then he saw Myssi come in and he paused it. He started it again, this time at normal speed. He saw her quick banter with Jeb, and then saw himself come through the door.

Myssi headed for the beverage section on the same wall the camera was mounted on, and so she disappeared from the frame. He saw himself talking to Jeb, and although there was no sound, he remembered the conversation:

"Hi there," he'd addressed Jeb. "This is a cool place you have here. I'm Nick O'Flannigan."

"I'm Jeb, the owner."

"Nice to meet you. I'm on a freelance travel assignment from *Travel USA* magazine, and I'd love to take a few photos and ask you some questions about your place if that's okay."

"For most people, the answer would be no," Jeb replied. "What are you going to do with them?"

"The magazine is putting together a book on all the state capitals, including the area around the Capitol building and local attractions," he said. "It will be good publicity for your place. I'll share on my social media channels too.

"Okay," Jeb told him. "Just be sure if you take any of the art you find back there, you give credit to the artist, okay? And let me review any of the photos you want to publish before you submit them anywhere."

Myssi reappeared as he disappeared into the back, and he could see them talking for only a moment before the door burst open.

It was Toby. But that was where he had seen something. He stopped the video and backed it up.

"What are you doing?" Sandra and Myssi asked at the same time.

"I saw something. Right there."

Nick advanced the picture one frame at a time. The door banged open, and, he saw it. The old truck, the one he had seen, or one just like it. He advanced a few more frames. The truck appeared to back away from the door. The black and white image didn't show him if it was the same once yellow color of the truck he had seen, but it had to be.

"That's the truck I saw," Myssi verified. "The one headed toward the freeway, just before you pulled in."

"Why would it come back?" Sandra asked.

"A better question would be, who was driving?" Nick said. "And why did they not stick around? Whoever it was must have seen Toby charge inside."

"Unless the driver already knew what would happen," Myssi said. "What if they gave Toby the drugs, and then sent him inside?"

"How would they know what he would do?" Nick asked.

"Well, they might not know exactly, but if they knew Toby, they would know he got a bit crazy when he was high. One of the reasons he got in trouble, and the reason he got clean."

"How many people knew how they affected him?"

"Me. A few other friends."

"Mr. Finbar?"

Myssi nodded without correcting him. "Maybe."

"Who else?"

"His parents."

Then it clicked. Nick hit play on the video again, but not because he needed to see the rest.

He saw the pistol appear in the man's hand, saw his head come into the frame at the bottom right, and then saw Myssi from behind, talking to him. He saw Jeb try to knock the gun away with the baseball bat, saw it fall from his hand, and then saw Myssi move, almost a blur on the low-resolution camera.

He saw a flash before his own head left the frame. After a blurred kick, Toby, still masked, straightened as Myssi pushed him causing him to stumble. He stopped and slowed the video down. Toby's eyes crossed, he lunged forward, and Myssi kicked him in the chest. He tried to zoom in, but the resolution was horrible. Toby's face went slack, his eyes glazed over, and they closed as he fell.

He stopped the video when the police rushed in through the door.

Myssi wiped her eyes.

"You okay?" he asked her. He found his eyes were watering, too. He'd just watched a young man die way too soon.

"I will be," she said. "Did you see any clues?"

"I think so," he said. "I think I know who gave Toby the drugs. I just have to prove it. The first thing I'm going to do is call the police."

"Who do you think it was?" Sandra asked.

"I'd rather not say. Not until I have more information," Nick said, looking at Myssi.

"I get it," she said. "You don't trust me."

"It's not that, it's just--"

"Just what, Mr. O'Flannigan?"

"I just want to be sure."

16

A MAN OF FAITH

"So, Mr. O'Flannigan," Detective Peabody said. "How did you get this footage again?"

The cops were standing in his hotel room, even though Nick has offered them a seat. Sandra sat beside him on the end of the bed and held his hand. They'd sent Myssi home before the police arrived, something she seemed happy about.

"Jeb, the store owner emailed it to me."

"Why would he do that?"

"I asked him too."

"Why?"

"We wanted to help," Sandra said.

"I thought you were going to keep your boyfriend out of trouble," Detective Jenkins interrupted.

"Look, we don't want to get involved," Nick said. "Believe me. I have enough to deal with my head and all. But I did see something in this video, and it helped me remember something both Myssi and I saw."

"Myssi? Have you been in touch with a witness, Mr. O'Flannigan?"

"We had a short conversation. Can I tell you what I saw and found?"

"Sure," Peabody said. She folded her arms over her ample chest.

"There was an old Ford truck, kind of yellow-ish, driving slowly toward the freeway when I exited and headed toward Jeb's."

"And you say Myssi saw it, too?"

"She says she did but said it didn't come from the parking lot of Jeb's."

"And you say she didn't see the boy outside when she went it, but you did?"

"Yes, sir."

"And what did you see?"

Nick pulled up the video on the hotel room television, and stopped it at the key moment. "There."

On the screen, the old truck was visible through the open front door, and Nick advanced the frames, showing it backing away before the door slammed shut.

"That's the truck? You can't even see the color. How can you be sure?"

"I just am," Nick said.

"Go back?" Jenkins asked.

Nick did and stopped when instructed.

"We can't read the plate. It's obscured and a little small. Maybe we can look at it on our copy, have our guys blow it up?" he said, looking at his senior partner.

"Hmmmff. Maybe," Peabody said. "Still, who do you think the owner is, *Detective* O'Flannigan?

"*Cui bono?*" Nick said. "Who benefits? Either a dealer who sold Toby drugs, but I kind of doubt that. Nick pulled out his phone and showed them the photo he'd taken. "Look, a prescription bottle cap, on top of this paper."

"You think prescription drugs made him do that?" Peabody gestured at the video.

"Maybe he thought it was his prescription. I know you found something in his bloodstream. A full autopsy should tell you more, right?"

"Okay, so he unknowingly ingested too much of a drug that caused him to overdose. You think someone gave it to him on purpose."

"Maybe they didn't want him to overdose," Nick said. "They might've wanted him to start hallucinating and turn to someone for help."

"And he would turn to?"

"Maybe his parents," Nick said. "Who would you have called if you found him drugged out in the store, and he hadn't tried to hurt anyone and hadn't died?"

"Well, his dad probably."

"Not the priest from the Satanic church where he hung out, or his ex-girlfriend, Myssi, though," Sandra said. "Right?"

"You are saying his dad poisoned him, trying to get him hooked on drugs and back under his control?"

"Maybe," Nick said.

Both detectives laughed at the same time. It went on for a few moments, and Nick watched them quietly, looking at Sandra who did the same.

"Look, Toby's dad is one of the biggest televangelists in Oklahoma. His son was an embarrassment," Jenkins said. "Once he left home, the reverend wanted nothing to do with him. Why in the world would he want to bring him back, especially all drugged up? Do you think he wanted to be embarrassed again?"

"No," Nick said.

"You see, no motive."

"Unless he wanted a prodigal son," Sandra said.

"Really?" Jenkins said. "I go to his church. I've heard his sermons. Not all of them, but a lot of them. No way would he tell anyone to go out and sin, and then come back so they would have some kind of story to tell."

"Maybe not usually, but maybe in this case, it would increase his reputation if he could lure his son back into the fold," Sandra said sarcastically.

"Not a chance," Jenkins said. "You got the wrong idea about Reverend Ayunda."

"How sure are you?" Nick asked quietly.

"Positive, Mr. O'Flannigan," Peabody said. "We'll look at this section of the video. Thanks for the help, but we'll take it from here."

Everyone shook hands, and the officers left.

"What was that about?" Sandra asked.

Nick sighed. "It's always that way. They don't want to listen to an amateur photographer or anyone else. And it seems the Reverend Ayunda is one of their own."

"But I think you are on to something."

"Well, there are only two things I have found to do in these cases that actually works."

"Oh, yeah? What are those?"

"Either we find some proof and deliver it to the police, or we get the reverend to confess."

"Like what we did in Denver?"

"Like what we did in Denver, only this time it will be harder. The reverend knows who both of us are, he knows who Myssi is. We'd have to trick him into a confession."

"Maybe we can do just that."

Just then, Nick's phone rang, an Oklahoma number. He answered.

"This is Nick."

"Nick O'Flannigan, this is Matt Grant, a freelance journalist. I wonder if you would be willing to do an interview with me?"

"Regarding?"

"Well, your trip overall, and your experience in Oklahoma City."

"My experience?"

"Your involvement with the incident at Jeb's. That would just be part of a larger story, of course."

"Freelance? Who are you selling this story to?"

"You know how it is, whoever will buy it. Will you do it? I'll buy you dinner or drinks."

"How about breakfast tomorrow?" Nick asked. "I think that would work perfectly."

"You bet. Eight too early?"

"Perfect," Nick said. Text me the place, and we will be there."

He ended the call. "What was that?" Sandra asked.

"Option three," Nick said. "The one I forgot about for a moment."

"What option is that?"

"The local media." He filled her in on his plan.

Sandra smiled. "You're brilliant, you know."

"I do, but thanks for the confirmation," he said, smiling back.

"Okay, let's look through what we have for photos. We have tomorrow to finish up. I think we should head for Topeka first thing Saturday."

"But it's only a four-hour drive."

"Yeah, but I have plans for you. You need to start enjoying this job a lot more," she said.

"Deal. You are my new navigator."

Nick had no idea what she had in mind, but he found that he trusted her.

And really, that was all that mattered.

By the time they were done looking through photos and had made notes of what they missed or needed to take again, it was after ten, and both fell asleep in an instant.

They woke the next morning to Nick's alarm and grabbed their cameras and headed out for breakfast. Nick brought his laptop along.

Their new reporter friend was going to get a bigger story than he bargained for. If he would publish it.

17

IF IT BLEEDS, IT LEADS

"Nice to meet you," Nick said. "Thanks for the invitation."

They were at Hatch Early Mood Food, reportedly one of the best breakfast spots in Oklahoma City.

"Of course," Matt Gant said. "And pleased to meet you, too, Sandra."

"You, too," she said, shaking his hand. "So glad to see the media interested in what Nick is doing."

"Hey, I would love to get a travel assignment like this. I think it would be the best," Matt said. "I can't imagine traveling the country for an entire year."

"It is pretty sweet," Nick said. "It does have its drawbacks."

"Like nearly getting shot, getting concussions, and taking accidental acid trips?"

"Um, yeah," he replied, a little uncomfortable. "You seem to know a lot about my trip."

"Been following you, through local papers and the web, when I can," he said. "You're also a helluva photographer."

"Thanks," Nick said.

"Let's talk about your time here," he said once their coffee had arrived and they'd each ordered chicken and waffles, at Mark's recommendation. "The first day in town, not even quite in town, you get gunned down."

Nick laughed. "Sort of. An interesting greeting for sure."

"And you, Miss," Matt said. "You rushed right in to help out. You've done that once before, haven't you?"

"I did. That's kind of how we met up," she said.

The reporter asked a few more questions about that, and Sandra told him of meeting Nick in Salem, and how she'd rushed to help him in Sacramento when his camera was stolen. "We've been dating ever since," she said.

"You were in Denver, too, right?"

"How do you know that?" she asked.

"I have my sources," he said. "From here, where to?"

"Headed to Topeka," Nick said. "My route hasn't been publicized, but I am sure anyone looking at a map for a bit can figure out the most efficient way for me to go."

"I'd imagine so," Matt said. "Tell me about Oklahoma City. What is your favorite part so far?"

"We loved the National Memorial. I wish I could spend more time there," Nick said. "Although it is a sobering experience. I wish I hadn't spent my first couple of days here in the hospital. I'd love to explore the area a bit more."

"Why don't you?"

"Deadlines. Commitments. But I am already making other plans to come back to some cities and visit when I can be more of a tourist."

"I'm sure my readers will love to hear that," Matt said. "Now what about the mystery here? Have you solved it yet? Do you know how Toby Ayunda died?"

"I'm not sure how much we should tell you," Nick said. His intention was to tell this reporter everything and let him break a great story. But he needed to bait him a little, set the hook. If he was too eager, this might not work at all.

"Hey, I'll only report the facts," he said, his voice showing some eagerness. "What do you know?"

"Well, let me show you something, and then I'll explain." Nick opened his new laptop, pulled up the video, and spun it around.

"Whoa! Where did you get this?" Matt asked.

"Jeb, the owner of the store emailed it to me."

"Ah." The reporter watched the scene unfold, and then Nick stopped the video.

"Now, watch carefully." Nick advanced the frames, showing the truck, and then duplicating what he had done the night before, showing Toby hitting the ground.

"And the cops have this?"

"Yep. I showed them what we found, but they just said they will look at it."

"I get the idea you know something else, not only this."

"I have guesses."

"And that is just what they are," Sandra interjected. "We don't have definitive proof."

"Hit me with it," Matt said. "Maybe I can help."

Nick explained his conversation with Jeb, his talk with the priest, and their interactions with Myssi and the reverend.

"You've been busy."

"Not intentionally."

"I get that. And I take it you want to be left out of the headlines about this story."

"We just want someone who will run with it," Sandra said. "Investigate, independently. The cops really like the reverend, and even if he did it, they will probably not go after him."

"True. We are in the Bible Belt, and the High Priest of a Satanist church certainly makes a better target. Or one of his followers, Myssi or Toby himself."

"And you?" Sandra asked.

"I'm not a fan of either one, frankly. I, like you Nick, just want the truth."

Nick nodded. "How will you get it?"

"First, I'll go interview the reverend himself. I'd also love to know if he owns an old Ford truck."

"Sounds good," Nick said, taking the last bite of his breakfast. "Keep us posted, alright?"

"Of course. If the story is juicy enough, I am sure I can get it on the air."

"Why do you say that?" Sandra asked.

The reporter shrugged. "You know the saying, 'if it bleeds, it leads.' If the reverend turns out to be involved, that is about as juicy as it gets."

Matt shook both of their hands and left.

"What now, Nick?" Sandra asked.

"We finish our jobs," Nick said, rubbing the bandage on his head lightly. "And we hope for the best."

"Should I tell Myssi anything?"

"Not yet. What do we really have to tell her?"

Sandra nodded, and they headed for the door.

By the time they got to the capitol, Nick felt a lot better about the situation overall. Either something would come of the reporter and his story, or it wouldn't.

But he had an uneasy feeling things would not go exactly the way he wanted them to.

18

THE BEST LAID PLANS

Nick's phone rang as he walked toward the capitol, setting up for a shot from the southwest he really wanted to redo in the better light of the afternoon.

"Hi, Mom," he said.

"How are you?" she said. "We haven't heard from you since the hospital!"

"I'm okay mom," he said. "Sandra is a huge help, and we are almost done here in Oklahoma."

"Thank goodness. Where to after that?"

"Topeka," he said. "Sandra is coming for at least that week to keep an eye on me."

"You guys should just team up for the trip."

"I don't think that would work, Mom." Up ahead, he saw Sandra enter the capitol building. She only had a couple of shots to get inside, and Nick was taking care of the outside. They would be done early enough for a nice dinner, this time at Cheever's.

He couldn't wait.

"Sure it would."

"How's dad?" Nick asked, changing the subject.

"Napping at the moment but doing really well," she said. "They released him from physical therapy this week."

"That's great, mom." He'd been worried about his dad's recovery from a stroke he'd had several weeks ago, but it seemed like things were going well.

He wished he could visit, just to see for himself, but his schedule made it impossible.

"He's back to his old self. Hey, Nick?"

"Yeah, mom?"

"I worry about you. I love you. Be careful out there on the road, alright?"

"I will, I promise."

"Talk to you late."

"Bye, Mom."

He ended the call and then raised his camera, snapped a photo, checked it for light, and took a few more.

Glancing at his list, he moved toward the next location he needed to shoot from.

"O'Flannigan!" he heard a booming voice say.

He turned and saw a man walking his way. He quickly recognized Adrial Finbar. The man's crimson face and bunched fists betrayed his anger.

"What the hell, O'Flannigan?" he said.

"What did I do?" Nick asked.

"You talked to Myssi?"

"I did. She told us about you, and your group, and how you helped Toby. Between the two of you, I believe it."

"That's not what the cops say."

"What?"

"They showed up at my home today, asking all kinds of questions about where I was that day, what I was doing, and if anyone but my family could back up my alibi. They all but accused me of giving that boy drugs, or worse selling them to him."

"That's not what I told them at all."

"I don't think they believed you."

"I pointed them elsewhere," Nick said. "I told them to look at Reverend Ayunda."

"Thank you! I have been saying that from the start, but the man is untouchable."

"Maybe. I have another plan in the works, but I can't tell you about it yet."

"Look, I know you are trying to help Myssi, or whatever Mr. O'Flannigan. But you're not from here. You don't know what it's like."

"No, I get it," Nick said.

"No, you don't. And you probably never will. Now just leave it okay? Finish what you are doing and go."

"That's the plan."

"Reverend Ayunda and I have been at each other for years, and if he can pin this on me or anyone around me, he will. And most of the city would back him."

"Unless he got caught red-handed."

"How would that happen?"

"I don't know," Nick said. "But keep an eye on the news, okay?"

"Okay," the priest said, clearly suspicious. "I hope you didn't royally mess things up O'Flannigan."

"I didn't."

Adrial Finbar just waved his hand and walked away, head down. Nick looked after him, hoping he'd told him the truth.

He moved on to his next shot, hoping Sandra was doing well inside. This was the last push, and then they would be done. He couldn't wait to head out in the morning and put Oklahoma behind him.

At four more locations around the building, Nick stopped to take photos. About 40 minutes after the priest had stormed off, he came around the north side of the building for one final setup. Just then Sandra walked out.

"Nick, we have to go," she said.

"Go where?" he asked.

She held up her phone, and he saw a message from Myssi with a link. "Help!" it read.

"What is that?" he asked.

Sandra clicked on the link and turned the phone around again.

A reporter filled the frame. "--at Jeb's convenience, the site of a foiled robbery that resulted in the death of the son of prominent Reverend Adam Ayunda earlier this week. Reports tell us the reverend is inside, and he has two hostages. Police are on the scene behind us and keeping the public at a distance.

"At least one hostage has been identified, Myssi Renata, the young lady who stopped the intruder, and who the police threatened with prosecution for involuntary manslaughter. The other hostage has yet to be identified."

"We have to go," Sandra said.

"Why?" Nick answered. "They aren't going to let us near the place."

"Oh, I have a feeling they will," she said. "Once they recognize you."

"Really?" he said. "I don't understand."

"She asked for our help," Sandra said, tapping her phone. "There has to be a reason she thinks we can do something. We have to at least try."

"Okay," he said. "Let's go."

They packed up their cameras and headed for Nick's car, but he had a sinking feeling they wouldn't be any help at all.

And even if they could, by the time they got to Jeb's, it would be too late.

19

——————

OFFERED

Nick's stomach tightened as they drove. His gut screamed at him that this was wrong, all wrong.

When they pulled in, the place was roughly as he remembered it from his two previous visits. But there was a critical difference. First, the parking lot was filled with news vans parked in a ring around dozens of police vehicles, their lights all flashing.

And in the center of the circle, right next to the store, was a once yellow Ford pickup and a light blue compact, an older Geo Metro, Nick guessed. Next to that was a scooter he recognized right away.

The other hostage had to be Jeb, he thought, just before he saw the store owner, a large camera pointed at him as he gestured toward his place of business.

He wasn't inside. Nick stood as he got out of the car, suddenly very self-conscious.

Not only was he a six-foot-six redhead, something that made him easily recognizable all the time, but he also had a huge bandage still on his head.

There would be no hiding.

He walked past the media vans, Sandra holding his hand when he heard the whispers. "There he is!"

"There's the guy who got shot."

"What's he doing here?"

"Did the police call him?"

"Go ask him."

No one moved to stop him though before two figures detached from the police lines and walked his way.

"O'Flannigan," Detective Peabody said. "I don't know why you are here, or how you even knew what was going on or to come here, but the reverend is asking for you."

"For me?"

"He wants to talk with you."

"Why?"

"Does it matter? Look, that girl Myssi is inside along with some freelance journalist, Matt somebody."

"Matt Gant."

"Yeah, how did you know?"

"He interviewed me."

"About what?"

"Well, mostly my trip, but also about what happened here."

"What did you tell him O'Flannigan?"

"Enough for him to make some assumptions," Sandra interjected. "That still doesn't explain why the reverend wants to talk to Nick."

"We don't know either. We wouldn't normally do this. But we'll fit you with a vest. Get you inside. We have S.W.A.T. standing by, and a sniper team with eyes on the inside. All you need to do is separate him from the hostages and try to talk him out of there."

"And if he won't come?" Nick asked.

"Then we will have to--take action," Jenkins piped in. Peabody glared at him.

Nick turned to look at Sandra. She shook her head no, but then shrugged.

What else am I going to do? he thought to himself. Sandra's words echoed in his head, the thing she'd said at the capitol. "We have to at least try."

"I'll do it." His head throbbed.

Jenkins clapped him on the back. "That's what we wanted to hear."

Ten minutes or an eternity later, Nick found himself wearing a Kevlar vest with 'Police' stenciled across the front.

"Remember, separate him from the hostages, and keep your distance from him, just in case," Detective Jenkins said.

"Got it," he replied. Sandra appeared in front of him. She hugged him, hard, and then kissed him on the lips.

"Don't do anything crazy," she told him.

"It's a little late for that," he said. But he moved forward, keeping his hands up as the police had told him. When he got to the front door of Jeb's an odd sense of Deja Vu washed over him, but he pushed the door open anyway and went inside.

"Hi, O'Flannigan," the reverend said. Nick looked over to see him holding Myssi with a tight grip around her arm, a knife at her throat.

"Hi, Nick," Matt said. "Sorry about this."

"What did you do?" Nick asked.

"I offered to interview him, here," the reporter said. "And her, too. I figured I could kill two birds with one stone, so to speak. Interview both, at the scene of the crime, and find out the truth."

"And what is the truth?"

"I didn't mean for any of this to happen," the reverend said. "I just wanted to scare Toby into coming back home."

"What?"

"The Satanists, and this--this girl were taking my son away from me. Away from my church where he could be safe, protected."

"But he got clean."

"It doesn't do any good to get clean if you hang out in the mud," he said. "Toby would just have moved from one kind of trouble to the next."

"What did you do?"

The reverend looked from Matt to Nick and then to Myssi, who wasn't struggling, but just allowed herself to be held.

"He called me for help. Money of course. Boy couldn't hold a job, and I didn't want him to start stealing again, so I agreed, on one condition."

"What condition was that?" Nick asked.

"That he go back on his depression medication. I brought him the money and the pills, here. He brought his little friends to feel safe, I guess."

"Here?"

"He left his friends got in the truck with me, and he took his first pills with some water, but we argued right away. I wanted him to attend church, my church, as part of the deal, but he refused. He said he'd come home, but there was no way he would attend a Christian church again.

"I insisted. As soon as I slowed down, he dove out of the truck and ran."

"Did he have the pill bottle with him?"

The reverend nodded.

"But the pills were not his prescription, were they?" Nick asked quietly.

The reverend shook his head.

"What did you give him?"

"I thought if he got hooked again, I could put him in rehab. He would have to come home then."

"So you drugged him."

"I never imagined this would happen. It's her fault!" He shook Myssi. "It's her fault for taking him to that church. I offered my son, my only son, a simple way out."

Myssi stayed limp as he shook her, but Nick her eyes betrayed her. Anger gathered in them like thunderclouds.

"He's right," she said quietly. "It is my fault. He never would have found the Church of Ahriman and gotten clean if it hadn't been for me."

Her words were sharp. Biting. Nick saw the future a moment before it happened.

Then reality caught up with him. Myssi moved, breaking the reverend's grip easily. He swiped at her with the knife, but she ducked, grabbed his hand as he turned, and used his momentum to send him to the ground. As he fell, she jumped on top of him and grabbed his hair.

Myssi slammed his face into the hard floor once, twice, three times. Each time it echoed with the sound of a melon struck with a baseball bat.

Nick rushed forward and grabbed her arm before she could strike again. She let the reverend's hair go, and Nick swept her into a bear hug. He lifted her the best he could, staggered to his feet, and kicked the knife away from the now still reverend.

"Shhhh," he said. "It will be okay."

He turned for the door and saw Matt, the freelance journalist with his phone held up.

"Are you filming this?" Nick asked.

"Of course. This is the story of a lifetime."

"You set this up, didn't you?"

"I didn't know this would happen, but I knew something would."

"Get out of here," Nick said. Myssi struggled against his grip and he set her down. "Let's go outside," he told her.

She reached out and held his hand, and Nick walked her out to the sunlight. A cheer went up from the police and the media gathered, and Sandra rushed over, throwing her arms around him.

Nick leaned into her hug, and over his shoulder, he saw Myssi run toward the crowd. Adrial Finbar knelt and wrapped her in a huge hug.

As he did, the police surrounded the pair. They pulled Myssi away, and several officers rushed past him into the store.

"We'll need a statement," Detective Peabody said as Sandra finally released him and stood by his side. Nick reached to take the protective vest off, and carefully lifted it over his bandaged head.

"Of course," he said. "As soon as you let that girl go."

Out of the corner of his eye, he saw Matt come outside and go straight to the closest network van.

"He filmed the whole thing," he told the detective. "You need to get that video from him before he sells it."

Detective Peabody shook her head. "We can't. But we can use it as evidence."

"Good. The reverend drugged his son. I don't think he meant for him to die, but no matter what his motive, the result was the same."

"And Myssi?"

"She took the reverend down, but the video will show he was holding her hostage. It was self-defense."

"Thanks. If you can fill this form out with more details of what you witnessed, that would be helpful."

"Then I am free to go?"

"Yes, Mr. O'Flannigan, you are."

Nick smiled. "Thanks."

He wandered over to the picnic tables to one side of the store, and filled out the police report, including his phone number and contact information. Sandra sat quietly, reading as he wrote, and helping him fill in some of the blanks, adding her contact information as well.

"Are we done now?" she asked finally.

"Yes, we're done. We've given them everything we can. Now it is up to the police to sort out what happens next."

"And we're done with our assignment, too," she stated. So we can move on tomorrow, bright and early?"

"Yes, we can," he said.

Just then he saw Myssi break away from Adrial. She sprinted toward him and Sandra. "Thank you," she said, throwing her arms around him. "And thank you, Sandra. You didn't have to help me, but you did."

"No," Sandra said. "We did have to help. And it was our pleasure."

The girl turned and walked away, and Nick saw Detective Jenkins intercept her, clearly asking her questions.

"Nick?" Sandra said, grabbing his arm. He turned to face her.

"Yes?"

"I think I finally understand you. Why you get involved in these mysteries even when you don't have to."

"Thanks. I appreciate it."

"I love you."

"I love you, too."

"Now let's go get dinner. I'm starving."

She put her arm in his, and they walked toward his car. As they did, a weight lifted off Nick's shoulders, but he still felt very tired.

At least tonight he would sleep peacefully.

20

HEADED OUT

"I've got a surprise for you," Sandra told him the next morning over coffee.

"And what would that be?"

"Well, we're stopping in Tulsa. It is only a short drive, but we will be spending the night there."

"Why is that?"

"Well, we are booked for a visit to the famous Philbrook Museum of Art."

"That is awesome! I have always wanted to see that place."

"Well, it gets better. I have booked us an after-hours photography session this evening from 5 until dusk."

"What?" Nick said. "That's incredible."

"I know, right? You should be able to stay out of trouble in the museum, and we will still arrive in Topeka early enough on Sunday for you to rest before we start work on the assignment there."

"Oh, I've already started my research," he told her.

"Me, too," she said. "I can't wait."

Nick saw the television over her shoulder switch to the news. There was a part of the clip Matt, the reporter, had taken inside Jeb's the day before."

"Because of this footage, Reverend Ayunda has been charged with involuntary manslaughter, although sources tell us there will likely be a plea deal, as he is a prominent local figure with no previous criminal history.

"Charges have also been filed against Myssi Renata for aggravated assault, although the same source tells us those charges may be dropped. But the prosecutor is no longer considering prosecution against her for the death of Toby Ayunda last Sunday."

"And what about the photographer from out of town, Nick O'Flannigan?" the anchor asked.

"Mr. O'Flannigan is a material witness," Detective Peabody filled the screen. "But he had no official involvement in our investigation, or in any way except as a victim of the original crime."

"The police offered no additional comment," the reporter on screen said. "And Mr. O'Flannigan has not come forward to comment."

"Well, that's that," Nick said. "Hopefully, this isn't the type of story that will get national attention."

"Either way," Sandra said. "We're just going to avoid this kind of thing going forward, right?"

"I'm trying," Nick said. "And I'm really hopeful."

As they walked out of the restaurant and to his car, Nick looked around the parking lot and saw a familiar-looking blue compact. He hadn't seen the freelance reporter, Matt, inside. But the car looked like his.

He would have loved to give him a piece of his mind but it looked like he wouldn't get the chance.

"Plug the museum into your phone," Sandra said. "Let's go."

Nick obeyed, and a moment later, Oklahoma City was in their rear-view mirror as they raced along I-35 north toward the turnoff on I-44 that would take them to Tulsa.

"Until next time," he muttered. Sandra cranked up the radio, and he laid his head back and closed his eyes. He might as well rest while he had the chance.

THE END

FACTS ABOUT OKLAHOMA CITY

Oklahoma City is a fascinating place, one of the many cities built during the historic land run in 1889 and the oil boom that followed. The population grew to more than 10,000 in a single day.

In land area, it is the 3rd largest in the nation, and covers over 10 counties, even though it is the 42nd most populous city in the country.

I-35, I-44, and I-40 all intersect in Oklahoma City. That, and Tinker Air Force Base, the second largest air depot in the country, make it a major interstate center.

There are 18 colleges and universities in the area, and Oklahoma City is the home of the very first Hobby Lobby store, a 600 square foot storefront in the northern part of the city.

Oklahoma City National Memorial honors the victims, survivors, rescuers, and all who were changed forever on the site of the bombing in Oklahoma City April 19, 1995. It is arguably one of the most notable and moving memorials in the United States, and why we have dedicated an entire chapter to it in this book. It's a must visit if you are in Oklahoma.

The Oklahoma State Capitol Building itself is unique in that it sits on 100 acres and has several active oil wells on the property. There is a lot of art in the building, as mentioned in the book, and a great deal of time can be spent exploring the building itself.

And of course, if you do get to Oklahoma City, check out some of the many great restaurants downtown. There was no way to highlight all of them here, thanks to Nick's head injury, but should you see a tall red head, former basketball star when you go, say hi. Nick will be headed back to many of the cities he visited on his trip once his assignment is over, and you'll have to keep an eye out for him.

Thanks again for reading, and happy travels!

Troy Lambert, August 2021

JOIN THE CAPITAL CITY CRIME SOLVERS, AND GET FREE PRIZES!

Nick is now on the assignment of his life.

Fast forward from *Fast Break*, and you'll find Nick O'Flannigan traveling the country from state capital to state capital, photographing capitol buildings and finding murder in each city.

> "At a time when we can't travel, Nick's story is a great escape."
> B. Worley, Amazon Reader

If you loved this book, I would love it if you would leave a review. It's one of the things we as authors love most.

If you want to keep up with Nick and his adventures, subscribe to our newsletter here. We'll only send you bargain books and let you know when new stories are coming. You'll never miss a release.

We also have audiobooks! Lots of them. Check those out here, and enjoy. Our narrator, Joseph Stevenson and the team at Larson Sound Studios do a great job on them.

If you want to join our exclusive review team, follow this link. (There is a test, but it's an easy one, I promise!)

In the meantime, be well. Nick and I will see you as we travel the country together!

THE "CAPITAL CITY MURDERS"
SERIES

"Introduction to Nick"

Book #1 "Overdoses in Olympia"

Book #2 "Slaying in Salem"

Book #3 "Strangled in Sacramento"

Book #4 "deCapitated in Carson City"

Book #5 "Buried in Boise"

"The Wicked West"—a compilation of books 1-5, available in both e-books and print

Book #6 "Hanging in Helena"

Book #7 "Branded in Bismarck"

Book #8 "Parricide in Pierre"

Book #9 "Carnage in Cheyenne"

Book #10 "Defenestration in Denver"

"The Nick of Time"—a compilation of books 6-10, available in both e-books and print

Book #11 "Silenced in Salt Lake"

Book #12 Poisoned in Phoenix

Book #13 Stung in Santa Fe

Book #14 Axed in Austin

Book #15 Offered in Oklahoma City

All the books in the "Capital City Murders" series are available at www.CapitalCityMurders.com and your favorite e-book seller.

ABOUT THE AUTHOR

Troy Lambert and Stuart Gustafson are each successful authors in their own rights. As residents of the Great State of Idaho (Troy lives in Meridian, and Stuart is in the capital city of Boise), they have teamed up to bring to you, the reader, this new and exciting series of novelettes **set in each capital city** of the United States of America!

And yes, a total of fifty states means a total of fifty novelettes. Are you ready?

Troy Lambert is a full-time writer and author. Having written over two dozen mysteries and other novels, Troy is well-versed in story creation, and he knows what it takes to make a fictional story real! Troy's hobbies and pastimes (when he's able to break away from the computer) include hiking into the mountains of Southwest Idaho, fishing in a fast-rushing stream, and going for a drive where his mind can work on creating that perfect twist to the book he's currently writing. A native of Idaho Falls, Idaho, Troy and his wife live in Meridian, Idaho. You can find his other works, including his latest book, *Harvested*, at fictionupdates.troylambertwrites.com.